Praise

"A fast-paced adventure into a modern heart of Balkan darkness… A truly original take on the blood-sucking undead."

–*Publishers Weekly*

"In the glut of vampire-themed novels now on the market, Lyon's debut stands out… skillful… authentic… fascinating… inspired… Lyon executes it perfectly... vivid... engaging... sophisticated."

–*Kirkus Reviews*

"Lyon shapes his vampire from Balkan folklore… Well written and at times lyrical… A good read!"

–*Professor Elizabeth Miller*

"Not your usual vampire book. It shows a different vampire than people are used to seeing… a very good story… rich and fascinating."

–*Vampire Romance Guild*

"A wonderful surprise…the modern day vampire mythos is completely shattered and restructured as a truth, backed by historical fact…My heart and spirit stirred."

–*Horror-Web*

"Deeply rooted in Balkan vampire lore…this guy knows his stuff…It's a great read…You'll want to add it to your collection."

–*The Vampirologist*

"A denouement of action and heart-pounding resolution… It was a wild ride to the ending,… If you liked "The Historian", you'll love Kiss of the Butterfly."

-Vampire Romance Books

"In one word: fascinating…Completely unique and unlike anything I've experienced before… A much-needed dose of reality amid the craziness that is the vampire genre."

–*Respiring Thoughts*

"An exciting read… A well-crafted mix of fact in fiction… fascinating… I can highly recommend *Kiss of the Butterfly*."

–*Magia Posthuma*

ABOUT THE AUTHOR

James Lyon has over three decades of experience with the Balkans and the lands of former Yugoslavia: Bosnia and Herzegovina, Croatia, Kosovo, Macedonia, Montenegro, Serbia and Slovenia. Although he calls San Diego home, he has lived and studied in Massachussetts, Florida, Germany, Utah, the Soviet Union, and England. He has a Ph.D. in Balkan History from UCLA and has lived in the Balkans for more than 18 years, during which time he has worked for international peacekeeping efforts, civil society organizations, and as a business consultant. A well-known political analyst, he divides his time between Belgrade, Sarajevo and the Dalmatian coast.

Follow ***Kiss of the Butterfly*** on Social Media:

Facebook
https://www.facebook.com/pages/Kiss-of-the-Butterfly/203838056294407

Goodreads
http://www.goodreads.com/book/show/15776662-kiss-of-the-butterfly

Twitter
https://twitter.com/KissoftheButter

Pinterest
http://pinterest.com/kissofthebutter/

Kiss of the Butterfly

JAMES LYON

First print edition published in 2013.

This is a work of fiction set against the background of actual historical events, namely, the breakup of Yugoslavia. All incidents and dialogue and all characters, with the exception of some well-known historical and public figures, are a product of the author's imagination and are not to be construed as real. Where real-life historical or public figures appear, the situations, incidents and dialogues concerning those persons are entirely fictional and are not intended to depict actual events or to change the entirely fictional nature of the work. In all other respects, any resemblance to persons living or dead is entirely coincidental.

ISBN: ISBN-13: 978-1483921358

ISBN-10: 1483921352

Front and back cover art by David Grogan of Head Design
www.headdesign.co.uk

To My Elusive Butterfly

March 1991
YUGOSLAVIA
International boundary
Republic boundary
Autonomous province boundary
National capital
Administrative capital
Kiss of the Butterfly
0 50 100 150 km
0 50 100 mi
AUSTRIA
ITALY
HUNGARY
ROMANIA
BULGARIA
GREECE
ALBANIA
SLOVENIA
CROATIA
SLAVONIA
BARANJA
KRAJINA
VOJVODINA
BOSNIA AND HERZEGOVINA
SERBIA
SANDŽAK
MONTENEGRO
KOSOVO
MACEDONIA
ADRIATIC SEA
Gulf of Venice
Venice
Trieste
Rovinj
Pula
Ljubljana
Kranj
Celje
Maribor
Ptuj
Novo Mesto
Rijeka
Zagreb
Varaždin
Bjelovar
Virovitica
Daruvar
Kutina
Sisak
Karlovac
Kostanjnica
N.Gradiška
Slavonski Brod
Osijek
Erdut
Vukovar
Vinkovci
Pécs
Szeged
Subotica
Sombor
Bečej
Novi Sad
Petrovaradin
Sremski Karlovci
Zrenjanin
Timişoara
Arad
Vršac
Belgrade
Ram
Kisiljevo
Požarevac
Smederevo
Velika Plana
Negotin
Zaječar
Ćuprija
Kraljevo
Čačak
Užice
Šabac
Loznica
Aleksinac
Niš
Leskovac
Vranje
Priština
Kosovska Mitrovica
Peć
Đakovica
Prizren
Skopje
Tetovo
Gostivar
Kumanovo
Petrovec
Kočani
Titov Veles
Štip
Kičevo
Prilep
Ohrid
Bitola
Lake Ohrid
Lake Prespa
Lake Dorian
Tirana
Durres
Bar
Titograd
Cetinje
Nikšić
Ivangrad
Pljevlja
Priboj
Lake Scutari
Ogulin
Slunj
Velika Kladuša
Rakovica
Senj
Bihać
Prijedor
Sanski Most
Banja Luka
Kulen Vakuf
Gospič
Udbina
Gračac
Maslenica
Zadar
D. Zemunik
Bribirski Mostine
Šibenik
Primošten
Knin
Vrbnik
Divulje
Split
Sinj
Bosansko Grahovo
Mrkonjić Grad
Jajce
Travnik
Donji Vakuf
Vitez
Gornji Vakuf
Livno
Prozor
Jablanica
Konjic
G. Drežnica
Mostar
Metković
Ploče
Dubrovnik
Previaka Peninsula
Zenica
Vareš
Visoko
Sarajevo
Pale
Goražde
Doboj
Maglaj
Brčko
Bijeljina
Tuzla
Zvornik
Srebrenica
Žepa
Krk
Rab
Lošinj
Pag
Dugi Otok
Kornat
Šolta
Brač
Hvar
Vis
Korčula
Lastovo
Pelješac
Mljet
Mura
Drava
Sava
Una
Vrbas
Bosna
Drina
Neretva
Tara
Piva
Tisa
Danube
Morava

CONTENTS

Pronunciation Guide

Professor Nagy	Nadge (like badge)
Dusan Popovic	Doo-shaun Po-po-vitch
Miroslav Ljubovic	Meer-o-slav Lyou-bo-vitch
Rade Lazarevic	Ra-day Lazar-evitch
Katarina Lazarevic	Katarina Lazar-evitch
Mariana Lazarevic	Mari-ana Lazar-evitch
Teofil Simic	Tayo-phil Simitch
Vesna Glogovac	Vesna Glogovats
Milica	Militsa
Ljubodrag Stojadinovic	Lyou-bo-drag Stoya-deeno-vitch
Danko Niedermeier	Dan-ko Needer-meyer
Natalija	Nataliya
Srebrenica	Srebren-itsa
Sremski Karlovci	Srem-ski Karlov-tsee

ACKNOWLEDGMENTS

Any book requires input from others, and *Kiss of the Butterfly* is no exception. Many people assisted me with proofreading and offering suggestions, including Neil MacDonald, Kevin Sullivan, Christopher Bennett, Christen Farmer, Barkin Kayaoglu, Roger LaBrie, Paul Fedorko, Mark Wheeler, Therese Nelson, Mary Theisen, and James K. Lyon. David Grogan did a superb job of translating *Kiss* and my ramblings into two fantastic book covers. I owe a great deal to my wife Maja, for pushing me forward. I also wish to thank countless individuals throughout the former Yugoslavia, who over more than three decades have given me many rich and wonderful human experiences that provided material for this book.

The creatures depicted in this book – popularly known as *vampires* – are based on authentic descriptions from Balkan folklore recorded by ethnographers in the 18th, 19th and early 20th centuries, and they differ significantly from pop-culture stereotypes. Most historical references to vampires in this book are factual. For further details, see the Historical Note at the end of the book.

Documented reports of vampire-related activity continue throughout the Balkans to this day, the most recent having occurred in 2011 in Serbia.

- Sarajevo & Belgrade, March 2013

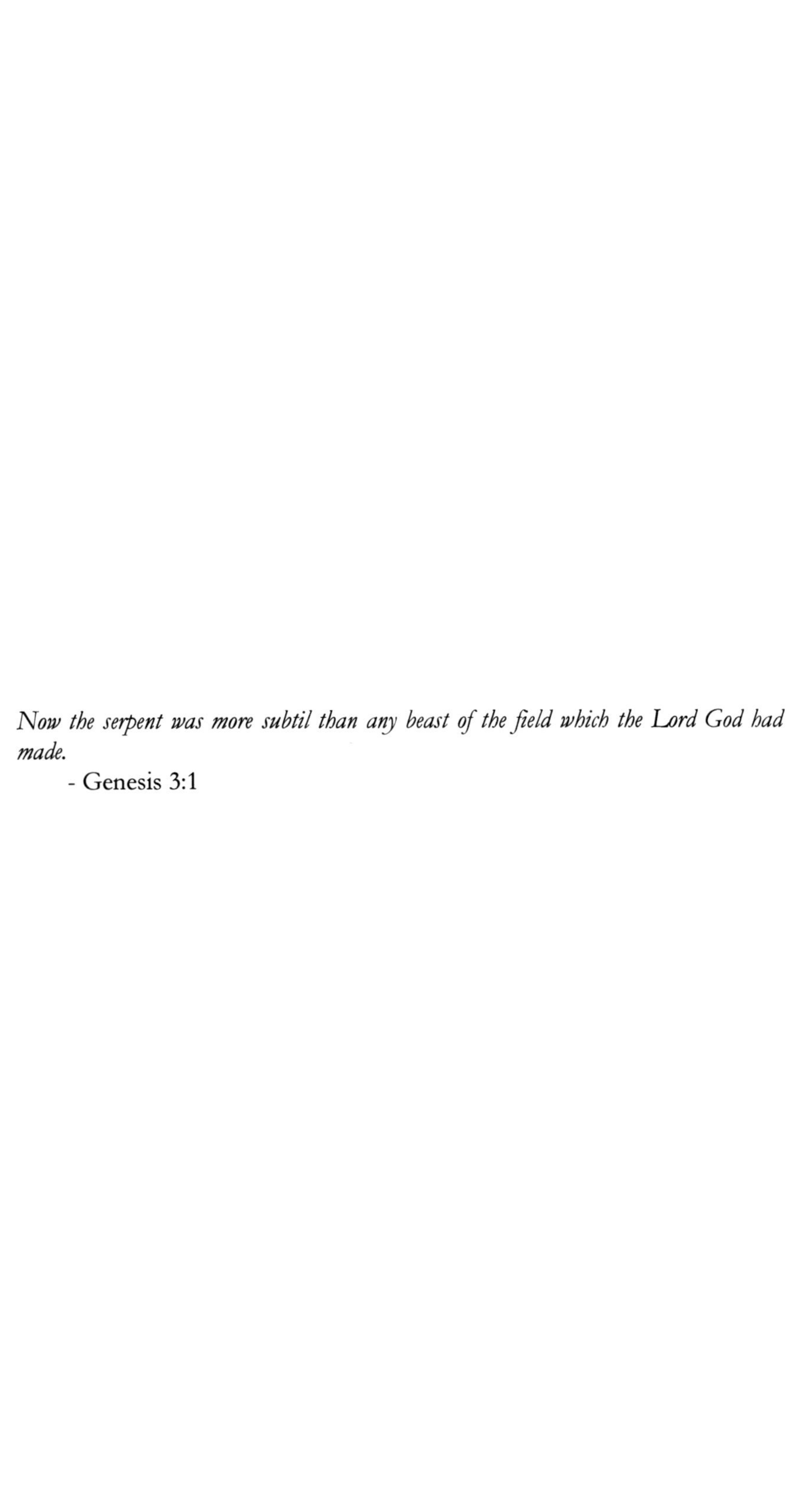

Now the serpent was more subtil than any beast of the field which the Lord God had made.

- Genesis 3:1

PRELUDE

February 1476

The victorious army followed the Drina River upstream, Serbia on the left bank, Bosnia on the right. As the host advanced, mountains rose along the river, their snowy forests thick and foreboding. Grey mists stretched forth their tendrils from the undergrowth, ascended from the emerald waters and tumbled down the mountain slopes in avalanches of billowing cloud.

The morning fog's caresses gave way to a stronger embrace that drove the sun from the valley's depths and brought twilight at midday. The vapor entered the soldiers' nostrils and lungs, under their armor, beneath woolen undergarments, as it whispered that the valley belonged to no man, that evil awaited those who dared desecrate its precincts. But the army paid scant heed, blinded by greed.

The host's armored mass cut everything before it, like the blade of a mower's scythe slicing its way through wheat that is white and ready to harvest. Outriders scouted ahead of the main body, followed by heavily armored knights, archers, infantry, retainers, baggage wagons and pack horses, closely pursued by the myriad scruffy camp followers: blacksmiths, leatherworkers, cobblers, beer and wine vendors, prostitutes, cooks, washerwomen, gamblers, con artists, scavengers and money lenders. What the soldiers left the camp followers swept clean in the army's wake as winged scavengers circled overhead, ready to swoop and gorge themselves on corpses abandoned in the mud. All reaped what they had not sown, while sowing seeds of a harvest their children's children's children would one day reap.

The army had rested briefly after its victory over the Turks at Sabac, and was once again on the move southward, albeit greatly reduced in size after Hungarian King Matthius Corvinus had departed with his court and most of the knights, infantry and spoils. He left behind a vassal, the Prince of Wallachia, Vlad III, to command 5,000 Serbian and Wallachian feudal levies, mixed with Italian and German mercenaries. This smaller army swept across the snow-covered Macva plain, past Mt. Cer and across the runoff-swollen Drina into Bosnia, setting torch to farm houses and villages, putting to the sword or enslaving the men and children, while taking the women for their pleasure.

Vlad halted the army at the approaches to the city of Zvornik, where the valley narrowed while his cavalry scouts overran the lightly guarded fortifications on the heights overlooking the city. Early on the morrow as the sun wrestled the mists, Vlad sat astride his horse and watched smoking chimneys rise up out of the cloud below, as a city once hidden now materialized from the morning fog. He flung back a dark green cape fastened around a bull neck to reveal full armor and a large sword with six golden dragons emblazoned on the scabbard.

A rider approached. 'Your Highness,' he spoke archaic Romanian. 'The Turkish commander will surrender the city, in exchange for a pledge that the garrison leave in peace. He asks that you spoil neither the city nor its inhabitants. The Christians of this place have pledged to swear allegiance to His Apostolic Majesty, the King of Hungary and to the Holy Father.'

Vlad looked at him with green eyes, blinked his dark lashes and sniffed curiously, as if scenting food nearby. 'And the troops?' he asked.

'They seek prizes, my prince. His Majesty did them great injustice by taking the plunder with him to Hungary.'

'Yes,' muttered Vlad pensively as he stroked his long bushy moustache. 'The Turks will have their safe passage, but without weapons. They must swear never again to fight against the Holy Cross. Then hurry to Mircea, and tell him to take the German and Italian mercenaries to the south of the city.'

'Yes, Sire.'

'We will take much spoil in this place,' Vlad thought to himself. 'I will enjoy this greatly.'

* * *

His stocky body wrapped in silks, Vlad reclined against velvet cushions set on a lush carpet, sipping blood-red wine from a gem-encrusted goblet. He could smell himself from the blood and human gore that soaked his clothes following two days of unfettered indulgence. 'Tomorrow I shall bathe in the thermal springs,' he thought. 'And I shall order the troops to do the same.'

It was late and the orgy of bloodshed had exhausted him. Oil lamps cast a dim light on oriental decadence that flickered between shadows: cushions, rugs, bolts of silk, all doused in the splendiferous nuances of brilliant golds, purples and scarlets. A naked girl whimpered softly at his side where he had tossed her, iron bands around her wrists and ankles, bruises on her body, her face swollen from blows, trickles of blood running from her nose, lips and thighs.

Although Vlad had promised safe passage, his mercenaries had fallen upon the unarmed Turkish soldiers and the heavily laden wagons of the merchants and artisans. They had separated the men from the women: the men he had impaled on stakes along the roadside as warning, the women he had given to his troops. And the Turkish commander, yes…he had taken such delight in torturing him. 'Impalement is so time-consuming,' he thought. 'But the Turks understand only that.' Even now some of the victims clung painfully to life, the night breeze carrying their faint moans to Vlad's tent. He had set his soldiers loose on the city, running amok among the Christian inhabitants, looting, burning, raping. When the town's priest complained, Vlad had strangled him with the very chain from the priest's own cross. Not a soul had escaped south to warn the Ottoman garrisons in other cities and towns.

Firelight danced around the entrance of Vlad's captured Turkish tent to highlight an approaching shadow. The guards challenged it, then permitted it to pass, and the shadow emerged into the dim light, a tall, dark-haired man with handsomely cruel features, his bearing unsteady. The nostrils of Vlad's thin nose flared as he sniffed: the newcomer smelled of wine and human blood.

'My prince,' he uttered with slurred speech. 'You called.'

'Mircea,' the prince said softly, brushing his dark curly locks from his face onto broad shoulders. 'You have served me well.' He extended the bejeweled chalice to Mircea: 'Take wine from my cup. It was found in the cellar of the garrison, a *Pavlovac* from the slopes of Mt. Kosmaj in the coasts south of Belgrade. It is so thick that one does not drink it…rather, it must be eaten.' He laughed at his own little joke; Mircea laughed along and took the proffered goblet. 'Isn't it funny how the soldiers of Allah drink the fruit of the vine like Christians?' Vlad poured himself more wine, and then struck the girl across her face. 'Silence,' he said viciously. She curled up in a ball and wept quietly.

'Mircea, tomorrow we raise camp and move towards Kuslat. From there we will move towards Srebrenica. Have you heard of Srebrenica?'

'Yes, Sire. Isn't it an old Roman town, fabled for its mines of silver? It will make us wealthy. The troops speak only of this.'

'Hasn't Zvornik offered sufficient for their needs?' inquired Vlad.

'My Lord, the city is small, and we are 5,000,' Mircea answered.

'Yes, you're right. Tomorrow I'll lead the army to Kuslat. But take 150 riders, disguise them as Turks, and take them to Srebrenica. Tell the garrison commander there that the Christians have been defeated and withdrawn. On market day, we'll surround the city walls. Then strike fear in the hearts of the people and open the city gates.'

'Yes Sire.'

'And what says Monsignor Rangoni?' The expression on Vlad's narrow face showed his distaste for the Papal Legate accompanying the expedition who had proven difficult from the very beginning.

'He has a delicate constitution, Sire, and the reality of war troubles him,' Mircea's sarcasm was evident. 'He tried to stop us from plundering the Christians, and he got angry over the death of the schismatic priest. But now he's drunk, and I sent a Turkish boy to his tent.'

'What about you? Have you taken your fill of pleasure?' Vlad wore a sinister grin on his face.

'Sire, can man ever satiate himself?' Mircea answered, grinning back.

Vlad laughed again, his green eyes surveying the ruined girl. 'Take her. Give her to your men.' His smile was now vicious. 'When they're done, have her join the others on the stakes.'

'With pleasure, Sire.' Mircea rose to leave.

'Mircea, stay with me a little longer,' Vlad grabbed Mircea's blouse. 'Within these hills lies a power dark and terrible. It's in the mists… it draws me closer,' he smiled darkly as he sipped from the goblet. 'It calls and nourishes me.' A red droplet ran from the corner of his mouth, down his chin.

'When we descend on Srebrenica our victory shall be complete and the bards will praise the name of Vlad III, how I defeated the Turks and rode through Srebrenica in might and glory. We will gorge ourselves with gold, silks, spices, slaves, blood and flesh… all will be ours. We will feed on the city and it will give us new life. The valley speaks to me with a kindred voice and I will partake of that power.'

'Yes, Sire,' Mircea nodded.

'My dear Mircea,' the expression on Vlad's face grew suddenly distant and his eyes clouded as though covered in the valley's swirling mists. 'We will leave here changed men. I feel it. And the Order of the Dragon will finally accept me as it did my father.'

'Yes, my Lord,' Mircea answered. 'The Order will indeed accept you, and the world will never forget your name, nor that of your father. May the house of Dracul and his son Dracula stand forever as a token to posterity of your power and might and greatness.'

CHAPTER ONE

A LETTER FROM A DISTANT SHORE

San Diego: Late August 1991

He arrived five minutes late for the start of the first day of class, and when he entered the students in the lecture hall were fidgeting and talking loudly. From the doorway at the back he surveyed the crowded room and twitched his nose slightly, catching the acrid musk of meat-fed bodies, the sharp jolt of Eucalyptus oil, tanning lotion and sea salt, all blended with odors of newness: new paint, new carpet and new furniture. Hazy late-morning sunlight flooded through the south-facing windows, spreading a sense of relaxed cheer. After a moment's pause, he sauntered briskly down the steps to the front of the hall, placed a battered leather briefcase on the table, removed a folder and laid it on the podium, followed by a stack of papers.

The room quieted. When it was completely silent he removed the iridescent blue sunglasses from atop his head and placed them on the podium, cleared his throat with a guttural rumbling that could be heard even at the back of the lecture hall, and removed from his coat pocket a tarnished silver pocket watch graven with ornate inscriptions. He glanced at it, and placed it on the podium. He looked at the folder as if double-checking something, then raised his head.

'Good day, class. I am Professor Doctor Marko Slatina,' he announced formally with a slight, yet indeterminate eastern European accent. 'This is History 240, section 3, the Medieval Balkans. If you are in the wrong class, please leave now.'

He was met by silence.

He appeared relatively young for a professor – somewhere in his early thirties – and not at all scholarly. He was far too stylish, in an Italian GQ sort of way, from the hand-stitched shoes with leather tanned the color of burnished pine wood, up past the pressed jeans and red-striped white button-down shirt, to the iridescent teal two-button coat. He was quite tall, with short-cropped dark hair, strong features, olive complexion and a deep tan that looked Mediterranean. Already several of the female students were taking favorable notice of his taste in accessories.

'I apologize for being tardy. As our German friends are fond of saying: *fünf minuten nach der zeit, ist Balkanische punktlichkeit.*' He looked for a flicker of comprehension among the students, but they stared back at him blankly. 'That means – five minutes after the appointed hour is Balkan punctuality.' Although he smiled, nobody laughed. 'I can assure you that in the future I shall be punctual, as I expect you to be.'

No one studies foreign languages anymore, he thought to himself.

Through the windows Slatina noticed a red and blue hang-glider as it circled lazily over the groves of Eucalyptus and Torrey Pine trees on the university campus. He looked at the assembled students, many of whom resembled extras from a surfing movie. Some had spent significant sums of money trying to appear casual, only to be betrayed by expensive haircuts, manicures and jewelry.

'I thank you all for coming today. I am most flattered that you found my class more important than the beach. It is truly a lovely day outside, not at all conducive to indoor education.' Although accented, his English was grammatically precise, delivered with an old-world charm and a slight inflection that hinted at a British education. Clearly he expected people to pay attention when he spoke.

The enrollment form in his folder told him that this semester would be similar to previous semesters – student athletes, history majors, the curious, and as usual, a large number of his students' surnames indicated Albanian, Bosnian, Bulgarian, Croatian, Greek, Macedonian or Serbian backgrounds. He read the roll in alphabetical order:

'Ahmeti.' 'Here.'

'Albijanich.' 'Here.'

'Anderson.' 'Here.'

'Barber.' 'Here.'
'Byelitsa.' 'Here.'
'Christensen.' 'Here.'
'Chorovich.' 'Here.'
'Mr. Chorovich, is your family from the Sandzhak, Herzegovina or Zlatibor?'
'Uh, I don't know. They're from Yugoslavia somewhere.'
He continued down the list, taking particular notice of the Balkan surnames: Brankovski… Georgevich… Hadjiahmetovich… Kayaoglu… Konstantinov…
'Lazarevich.'
'Here.'
He paused, looked up at the student and smiled gently. 'Could you please come see me after class?'
She nodded and he continued: 'Matkovich… Musliu… Nemarliya… Omerhodjich… Pappas…'
'Pesek.' 'Here.'
He glanced up to see a tall chestnut-haired girl with large brown eyes and a radiant smile sitting on the third row. 'Miss Pesek, is your family from the island of Hvar in Dalmatia?'
'Yes, Professor Slatina, from Stari Grad.'
'Are they *Nanetovi* or *Girotovi*?'
'Both.'
After finishing the roll he asked: 'May I please see by a show of hands, how many of you come from a Balkan background?' As the students looked around at each other, nearly half the class raised its hands.
Slatina looked at them, children of the Diasporas, raised on the shores of the new world, yet poisoned by their parents with shadows and memories of the old. From experience he knew that their parents felt deep guilt for having left their mother countries; guilt for abandoning their families; guilt for enjoying the bounties of democracy, capitalism and enlightened government, while the mother countries still groaned under the stifling burdens of oppressive tradition and communism. To compensate, they had indoctrinated their children with the very evils and obsessions they themselves had fled.
He had seen how they spoon-fed their young from the cradle with tales of atrocities and injustice. How the Turks impaled a great-great great grandfather for leading a peasant uprising; how the Serbs took away all the men from the village, none of whom were ever seen alive again; how the Croats slaughtered one third of the village residents, drove off a third, and forcibly baptized the remaining third; how the Albanians burned down the village church and roasted the priest alive on a spit; how the Bosnian Muslims cut off the genitals of a great-uncle and stuffed them in his mouth;

how the Greeks massacred an entire village on market day. There was suffering enough to go around, and even now, far removed in the United States the parents beat the drum of ancient grievances, each painting a picture of how their victim-hood and suffering was unique and entirely unjustified, as they prepared the next generation to avenge the family and national honor that earlier generations had long ago tarnished with the blood of innocents.

Now the children uncertainly carried the dark mantle of their parents' sins and guilt, a legacy that lingered in the light of the modern world. And it was Slatina's job to undo the lies, myths and propaganda.

He picked up the stack of papers and handed it to a tall auburn-haired young man, who began distributing it to the students. 'Steven Roberts, my Teaching Assistant, is passing around the course syllabus. It contains a list of books and readings for each class session. I expect each of you to take and pass a mid-term essay exam, as well as a final essay exam. There are no multiple choice tests. I require a 15 page term paper from each of you. You must receive my approval for the topic.' Unless he forced them to get his approval they would end up writing papers parroting their parents' prejudices.

'In this class we teach Balkan history. Not mythology. Not propaganda. Not legend. You will hear many things that will contradict what you learned at home from your parents. As you are all most certainly aware, a war has begun in Yugoslavia, and the country is tearing itself apart. There is no room for the war in this classroom. Nor is there room for a Greater Croatia, Greater Serbia, Greater Greece, Greater Bulgaria or Greater Albania, et cetera, et cetera, et cetera. Our work shall be based entirely on historical fact. In the course of our study we shall discover many things that undermine the claims made by the various national programs of the Balkans. Leave your prejudices behind, and please, do not attempt to use history to wage war in my classroom. I expect you to come to class with an open mind. Prepare to be challenged. If this disturbs you, please see me after class and I will sign your drop slip.'

He was met with silence.

'Well, then. My office hours are from 12:00 until 13:45 Mondays, Wednesdays and Fridays. Or you may make an appointment with me. Steven will also be available to help you. Any questions.'

A hand shot up: 'Professor, will this class count towards fulfilling my requirement for an area studies minor?'

'I do not know. You must consult your department secretary or your faculty advisor. Any other questions?'

From the back came the sound of giggling, a loud thump, and a muffled grunt of pain.

'Yes? You in the back…do you have a question for me?'

Two students with the blonde hair and deep tans that come from spending long hours on surfboards sat on the back row, punching each other on the upper arms. 'You ask him, dude,' said the one in a Hansen's Surfboards t-shirt. 'Dude, stop hitting me, I'll ask him,' said the other, who wore a t-shirt advertising Mitch's Surf Shop. His embarrassment was palpable. 'Uh, Professor Slatina, will, uh, like we be, uh, like, learning…you know…about, uh, vampires?' The entire class broke into peals of laughter and the student blushed.

Slatina stood silently and waited for the laughter to subside. He drew himself up to his full height and squinted, his eyes darkened slightly, while a grim expression flashed briefly across his face. A cloud drifted suddenly across the sun, darkening the room and sending a chill through the students. Outside the hang-glider circled closer. 'You should be careful what you say,' Slatina admonished gravely. 'In the Balkans we have centuries of experience with vampires and we take them very seriously. Do not speak of them lightly.' The students watched him with nervous expressions, unsure at this sudden change of demeanor.

Then he smiled. The hang-glider disappeared, replaced by a muted roar that chased a flight of US Navy F/A-18 aircraft streaking low overhead on their way from Miramar Naval Air Station to an aircraft carrier out at sea, somewhere over the western horizon. As the sun re-appeared from behind the cloud, his face relaxed and his eyes cleared. 'You see? It is only a cloud. Of course, there are no such things as vampires. No vampires. None. They do not exist, at least, not anymore. So you have no need to fear.'

'However,' a mischievous expression appeared suddenly on his face, 'since it is a well-established historical fact that vampires originated in the Balkans and that Dracula was a late-comer to the vampire scene, I will offer you an extra credit assignment. Whoever completes this assignment successfully, I will raise his or her grade an entire point. But to get the extra credit, you must answer the following questions.' The students began scribbling notes hurriedly.

'What shape and color are a vampire's eyes? What are a vampire's teeth made of? Where does a vampire's power reside? What do vampires look like? What is the first recorded reference to vampirism in the Balkans? What side of the body do they feed from? What are they made of?'

A voice from the center called out: 'Professor, could you please speak a little slower? I'm having trouble writing all this down.'

'Of course, I apologize.'

He continued: 'how does someone become a vampire? How do you kill one? Where do they sleep? Are they afraid of daylight, or can they solve their problems with sun block and Ray Bans?' A few students laughed lightly. 'What time of year are they most active? Where do they like to hang out? And no, the answer is not the blood bank.' More students laughed.

'How many people can attend a vampire party, and what do they eat? Where can you find vampires on Good Friday? What is the historical connection between the Vojvoda of Wallachia, Vlad III – also known as Dracula or *Tsepeş*, the Impaler – and the Balkans? What are the most common professions for vampires, bearing in mind that telemarketers, attorneys and IRS agents do not count.' The entire class laughed at this last comment and Slatina smiled. 'And because you have all been raised on MTV and are seething with the fiery, volcanic passions of youth, we must also have a question that is relevant to popular culture. Therefore, you must discover if vampires can have sex.'

'They can, just ask my ex-girlfriend.' The high-pitched squeaky male voice from the back of the room sent the classroom into spasms of laughter.

When the laughter died down, Slatina smiled sternly: 'Young man, are you claiming to be a vampire?' The students laughed once more. 'Or are you imputing these characteristics to your ex-girlfriend? If so that is a most ungentlemanly thing to do, seeing as she is not here to defend herself.' The student appeared somewhat embarrassed and a female student turned her head towards him and muttered: 'What a jerk' very loudly.

Slatina continued: 'And finally, you must discover the relationship between a vampire and a butterfly.' The students looked at Slatina with bewilderment. 'Yes, a vampire and a butterfly. Next month the Monarch and Painted Lady butterflies will make their appearance in the Eucalyptus trees of our campus in the course of their annual southward migration. So, what is their relationship to vampires?'

'Please remember that we are not talking about Hollywood vampires. Do not tell me that vampires sleep only in coffins, or that you become a vampire after being bitten by a vampire, et cetera, et cetera, et cetera. I do not wish to hear stories of Bela Lugosi or Christopher Lee or Van Helsing: do not regurgitate Bram Stoker or Anne Rice. They described imaginary creatures with little basis in history. They appealed to bored middle class teenagers and housewives, longing to escape the drudgery of daily life and find forbidden pleasures and excitement that come from breaking social taboos. They played to the sexual neuroses of a bored bourgeoisie. I am interested in real vampires, Balkan vampires, and they existed long before Dracula. The answers to the questions I have posed bear no resemblance to popular imagination. To find your answers you must undertake solid, academic research. You must comb through Balkan folklore, history and ethnography. You must find what the people who actually experienced vampires have to say. Find out how peasants, priests and soldiers fought against these dreaded creatures and what they had to do to vanquish them.'

'Are there any questions?' The room was silent. 'Do not worry. I doubt that any of you will find the answers,' his smile was relaxed and he exuded old world charm. 'And you should not wish to. After all, this is sunny

California, life is a beach – I believe that is the expression – and you should not trouble yourselves with mistakes from a grey and distant past. For now we see through a glass, darkly, et cetera, et cetera, et cetera.' He relished letting the 'R' of 'et cetera' roll from his tongue. 'You should concentrate on the more pleasant pursuits of youth while you are still young.'

'And now, we shall use what little time remains in today's period and turn to a more important topic,' he picked up the folder. 'Let us discuss the Roman Emperor Diocletian, who is famous for dividing the Roman Empire into two parts, persecuting Christians, building himself a lovely and not very modest seaside retirement palace, and raising the world's best cabbages. This will be on the first mid-term exam,' he added with a twinkle in his eye, 'especially the part about the cabbages…'

* * *

The university had invested enormous capital to give its faculty the newest facilities, and Slatina's office was no exception: a freshly constructed building with everything painfully new and sterile – book shelves, industrial carpet, filing cabinets – even the air filtering through the vents.

It was near the end of office hours, which had been taken up with the usual first-day-of-class activities, students wanting him to sign add or drop slips or asking for advice. The office was now empty, the door open a crack, and Slatina had just leaned back in his new chair. Looking out the window as he finished adjusting his class roster with adds and drops, he saw the same hang-glider that had been circling during his morning class. A slight knock on the door interrupted him. 'Come in,' he called.

A tall girl with bright green eyes and a canvas military backpack entered.

'How may I help you?' he inquired politely, intrigued by eyes that seemed somehow familiar.

'Professor Slatina?' she asked shyly, tugging nervously at the sleeve of her cotton blouse.

And then it dawned on him. 'Ah yes, Miss Lazarevic…Katarina. I thought it was you.' His face lit up as he switched to a Dalmatian island dialect of Serbo-Croatian. He stood up, hugged and kissed her three times on the cheeks. 'And how is my god-daughter? When did you get in? Please have a seat, won't you? I haven't seen you since you were three years old. I won't embarrass you by telling you how grown up you have become. It is so good to see you again. Your parents have written so much about you.'

'Professor Slatina,' she was hesitant, 'my father asked me to come by and give you his greetings.' She spoke Serbo-Croatian with a northern Serbian Vojvodina accent.

'How nice of your father to remember me. And how is he?'

'He died only two months ago, just before I left for school.'

Upon hearing this news, Slatina collapsed backwards into his chair, stunned. 'But he was so young…' He paused, visibly disturbed. 'And no one told me…and…and…such a terrible pity. And how is your mother?'

'Not well. She pretends to be okay, but I can tell it's hard on her. She loved him very much.' Her eyes moistened.

'You are your father's daughter…I can see it in your eyes. But you have your mother's beauty. She is a good woman, in the truest sense of the word. She loved light and truth, and that is everything your father stood for. That is why she fell in love with him and married him. And I hope that their daughter is like them.' He smiled generously. 'What did he die of?'

'The doctors aren't certain. He always looked so much younger than his years, and he was always so healthy.' She gulped back tears and fidgeted with her long, dark tresses. 'But sometime during January he got sick. The doctors performed many tests, but couldn't find anything. You know how our doctors are…and since Milosevic cut off trade with Slovenia there have been fewer medications, and then the economy and hospitals fell apart and hyperinflation and the war…well, Papa just got worse. When he finally died the doctors said it was from a broken heart.' Tears began to run down her prominent cheekbones.

He handed her a tissue and motioned for her to continue.

'He said that he sent you a letter sometime in February, but we never heard back from you and it probably didn't arrive. He asked me to give you this.' She handed Slatina a large manila envelope with a red wax seal. He picked it up, weighed it with his hand and placed it on the desk.

They sat and talked: of life in Yugoslavia; friends; the trip across the Atlantic; where she was staying; what her study plans were. It all flooded out in what seemed brief moments, but lasted an hour. Suddenly he glanced at his watch and interrupted her abruptly.

'Katarina, I must apologize, but right now I am very busy, it being the first day of classes. I would very much like to continue this conversation at a later time. Perhaps I could have the pleasure of your company later this evening.' She looked at him and hesitated. 'I shall be taking a group of medieval history graduate students to dinner, and I would quite like to have you join us. We shall meet for drinks and dinner at 7:00 PM at the Fire Pit Restaurant at 17th Street in Del Mar. It is on the beach, so you may dress casually.'

'Thank you.'

He removed his business card from the top drawer of his desk, wrote something on the back and handed it to her. 'This is my home telephone number. If there is anything I can do to help the daughter of my dearest friend, please feel free to call me anytime, day or night. After all, I am your *Kum*,' he smiled generously and sincerely as he stood. 'And if either you or your mother experience financial difficulty, do not hesitate to let me know.'

'Sure,' she smiled.

'Until this evening then.'

After she had left, Slatina closed the door, jiggled the knob to make certain it was locked and sat down. He took a dagger from his desk and broke the wax seal on the envelope, sniffed the contents, gently removed a large black and white photograph and placed it on the desk. In the photograph two men stood on top of a hill next to a Baroque clock tower. Between them stood a woman with thick blonde hair, her arms wrapped around both men. All three were smiling. The caption read *Petrovaradin, 5.viii.1960.*

A yellowing newspaper article fell out, printed in the Cyrillic alphabet. He picked it up and saw it was from a Novi Sad newspaper in northern Serbia, and that the story was about a night watchman from the Petrovaradin fortress whose body had been found after it had been savaged by a pack of feral dogs and left horribly disfigured. As he read the story Slatina learned how the dogs had completely gnawed the entire left side of the watchman's body from head to ankles. The article was dated 15 January 1983, two days after the Serbian New Year.

There was also a letter, handwritten in the Cyrillic alphabet on lined paper torn out of a bound notebook. It was written with a beautiful flowing hand, one in which the author had obviously taken pride, and was dated 6 May 1991. Slatina picked it up and began to read.

My dear Marko,

Happy St. George's Day. I hope this letter finds you well. Unfortunately my health is failing and I know in my heart that I will not live to see the next snowfall. It comes from too many cigarettes and bottles of Vermouth. As you well know, old habits are difficult to break, and unfortunately I developed these vices prior to meeting Mariana and confronting my own mortality. She always tried to get me to stop, but what could I do? By now you have met my Katarina. She is all that Mariana and I have, and I would ask that you take care of her as though she is your own child. After all, you are her Godfather. Please watch over her and see that she learns to treasure truth and light. I have entrusted this letter to her, knowing it will take longer to reach you, but also knowing that this way it will avoid prying eyes.

Since 1987 I have watched events unfold with fear and trepidation, but mostly with disbelief, as people sacrificed their reason at the altar of Slobodan Milosevic. I have had difficulty believing that one man can lead a people so quickly into darkness. What I have found even more difficult to believe is that this people would follow him so blindly, and so willingly assist in their own destruction, all the while blaming it on others. And they are doing it all in the name of Serbia, a horribly distorted Serbia built on old myths and new lies. I do not recognize this Serbia as the country that we once knew. Something noble has become horribly polluted by those with the greatest duty to protect it. The Church and the Communist Party have played key roles, and both have deprived man of his ability to think clearly, proving they are identical in behavior and ideology.

The people labored and were heavy laden. And when Slobo said 'come unto me' they did so, blindly. The yoke they have taken upon themselves is neither light, nor easy to bear, and they have shouldered it just when others wished to cast it off. At first I thought Milosevic to be merely a demagogue and tyrant, but now I fear he may be much worse. The smell of blood is in the air, I sense it even now. People thirst for it; the entire country is mad with desire for it. And now we are going to war with our brothers because they look like us, and because we can smell our blood coursing through their veins. It is madness. I know not what will come of it.

I have tried to carry out my duties as charged. Unfortunately my health no longer permits me to do so. I sometimes wonder whether the seals have been broken. I have not checked them these last several years, but when I last went there the entrance was flooded and inaccessible. I know of no effort to pump out the water, and as my friends have told me, the water level has only risen with time. I have enclosed an article about the death of the watchman, which puzzles me. Please do what you must. Katarina knows everything, so you need keep nothing from her.

I send you my most heartfelt greetings, as well as love from Mariana. Her health is also poor, and although she is too proud to seek help, she would benefit greatly if you would send her medications. Katarina can tell you what is needed.

My dearest friend, I recall with fondness the warm summer days of long ago, you and Mariana and I basking in the warmth of the sun on the grassy banks by the Danube under the Cottonwood, Linden and weeping willow trees, watching ducks and geese paddle lazily, while sipping from a bottle of Smotrina Kapljica wine. Yet now I grow ever colder, the sun can no longer warm me, and the Tambouritsas sound strangely out of tune. Perhaps we shall see each other once again, hopefully then face to face, and then shall we know even as also we are known, for we know now in part.

As the song says, 'Here is dawn, here is dawn, I will pray to God, it is St. George's Day…' I still remember that St. George's Day when I decided to give up everything for Mariana. It is true that I have sacrificed much and have since experienced great pain, but I gained far more in return. And I felt true joy for the first time in my life when Katarina was born. Joy far greater than any that you – my dear friend – will ever know, unless you choose to one day follow in my footsteps. I pray to God every day that you will do so. But you have chosen a different path that has taken you far away. I had hoped to celebrate one more St. George's Day together with you and Mariana, but it is not to be. I fear we shall not see each other again in this life.

O quam misericors est Deus, Justus et Pius.

Your loyal and eternal friend,

Rade

Slatina looked at the back of the letter, held it up to the light, and then returned it to the envelope. Mortality…, he thought, suddenly feeling old. At least he leaves behind something for the future, a legacy of hope. He looked at the photo once more. I have chosen a different path, and I feel increasingly damned for it.

From the bottom drawer of his desk he pulled a bottle of red wine and a wine glass, removed the cork and poured himself a glass. He placed a cassette in a tape deck and pressed the play button, flooding the small office with the sounds of Tambouritsas, accompanied by the melancholic tones of a group of men singing:

Bring me some red wine,
I yearn to recall the tales,
Right on this lovely spot,
Where I saw her eyes.

The three people in the photograph blurred as tears flooded his eyes. He sniffed the air above the glass lightly. 'Rade, I drink to you and our love for each other.' He lifted the glass high and drank nearly half. He continued looking at the photograph, and began to sing along with the tape:

Halt the Danube,
And the old clock hands,
That is my song,
And the song of my beloved…

Let me always be followed,
With songs of red wine.
By eight Tambouritsa players,
From Petrovaradin.

He looked out the window at the groves of flaking Eucalyptus trees, whose falling oil had killed the vegetation underneath, making the surroundings barren so that their roots could drink in all the rainfall, a survival mechanism for a desert tree. He longed for the Cottonwoods and Linden trees lining the Danube and the grassy river banks. I am exiled in a desert paradise, he thought to himself. And there is so much I must now do. He picked up the newspaper article and looked at it once more. My dear Rade, you couldn't have died at a worse moment. Madness is descending, and there is so little I can do from here. He began pacing the room, looking at the books, pondering, as outside the window a hang-glider circled.

* * *

The music had stopped long ago, the bottle of open wine sat next to the half-finished glass, and Slatina sat hunched over the desk, his face buried in his hands, moist with tears.

A knock at the door interrupted his thoughts. He opened it to find his Teaching Assistant, Steven Roberts, a young man in his mid-twenties, with auburn hair and a troubled expression. He stood only slightly shorter than the professor, but was broader across the shoulders and chest.

'Ah, Steven, how good to see you. Please come in and take a seat.' Slatina closed the door behind them, regaining his composure. 'What may I do for you?'

'Professor, I've got a serious problem.' Steven fiddled with his backpack, clearly agitated.

'Ah, can it wait for a glass of wine?' Slatina smiled as he removed a second glass from his desk and handed it to Steven. 'Did you know that in 1777 the German traveler Friedrich Wilhelm von Taube visited the Vojvodina city of Sremski Karlovci, where he described their excellent Vermouth? Well, actually he called it *Tropf-Wermuthwein.* The merchants of Karlovci made a great deal of money selling it to the Imperial Austrian court, and to the nearby fortress of Petrovaradin. Today they call it *Bermet.* Perhaps I could interest you in a glass of 1934 *Marinkov* Bermet?' Slatina filled the glass nearly to the brim and handed it to Roberts.

Steven hesitated momentarily, then took the glass. 'Thanks, Professor.'

'So, young Steven, shall we toast the beginning of a new school year?' They clinked their glasses together and sipped. 'Now, tell me the nature of your problem.'

'Professor, I'm supposed to choose a dissertation topic this year, but with the war in Yugoslavia…' He studied the industrial carpet, his sentence unfinished, then continued. 'All research grants and scholarships are frozen, so work in Yugoslav archives is out. Without archival research, there's no way I can write a dissertation, and without a dissertation I can't get a Ph.D. So it seems I've basically wasted two years of my life. I don't want to sound like a quitter, but I'm starting to wonder what the hell I'm…'

'Yes, yes, of course,' Slatina cut him off with a wave of the hand. 'You are correct. This is a bad moment to study Balkan history. Yugoslavia is falling apart, and it is difficult to get permission from the Croatian and Serbian governments to work in their archives. They are very protective of their newly falsified nationalist histories, so they will be reluctant to have someone poking around trying to find out what really happened. And I am uncertain how much longer Bosnia will be safe. And we face the problem of funding your dissertation research, et cetera, et cetera, et cetera.' He grinned at Steven. 'Am I boring you?'

'No, no,' Roberts nodded. 'I'm listening.'

'Well, I may have an answer to your difficulties,' the Professor said, suddenly serious as he looked Steven directly in the eyes. Steven felt uncomfortable, as though the Professor were rummaging around inside his head, reading his thoughts, but he didn't dare avert his eyes.

'Ethnography!' Slatina exclaimed suddenly, breaking his uncomfortable gaze. 'The answer to your problems is ethnography. Everybody loves their folklore, and it is not as controversial as history.'

'Ethnography?' Steven spluttered, clearly perplexed. 'Are you serious?' he spluttered. 'Do you want me to leave the History program? But I've spent two years…'

'Now, now, young Steven,' Slatina interrupted, lifting a hand. 'You haven't lost two years and you needn't change majors. Ethnography and History have a great deal in common. You see, I know of a private foundation that funds ethnographic research inside Yugoslavia. It offers research scholarships. Do you like the wine?'

'Yes, it *is* good.' Steven perked up and smiled at the mention of a scholarship.

'You should, it is Vojvodina's best. Anyway, the foundation pays all expenses for one year, including air fare, housing, et cetera, et cetera, et cetera. It will give you access to archives in Bosnia, Croatia and Serbia and permit you to research without being subject to the usual suspicions.'

'Of course I'd like that,' Steven said enthusiastically, his gloom washed away by the new opportunity. 'What are they looking for? I've never applied for an ethnography grant before.'

'Do nothing. Leave it to me. I shall call and tell them that you are interested. Can you leave right after Christmas?'

Steven nodded affirmatively.

'Of course I will have to find a new TA for winter semester,' Slatina thought out loud. 'It is settled then. Prepare to travel.'

'Really? I mean, how? We don't even know if I'll get a grant,' Steven muttered, skeptically.

'Consider it done,' Slatina said confidently. 'I shall speak with them. As I recall, you studied Serbo-Croatian for four years, is that correct?'

'Yes.'

'And you have also studied German, Latin and Old Church Slavonic, No?'

'Yes.'

'Oh, and one more thing,' Slatina added, almost as an afterthought. 'Young Roberts, do you believe in God?' The professor looked directly in his eyes, his expression suddenly very serious, again with that piercing gaze.

'Uh, yes,' Steven was taken aback. What's the professor getting at? he wondered to himself, thoroughly confused by what had just taken place.

'Good. You must pray often. I will see you this evening at 7:00 at the Fire Pit. There is someone I would like you to meet.'

Slatina's last question haunted Steven after he left the office: Do I pray often? Has the professor had too much wine?

* * *

Slatina sat at a table on the beach deck, surrounded by four graduate students, watching the sun set over the Pacific. All were male – for some reason medieval history attracted few women. The early evening shadows and pounding surf created a soothingly dull background as meat and fish cooking over a mesquite grill added flavor to the sea-side smells. Although the sinking sun lit the western sky with deep oranges, the conversation centered on the murky greys of medieval Europe's kings, dynasties and wars.

As one graduate student droned pompously about Gnostics and Bogomils, Slatina sat and nodded, a slight smile on his face, enjoying the anachronistic nature of the conversation. Here they sat watching the last few die-hard surfers catch the last wave of the day, all the while discussing topics from which they were separated by nine time zones, an entire continent, one ocean, and five hundred years. Slatina sniffed the salt air with pleasure, noting the subtle smell of decaying seaweed and dead fish mixed with salt.

'You know,' Slatina interrupted, 'in my student days we spent our spare time enjoying life. Forget medieval Europe for one short evening and think about other more pleasant pastimes. After all, our lives are tragically short. Enjoy this sunset! Enjoy this beach! Enjoy this moment! And enjoy this company. But also, try not to bore each other too much. Otherwise you will never successfully charm a woman and get married. Remember that we historians are very boring by nature…what is it you say – nerds? So we must work very hard to attract the opposite sex. Do not take your studies too seriously or you will end up a lonely old man like me. You surely don't think that medieval rulers secured the continuation of their dynasties by discussing history? No, they wooed as many women as possible to ensure there would be no shortage of heirs. I would be remiss in my duties as a mentor if I permitted any of your dynasties to die out.' The students chuckled politely.

'Permit me to draw your attention to the young lady who has entered the restaurant.' All heads turned to see a beautiful girl with long dark hair standing at the door, talking to a waitress. She was tall and slender, yet full-figured, with high cheekbones, a strong nose, and wore an olive green silk blouse. 'Because we are historians, we shall never have much chance of wooing a woman as lovely as her. We are simply too boring, and it is unlikely that any of you will ever interest her by speaking about Bogomils. However, I shall see if I can coax her to join our boring group.' He arose and walked towards the entrance. The graduate students stared, unable to believe their professor had invited them to dinner in order to give them lessons in chasing women. Some exchanged glances with each other, rolling their eyes at the professor's old-world male chauvinism.

Slatina approached the girl and said something to her. She flashed a warm smile in response, said something back and offered him her hand. He took it in his and kissed it gallantly, causing a bright red blush to rise to her cheeks. He spoke with her for a few moments, then motioned towards the group, said something, and she once again smiled and nodded. He offered her his arm, which she took, and he then proceeded to escort her towards the patio. The students stared in amazement, stunned by their professor's behavior. As she approached, they all stared at her. She was even more beautiful up close and her translucent green eyes matched the silk of her blouse.

'Gentlemen,' Slatina said formally. 'It is customary to stand when a lady enters the room.' The students jumped awkwardly to their feet, causing the girl to smile once more. 'Ah, that is better. Gentlemen, I have the great pleasure and privilege of introducing to you the loveliest woman in the world. May I present my god-daughter, Katarina Lazarevic.' Katarina smiled shyly and nodded hello. Some of the students sighed, relieved that the professor's chauvinism had only been in jest. Slatina then went around the group and made introductions.

'Katarina is just beginning her freshman year at the university and will probably be majoring in either anthropology or biochemistry. She is from Novi Sad in Yugoslavia's northern province of Vojvodina.' They all stood nodding silently. He looked around at them. 'Gentlemen, protocol states that we remain standing until such time as the lady has taken a seat, and I do not wish to stand all evening. Steven, would you be so kind as to offer Katarina a seat.' Steven rushed over and pulled out a chair and Slatina motioned for Steven to sit next to her.

When they had sat, Slatina continued: 'Katarina, you will be interested to know that after Christmas, Steven will travel to Serbia to conduct ethnographic research. Just this afternoon I learned that he received a one-year fellowship from the Balkan Ethnographic Trust that will permit him to conduct research in Novi Sad and Belgrade.'

Steven sat in silence, stunned at the speed and efficiency with which Slatina had arranged the fellowship: often it took nine months to get a grant. The other graduate students congratulated him warmly and asked questions about his plans and the fellowship, none of which he had even the slightest idea how to answer.

'Katarina, perhaps you can take some time away from your busy schedule this semester and acquaint Steven with Novi Sad,' Slatina added. 'He also needs help practicing Serbo-Croatian.' She nodded silently and the other students looked at him jealously as he attempted to hide the slight blush that rose in his cheeks.

'Professor, is there any way we can apply for this scholarship?' asked one student.

'I am sorry Joshua, but the grants are available only for Balkan studies and places are limited. I fear your concentration on the Italian city states will not qualify you.'

'Professor,' said another. 'I heard some students from your 240 class talking about the lecture you gave today. You really left them curious…they just couldn't stop talking about it.'

'Well, Jeffrey, Diocletian is an interesting Emperor. You should go some day to Split and see the seaside palace he built. After he divided the Roman Empire in two parts and abdicated, he retired to his palace. As the empire began to experience difficulties, the Roman Senate sent a delegation to ask him to return and become Caesar once more. When they arrived at the palace, they found him in the garden on his hands and knees, weeding the cabbage plants. They made their presentation and asked him to return. Without standing he picked up a cabbage, looked at them, and said: "why would I want to be emperor when I can grow cabbages like this"? So he stayed in retirement. May we all have such wisdom.'

'No Professor, not Diocletian,' said Jeffrey. 'They were talking about vampires. They said you offered them extra credit if they could answer certain questions about vampires.'

'Ah, so I did,' he sighed.

Katarina and the graduate students were listening attentively. 'It is a long, complex question. But since you are students of medieval history, you should know that legends of vampires are an old phenomenon. There are ample accounts of vampirism in the folklore and legends of the Balkans, going back to before recorded history. I merely wished to pique the students' interest in history by using a popular topic. Now of course there are no such things as vampires, but as the students research the folklore surrounding vampires, they will learn much about medieval history. But enough of that. Let us discuss more pleasant matters, such as your fleeting youth and this beautiful sunset. The melody the waves are playing on the sand…I believe I have heard it somewhere before.'

* * *

Interlude I: The Labyrinth: Friday, 28 February 1733

'Careful…slowly now…you don't want to drop the Emperor's new pets.' The Captain's voice rang loud, yet calm as he sniffed and caught the smell of newly-fired brick and damp air. Behind him eleven coffins floated down the tunnel, borne on the shoulders of Imperial Grenadiers in grey-green greatcoats that rendered them nearly invisible in the darkness, eight men to each coffin as they trudged in disciplined silence, grunting occasionally, sweating under their heavy loads in the chilled humidity. Between each coffin a Grenadier carried a lantern and a bundle of thorny branches.

'Don't straggle…stay together. If you get lost in the Labyrinth we may never find you.' The Captain spoke authoritatively in German with a slight Italian accent. 'You will probably die of starvation, or perhaps if you are unlucky the Emperor's pets will escape and have you for lunch.' He walked ahead of the column in his high-collared greatcoat, his oil lantern held aloft on a stick.

Flickering lanterns cast shadows over the Latin crosses carved in relief on the lids and sides of each coffin. Each man loathed the burden, yet each knew what was inside, and that knowledge enabled them to carry the heavy loads all the further. They came first to one tunnel junction, then to another, then yet another. At each the yellowish lantern light rushed faintly down the side passages until darkness swallowed it. The Captain examined markings painted on the wall in Gothic script and led the way. After 15 minutes he called a rest and the Grenadiers put down their loads and sat on top of the coffins.

The Captain removed his three-cornered officer's hat and wiped the sweat from his forehead. 'Be patient, we're almost there,' he called, a severe expression on his unshaven face. His eyes betrayed his worry.

'Just a little farther. Then we shall forget everything we have seen these past years.' The troops looked at him silently, steam issuing from their mouths and nostrils. 'Now, let us finish,' he said as he tucked his ponytail up under his hat.

Once more the Grenadiers hefted their grim loads and followed their Captain down the tunnel. After several more turns he came to a marble slab painted with Gothic letters that read *IV/500 Kom. Gall.* The Captain studied it intently and ordered the men to rest their loads again. 'You will wait here,' he ordered, as the Grenadiers sat obediently on the coffins. Shouts and pounding emanated from inside several.

The Captain turned into a small corridor that came to a dead end. Turning to the wall on his right he faced the lock and pressed his hand firmly against it and then crossed himself in the Latin manner – first the forehead, then the stomach, then the left breast, then the right. He heard the muffled sound of a latch being sprung, and saw that the brick wall at the end of the tunnel had swung open a crack. He walked to the wall and pushed it open to reveal more darkness. He entered and descended broad brick stairs that curved down and away to the right, looking with satisfaction at the bricklayers' workmanship and the near seamlessness of the joints.

After forty feet he stopped, his path blocked by an underground stream that cut across the foot of the stairs, a brick wall on the far side. The Captain waded across the stream and illuminated another lock with his lantern. He pressed it, now crossing himself after the Eastern Orthodox fashion and listened as another latch sprung open. He nodded with approval as he pushed the wall and watched it silently swing inward.

He stepped inside, his lantern held aloft. Its light was too dim to fill the void, but it reflected faintly off a host of luminescent white crosses floating in the air, some closer, others distant. Latin crosses, Rosy crosses, Celtic crosses, Orthodox crosses, Russian crosses, Georgian crosses: every type of cross imaginable glimmered, suspended in the darkness. As the Captain's eyes grew accustomed to the emptiness he saw that he stood at the entrance of a large vaulted chamber with a high domed ceiling covered in red plaster with luminescent white limestone crosses in relief, making them appear as though suspended in the air. He crossed the white limestone floor and examined the red granite paving stone that radiated from the chamber's center to form a large Maltese cross. He continued to a large red stone cross that rose nearly ten feet in height from the center of the chamber. He sniffed the air, unable to smell any mold or damp. 'Very good,' he smiled as he examined the masonry. 'There is nothing like German workmanship.'

Returning to his troops he led them into the chamber, where they placed the eleven coffins in a circle around the center of the upright cross. He knelt before the cross, looked in a large wooden chest at its foot filled with eleven folded sheets, crossed himself and closed the lid. He ordered the Grenadiers to place thorns over the chest, in a circle around the coffins and in front of the doorway, then turned to face his men.

'You have two hours to clean up. Then present yourself at the St. George monastery church. I have paid the Abbot to say a *Te Deum* mass. You will be sober when you come to the church. God save the Emperor.'

'God save the Emperor,' they answered in tired unison.

As the Grenadiers filed from the chamber, the Captain counted the coffins. 'Only eleven,' he thought to himself. 'We still need to find the twelfth.'

He waited until their boots faded through the door, across the stream and up the stairs. When he was alone the Captain sniffed the air uncertainly, turned and crossed himself once more, uttering a silent prayer under his breath. He withdrew a waxed oil-skin package from his pouch and placed it in an alcove high in the back of the upright stone cross.

He then walked to one of the coffins, placed his fingers on it and stood silently, trembling. A bone-chilling shriek came from inside, followed by cursing, pounding, scratching and finally a heart-wrenching wail. He whispered under his breath as his fingers transmitted his words through the thick wood.

'Please forgive me, Natalija.'

CHAPTER TWO

THE ORDER OF THE DRAGON

San Diego, Budapest, Belgrade: Fall and Winter 1991-1992

The unrelenting thumpity-thump of the railroad car was making Steven drowsy. The hazy early afternoon light of a Central European winter cast uncertain shadows across the filthy train compartment, bleaching already dull colors into shades of grey that made everything appear dirty. He had never realized that grey came in so many different hues. He gazed out the dirt-streaked window at the snow-covered fields, interrupted every so often by the pastel Habsburg towns and villages that dot the Pannonian Plain, clustered around tall church steeples, wood and coal smoke pouring from the chimneys. As he watched the monotonous scenery he thought back over the events that had marked the previous four months. Slatina's surprise announcement of a research fellowship, the extra reading assignments in preparation for the trip, his graduate studies, his language tutorials with Katarina and his work as a TA for Slatina.

He recalled watching CNN in anger and disbelief as the Yugoslav Army – known by its initials as the JNA – shelled the medieval walled port city of Dubrovnik until smoke billowed over the white walls across the Adriatic Sea. Vukovar also haunted him, as the JNA shelled that Danubian city into rubble. And then there were the late night discussions with Slatina and Katarina about the ongoing breakup and war in Yugoslavia as they watched that country's blood pour out onto the world's television screens…everything blurred together now in a mass of convoluted memories.

But the memories that were most distinct were the times he had spent with Katarina, practicing Serbo-Croatian. They had met regularly in the library after Slatina's class and she never called him Stevie, as did his mother, or Steven, as did Professor Slatina, or Steve, as did his friends in High School and College, but always Stefan, after the Serbian fashion. He had always thought of himself as Steven, and when people called him Steven, he felt he behaved differently, more responsibly and mature. And now Stefan? He responded differently and felt that it somehow brought an intimacy to their relationship that otherwise would not have existed. What *was* in a name? Did what we call someone change who they were, how they behaved and how we perceived them?

Speaking a foreign language frustrated him and locked his normally outgoing character into a linguistic prison whose rules and nuances he understood only with difficulty. Sometimes, even the simplest thoughts proved impossible to express. When he spoke Serbo-Croatian he behaved with more reserve than when he spoke English, something he hoped would change as his fluency increased. He was embarrassed by his accent and the way he butchered the language's seven grammatical cases. Yet Katarina was always patient, laughed sweetly at his many mistakes, corrected his errors, and helped him with pronunciation. Still, no matter how hard he tried, he just couldn't grasp the subtle difference between č and ć and pronounced both as *ch* in *ch*eese. Although he tried to concentrate on his studies, with each session he felt an emotional bond developing between them, something for which he was unprepared.

Watching the drab winter landscape from the train, he let his mind wander over the previous four months.

* * *

Three months earlier on a sunny late September morning, Slatina had walked him to the hill at the base of the university library, a silver-grey saucer that hovered over the Eucalyptus groves. 'Here we have an allegory of life's choices, of the struggle between good and evil.' Slatina pointed to a paving-stone sculpture of a serpent that wound its way through a lush garden, crisscrossing the sidewalk leading up the hill to the base of the library, wrapping itself finally around the base of a Pomegranate tree set in a lush semi-tropical garden.

'Notice this serpent. How it coils up the hill towards the Tree of Knowledge of Good and Evil. It is a symbol, something that is important in your study of the medieval period, where allegories were common, and symbolism meant everything. It will also be important in your study of ethnography. Watch for types and symbols. God commanded Adam and Eve not to eat of the fruit of the tree because it would cause them to die. The serpent told Eve otherwise, saying it would open her eyes and make her as the Gods, knowing good and evil. It appears the serpent had more persuasive marketing than God. The clear message is that to attain knowledge of good and evil, and to become like the Gods, we must cross paths with the serpent. And the more knowledge we acquire, the greater responsibility we have to do good. New responsibilities are thrust upon us as we acquire greater knowledge. Remember this as you conduct your research, for the things you discover may require you to take action you otherwise never would have contemplated.' They continued further up the hill, past a stone inscribed with a quote from Milton's *Paradise Lost.*

'Watch closely for the serpent in your work. Throughout history it has represented two opposite ideas. On the one hand it is associated with the devil. When God asked Eve why she ate of the fruit of the tree, Eve said 'the serpent beguiled me, and I did eat.' Saint George slew the fiery serpent, what we would call a dragon. The serpent or dragon is frequently a personification of the Devil himself, particularly in medieval literature. On the other hand the serpent is also a symbol of *Jahweh*, the God of the Hebrews in the Old Testament whom we call Jehovah. When *Jahweh* sent fiery serpents to chasten the disobedient children of Israel in the wilderness, he told Moses to create a brazen fiery serpent and place it on top of a pole. All those who looked on Moses' serpent would be healed of the bites of the fiery serpents. On many ancient graves – Christian and Pagan alike – you will find a snake with its tail in its mouth, representing eternal life. Unfortunately most people forget that the serpent is also a symbol of God.'

'What you must pay close attention to in your research are references to the serpent as the personification of Satan,' Slatina faced Steven and looked directly in his eyes. 'If you come into contact with them you may well be facing the Adversary himself.'

The Professor's impromptu lecture troubled Steven. Why was Slatina explaining the knowledge of good and evil and the symbolism of the serpent? Steven felt the professor was trying to tell him something indirectly, but was uncertain just what, unable to put his finger on what troubled him.

Later that day Steven stumbled upon Katarina, sitting alone under a tree in a Eucalyptus grove, its branches alive with a shimmering orange and black shroud of Monarch butterflies. She stared at the sky, pale clouds reflected greenly in the moisture of her tears.

'Katarina, what's wrong?' he asked, crouching beside her. 'Did someone hurt you?'

She held up her hand, motioned for him to stop talking and waited. After a few moments she took a deep breath, then spoke in a quivering voice: 'Today marks one hundred days from the death of my father. I should go with my mother to visit his grave. Instead I'm thousands of kilometers away. It's wrong. It's all wrong. I feel so empty without him,' she sobbed.

Steven placed an arm around her and hugged her. 'I'm truly sorry for your loss.'

She reached up and placed her hand over his, softly: 'At least he has someone to take care of his grave. But who will take care of their graves when my mother dies and I'm here?'

'I know what it means to lose someone close,' he said softly, strongly. 'I understand.' His hand tingled at her touch and goose bumps appeared along his arm. The softness of her shoulder and scent of her perfume heightened his senses to her closeness. His hormones and instincts told him to take advantage of her vulnerability and draw closer to her, while his conscience argued for virtue. Although his conscience won, guilt gnawed at him for permitting baser desires to enter his mind at a time when she needed compassion. Memories of his own loss also flooded in to cloud his mind. 'Has it been almost two years?' he thought to himself. It still seemed like only yesterday.

Steven sat silently with her for another half hour, and when he said he had to leave for class she said 'thank you for sitting with me. It means much to me,' and then kissed him on one cheek.

He blushed as he strode away through the Eucalyptus groves, his thoughts confused.

* * *

Watching the fields rush by through the dirty window, Steven saw no Eucalyptus trees: instead a thick layer of low-lying winter clouds hid the sun. Nor were there any serpents: only snow and lines of telephone poles disappearing into the distance. As he watched the Pannonian plain stretch away until it merged seamlessly with the horizon, it reminded him somehow of looking out over the Pacific, watching the fog banks.

He thought back to a warm sunny day in mid-October, sitting under the shade of a gnarled Torrey Pine tree on the sandstone cliffs above the beach, barefoot, Katarina forcing him to speak only Serbo-Croatian, refusing to answer in English. The sun, sea and Katarina's closeness made concentration difficult and the parade of hang-gliders distracted him as they hovered in the updraft from the cliffs.

'Make it easier, talk about yourself. Tell me where you are from and why you study Balkan history.' She spoke brightly, the Vojvodina dialect gentle on her lips.

'I'm an Air Force brat.... lived all over. My dad's last post was Hill Air Force Base in Utah, and when he left the service he got a job at Morton-Thiokol working on space shuttle booster rockets.'

'Isn't that where Mormons live...in Utah?'

'Yeah.'

'What are they like?' her face was curious.

'Just like anybody else,' he grinned. 'Except the men wear ties and the women wear big hair...think of 1950's America.'

'So why are you studying Balkan history?'

'I went to the University of Utah on a wrestling scholarship and then to the University of Wisconsin. My history professor was a Serb, and he got me interested in Yugoslavia. I studied language in Zagreb and Dubrovnik for a year, then my professor recommended me to Professor Slatina for graduate work.'

'You wrestled?' her eyes widened. 'Did you wear a mask and funny costume like on television?'

'Nope, real wrestling. I was All-State in High School for two years.'

'All-State? What's that?' she asked.

'It means I was the best in the entire state.'

'Oh,' she said, thoroughly unimpressed.

'So, do you believe in God?' she changed the topic abruptly.

'Well...you know...' he looked at his feet, puzzled as to how the conversation had suddenly jumped from wrestling to religion. Why had she brought up religion? 'I believe there's a higher power... a god of some sort, but I'm not that big on organized religion.' He shifted his gaze from his feet to her face and found her eyes, shining greenly. Sitting this close to her wasn't conducive to contemplating religion. 'What about you?' he asked out of curiosity.

'I'm Orthodox,' she answered matter-of-factly. 'But it's my tradition. I don't really believe in it. If you're a Serb, you're supposed to be Orthodox.'

'So, what do you believe in?' he asked.

'Hmmm, that's a good question. God. His love. My parents. Family. Marko.'

'Marko? You mean the professor?'

'Yes. He's a good man. He would never let anything bad happen to me, and I know he has a good heart.'

'What about me?' Steven grinned, trying to lighten the subject. 'Do I have a good heart?'

'Of course,' she said matter-of-factly. 'If you didn't, Marko wouldn't have chosen you for this trip.'

He stared at her, puzzled. 'What does that mean?'

'Do you have faith?' she asked.

'Do I have faith?' he repeated, puzzled why she kept steering the conversation towards religion. 'Well, I mean…'

He didn't finish the sentence as he thought back to high school, his mother, a staunch Presbyterian, the arguments around the dinner table as she scolded his father, a relaxed Methodist, that they never should have settled in Utah. His father would respond by defending Mormons, arguing that there was good in everything, but each meal would finish with her angrily declaring: 'I don't want my children to become damn Mormons!' And then in high school, Steven did the unthinkable and converted to the Church of Jesus Christ of Latter-day Saints against the explicit wishes of his mother. His mother didn't speak to him for almost six months, while his father tried unsuccessfully to mediate.

After his freshman year at college, Steven eagerly volunteered to serve a two-year mission for the Mormon Church, took a vow of celibacy for the duration, and was ordained a minister. After two months at the Missionary Training Center, a spiritual boot-camp located next to Brigham Young University in Provo, Utah, he stepped off the plane in Hamburg, Germany, eager to make converts. Yet two weeks later he was back in Utah, disgraced and shunned.

At the end of his first week in Hamburg, a woman's hushed giggles had awoken him during the night. Peering into the sitting room he had seen his half-clad mission companion locked in the embrace of the girl from across the hallway. Steven reported the conduct to the mission president, who ex-communicated Steven's companion and, uncertain whether to believe Steven's protestations of innocence, released him from his mission and sent him home. Returning to Utah in disgrace he was shunned at Church, an outcast in the predominantly Mormon community. He soon stopped attending weekly meetings, angered at the hypocrisy and injustice, then transferred to the University of Wisconsin, relieved to be in a place with few Mormons. Over time he abandoned the outward trappings of his religion and began drinking coffee, tea and alcohol, taboos for Mormons. He was finished with organized religion.

Katarina studied Steven's face with empathy, sensed she had hit a raw nerve, then picked a pine cone from the ground, gently placed it in his palm, startling him from his reverie. As she tenderly closed his fingers around it, one at a time, a current of energy flowed slowly from her fingers to his, through his hand, up his arm to his heart, causing it to skip a beat.

'Stefan, you will find faith. Here is its seed. Nurture it and it will grow. Perhaps you may not have faith in God now, but He has faith in you. I have faith in you and I know you'll find your own faith.'

'You're quite the philosopher,' he grinned at her. She smiled back, he talked about his glory days of high school football, and then she read his palm, which sent tingles up his arm and made him blush.

As they stood to leave, she reached out, ran her fingers across his left cheek, and then kissed the spot where her fingers had been. He left exhilarated at the increasing closeness between them, and troubled by her questions about faith.

* * *

But faith eluded him throughout the autumn and early winter, even though he kept the pine cone on his nightstand. Steven couldn't remember the last time he had prayed or what it was he said, except that his words had been angry and defiant. Now he was journeying into a strange country gripped in war and madness, and suddenly questions of God and faith seemed more important. 'Do I have faith?' he asked his faint reflection in the train window.

'At least it's stopped snowing,' he thought as he gazed through the glass at the darkening landscape. He had spent the previous four days in Budapest, and it had snowed much of the time, a contrast to the rain of La Jolla.

It had been a rainy Saturday back in November when Steven visited Slatina's house for dinner. The professor's Spanish style art deco home sat in a pricey La Jolla neighborhood of multi-million dollar homes, with a stunning view of the Pacific, now obscured by the pouring rain. As he parked his ten-year old Toyota Tercel, Steven wondered how Slatina could afford the view and address on a professor's salary. He ran through torrential rain and wind that lashed the Palm and Torrey Pine trees in the front yard, catching his sleeve on the thorns of a red-berried Hawthorne. Katarina answered the door with a smile, as breathtakingly beautiful as when first they'd met.

She invited him in, and throughout the rest of the day she and Slatina spoke Serbo-Croatian, forcing Steven to practice the language, encouraging him when he made errors. The three of them prepared the meal, a simple Adriatic dish of large prawns cooked in a spiced tomato sauce served over pasta, along with a refreshing salad of mozzarella cheese, rucola and sliced tomatoes, mixed with fresh basil leaves, olive oil and a smattering of pesto. They washed it down with a pitcher of juice Steven had squeezed from blood oranges and a bottle of Dalmatian wine. For dessert Slatina had prepared *Tiramisu.*

After the meal, Steven and Katarina volunteered to do dishes, while Slatina excused himself to make telephone calls in the study. As the two of them washed the dishes they made small talk, which was difficult for him in

Serbo-Croatian, so she ended up doing much of the talking. 'You only know academic words,' she said with an accusing look that made her even prettier than usual.

'You must learn more. Today I will teach you some new vocabulary. *Serpa* - pan. *Lonac* - pot,' she held each one up in turn. He dutifully repeated each word after her. As he listened to her pronounce the words, first in Serbo-Croatian, then in English, he watched her lips move and imagined them brushing against his. Her slender fingers and hands dipped the plates in the dishwater, and then she would hand him a dish to dry. He watched her hair fall over her face as she bent over the sink and thought he had never seen a more beautiful girl in his entire life. He stood and stared, only to be startled out of his trance by her words: '*Daj mi krpu.*'

'Huh?'

'*Krpa* - dishcloth. I am finished. Give me dishcloth so I can dry my hands.' Her strangely accented English made the words somehow magical. '*Daj mi viljuske* - give me forks,' she motioned. He watched as she began to dry each one and put them in the silverware drawer. She noticed him staring at her hands and said '*deterdzent za pranje posudja* - dishwashing liquid,' which caused his heart to skip. Yet he said nothing and kept on drying. '*Deterdzent za pranje posudja*,' he repeated softly to himself as he looked in her eyes and saw a flicker of something he thought he recognized.

The dishes done, Katarina grabbed both Steven's hands, looked in his eyes and kissed him gently on his cheek, smiled and pulled him towards Slatina's study. 'Come, the professor's waiting.'

They entered a cozy room with overstuffed leather furniture and glass doors looking out on a rain-swept terrace facing the Pacific, its smell of old leather and mildew presenting a sharp contrast with the newness in Slatina's office. Steven rushed to the bookshelves lining the walls and gaped in awe at the treasure trove of rare Slavic literature: Juraj Krizanic's 17th century treatise *Politika*; Mauro Orbini's 1601 *Il regno degli Slavi*; Vinko Pribojevic's 1532 work *De origine successionibusque Slavorum*; Petar Hektorovic's 1568 edition of *Ribanje i ribarsko prigovaranje*; and Ivan Gundulic's 1626 edition of *Osman*.

'Professor, are all these original?' Steven asked in amazement, envious of the priceless collection of Balkan literature.

'Of course. Family heirlooms,' Slatina answered with a smile. 'Our family brought them with us when we fled the communists. Please use care when you handle them.'

Steven approached a darkened oil portrait of a gaunt monarch with a blonde goatee in a dark green cloak, a St. George cross at his neck. He examined the painting and saw the words *O quam misericors est Deus* ran from the top of the cross, while the cross-piece bore the words *Justus et Pius*. A dragon pin fastened the monarch's cloak, its tail looping underneath its body to wrap back around its neck, forming a circle. The monarch's sword was sheathed in a scabbard emblazoned with six golden dragons. Steven silently counted the coats of arms painted in the background: twenty one.

'Who's this?' Steven asked. 'I don't recognize him.'

'Sigismund, King of Hungary, from 1408.'

'Another heirloom?' Steven asked.

'But of course.'

Next to it hung a small, oval portrait of an attractive noble woman with high cheekbones, a high forehead and dark eyes, posing in front of a landscape. Steven guessed it to be from the late 17th century.

The professor watched Steven carefully as he moved excitedly from the bookshelf to the paintings, then back to the bookshelf. He noted Steven's care and reverence handling the old volumes. He nodded his head in satisfaction at Steven's enthusiasm and pointed towards a large yellowed map that filled the wall above his desk, a cryptic smile on his face.

'Do you like it?' he asked. A hilltop fortress guarded galleys in the harbor of a walled port city next to Latin inscriptions, a winged lion and the word *Pharos, 1714*. 'It is my home town, the city of Hvar on the island of Hvar in Dalmatia. Perhaps someday you will visit…but it looks a bit different now…no more galleys…just yachts and tourist hotels.'

Slatina smiled, then walked to a shelf and removed a bottle filled with dark liquid containing sprigs, grasses and leaves. He opened the cap, sniffed it and took three small shot glasses: 'May I interest you in a glass of homemade *rakija*? It is purely medicinal…made from herbs to assist digestion.' He smiled and filled the glasses, handed one to Katarina and Steven, and then raised his in a toast.

'My friends, thank you for coming and making this meal so pleasant. May there be many more meals such as this one, and may we live to see them in good health and happiness, and with the joy that comes from being surrounded by those we love. And may we also drink to those whom we have loved and who loved us and who cannot be here.' He looked them each in the eyes as they touched glasses.

'Steven, I have been in contact with the Balkan Ethnographic Trust. They have asked that you conduct research on witches, fairies, and other mythical creatures in what is increasingly becoming the former Yugoslavia. They have asked that I supervise your research, so you will report to me.'

'I may also ask you to undertake some tasks of a personal nature for me. As you know, it has been difficult for me to return with the communists in power. Perhaps time shall change that, but in the meantime I may seek your assistance. I shall give you letters of introduction to professors in Budapest and Belgrade and for the archives in Novi Sad and Belgrade. I have asked my old friend Dr. Ferenc Nagy to do the same for the Budapest archives.'

'Professor, you forget, I don't know Hungarian.'

'Now Steven, you know that Latin was the official court language throughout most of medieval Europe.'

I hate Latin, Steven thought. He had struggled with the History program's Latin requirement.

Afterwards Slatina had put on a video and Steven sat next to Katarina on a large overstuffed sofa, watching a film about three friends who had fled communist Yugoslavia by rowing across the Adriatic Sea to Italy. During the film Katarina placed her hand in his, gradually leaned against his shoulder and fell asleep. It felt pleasant, and he put his arm around her, letting her head fall against his chest, enjoying an intimacy he had long denied himself. As he did so, recent memories returned to haunt his new feelings.

From the armchair, Slatina watched from the corner of his eyes, a slight smile on his lips.

* * *

Steven shifted uncomfortably against the hard-backed train seat. Professor Slatina's leather sofa had been far more comfortable. As the telephone poles rushed hypnotically past, Steven wondered if he might find answers here, away from everything that was familiar to him.

He thought back to his departure from the US and his arrival at the Budapest airport only six days ago. Katarina and Professor Slatina had both seen him off at the San Diego airport the day after Christmas. The departure terminal was crowded with lightly-clad vacationers enjoying San Diego's winter sun: Steven carried a heavy winter coat and a fur hat in his arms. As he left Professor Slatina hugged him, kissed him once on each cheek and wished him luck. 'And watch your temper. You'll be in a strange country that is at war. Injustice will be everywhere. Discipline your emotions'.

Katarina kissed him three times, once on the right, left and again the right cheek. 'Serbs kiss three times,' she whispered to him. And then she kissed him a fourth time, long, passionate, squarely on the lips, sending an electric charge through his body.

She then fished in the pocket of her jeans and brought out a small wooden cross affixed to a piece of rough twine. Reaching up she placed it around Steven's neck. 'This is to you from me and it is for your protection. It's made from the Hawthorne tree and was blessed at the monastery church of Zica, the blood red church where a piece of the true cross lies. You must wear it around your neck at all times: it'll protect you from whatever evil you encounter.'

Overcome by the kiss, Steven spluttered: 'but…its just superstition…'

'Please do it. For me.' Her look was earnest. 'It would mean a lot to me.

And maybe one day it may mean something to you. Think of it as a good luck charm, not a religious symbol.'

He nodded, looking into her eyes, now a dark impenetrable green, wondering what the kiss had meant.

'Hurry, you'll miss your plane.' She shoved an envelope in his hand, kissed him again once on the cheek, turned around and walked away. 'And remember me when you wear it,' she added as she glanced over her shoulder. Slatina smiled and nodded silently.

As Steven walked away he realized that his feelings towards Katarina had grown stronger than he wished to admit. Confused, he tenderly touched the cross around his neck as he boarded the airplane.

Due to the war, flights into Yugoslavia were sporadic, so Steven flew into Budapest, from whence he planned to take a train to Belgrade. He disembarked from the *Malev* airliner down a metal stairway onto the tarmac – the wind driving snow into his face – and was then herded with the other passengers into a decrepit communist-era terminal labeled *Ferihegy*, where the centrally-planned heating made him sweat, and the stench of tobacco brought on nausea.

The border guards had not yet heard that Hungary had cast off the dual yoke of Marx and Moscow and was making its uncertain way towards democracy. Irritated that they had to work between Christmas and New Years, they acted out their aggression on the arriving passengers. Steven noticed that those with Yugoslav passports received the worst treatment. By the time he cleared customs, his head was swimming from cigarette smoke and exhaustion. He took a taxi through the decaying center of Budapest, sucked dry by 45 years of Marxism, to a cheap hotel on the Buda side of the river near Moskva Ter, where he collapsed into a deep sleep.

The next day didn't dawn, as much as it gradually grew less dark. He crawled from bed and walked to the bathroom to find lukewarm water, soap that burned his skin, sandpaper masquerading as toilet paper, and bath towels only slightly larger than washcloths. After his morning routine of pushups and sit-ups he ate breakfast in a socialist-chic dining room that probably looked shabby the day it was remodeled in the 1970s. Breakfast consisted of a barely palatable hard-boiled egg, two pieces of bread with a slab of butter and marmalade, accompanied by a metal cup of warm milk with curdled skin floating on the surface. Steven was the only guest at breakfast, and the waiter spent most of the time glaring over his bushy moustache, frustrated at having to work over the holidays.

After breakfast Steven put on his winter coat and fur hat, left his hotel room and slogged through the lightly falling snow into the city, still groggy from jet lag. Map in hand, he took the subway to the Pest side to an old neighborhood near the National Opera, to a crumbling Habsburg-era apartment building. Steven walked through the main doors into the courtyard, tripped over snow-covered garbage, and entered a stairwell. As he climbed the dark unlit steps, the sounds of conversations, domestic arguments and television mingled with the smell of *paprikash*, urine and human feces. Reaching the fourth floor, he walked around the open walkway, holding tightly to the wobbly rusted iron railing, taking care to avoid sheets of ice. He stopped and knocked at a door. There was no answer.

As he knocked again, faded blue paint from the door came off on his glove. Steven heard a shuffling sound from inside, saw a light appear in the transom above the door, and heard the lock click. A white-haired man opened the door part way, looked out at him from under bushy white eyebrows, rubbed his red nose and barked something unintelligible in Hungarian.

'Guten tag,' Steven answered. He hoped the man spoke German. '*Sind Sie Professor Doktor Nagy* – Are you Professor Doctor Nagy?'

'*Ja, Ich bin Doktor Professor Nagy* – Yes, I am Doctor Professor Nagy.'

'*Ich habe für Sie ein Brief von Professor Doktor Marko Slatina* – I have a letter for you from Professor Doctor Marko Slatina.' Steven handed him an envelope.

Nagy opened it and read it slowly. He then looked at Steven and said in thickly accented English: 'It is cold outside. Please do come in and make yourself at home.' He opened the door. 'Permit me to take your coat.' He stripped it from Steven's back and placed it on a coat rack before he could react. 'Marko wrote me about you. I expected your arrival much sooner.'

Nagy's house slippers and woolen sweater made him appear overstuffed. He ushered Steven down a short hallway to a tiny sitting room that appeared to also serve as a sleeping area and study, cleared a pile of books from a folded sofa bed and placed them on an end table hidden under even more papers and books. A television glowed silently as folk dancers in colorful Hungarian costumes leaped cheerfully across the screen, accompanied by a radiator hissing against the wall.

'Sooooo,' Nagy drew out the word as though it had several syllables. 'How is my dear friend Marko?'

'Professor Slatina is well,' Steven said formally. 'He asked me to give you his warmest regards and thank you for the hospitality and friendship you've shown him in the past, and said that he appreciates your correspondence.'

'Aahh, that is too nice of him. He is a good man, you know? I recall him fondly from happier days. He could certainly turn a young lady's head, you know. May I make you some tea?' Steven nodded. 'Would you like black or chamomile?'

'Chamomile, thank you.'

Nagy disappeared into another room, and Steven watched folk dancers gyrate across the TV screen. He waited through a short harvest dance, as well as a longer courtship dance. Why do the women folk dancers wear red rubber boots? he asked himself. Nagy finally returned bearing a silver tray with old porcelain cups, steam rising from the surface. 'Sooo, tell me now, what you are doing.' He enthusiastically passed a cracked sugar dish to Steven.

'Professor Slatina arranged a fellowship from the Balkan Ethnographic Trust. I'll be spending the next twelve months in Serbia. If things calm down I might go to Croatia, perhaps even the Dubrovnik archives, if the siege lifts.'

'Hmmm, the Balkan Ethnographic Trust. Never heard of it. But then the communists kept us far from the academic mainstream. Too much knowledge was always dangerous, so they tried to limit people's access to all types of information, forcing them to place all their faith in the infallibility of the party. In his letter Marko tells me that he wishes you to examine certain documents in the national archive. Unfortunately you have arrived between Christmas and New Year, and everything is closed. The archive will remain closed until the end of the first week of January. And even if you wait until then, there may not be much heat, as they are short of funds.'

Steven looked dismayed.

'However, not to worry, I have already taken care of things through some connections and have had photocopies made,' Nagy smiled triumphantly. 'But first you must finish your tea, and then we shall turn to business. *Egészségedre*' – Cheers!' He lifted his tea cup.

Nagy spent the rest of the day going through photocopies of old documents with Steven, most of them in Latin, most relating to the medieval Hungarian kingdom during the reigns of Sigismund I, Janos Hunyadi and Matthius Corvinus. Steven was exhausted from jet lag, the stale air of the cramped apartment was tiring him and the silent folk-dance marathon had a distracting, yet hypnotic effect. As they pondered royal charters, land deeds, grants, endowments, testaments and other documents, he became increasingly confused…noble houses, royal blood lines, treaties, marriage alliances, wars with the Turks, feuds between nobles, court intrigues, international diplomacy, the Holy Roman Empire… He wondered how 15th century Hungarian history was relevant to ethnography and the study of monsters in folklore. As jet-lag hit he fought to stay awake and rapidly lost interest. He repeatedly asked for more tea, but by 3:00 PM his head was swimming and his eyes lost focus as he began to nod off.

'Wake up young man,' Nagy nudged him. 'We are here to study, not sleep.' Steven excused himself, and asked if they might continue the next day.

He went back to the hotel restaurant and ordered a bowl of fiery red fish *paprikash* stew with black bread, under the scowling moustachioed supervision of the same waiter who had served him breakfast, then returned to his room and plunged immediately into a deep sleep, only to wake up around 3:00 a.m. Jet lag, he thought. He lay in bed for hours, trying futilely to sleep. Sometime around 5:00 a.m. he drifted off, only to dream that he was the King of Hungary, sitting on a throne in the middle of a university lecture hall, surrounded by moustachioed nobility, all staring at him and speaking in a strange language while jumping back and forth performing folk dances. He tried to get them to quiet down, but to no avail. Finally he stood to address the nobles and noticed that he was clad only in underwear and red rubber boots, which caused the nobility to laugh at him. He picked up his royal scepter to strike out at them, but it somehow transformed into the steering wheel of his battered Toyota Tercel, and he was now driving Katarina home to her dorm in the middle of the day. As he stopped the car she smiled, squeezed his hand, kissed him on the cheek, and whispered softly: 'Clean the pots and pans with dishwashing liquid, then dry them with a dish rag.' He then dreamt that Professor Slatina was giving a lecture on the best way to prepare meals made from serpents, dragons and Vojvodina wine. Steven awoke, confused and disoriented. 'I'll never eat fish *paprikash* again,' he swore to himself.

En route to Nagy's apartment he purchased a kilogram of coffee and a bottle of Tokaji wine, which he presented to the professor. Given Nagy's obvious poverty Steven suspected he didn't have much money for coffee, and Steven hoped the coffee might help keep him awake. Nagy was waiting anxiously, papers in hand. 'Today we will review documents pertaining to one of the more interesting phenomena in Hungarian history, and I am certain it will keep you awake. And you will not need coffee. You see this document here? What can you tell me about it?'

Steven squinted at the handwritten Latin text. 'Well, it looks as though it is the founding charter of a knightly order…it is dated 12 December 1408 by Sigismund I, King of Hungary. The co-founders consist of twenty one *Barones*, which I assume to be nobility or Barons. Now this is interesting… Barbara von Cilli is listed as a cofounder,' he exclaimed. 'Isn't this unusual to have a woman belong to a knightly order, much less co-found one?'

'Yes, most unusual,' Nagy agreed.

'And who is Barbara von Cilli?'

'The second wife of King Sigismund. She was the daughter of a Slovenian nobleman. But she is tangential, unless you like stories of lesbian vampires,' Nagy smiled as if sharing a secret.

'A lesbian vampire?' Steven woke up suddenly as lurid images from puberty flashed through his head.

'Yes. After the death of Sigismund, Barbara moved to Bohemia, where the Habsburgs accused her of drinking human blood during Holy Communion and holding sexual orgies with young girls. I am certain that someday Hollywood will make a movie about it. But that is beside the point,' Nagy gestured at the photocopy. 'Please, would you continue with the document?'

'It is called the *Societas Draconis*, the 'Society of the Dragon,' it has as its emblem the *Signum draconis*, 'Sign of the Dragon,' and its motto is *O quam misericors est Deus, Justus et Pius*, "O how merciful is God, Just and Faithful".' He thought to himself: 'Haven't I seen that somewhere?'

'Professor Nagy, why are we examining this particular Order?' Steven asked.

'The younger generation is so impatient. You have no concept of the work required to get good answers,' scolded Nagy. 'Marko asked me to educate you about the history and importance of the Order. Did he not tell you? No, of course not, he likes his little surprises. You will find that out in the course of your research. Now, let us examine other documents to discover more answers.'

They spent the remainder of the morning examining documents pertaining to the Society of the Dragon. During their brief lunch break Nagy turned on the television and they watched a 100-piece Gypsy all-violin orchestra perform Strauss, Liszt and Brahms in a madcap, enthusiastically undisciplined fashion that reminded Steven of a sprint to the finish of the *Tour de France* or Spike Jones playing the Blue Danube Waltz. But the musical chaos was a welcome relief from the folk dancers. Lunch was homemade and modest: cucumber and ham sandwiches served with plain yogurt, followed by steaming cups of strong Turkish coffee. After they drank their coffee thick sludge remained in the cups. Nagy turned his upside down on his saucer, waited a few moments, removed the cup and pointed at the brownish-black streaks on the saucer and in the cup.

'You know, Steven, there are women in the Balkans who can read your future from the patterns they see in the sludge.'

They continued reading documents all afternoon, and Nagy had to help Steven with the more difficult passages of Latin. The work was tedious, but Steven stayed awake and focused, thanks largely to the strong Turkish coffee. Around 5:30 PM, after they had put away the photocopies and Nagy had brought out some sliced *kobasica* and cheese and poured them each a glass of Tokaji, he asked Steven: 'What have we learned thus far about the Society of the Dragon?'

'Well,' Steven said, 'it's a rather murky organization. Although the charter dates from 1408, it appears that it may have been in existence as early as 1381, or perhaps in 1387 at the time Sigismund was in exile.' He looked to Nagy for approval.

The professor nodded and smiled. 'Continue.'

'It was called by several names depending on the time period.' Steven thumbed through his notes. 'Various documents refer to it as *Societas Draconis* - the "Society of the Dragon", *Fraternatis Draconem* - the "Brotherhood of the Dragon", *Ordo Draconis* - the "Order of the Dragon" and *Societatis Draconistarum* – once again the "Society of the Dragon". And judging by the two different spellings of the words 'society' and 'dragon', I'd say that I'm not the only person who had difficulty with Latin in school.'

'Yes, yes, quite right. In Hungarian we call it *Sárkány Rend* - the Order of the Dragon. Please continue.'

'Each member had two different capes, one dark green, and the other black. They wore the black cape on Fridays to signify penitence, and the green cape the remainder of the time. They also wore a cross around their necks with the Order's motto on it. They were supposed to wear the Order's dragon insignia prominently at all times and to include the Order's insignia in their coat of arms. There was an inner circle of 24 nobles and an outer circle with unlimited membership. It had some rather interesting members. There is Hrvoje, the Duke of Spalato in Dalmatia; Stefan Lazarevic, the Despot of Serbia; and I noticed that Vlad II, Vojvoda of Wallachia, was made a member of the inner circle in 1431…isn't that Dracula?'

'No. Dracula was Vlad III, Tsepeş. This was his father, Vlad II, who was known as *Dracul*. The name *Dracul* means 'Dragon' in Romanian and Vlad got his nickname because he displayed the Order's dragon insignia. His son, Vlad III was called *Dracula*, meaning 'of Dracul.' It was also a play on words, as the Romanian word for 'devil' is almost identical to the name '*Dracul*,' and may have reflected the Romanians' true feelings about the behavior of their Vojvoda.'

'Oh.'

'Now, tell me, what was the purpose of the Order?'

'I haven't the faintest idea.'

'Excellent, excellent. Your honesty is most admirable. And you stand in good company. You see, no one really knows the reason the Order was founded, and part of the answer may depend on when it was founded and by whom.'

'I don't understand.'

'Excellent, excellent. Please bear with me. If the Order was founded in 1387 or 1408 by Sigismund then we may believe that its purpose was to strengthen Sigismund and the Luxembourg dynasty's claim to the throne of Hungary, and there is no question that he used the Order to do just that and buy off his nobles. But he also used it to protect Hungary's southern borders against the Turks. In some instances we see both motives at work, such as when he granted the famed silver mines of Srebrenica to Despot Stefan Lazarevic in 1412. At that time Hungary held title to the area, but had long ago lost effective control of it to local magnates, backed by the Bosnian kings. Sigismund deeded the mines to Stefan under the conditions that they be placed back into production and that the crown received a percentage of the proceeds. The induction of Vlad II into the Order is also an example of how he attempted to pacify a potentially troublesome nobleman and form a bulwark against the Turks.'

Steven nodded his agreement: 'It makes sense. The king wanted to unite his nobles around him and strengthen his position on the throne, so, he formed an exclusive by-invitation-only club with 24 members, and bought off the nobility by giving them deeds to lands that are rightfully his, but over which he has lost control. I see nothing wrong with that explanation.'

'Well, you see, actually much is wrong,' Nagy was now getting excited. 'Firstly you must ask yourself what it means if the Order actually existed before Sigismund came to the throne in 1387. As you have seen there are references to it as early as 1381. I am told that it may have existed further south in Serbia even earlier than this and that several of its members may have been killed at the Battle of Kosovo Field on St. Vitus' Day in 1389. Thus, it may well have been an already existing Order that Sigismund took over and used for his own purposes. Remember, this Order is quite unusual in relation to other medieval knightly orders in that it had no headquarters or regular meetings that we are aware of. We must also ask about the name.'

'What's so unusual about the name?'

Nagy closed his eyes and began reciting from memory:

> *And there was a war in heaven: Michael and his angels fought against the dragon; and the dragon fought and his angels, and prevailed not; neither was their place found any more in heaven. And the great dragon was cast out, that old serpent, called the Devil, and Satan, which deceiveth the whole world: he was cast out into the earth, and his angels were cast out with him. And they overcame him by the blood of the Lamb, and by the word of their testimony; and they loved not their lives unto the death.*

'That is from the Revelation of St. John, the twelfth chapter. They overcame the dragon by blood…the blood of the Lamb. So if the Dragon is associated with Satan, why is the Order called after the Dragon. Why not the order of St. George, especially since the members of the Order wore the cross of St. George at all times? After all, the Dragon represents the evil one, Satan. Were they in fact Satan worshippers? Why name your order after your adversary?' Nagy waved a forefinger.

'Didn't some African and indigenous American tribes believe they could take on the powers and attributes of their enemies by eating their hearts?' Steven interjected. 'Perhaps this was something similar…name yourself after your enemy in order to take his power and defeat him.'

'That is precisely my point,' Nagy enthused. 'It is entirely possible that they were not originally organized to fight against the Turks or to strengthen the Luxembourg dynasty. In fact, they do not appear to have been visibly organized at all. Or, if they were organized, it was as a secret society about which little knowledge has survived. And why would they be organized in secret? Because they were formed to fight against the serpent himself, Satan. Therefore they took upon themselves the name of their adversary.' He stopped, pondered what he had just said, and added: 'but these are simply the musings of an old man. The only evidence I have is circumstantial. Whatever the purpose of the Order, it is well concealed to this day.'

Both sat silently for some time, sipping their Tokaji. Then Nagy asked: 'Tomorrow is Sylvester. Do you have plans?'

'Sylvester? What's that?'

'The day of St. Sylvester…New Year's Eve. You must come with me. Some colleagues and I are having a get-together to celebrate the New Year. Meet me here at 9:00 PM.'

Steven froze as he thought back twenty four months, when he sat in a wheelchair on New Year's Eve, keeping vigil at a hospital bedside, holding *her* pale hand as *her* life slipped away.

'Steven?'

'Oh, yes. I'll come. Thank you.'

Steven arrived the next evening at Professor Nagy's apartment to find him wearing a brown suit with a red waistcoat and a completely inappropriate broad green tie that had somehow survived the 1970s and now lay on top of his waistcoat.

'Welcome,' Nagy said, the smell of alcohol already strong on his breath. He wrapped himself against the cold, and led Steven several blocks away where they entered a dark doorway, descended stairs, knocked, a small panel slid open, words were exchanged, and a metal door swung open, hitting them with a cacophony of sound and tobacco smoke.

Steven entered a dimly-lit cellar of vaulted brick with paper decorations – stars, moons, suns, posters with unintelligible phrases he assumed meant 'Happy New Year' in Hungarian. At the far end a small jazz combo tried to follow a skinny blonde singing 'It's only a paper moon.'

Nagy pulled him to a table in an alcove, around which sat a group of elderly men and women.

'Great,' thought Steven. 'New Year's Eve with Hungarian retirees.'

Nagy said something to them in Hungarian by way of greeting and they all stood up and hugged and kissed him. He then changed to English. 'I would like you to meet Mr. Steven Roberts,' he was very formal. 'He is a student of Marko Slatina's at the university in California.' At the mention of Slatina's name those present smiled. Nagy made introductions all around…a professor from the Sociology Department, another from Anthropology, Chemistry, History, and their spouses. Some spoke battered English, others German.

As the evening wore on Steven attempted to match them glass for glass, but gave up after it became apparent the Hungarians had learned a few tricks about holding their liquor from the Russians during 45 years of occupation. All present knew Marko Slatina and had fond memories of him. One very nice lady, a retired professor of something-or-other with a butcher's command of English, insisted on monopolizing him for most of the evening. At one point she asked: 'has Marko found anyone yet? You know he was quite a catch…' The rest of the evening passed in an alcohol-fuelled daze, and the only thing Steven remembered was everybody joyously shouting '*Boldog Új Évet* – Happy New Year'. Steven had absolutely no recollection of how he returned to the hotel.

* * *

As he thought back to Budapest's massive Keléti Pályaudvar train station, Steven decided the Hungarians could teach Pavlov a thing or two about behavioral control. The enormous glass-roofed main hall built during the 19th century imperial heyday was crowded, and announcements were only in Hungarian. His head clouded by a hangover, it took Steven some time to find a train schedule, and when he did it appeared erratic, as though similar to the suspension of flights into Belgrade, Serbia's very existence now depended on the whim of the Hungarian state railway. He met a Serb who understood Hungarian and discovered that the next train was to leave at 12:10 PM.

Steven dragged his suitcases to the platform and joined a large crowd of people sitting on their bags, stamping their feet and rubbing their hands together for warmth. By 12:30 the train hadn't arrived, but a series of announcements in rapid-fire Hungarian caused the passengers to pick up their bags and run first to one platform, then to another, and then back again, until the announcer decided she had derived enough sadistic pleasure for one day and permitted the train to arrive. Steven found a compartment with the only other non-smoker in Eastern Europe and the train finally departed, an hour late.

'I've gotta stop drinking' he murmured as he gingerly rested his head against the back of the train seat, stretched out his legs and placed them on the seat opposite him.

The trip south was slow and uneventful, but by the time the train reached the border most of the seats had filled up with Yugoslavs, all of whom carried large boxes or overstuffed suitcases. From their conversations Steven assumed most were petty smugglers crossing into Yugoslavia with black market goods. Somewhere in southern Hungary the train's motion had lulled Steven to sleep, but a change in movement woke him as it slowed at the border. Green uniformed border police with the red white and green Hungarian tricolor, some carrying Kalashnikovs, customs agents searching compartments; it all passed quickly and the blast of a conductor's whistle sent the train moving forward.

In Subotica – the first station in Yugoslavia – a wild peasant mob was held restlessly at bay behind metal barriers, with police standing watch. The border guards, wearing bluish purple and black camouflage, were followed by green uniformed customs officers. One customs officer opened the compartment door and greeted the passengers, all of whom recognized him. He asked what they had in their luggage, and they all answered openly. 'I have 30 kilos of coffee and 20 kilos of laundry detergent,' said one. 'I have 10 liters of alcohol and 15 cartons of cigarettes,' offered another. 'I have nylons and chocolate,' chimed in yet a third. 'Everyone give me a little something. I'll be back in five minutes…and make sure you put it in a bag,' the customs officer said. Five minutes later he collected his tribute. Steven watched the events, shocked at the flagrant corruption.

When the customs check was completed the police pulled back the metal barriers and a wave of humanity flooded the train carrying bags, sacks, and boxes of black market goods. Steven's second class compartment – which had seating for eight – ended up with ten people on the seats and two sitting on boxes. Overhead luggage racks were stuffed full of every imaginable item, and people stood packed together in the hallway. Another whistle blast sent the train slowly lurching forward as Steven assessed his new traveling companions. Three old peasant women with skin the texture of rhinoceros-hide bundled in heavy woolen knit sweaters, three middle-aged men who immediately began smoking, and a mother with two children, who alternated between the boxes and the mother's lap.

The travelers were all Serbs returning from Hungary with black market goods, or from family plots and farms in the countryside. They shared methods of smuggling, close calls with the authorities, where they had purchased their goods, where they expected to sell them and for what price.

Two small children were told to come in and sit on laps, while their grandmother remained outside in the hall. The grandmother looked tired and tragically proud, almost heroic, with a strong and noble face that was creased, leathery, and sadly beautiful, reminiscent of a bust by the famous Croat sculptor Ivan Mestrovic. She seemed used to standing.

Someone pulled out a newspaper with an article saying Belgrade had run out of milk, dairy products and gasoline. Someone else mentioned that the government was going to revalue the Dinar by removing several zeros. All the problems, the paper's headline said, were due to "unprovoked and unjust sanctions against the Serbian people and state." Now, for the first time Steven felt he was entering a country at war.

Between Subotica and Novi Sad more people managed to board the train, even though the corridor was so crowded that the conductor never passed through to collect tickets. Steven realized only later that he could have ridden from Subotica all the way to Belgrade for free. The train crossed the Danube at Novi Sad, past the Baroque fortress of Petrovaradin, then the skeletal-frame steeples of the Sremski Karlovci cathedral, dark farmland, the outskirts of New Belgrade, and the Sava River.

The train arrived in Belgrade an hour before midnight and was immediately mobbed by an enormous crowd. People lined the tracks well outside the station and began climbing aboard the slowly moving train before it reached the platform, preventing passengers from disembarking. Even though Steven was in the compartment closest to the door, he needed almost five minutes of rough pushing and shoving to get off the train. He then ran around to the outside of his compartment where his fellow passengers handed down his luggage.

Late at night the Belgrade train station was a mélange of shadows and human bodies. Steven looked for a place to change money, but the only exchange office was closed and he changed money with a cab driver hustling passengers on the platform, receiving twenty times the official rate. Unable to find a working pay phone, Steven walked into a smoke-filled police station located on the platform, where he was met by a tired-looking policeman in blue and black camouflage, armed with a Marlboro and a Kalashnikov. He gruffly agreed to let Steven use the phone, and Steven dialed the number Slatina had given him.

'Hello, Dusan? Steven Roberts here,' he said in Serbo-Croatian. Even though it was a local call the connection was bad and he had to speak loudly, his accent attracting stares from everyone in the room. 'Yes, I am here in Belgrade. Yes, Belgrade,' he repeated, louder. 'Yes, the train station. Yes, the Belgrade train station.' He listened for a few moments. 'Okay, I am waiting here at the police station.' He hung up the phone, only to notice that he had attracted a crowd of policemen. A suspicious duty officer asked: 'Where are you from?'

'From America,' Steven answered.

'America? Which part?' asked the officer.

'All over, but I go to school in California,' said Steven. 'San Diego.'

'I have a cousin in America. He lives in Chicago. Is San Diego close to Chicago?'

'Not really.'

'Perhaps you know *my* cousin? He sells real estate in Chicago,' asked another policeman. All the officers had either family members or friends in Chicago.

'Don't you think our women are beautiful?' asked yet another.

'What are you doing here in Yugoslavia? You know there's a war on? It's not a good time to be here.' The tone was belligerent.

'I'm here to research ethnography, folklore, folk tales, etc. Serbia is famous for its folklore and poems.' Steven's response seemed to placate the policeman somewhat. The door swung open as another passenger came in and asked to use the telephone.

'Why do Americans hate Yugoslavia? I'm not a policeman. I'm a civil engineer, but the war makes me be a reserve policeman. It's because of you that Yugoslavia is falling apart and that we have a civil war.'

Steven looked blankly at him, trying to feign interest, yet unable to believe that the man believed what he had just said. 'Really?' he asked. The jet lag was killing him and it was all he could do to bite his tongue and refrain from telling the cop to go to hell.

'Would you like a cup of coffee?' the policeman asked, suddenly polite.

'Yes, thank you,' said Steven. The duty officer sent one of the police officers scurrying to fetch Steven a cup.

'It's the fault of America and the Germans that Croatia and Slovenia want to destroy Yugoslavia. The CIA worked with the German government. Also, the Free Masons are responsible. Did you know it was the Masons working together with the Croatian fascist Ustase that killed King Aleksandar Karadjordjevic in Marseilles in 1934? We're trying to protect our country against Islamic fundamentalism. Do you like the Ayatollah? Do you want the world to be over-run by Islamic terrorists? Don't you in the West know that Serbia is the last bulwark against the Turks and that we saved Christianity? If it wasn't for Prince Lazar and the Battle of Kosovo in 1389 you would all be Muslims today. We have fought to defend you against the Turks, and now you're turning your backs on us and are supporting the Albanians in Kosovo and the Muslims in Bosnia. The Masons and CIA and Vatican want to create a 'Green Corridor' of Islam through the Balkans. It's all there in Alija Izetbegovic's book.'

The coffee arrived: black, strong, sludgy Turkish coffee. Steven sipped silently, watching and listening, too tired to follow the policeman's convoluted train of thought, knowing that if he did he'd lose his temper.

'The CIA is working together with the Vatican to destroy Yugoslavia. You are helping the Croat Ustase, and we are simply trying to defend ourselves against this aggression. The only salvation for Serbia is Slobodan Milosevic. He knows what we have to do to them. He'll take care of them and save Serbia. Remember: "Only Unity Saves Serbs".' The policeman's discourse won approving nods from his chain-smoking colleagues.

The policeman continued his monologue, while his colleagues chipped in their comments. 'You know that the Muslims are all Serbs who left Christianity and joined Islam?' said one. 'You should read *Bridge on the Drina* by Ivo Andric, the famous Serb Nobel Prize author.'

'The Muslims have all become Turks, they have become vampires who want to suck our Christian blood,' said another.

'Did you know they impale people on stakes while they're still alive. They did it to poor Martinovic in Kosovo with a beer bottle, and they burnt

Serbian haystacks and barns and destroyed our graveyards. They won't even leave our dead in peace. They're vampires,' added another.

'And now they want to take Bosnia from us,' said the duty officer. 'But we won't let them. Vuk Draskovic and Vojislav Seselj will stop them. They've organized the Cetniks to fight against the Turks and Croat Ustase fascists. Do you know what Cetniks are?'

Steven nodded his head, knowing it wasn't wise to argue late at night with Kalashnikov-armed police in a foreign country at war. By now the conversation had deteriorated into a free-for-all of competing voices, as each policeman offered his take on news of the latest atrocities from the front lines and the character of Yugoslavia's other national groups. He simply sat nodding his head, waiting for it all to end.

After another 20 minutes of this harangue, the door of the police station swung open and a tall, dark-haired college-age male dressed in a cheap winter parka, jeans and woolen cap entered and inquired: 'Is there an American here?'

Salvation – in the form of Dusan – had arrived.

* * *

Interlude II: Grosswardein, Wasserstadt: Friday, 28 February 1733

The Austrian Imperial Grenadiers assembled on the fortress' frozen parade ground in the twilight of the short winter day, their dress uniforms concealed by the bulk of their greatcoats, heads swallowed by bearskin hats, muskets at parade rest in thickly-gloved hands. Snow crunched under the Captain's riding boots as he made his way down the ranks. He scented the air as he walked: it was crisp with a twinge of wood smoke. He stepped onto a wooden crate, steam billowing from his nostrils and rubbed his freshly shaven chin, his face far too young for a Grenadier officer. 'What shall I do without them?' he thought. 'How shall I find the twelfth?'

'My dearly beloved brethren,' he began, his Italian accent more pronounced. 'For you are truly my brethren, as you have proven time and again these past years in the most difficult of circumstances, where only God, the Devil and the Emperor knew we existed.' He wiped a tear from his eye with a handkerchief. 'I placed my trust in you, and you have been ever true. I asked you to follow and you followed, even when the very jaws of hell gaped open after us, and all the elements combined to hedge up our way. When we were encircled about with darkness and destruction, you stood fast. You have been true and faithful,' he said, his voice choked with emotion. 'Like unto Saint George of old you have fought against the Dragon. For this service, only God can give you the reward you so richly deserve. My heart, however, I pledge to you. I give you my most solemn oath that henceforth and forever, I shall be at your service, for you are my brothers.' The men stood silently, some with tears running down their face.

The Captain signaled to his Lieutenant, who handed him a large parchment with an official wax seal attached to a ribbon at the bottom. He cleared his throat with a deep rumbling sound. 'A message from his Imperial Majesty. Hats off!' They removed their bear-skin hats. 'Attention!' The entire company snapped ramrod straight in a well-drilled movement.

The Captain read the document out loud.

> *'We, Charles, by the grace of God, Holy Apostolic Roman Emperor, King of Hungary and Bohemia, Archduke of Austria, do hereby declare Our greetings to Our most loyal and trusted soldiers of Our Fourth Imperial Grenadier Company. You have served Us and the Holy Church with great devotion and sacrifice. You have engaged in the most perilous of duties in the service of our Lord and Savior Jesus Christ and have defended the Holy Cross against the Dragon as did all the holy saints and apostles. To reward your faithful service, We have sought from His Excellency the Holy Father in Rome, complete and full pardon of all your sins, which the Holy Father, in His mercy, has chosen to grant you as a reward for your service to the Holy Church.'*

The Captain paused to observe the reaction of the men. All stood expectantly. He continued.

> *'By Imperial decree We hereby release you and your posterity from your military obligations to the Emperor in perpetuity. We do hereby grant each of you the status of a freeman and declare null and void any bonds of serfdom or obligations which you, your wives or children may have to any person or institution in Our Imperial lands. We do also grant each of you a full state pension befitting the rank of lieutenant. We…'*

'Long live the Emperor; Long Live Charles; God save His Majesty;' the cries broke forth spontaneously from the lips of the jubilant Grenadiers.

The Captain once again cleared his throat with a deep rumbling and resumed reading.

> *'We have endeavored to grant you that which each man holds dearest: his own land.'*

A gasp went up from the Grenadiers.

> *'In agreement with His Majesty George I, King of England, We have arranged for the entire company and their families to travel to the British colonies of North America, where you shall be awarded a generous grant of land. His Majesty King*

> *George has agreed to give you a charter to establish your own free town in the colony of Pennsylvania, and there you shall live as free men, with all the rights and privileges of landowners.*
>
> *We shall also award each man a generous monetary gift sufficient to establish himself in his new life. Upon the reading of this proclamation, the Fourth Imperial Grenadier Company shall be disbanded. You are free men. So declare We this 8th day of December in the year of our Lord 1732. Signed, Charles.'*

The Captain looked at his men. The Grenadiers stood in stunned silence, steam issuing from their mouths in the cold evening air. 'Your loyalty, devotion and service to God and the Emperor have been richly rewarded. As of this moment I am no longer your Captain, only your former comrade in arms. I would like to spend this last night with you as my comrades and treat you to a night on the town. We shall meet at the *Sign of the Elephant*, where I have asked Herr Siegel to prepare a farewell feast for us,' he grinned. 'There we shall drink to His Majesty's health, and to our comradeship, and to your future lives in the North American colonies. Three cheers for His Imperial Majesty, Emperor Charles.'

CHAPTER THREE

IT'S ONLY FOLKLORE

Belgrade: Winter 1992

The Popovic apartment lay just up the road from Slavija Square, across the street from the concrete massif that was rapidly taking shape as a cathedral to Serbia's patron, St. Sava. A labyrinth of musty rooms, the apartment's high ceilings, elegant chandeliers, cut glass salon doors and parquet wood floors were relics of a bygone era, before a tidal wave of proletarian values had drowned bourgeois sensibilities. Now, three generations of family called it home. Steven's bedroom was a large converted pantry off the kitchen, and he shared a bathroom with Dusan.

'If anyone asks for me,' Dusan had told Steven the first night at the train station, 'tell them I've left the country. I don't want to get sent to the front to fight.'

The family had taken Steven in as a favor to Professor Slatina – who knew Dusan's father. His grandfather had placed a color portrait of Slobodan Milosevic on the wall of the living room, and Dusan told Steven it had replaced an earlier portrait of Tito. 'They're communists,' he said, shrugging his shoulders.

Each evening Steven and the grandparents dutifully watched RTS, the state television evening news broadcast, which inevitably led with reports of Milosevic's activities or the latest atrocities committed by Croats – the announcer always used the pejorative term Ustase – against Serbs. RTS told how victorious Serb forces were defending and liberating ancient Serbian lands from fascist aggressors, and how the Muslims in Bosnia were threatening to secede from Yugoslavia, create an Islamic fundamentalist state and drive the Serbs from their centuries' old homes. And whenever the story was about shortages of heating fuel, food, electricity, gasoline or food, the announcer always began with the mantra: "because of the unprovoked and unjust sanctions against the Serbian people and state..." It was brainwashing at its best, and Steven marveled at its effectiveness. The television mesmerized Dusan's grandparents as they helplessly watched the collapse of their world.

The winter was cold, and the government kept the central district heating at very low temperatures, claiming that sanctions were causing a shortage of heating fuel. Some days Steven could see his breath inside the apartment, and he constantly wore long underwear and woolen sweaters.

The archives, libraries and research institutes were closed until after Serbian Orthodox New Year on 13 January, so he read ethnography books, puzzled over his meetings with Professor Nagy, the Order of the Dragon, and wondered why Professor Slatina had wanted Steven to learn of it in such detail. He also spent considerable time walking around the icy sidewalks, getting acquainted with the city.

His impression of Belgrade was one of dirty decay. He choked on the coal smoke, leaded automobile exhaust, cigarettes and diesel fumes, yet admired the awkward mix of graceful neglected old buildings and concrete communist kitsch. Street-corner black market currency dealers buzzed about like swarming bees as they chanted endlessly the Serbian word for hard currency, '*devize, devize, devize.*' He was almost run over several times by new black Audis, BMWs and Mercedes with tinted windows, whose drivers braked for no one and rarely observed traffic lights, while the police stood by. And no one smiled.

One night before bed he re-read the letter Katarina had given him at the airport. The envelope contained a single sheet of paper and her photograph. It was simple and written in Serbo-Croatian.

> *Dear Steven,*
> *As you set out on your journey I wish you luck and good fortune. I will also pray to the Lord to protect you every day. Please keep yourself safe. This is a strange time when men are doing horrible things. The fabric of society and the hearts of men are*

failing and evil is everywhere. Please guard yourself against this evil.

I know that you are a good person, that you like truth and light. Please remember what you know is right and do not turn from it. You do not yet know it but you have a great task ahead of you. The work you do will be valuable and necessary and will help many people. Please use wisdom and good judgment in all you do and protect yourself from the adversary. And never fear to pray for help.

Thank you for listening to me when I was having a hard time. You are a good friend.

Kisses,

Katarina

P.S. Don't forget the pine cone.

'What does she mean, a "great task"? Does she know something I don't?' he asked as he thought back to Slatina's impromptu lecture on knowledge of good and evil and the serpent.

'Do I love her?' he wondered, looking at her picture on his nightstand. 'Does she like me? Am I ready for this again?' he asked, as he opened his journal and removed a smudged, white silky card. He ran his finger-tips over the richly embossed floral edges. As he opened it his eyes caught the words inside, words he knew by heart.

Harold and Margene Woodruff-Kimball
Are Pleased to Announce
The Wedding of their Daughter
Julie
to
Steven Preston Roberts
On Friday, the Twenty-Second of December, Nineteen Eighty-Nine

His blurry eyes looked at the photograph of a happy couple, posed against a mountain stream, gazing intently at each other as though nothing else existed.

He thought back to the day that had marked the end of an old year and the start of a new life…a day that just wouldn't seem to let go of him, any more so than he could let go of *her*. Maybe life in Serbia would help him let go of the past. Or maybe it wouldn't. He slipped the invitation back among the pages of his diary and looked at Katarina's photograph once more before turning off the light and closing his eyes. 'But if she's in California, what am I doing here?' he thought as he drifted off to sleep.

* * *

For Serbian New Year, an aunt, uncle and cousins came over and the family celebrated, the television glowing in the background. Food constantly arrived from the kitchen: *sarma* – filled cabbage leaves, roast pig, different types of cheese, corn bread, pickled vegetables, cold cuts, roast chicken, grilled meat, homemade *baklava*, homemade cakes, and lots of high octane *rakija*. Around 10:30 p.m. a heated argument erupted over the war, with the grandmother telling Dusan he was a coward for evading the draft and Dusan's mother getting angry and calling the grandmother a fascist for supporting Milosevic. 'He'll save the Serbian nation,' the grandmother retorted. 'He'll do things for Serbia no one else has ever done. Just you wait and see.'

'If we wait long enough he'll turn all of Serbia into another Vukovar,' the mother answered derisively, referring to the Baroque city in Croatia that Serb forces had just razed to the ground during a three month artillery bombardment. 'And my own son and your only grandson will be killed. Is that what you want?'

A crescendo of automatic weapons fire signaled the approach of midnight. '*Srecna nova godina*' – 'Happy New Year' they all shouted, clinking glasses together, hugging and kissing each other and momentarily forgetting the war next door in Croatia, the gathering storm clouds over Bosnia and all their misery.

* * *

The next week Steven set off to meet Professor Miroslav Ljubovic at the Philosophy Faculty building, a brick, glass and concrete monstrosity defiling the heart of Belgrade's old pedestrian district, where a suspicious doorman interrogated him before letting him enter. The doorman said the professor's office was located on the fifth floor, but the elevators were out of order, so Steven took the stairs, which were lined with smoking students whose cigarette smoke funneled upward, turning the stairwell into a chimney. By the fifth floor Steven was barely able to breathe. He found Professor Ljubovic's office in a darkened corridor and knocked.

'Come in,' he heard a voice call loudly.

A grey-haired man in his late 50s stretched up to return a book to its shelf. He smoothed his threadbare suit coat over a woolen sweater and equally threadbare trousers. 'Yes?' he asked.

'Good day. I am Steven Roberts.' He handed Ljubovic an envelope and looked about the office, yellowed with age and central planning. 'Professor Marko Slatina asked me to present his compliments and to give you this letter.'

Ljubovic smiled and shook his hand. 'Yes, I've been expecting you. It's so pleasant to meet you. Please have a seat.' He took the envelope, read the letter and then looked up. 'It's so pleasant to hear from Marko again. He's been unable to return because of problems with the authorities. I'm glad he's still teaching. His knowledge is valuable and should be passed on to new generations.'

'Indeed,' agreed Steven.

'Marko tells me that I'm to direct your research on monsters and mythical creatures in our rich South Slavic folklore. As you know we have many of them...witches, fairies, vampires, werewolves, the wild man and others. Some are old Slavic creatures that were brought here in the 5th and 6th centuries when the Slavs migrated from the north-east. Others appear to have already been here when they arrived, so I guess you can say that some of the creatures you will meet are local, while others are imported.' He laughed at what he considered a joke.

'We'll start you off here in the Ethnographic Library and History Library, and then when you're ready we'll send you across the street to the archive of the Serbian Academy of Arts and Sciences. There you'll find many living monsters. However, I'm afraid that they are primarily old communist academicians who bear a greater resemblance to political dinosaurs than to anything you'll find in the literature.' Once again he laughed, as if at an inside joke. 'When we have given you a good grounding in the folklore we'll send you to Novi Sad to work in the Matica Srpska archive.'

'In his letter Marko asked that you start with vampires,' Ljubovic continued. 'He always took an interest in them. So, here is a list of books to start with.' Ljubovic smiled broadly, revealing uneven teeth. 'Actually, the list is Marko's. He left it with me some years ago, urging me to look at it, but I never had the time. When you've finished with the books, you'll start in the archives.'

He handed Steven ten typewritten single-spaced pages. 'I think you'll have great fun.'

Steven looked at the list: there wasn't a single book in English. The winter would be long.

* * *

The following day Steven fought his way onto a battered and overcrowded electric trolleybus that somehow managed to take him to the heart of the city. In the Philosophy Faculty's sixth floor History reading room he ordered a book and began to work.

He quickly entered into a routine: a morning run, the reading room until closing time at 2:00 PM, a solitary cup of hot chocolate at the Aristotle café, then the trolleybus to the National Library where he perused back issues of newspapers in the cavernous reading room. He repeated this pattern, alternating between the Ethnography and History reading rooms in the morning and the National Library in the afternoon.

His social life…well, he had none, so for the first time in his life he grew a beard against the cold. He thought often of Katarina and wondered what she was doing, whether or not she liked him, and whether she had a boyfriend. Weekends he took refuge in Belgrade's unheated movie theaters to watch outdated films. Often the lights came on in the middle of a screening as Military Police swept the theater for draft dodgers. They never left empty-handed.

Rough men in camouflage uniforms sporting paramilitary insignias seemed omnipresent, and he avoided them, as did most Belgraders, terrified by their appearance and wild behavior. Students at the Philosophy Faculty whispered about horribly mutilated bodies floating down the Sava River. None of these stories appeared on state television, although RTS carried stories of horrible atrocities against Serbs by Croats, showing grotesquely disfigured bodies that were sometimes unrecognizable as human beings – limbs torn apart, ears, eyes and noses missing. Steven watched one news clip in disgust at it showed what had once been a person, but now resembled little more than a large mass of red meat. He was witnessing firsthand the collapse of an entire society and all its norms, and he felt darkness press him from all sides, a darkness that grew with each passing day.

As he read, Steven came across a case of vampirism on the Dalmatian island of Pasman, near Zadar, in 1403. Steven wanted to visit the Zadar archives in Croatia, but at the moment Zadar was besieged by Serbian forces, so he asked Professor Ljubovic if he knew of a facsimile that existed in Serbia. The professor said he'd look around, but a week later, Ljubovic told Steven that no one had heard of it. Then Steven came across an account of vampire trials held in Dubrovnik between 1736 and 1744. But Dubrovnik too was inaccessible, under siege by Serbian and Montenegrin forces, cut off by a blockade of steel and hatred.

The research was tedious, and his eyes grew tired easily because of the poor lighting. Sometimes he felt he could read no more. Gradually, he uncovered small pieces of what increasingly seemed to be a much larger puzzle. Some came from historical documents, while others came from collections of folk tales recorded by ethnographers… Ducic, Novak, Zovko, Klaic, Liepopili, Karadzic…the names blurred together. Everywhere he turned he found Serbian newspaper accounts of people who were arrested and tried for opening up graves and driving stakes through the hearts of suspected vampires. He had particular problems with one 15th century document written in the Glagolitic alphabet, a precursor to Cyrillic that resembled mangled bicycles, trapezoids and triangles. It took him the better part of three days to read a two page document.

Steven had become the favorite of Gordana, the librarian at the

Ethnography reading room, who had a son his age serving in the army in Croatia and a brother in Chicago. 'If I'd been smart I would've gone to America with him, but my parents weren't healthy so I stayed here to help them. Now they're dead and I'm too old to leave. But my brother has a big house and two cars and a swimming pool and an American wife, and his children are at the university.' She showed Steven photographs of her brother's family in suburbia. Once, when the military police came to the Ethnography reading room seeking draft dodgers, Gordana sprang to his defense and sent them packing.

As he read it became apparent that all the accounts had common elements, no matter whether they came from the furthest of the Dalmatian islands, the flat lands of the Pannonian Plain and Slavonija, or the wild mountains of Herzegovina, Bosnia, Pirot or Macedonia. But these vampires were unlike anything he had ever heard of and bore scant resemblance to film versions of Dracula.

* * *

One March morning, just when spring seemed to lurk around one of Belgrade's grimy street corners, Steven stood up from the table in the Ethnography reading room, stretched his arms, returned a book to Gordana, walked down the hall to Professor Ljubovic's office and knocked.

'Ah, Steven, how are you?' Ljubovic asked distractedly, staring out the window into space. 'I didn't recognize you with that beard. And you've let your hair grow. You look like Che Guevara.'

'My hand's cramped from writing, my eyes hurt from reading and I can't wait for spring,' Steven replied.

'Well, it could be worse…at least you're not in Sarajevo…it looks as though these fools will carry their nationalist madness into Bosnia…it's starting all over again…but this time it'll be much worse…Croatia was only a warm-up,' Ljubovic spoke as if drained of all emotion. 'But tell me what you've been up to.'

'I finished the list you gave me.'

'Really,' Ljubovic turned and looked at Steven. 'You have been diligent. Would you care to share some of your findings with me? I've always wanted to know what Marko found so fascinating about that list and how it all fits together.'

'Well, I need some time to put it all together.'

'Come to my apartment tomorrow. I'm having a group of students over for dinner. Perhaps you could present your findings.'

When Steven arrived home he found a letter from Professor Slatina that had taken a month and a half to arrive and appeared to have been opened several times. As he opened it he sensed a faint scent of leather and mildew that somehow transported him halfway across the world to La Jolla. In his mind's eye he imagined Slatina, sitting upright at his desk, surrounded by old books and portraits, writing the letter. At once a sense of melancholy set in.

My Dear Steven,

By now I am certain that you have arrived safely and have settled into your research. I wish you great success in all you do and feel confident you will find the necessary materials and arrive at the appropriate conclusions. I hope Professor Ljubovic is helping you.

I suspect that the direction your research is taking is somewhat different than what you expected.

Steven stopped reading and looked across the narrow room at his puzzled expression in the faded wall mirror. How did Slatina know what direction the research would take him? Did the professor know how much time he was spending reading about vampires? He continued with the letter.

Keep in mind that what you are doing is actually quite important, not only for the field of anthropology, but also for other related fields. And you should not underestimate its significance. It may well have results that you cannot foresee at this stage. And I am quite certain you will be able to use this material to publish several articles and perhaps even a book. Nonetheless, I would ask that you be very careful as you gather information and share it with no one, until such time as we see each other again.

What was this? He wasn't to share his information with anyone until he met Slatina? He shook his head in disbelief. Didn't the professor trust him? And why was Slatina acting so cryptic about the research topic? Did the professor think he was brain-dead? And now he had a presentation tomorrow at Ljubovic's place…he couldn't just back out. Steven grumbled under his breath as he returned to the letter.

Belgrade is a fun place for a university student. I would encourage you to socialize and enjoy your stay there. After all, you have adequate time for your research, and if you feel that you are falling behind schedule, then we can always speak with the Balkan Ethnographic Trust about extending your fellowship. Please, take time for yourself and enjoy student life. Remember, one must always think about continuing one's dynastic line, and Yugoslavia is full of beautiful and smart women.

I would encourage you to take the opportunity at your earliest convenience to visit Novi Sad.

I wish you a pleasant sojourn.

Your old professor
Marko Slatina

P.S. Katarina asked me to say hello and to ask how your Serbo-Croatian is coming. She likes you, you know.

Over the last few weeks Katarina had slipped further from his mind as he immersed himself completely in his research. He placed his hand on the cross around his neck and glanced at her photograph on the nightstand.

And then he penned a brief letter:

Dear Katarina,

I'm here in Belgrade, and the winter has been miserable. Cold, no heat, bad public transportation, and everyone is paranoid because of the war. Thank you for the help you gave me with the language: it's really been helpful, but I do miss our language sessions. You really helped me a lot and were very patient with me. Here it's easier to learn the language when everybody is speaking it, and I'm improving.

I hope you're enjoying life there in sunny southern California. It's certainly much different than Serbia. Be glad you're there and not here. Life here is crazy, as though the entire world has been turned upside down and all morals have ceased to exist. Right is wrong and wrong is right. Day is night, black is white, good is bad, virtue has become a vice.

Research is difficult but going well, and I'm making some progress. I won't bore you with the details, although I will say that one day I'll have enough material to write a screenplay for a really good Hollywood movie.

I hope you're doing well with your studies. Please give my best to Professor Slatina when you see him. If you visit here over the summer break, please let me know and we can meet up.

Once again, thank you for all the help you gave me. And thanks for your photograph. I'm wearing the cross you gave me and still have the pine cone. I think of you every time I see it.

Steven

* * *

En route to Ljubovic's, Steven struggled with Slatina's admonition to share his research with no one. He rationalized his upcoming presentation, telling himself it was only academic research on ethnography and was of no danger to anyone. He told himself that the professor was probably paranoid someone would steal his research topic and information.

A power outage meant the trolleybusses weren't working and he had trouble finding the Ljubovic's address near the famous Zeleni Venac open market. The elevator didn't work, so he climbed the stairwell using the flame from a Zippo lighter to find the door. He brought a bottle of Macedonian red wine and a bag with two kilograms of tangerines as a gift.

'Come in, come in,' welcomed Ljubovic as he opened the door to his apartment. 'We were worried you might have changed your mind and decided not to share the fruits of your research with us,' he said taking the bag of tangerines. 'But at least you brought some other fruits. May I introduce my wife, Dragana?' He gestured towards a large woman, slightly taller than the professor, and then ushered him into a sitting room lit with candles and crowded with students, most of whom Steven recognized from the reading rooms and library. 'Our guest of honor has arrived.'

Steven looked around at the shadowy faces and said 'Hello.'

Ljubovic made introductions all around, announced that dinner was ready, and invited them all to the adjoining room, where his wife – a professor of musicology – had set various dishes. They all helped themselves and took their plates back to the sitting room. Mrs. Ljubovic announced proudly: 'this is a sanctions meal. I've prepared everything here with food that is domestically available.' She looked around for approval, and then added: 'Actually, Slobo has screwed things up so badly that this is the only food at the green market. There's no cooking oil, so I had to do without. I'm also missing a few other crucial ingredients, including sugar, but hopefully you won't notice.' Everyone congratulated Mrs. Ljubovic on a wonderful meal, and Steven found it tasty.

After dinner some of the students helped with the washing up, while others rearranged the chairs. They then sat down, wine glasses in hand.

'As you all know, we have a guest with us this evening,' Ljubovic began. 'Steven Roberts is studying with my old friend Marko Slatina in California, and he's here doing research on mythical creatures in Balkan folklore. He's been researching vampires, and this evening he'll share some of his research with us.'

'Why in Serbia? Shouldn't he be in Transylvania?' asked one student, causing the others to laugh.

'Now, if we pay attention,' Ljubovic interrupted, 'we might all learn something. And without electricity the ambient will be appropriate. Steven, if you please,' Ljubovic gestured to indicate that Steven had the floor.

Steven prayed his Serbo-Croatian would rise to the occasion and cleared his throat.

'Vampires have a long history in the Balkans. One of the earliest mentions is in the 1349 Law Code of Serbian Emperor Stefan Dusan. Belief in vampires in his Empire was strong and people were digging up bodies and burning them, so he passed a law to prevent it. I quote Article 20: "*That village that would do so will pay the money price for killing a man and the priest who participates will be defrocked.*" This indicates that priests were taking part, contrary to Church teachings.' Looking around he saw that everyone was listening raptly.

'That's the famous Law Code that formed the basis of Serbian law,' the professor interjected.

Steven continued. 'In addition to this law, I've found numerous other references to vampirism in Yugoslavia. There was a case on the Dalmatian island of Pasman, near Zadar, in 1403, when a woman named Priba became a vampire and terrorized the entire island. Eventually the mayor of Zadar authorized her exhumation and impalement, after which the problems stopped. There's a Glagolitic manuscript from the 15th century, where the Senj Bishopric recorded a curse to protect people against vampires. There's also an account from the first half of the 16th century by a priest – Georgius Sirmiensis – that discusses a vampire named Pavle Kinjizi, who terrified his village for nearly a year after his death until the local priest and monks killed him. In a 17th century *Nomocanon* the Serbian Orthodox Church forbade burning the bodies of suspected vampires, and banned anyone who did so from taking communion for six years. In 1666 in the town of Ston on the Adriatic coast, a man named Stjepan Nikolin went around digging up graves of vampires and driving stakes through their hearts. I guess he was sort of a medieval version of Van Helsing.' Steven smiled.

Professor Ljubovic nodded his approval.

Steven continued. 'I found another case of vampirism in 1672 in Kranjska, where the village priest saw a man named Djura Grado – whom the priest had previously buried – walking about, terrorizing the villagers. The dead man even visited his own wife and sexually assaulted her. The priest and others opened his coffin, to find that the corpse was entirely red. As they looked at the corpse it screamed and everybody fled. Finally the village elders and priest regrouped the people and returned to the grave, this time carrying a crucifix with Christ crucified in front of them. When the vampire saw the crucifix he stood in his coffin and cried. Then they impaled him with a stake, filling the coffin with blood.'

'My, my, my…sex and impalement. I'm certain Sigmund Freud would have a field day,' Mrs. Ljubovic commented, evoking a slight blush from Steven and ribald whispers and snickers from the students.

Steven recovered his composure and continued. 'In 1716 Austria took control of large sections of what is today Serbia, including Belgrade. The Emperor Charles VI was a real nut about vampires and instructed Austrian officers and officials to report directly to the court about them, so a great deal of information exists.'

'In 1725 when Serbia was under Austrian rule, there was a famous incident in Kisiljevo, near Ram on the Danube that started a vampire sensation throughout Europe. It led to the publication of books on vampires in German and French. A man by the name of Petar Plogojowitz turned into a vampire and within two weeks ten people died. Each person suffered for 24 hours before death, and all declared that Plogojowitz had visited them in their dreams and strangled them. Plogojowitz's wife fled to a nearby village and claimed that her dead husband visited her and sought his shoes. The villagers convinced the Austrian district administrator to take action, and they also convinced two priests to participate. When they got to the grave they found that it had already been opened. I'll read you what one eyewitness, the Austrian district administrator wrote:

> *'We didn't sense the slightest smell from the body, nor from the grave. Nor was there that usual smell of death. The body, with the exception of the nose which was slightly depressed, had remained completely fresh. The hair, nails and beard, instead of falling off, had continued to regenerate. The place where his old skin had been light blue was now renewed with fresh skin. The face, legs and arms were so well preserved that they couldn't have been better in life. In his mouth I noticed with the greatest surprise a little fresh blood, which according to the general thinking of those present he had sucked out of those he had killed. Since the priest and I saw all of this, the people, with greatest haste, sharpened a stake and impaled the corpse in the middle of the heart. Upon impalement completely fresh and red blood appeared that flowed through the ears and nose. Afterwards, as is the custom in these cases, they burned the body.'*

Steven looked around to find the room completely silent. 'That's from the *Vossiche Zeitung*, Nr.98, from 1725. It was this well-documented vampire case of 1725 that led to the widespread use of the word vampire – which is a Serbo-Croatian word – in the West.'

'So the word vampire originated in Serbia?' Ljubovic asked, curiosity on his face.

'Yes. That is correct. And in 1730 the Orthodox Church held a Bishops' Council in Belgrade to discourage people from believing in vampires and declared that anyone who investigated vampires was to be anathematized and turned over to the Austrian Imperial Court authorities.'

'Reports emerged of vampires in the Serbian village of Medvedja, so in the winter of 1731-32 the commander in Belgrade sent the field surgeon of the Alexandrian regiment, Johann Flückinger, to investigate, along with a military escort. Flückinger found that eighteen people had been killed by vampires and he attended the exhumation of numerous alleged vampires and performed autopsies on thirteen of them. He found them all to be full of blood, even though they had lain dead for several months. He said that one corpse was "*complete and undecayed*," and that another was "*in good condition*," and all were in a "*state of vampirism*".'

'Flückinger wrote a bestseller entitled "*Seen and Discovered*" in 1732 that offered signed testimony by Austrian Army officers about the vampire phenomenon. His original notes were destroyed during World War Two, so we have to rely on his book and the report of a researcher who recorded this information prior to their destruction, one Stefan Novakovic. Flückinger described how the villagers killed one vampire.'

> *'They found that he was quite complete and undecayed, and that fresh blood had flowed from his eyes, nose, mouth, and ears; that the shirt, the covering, and the coffin were completely bloody; that the old nails on his hands and feet, along with the skin, had fallen off, and that new ones had grown; and since they saw from this that he was a true vampire, they drove a stake through his heart, according to their custom, whereby he gave an audible groan and bled copiously.'*

'That same year in the village of Kukljin, also near Ram, a vampire killed two brothers.'

'All this happened in Serbia?' Ljubovic exclaimed with disbelief. 'That's absolutely amazing.'

'Wait, it gets better. Between 1736 and 1744, the Dubrovnik court conducted criminal investigations of people accused of digging up bodies and driving stakes through the hearts. All of them were from the island of Lastovo. Things were so bad that on 23 October 1748 the Austrian Imperial War Council in Vienna ordered all priests in the Empire to dissuade people from believing in vampires. This order was relayed to the Metropolitan Bishop of the Orthodox Church, Moses Putnik, by the Slavonija General Command in Osijek, Croatia, on 6 November 1748. The Austrian Empress Maria Theresa also sent out a physician, Gerard van Swieten, in 1755 to investigate and debunk vampires.'

'And finally, I've found quite a few references to vampires in Serbian newspapers, some quite recent. For example, in the village of Cickovi near Arilje there was a case recorded in 1933, and another in Smederevo in 1934. Right here near Belgrade there was a recorded case in the village of Knezevac in 1938.' Steven shuffled through his notes. 'Or at least that's what *Politika* reported,' he said, referring to Serbia's most prominent government-controlled daily. 'But the newspapers stopped reporting on vampires when the communists came to power.' He looked around the room. 'Any questions?'

Ljubovic arose. 'Steven, this is marvelous. You've done a very thorough job. I congratulate you. Although I must say that with all these vampires I wouldn't be surprised if Dracula himself visited Serbia,' he commented with a smile on his face.

'Actually, he did,' responded Steven. 'In February 1476, less than a year before his death, Dracula took part in the Battle of Sabac as a vassal of the Hungarian King Matthius Corvinus. After defeating the Turks the King returned to Hungary, placed 5,000 of his troops under Dracula's command and sent him up the Drina River valley between Bosnia and Serbia. Dracula sacked Zvornik, Kuslat and Srebrenica and carried out horrible massacres.' Steven rummaged through his notes. 'I copied this account by the Papal Legate, Gabriele Rangoni, of Dracula's massacre in Srebrenica: "*he tore the limbs off Turkish prisoners and placed their parts on stakes…and displayed parts of his victims so that when the Turks see these, they will run away in fear*".'

'Well, that sounds quite a bit like what's going on now in Croatia,' Ljubovic commented. 'Perhaps Mr. Dracula has returned to Yugoslavia once more.' Several students laughed nervously. 'Perhaps we could open up the floor to discussion,' said Ljubovic. 'If there are so many references to vampirism in Serbia in particular, and in Yugoslavia in general, and if these references predate Dracula, then what does this tell us about the Dracula myth? After all, Dracula was a latecomer. Is it possible he became a vampire while he was here in Serbia? Did another vampire bite him?' He smiled at the students, all of whom sat absolutely silent. 'We know that myths and legends often are based on real historical events that are now lost to us. But if these stories continue up to the present, is it possible that there's substance behind the myth? Is there in fact some basis to the legends?'

A dark-haired female student crossed herself and spat three times. 'This is horrible. It's an unpleasant topic. Must we discuss it?'

Another student told her: 'Don't be superstitious. There are no such things as vampires.'

'In my grandmother's village near Pirot they still talk about vampires, especially during the winter,' commented a large, bearded student with his hair in a ponytail, who bore a striking resemblance to the Russian monk Rasputin. 'They say that they're most active between Christmas and the Feast of the Ascension in June.'

'My parents have a weekend home on Mt. Zlatibor,' added a thin girl with long blonde hair. 'The peasants there still believe in vampires. A lot of times at night when the animals go crazy and start making noise they'll say there's a vampire nearby.'

'But why are vampire tales so specific to this area?' asked Ljubovic. 'And what keeps them alive in the folk traditions for 700 years. Steven, do you have anything else to share with us this evening?'

'That's all I've prepared for now. I'm still working on the characteristics and behavior of vampires. I'm also trying to understand why a person becomes a vampire.'

'Isn't that well known? Doesn't a person become a vampire when they're bitten by a vampire?' asked a female student.

'No, not at all. If a vampire bites you on the neck, you simply die. A vampire's bite won't turn you into a vampire, at least not according to the folk tales and historical documents.'

'Well then how does one become a vampire?'

'I'm still working on that.'

'Steven, you've made an excellent presentation,' Ljubovic said. 'Thank you so much. Perhaps some other time, when you've been able to prepare some of your other materials, you'll be able to share these other things with us. Now let's adjourn to the other room where my wife has prepared an excellent "sanctions cake".'

And then the power came back on.

* * *

The next day Steven wrote Professor Slatina a long letter, describing his impressions, his progress with research, and the overall situation. At the end he wrote:

> *Given the large number of references I'm finding in newspapers and historical documents, as well as the similarity among recorded folk accounts from regions that are geographically separated, I suspect there might have once been some phenomenon that led to the establishment of these myths. In fact, there are days when I wonder if vampires might actually have once existed. Sounds silly, doesn't it, but after a while the sheer weight of the historical evidence makes one begin to wonder. How can there be so many consistent reports of a supposedly mythical phenomenon that keep occurring nearly up to the present day?*

* * *

That Saturday Dusan invited Steven to go out with him. Steven – feeling he deserved a break from research – accepted.

They met up with some of Dusan's friends at 10:30 PM and walked past a spray-painted Woody Woodpecker graffiti with a caption that read inanely: "*it never would have come to this if Woody had gone to the police in time.*"

'That's the moral of our story,' Dusan said, pointing at it.

'Huh?'

'Yeah…none of this ever would have happened if somebody had gone to the police in time,' Dusan said.

'I don't get it,' Steven answered.

'You will, you will,' Dusan smiled. 'Just stay here long enough.' Then he added: 'It means that we're really not responsible for any of this. Someone else is to blame because they didn't report us to the police in time. That's the way it is with us. Someone else is always to blame… There's no sense of personal responsibility.'

They fought their way onto an overcrowded trolleybus that took them to the Square of the Republic. Even though it was past midnight and cold, the square was filled with young and old as though at mid-day.

Dusan led them to a non-descript door in the side of an old building with a small plaque that read *INFERNO*, down an unheated dirty white hallway, increasingly enveloped by the ever-louder thump of a deep bass beat that intensified as they approached the head of a stairway. Out of the stairway thick clouds of tobacco smoke billowed up into the hallway and out a nearby window, partly obscuring a sign in Italian that read *Lasciate ogne speranza, voi ch'intrate*, urging those who entered to abandon every hope. And of course, they entered.

They descended into darkness and felt their way down through the smoke, groping at the flesh of shadowy bodies lining both sides of the crowded stairwell. The stairs felt slippery underfoot, and the farther they went, the warmer it became until Steven was sweating and gasping for air. An acrid ammonia-jolt of concentrated urine struck his nose and purged it of smoke as they passed the lavatories, doors hanging askew from hinges, fluids dripping down the steps. At the bottom of the stairs, dim lighting cast hellishly red shadows throughout a vaulted basement as wraithlike figures writhed in and out of focus. Human forms crowded the corridors, forcing Steven and Dusan to swim against a tide of human flesh. Hauntingly beautiful women in black sucked nervously on cigarettes, glaring at Steven with the look of those damned to eternal boredom, while leather-clad men glared fiercely with sunken cheeks. The passage reeked of sweat and cheap perfume.

The music overpowered and squeezed Steven's heart in a deep bass vice. Bodies everywhere, pushing, shoving, groping, squeezing...he could barely breathe as they fought their way forward like rugby players in a scrum. Unseen hands touched him, patted him, and some fondled him intimately. He couldn't see who the hands belonged to, and it wouldn't have mattered. A violent 10 minute journey took them 70 feet, until they halted in the middle of a crowded chamber, the bass vibrations penetrating his muscle, bone and skin. The amplified sounds of Yugoslav rock bombarded their senses. One song caught Steven's attention and he strained to make out the lyrics:

One day I won't be here,
And I won't ever come.
Friends that I know,
I no longer recognize when I pass.
As if I was never in this world,
As if her body didn't want me.

People wore the desperate smiles of drunks facing a firing squad, singing at the tops of their lungs. The men all appeared to have long ago lost hope in God and life, and were now seeking any possible escape from this world and the war, short perhaps of death. The women, the most beautiful Steven had ever seen, drifted as apparitions in and out of the light, ghostly and ghastly with unsmiling faces, flowing to the throbbing rhythm, glancing about furtively as the music continued to pound. Everybody shouted the song's refrain in unison:

Balkans, Balkans, My Balkans,
Be powerful and stay well.
Balkans, Balkans, My Balkans,
Be powerful and stay well.

And they seemed to be finding escape, however temporary: the smell of marijuana and hashish mingled with the stench of tobacco, spilled beer and alcohol-rancid breath. Yet to find it they had imprisoned themselves in this dungeon, without light, air, sun, God or hope. In one voice of alienated desperation they all sang frenetically:

We are people,
Gypsies damned by Fate.
Someone around us always
Comes and threatens us.
Not even the gangs
Are what they used to be.
My people are amateurishly
Preparing to play…

They were escaping from a hell they had neither chosen nor sought, into one of their own making, if anything worse than what they were trying to escape. All were held captive by a power that encouraged physical and spiritual degradation as the only release. And here they found solace, after a fashion.

Balkans, Balkans, My Balkans,
Be powerful and stay well.
Balkans, Balkans, My Balkans,
Be powerful and stay well.

The music was too loud for conversation, so Dusan and his friends just stood rocking back and forth with beer bottles in their hands, the vaulted brick ceiling arching scant inches overhead, holding them tightly. Steven felt disembodied and estranged. After half an hour he put his mouth next to Dusan's ear and yelled: 'How long will we stay here?' Dusan smiled and yelled back: 'In just a little while it's gonna get really good.' So Steven waited. Fifteen minutes later he once again put his mouth next to Dusan's ear and yelled: 'When's it gonna get good? What's gonna happen?' Dusan once again yelled: 'Just a little…it's gonna be really good.' This continued for the next hour, and Steven finally realized that Dusan had now become like all the others…oblivious, feeling no pain. For him it was really good.

'This sucks. I'm leaving,' Steven shouted at Dusan, who smiled vacantly.

Steven fought his way across the room, up the stairs and into the refreshing chill of the winter night. His lungs burned with pain as he sucked in the cold and his head spun from the noise, beer and poisoned air. He sat down on the steps outside *INFERNO*, holding his face with his hands, trying to regain his senses as vomit lapped at the back of his throat.

The sound of retching turned his attention to a thin blonde girl bending over a dark haired girl who was crouching and vomiting on the sidewalk. She stopped vomiting, coughed several more times, and struggled to her feet, assisted by her friend, then turned to Steven and spat sarcastically: 'Aren't vampires enough for you? Do you also get your thrills watching people get sick?' She was absolutely beautiful – in a fallen angel sort of way – and Steven realized he had seen the two before, at Professor Ljubovic's place.

'I'm Tamara,' the blonde approached Steven apologetically. 'This is Vesna…she's sick.' The dark-haired fallen angel smiled wanly. 'It's really bad down there. I don't know why we keep going back, but we do.'

'Yeah, it's pretty bad,' he agreed. 'I'm going to get a sandwich. Are you hungry?'

'Whenever you get sick like this you need to eat,' Tamara urged Vesna.

'Come with me, then. My treat,' Steven said.

They went to an all night sandwich shop, then headed slowly towards the Square of the Republic. As they walked Tamara placed her hand tenderly around Vesna's arm and snuggled up to her.

'Your presentation really was excellent,' said Tamara, between bites of bread, cheese, ham and lettuce.

'I didn't like it… it didn't make me feel good,' Vesna said, food spurting from her mouth.

'But it was good,' rejoined Tamara. 'You looked at something that everyone thinks is a joke and showed how integral it is to our culture. I can't wait to hear more.'

'I'm glad you liked it. I think my next presentation will be even better,' Steven said. 'At first I thought vampires weren't a serious topic, but it's turned out to be quite interesting.'

'You've found a real gold mine. Everything you've discovered is original and completely unknown,' Tamara gushed. 'It's what every graduate student dreams of. You could base your entire academic career on vampires. I wish I could find such a good topic for my dissertation.'

'Well, I got lucky on this one,' Steven said.

'And you got lucky bumping into us tonight,' Tamara teased.

Steven looked at Vesna's face, pale, drawn slightly sickly looking, and realized that there was something in her eyes that he found attractive.

'I still think it's terrible,' Vesna said. 'There's nothing good about it. There are too many unpleasant things happening and we don't need more. Don't you sometimes think that there just might be vampires? What about all these mutilated bodies floating down the rivers and everything on television? Something horrible is going on in Croatia, and nobody will speak honestly about it. I feel as if evil has swallowed our country and there's nothing we can do, as if vampires are running the country. What if Milosevic is a vampire? What if all the generals are vampires? What if all of Milosevic's cronies are vampires? What if the paramilitary formations are vampires? What if Croatia's President, Franjo Tudjman, is a vampire? What if the DB are vampires,' she said, referring to the secret police.

'What if you're a vampire?' Tamara shot back: 'the way you're drinking Stefan's blood right now you're the vampire.'

'She's not drinking my blood,' Steven said.

'I didn't mean it literally. That's our expression for when someone is nagging someone else,' answered Tamara.

'I still don't like it,' Vesna continued. 'There's blood everywhere…in the rivers, the newspapers, the television, and here on the streets. Did you hear about the body they found last week in the Botanical Garden that was missing its kidneys? Or about the girl's body they found under the Brankov Bridge without any blood in it? I think there are real vampires and that they're having the biggest feast of their lives, and no one notices because of the war. If I were a vampire I'd be enjoying all this chaos and would do nothing but eat, because no one would ever find out…they'd just blame it on the war.'

Steven smiled at her, silently. He liked her fire.

'Vesna, enough. Stop it,' Tamara ordered.

At the Square of the Republic, Vesna and Tamara gave him their telephone numbers and suggested they meet for coffee. 'And if you're not doing anything next Saturday, then perhaps we can go out to a place where we won't get sick,' Tamara said.

'Ladies, it will be my pleasure,' Steven said, bowing in an exaggerated fashion.

'But leave the vampires at home,' Vesna cautioned.

'Okay, okay,' Steven laughed. 'No vampires…at least, not this time.'

The girls drove off in a taxi leaving Steven alone in front of the National Theater. He walked slowly across the street towards the trolleybus stop and thought about Vesna's outburst. 'She's right,' he thought to himself. 'If I were a vampire this'd be the perfect time to feed. There's war, lawlessness, the complete disintegration of society, economic disruption, ethnic cleansing, lots of dead bodies, complete and utter chaos. It would be a vampire's paradise.'

'I'm living in a vampire's paradise,' he suddenly spoke out loud in English to nobody in particular, causing the other person waiting at the bus stop to stare at him.

A derelict red trolleybus with one working headlight and a loud air compressor crawled towards the bus-stop, driven by a pale, middle-aged ghoul. Steven climbed aboard and sat at the back of the nearly deserted bus. 'A vampire's paradise,' he thought once more. The thought made him giggle softly to himself. The more he thought about it the more he giggled, until finally other passengers began to turn and look at him, but saw just one more drunk coming home from a night out on the town.

He began singing softly to himself:

We are people,
Gypsies damned by Fate.
Someone around us always
Comes and threatens us...

Balkans, Balkans, My Balkans,
Be powerful and stay well.
Balkans, Balkans, My Balkans,
Be powerful and stay well.

When he got home he removed his smoke-drenched clothing and cast it aside. Then, for the first time since he'd arrived, he felt the need to bow his head and seek out God in prayer.

* * *

Interlude III: Vienna: Tuesday, 12 May 1733

The gaily attired Watch Commander of the Imperial Household Guard escorted the Captain, stepping carefully to avoid dirtying the trousers of his dress uniform, his pace slowed by knee-high riding boots. 'My Captain, much has happened since you left', the Watch Commander said.

'Did I see horses stabled in the Maximillian Palace?' the Captain asked in astonishment, glancing over his shoulder. 'So much has changed.'

'Those are the Lipizzaners for the Riding School,' the Watch Commander gestured, 'which they say will be finished soon, but the contractors...thieves, the lot of them.'

The Captain nodded knowingly.

'Since you left they completed the new wing of the palace…it's to be the Reichskanzlei.' The Watch Commander gestured at a large building pierced by gateways. He led him to an archway in the Leopold Wing, past some guards who snapped to attention, up a flight of stairs, and down a corridor.

'Vienna grows because we've secured the southern marches,' the Captain smiled. 'Each year we push the Turks further south.'

The Watch Commander nodded affirmatively. 'And here in Vienna everyone is building...new palaces are sprouting like mushrooms. Have you seen what our old general Prince Eugene of Savoy has built for himself, his Belvedere? Do you remember the prizes we took from Damad Ali Pasha's army at Tekije? Well, I've invested mine in two new apartment houses just outside the old city walls, so now I have a hefty income.'

'Yes, and a waistline to match,' the Captain laughed good-naturedly.

'Well, my Brigitta is a wonderful cook, and palace life is not as harsh as the military frontier. All I have to do is keep from getting too drunk and make certain I don't fall off my horse when someone's watching,' he laughed. 'But what about you? You haven't aged a day since you led us against the Janissaries eighteen years ago. How do you keep the pace of a front line soldier? I must insist you come to dinner. Brigitta will put some meat on your bones.'

'Frontier life is healthier than city life. The air's fresh, the food's good and there are fewer impure vapors to pollute the body's humors. I'll accept your invitation with pleasure, if His Majesty permits.'

'Yes, well, here we are.' The Watch Commander stopped at a richly inlaid wooden door, music seeping from behind. 'Be quiet when you enter. He dislikes interruptions.' He pushed gently on the brass knob and opened the door, permitting the Captain to slip through.

The Captain squinted at the bright light of the high-ceilinged hall, its windows thrown open to the spring air. The late morning sun glistened off the richly inlaid parquet floor as the light danced from tall, narrow mirrors, their ornate gold-leaf frames set in rich red velvet wallpaper with stylized Pomegranates. Through the windows he saw the massive Burgthor, the city wall and the new suburbs spreading outward towards the Linienwall. He sniffed: the air smelled of wood polish and snuff.

In the center of the hall a robust, bewigged man with an expanding belly exuberantly directed a small string ensemble from an ornately decorated harpsichord. Charles VI's droopy eyes took pleasure in each note, his long nose and protruding Habsburg chin bobbing with the tempo. The Emperor squinted at the sheet music as the minuet danced enthusiastically towards its climax. Catching sight of the Captain from the corner of his eye, he jerked his head, lost his concentration and missed several chords.

'Damn it,' he shouted, and the ensemble stumbled to a halt in mid bar. He stood and faced the Captain, who removed his three-cornered hat and bowed deeply.

'Your Majesty,' he said.

Charles squinted at him, nearsightedly. 'Is it really you?'

'At your command, Majesty.'

'Out, out! Everybody out. Out at once,' the Emperor shouted and clapped his hands at the musicians. 'Leave us alone.' They hurriedly fled the room as an anxious courtier barged in. 'Out, We said! Out! We will be left alone! At once!' The courtier fled, leaving the Emperor alone with the Captain.

'Pray forgive me, your Majesty, for the interruption.'

The Emperor looked at him, then advanced and gave him a hearty handshake. 'My dear Venetian friend, how good to see you.'

'The pleasure is mine, your Grace.'

'And you have succeeded?'

'I trust so, Sire.'

'Excellent. Excellent…..' the Emperor trailed off into silence. The Captain waited respectfully. 'Now, tell me about the project.'

'All was done as you instructed. You have received my dispatches, yes? As you know, it took us some time to select the proper men for the task and then to train them. After a year of preparation we began the hunt in 1729.'

'And? Did you find them? How many did you get?'

'We have cleansed Your Majesty's lands as far south as Skopje. We killed all those we encountered, except for those deemed most powerful. We have interred eleven of them in a tomb most secret and impenetrable, as you did command.'

'Eleven? I thought you told me there were twelve.'

'There are, but we can't find the twelfth, the Vlach. He has gone to ground and may never reappear, or perhaps been killed. We heard rumors that he was last seen near Srebrenica in Bosnia, so we scoured the area, but to no avail.'

'And the men?'

'They have embarked for England. From thence they journey to the New World.'

'That is good. Yes, yes, quite good,' the Emperor looked out the window at the growing city.

A silence followed.

'Majesty', the Captain looked him directly in the eyes. 'I have always been your faithful servant and done your bidding. No other has served you as have I. My loyalty and faithfulness are not to be doubted.'

The Emperor nodded in agreement.

'Sire, I fear it may be folly to leave the eleven there. Please, you need only give the order and I shall finish them.'

'Was it not your idea to inter them? Were you not the one who suggested we find another way to deal with them, to help them repent of their sins and find redemption?'

'Yes, Majesty. But alas, we have not yet discovered a means, and when I think of them entombed alive – if they are indeed alive – alone in eternal darkness, tormented by their sins, my soul shudders in horror. And what if they should escape?'

'I feel your initial impulse was right and just: we must find a way to save these lost souls. If we can redeem them from the devil's grasp, we will be doing the Lord's will.'

'But Majesty, if they…'

'Please,' he fixed his gaze firmly on the Captain. 'As your brother in the Order I implore you and as your Emperor I command you. Promise me.'

The Captain knelt on one knee and kissed the Emperor's extended hand. 'My Lord, it will be as you say.'

'And the funds for the Order?'

The Captain rose to his feet. 'I placed some with the Jews – the Rothschilds – both here and in Paris, some with the Fuggers in Augsburg, some with Dutch merchants and the Honourable East India Company in London. The remainder I have secreted in bullion, coins and precious stone as you commanded. The Order will not perish for want of funds.'

The Emperor hit several keys on the harpsichord, the notes echoing dully across the empty hall, then looked directly at the Captain. 'You must supervise the funds carefully and make certain the Order can sustain itself. The Adversary is not defeated. There will be future struggles. You understand this, do you not? Without the funds, our struggle against the Evil One cannot continue. Evil will be present as long as the Sons of Adam and Daughters of Eve walk this earth in sin and mortality. As God's anointed Emperor, it is my duty to continue the fight until our Savior comes again in His Glory. I shall not be found wanting.'

'Yes, Majesty.'

'What about the one who escaped?'

'I shall maintain vigilant watch, Majesty. My spies are active throughout the land. I have a reinforced company of Grenzer, mostly Serbs and Vlachs, who are garrisoned at Grosswardein, but we use Belgrade as a forward post.'

'And you, do you not wish to return to Venice? Have you not had enough of this life?'

'Venice's sun and islands are now distant. It is no longer mine, Majesty. Perhaps, someday…but not now. My service to the Order continues. Until when, I know not.'

'My dear Venetian friend, be watchful, for the Dragon is Evil. Like unto our Savior, no man knoweth the hour or day of his coming…he cometh like a thief in the night to steal away the souls of Man. I am the anointed Arm of the Lord, and you are the sword that I wield. Justice and the Word of the Lord shall prevail. You shall see to this, will you not?'

'I serve none but thee, Majesty. I have served the Order long and will continue in faithful service all my days, as God sees fit to grant me strength of limb and clarity of mind. O how merciful is God, Just and Faithful.'

CHAPTER FOUR

A MISSING LIBRARIAN

Belgrade: April 1992

April in Belgrade is an enchanted month. Spring elbows winter aside for lovers. Warm weather draws couples to the leafy streets and parks as fresh winds cleanse the coal smoke and automobile exhaust from the air with a promise of summer. This particular April, sunlight and passion blinded the eyes of lovers to the city's decay and signs of war.

In parks throughout the city – along the Danube and Sava quays, at Usce and Ada – every bench was taken by grappling couples, oblivious to passersby. Grass sprouted, leaves burst onto recently-barren branches, and flowers appeared in gardens. Tables and chairs sprouted from the concrete and asphalt in front of Belgrade's cafés and restaurants, even though the weather was still brisk and often chilly. Yet darkness weighed heavily over these bright spring days.

Steven sat in the Aristotle café near the Philosophy Faculty with Vesna, Tamara and the bearded Rasputin look-alike he had met at Professor Ljubovic's, whom everyone deservedly called "Bear". A brisk breeze made them shiver, even though they wore heavy coats. So too did the topic of conversation, the new war in Bosnia.

'I can't believe it's happening again,' Vesna exclaimed emotionally, her high cheekbones flushed with emotion. 'First Slovenia and Croatia, now Bosnia…its *déjà vu* …and Bosnia will be far worse. It's all so immoral. Evil has been unleashed and no one's doing anything about it.'

'They're shelling Sarajevo,' Tamara said, shock written across her slender face. 'My parents took me there for the 1984 Olympic Games… we used to ski there every winter… my father took me to the old *Bascarsija* market to eat the spiced *cevapcici* sausages...' Tamara began to cry. 'My mother is there now… she remarried a Bosnian Muslim and refuses to leave…' Her voice trailed off as tears rolled down her cheeks. 'I don't know what's happening to her, if she's alive, if she has food…' she sobbed. Bear hugged her.

'Slobo says the Muslims want to create an Islamic republic, but his propaganda's the same as at the beginning of the war in Croatia,' Vesna said, irritated. 'They're calling the Muslims fundamentalists, but we all know that they drink and smoke and eat pork and go to the mosque as often as Serbs go to church. Their women don't wear veils and they dress in modern fashions like other women in Yugoslavia. It all seems like a big lie.'

'Why don't people protest?' Steven asked.

'We tried on March 9th last year,' Bear muttered, 'but Milosevic sent police on horseback and water cannons against the demonstrators, and when those didn't work he sent tanks. Two people were killed. And then we occupied Terazije, but that didn't work either.'

They sat in silence for a long while.

Bear broke the silence: 'The Military Police came for me at my parents' home this week.'

'What happened?' asked Steven.

'Obviously they didn't find me. I was spending the night somewhere else,' he grinned, squeezing Tamara's hand.

'Why didn't you tell me about the police?' Tamara demanded, withdrawing her hand abruptly.

'Tamara? Bear? Are you two dating?' Steven asked with a grin.

'Yes, for over a year, but please don't tell anyone,' Tamara said, her stern expression indicating concern.

'It's okay to tell people,' contradicted Bear. 'We're in love and I want everyone to know. It's just that Tamara's afraid of her father.'

'He doesn't want anything to disrupt my studies,' Tamara interjected. 'As if the war and all this chaos are helping. My older sister got pregnant, got married and never finished the university. And then she immigrated to South Africa. If my dad finds out about Bear and me, the Military Police will be the least of Bear's problems. My dad's a difficult person…' her sentence trailed off.

'Difficult is right. He's an SPS party official,' Bear added.

'Where will you stay?' Steven asked Bear.

'At my Uncle's place on Banovo Hill.'

'So you're a draft dodger,' smiled Steven.

'Yeah, it's an old Serbian tradition. Everyone makes a big deal about how we're such warriors, but nobody wants to fight, just a few crazies,' Bear answered.

'How's your research?' Tamara asked. 'Anything new?'

'Well, I finished with vampires and moved on to fairies…'

'That's good, fairies,' interrupted Vesna. 'They're common in our folklore, and they aren't as horrible as vampires.'

'I started on fairies, but everything led back to vampires. Then I collected material about witches, but once again, vampires kept popping up. I'm surprised there's so little mention of vampires in Yugoslavia, because they're really prevalent in folklore. No one would ever know there'd been vampires in the Balkans. It's like they've been erased from public discourse,' Steven said.

'The communists did a good job erasing superstitions,' Bear remarked. 'In fact, they did better than the Church.'

'Stefan, Professor Ljubovic told us you'll present more of your findings at a round table next week,' Tamara said, eagerly. 'Will it be about vampires again?'

'Yes, but this time I'll talk about their characteristics.'

Vesna's face registered her displeasure.

'Don't make faces, Vesna,' Steven smiled. 'It'll be fun. If you come you'll learn something.'

'Oh come on Vesna, don't be superstitious,' Bear said. 'No one's going to bite you. After all, vampires don't exist, isn't that right Stefan?'

'Of course not, they're just folk tales.'

'It'll be fun,' Tamara said, smiling. 'Your last presentation really had people talking.'

'Will you come?' Steven asked Vesna, cocking his head playfully. 'I promise I'll keep it safe for families and small children.' He winked at Tamara.

'Well, okay, but promise you'll not be scary.'

'Well, I can't promise it won't be scary, but I promise that if a vampire appears I'll come to your rescue.'

'Great. Just what I need, my own personal vampire-slayer. Okay, if you insist. But I'm doing it only for you.'

'Great. And bring rotten tomatoes to throw in case you don't like it. I'm definitely going to write my dissertation on this.'

'Don't even think about that!' Vesna said bluntly.

'Why not?'

'I really mean it. Don't think about it. There are so many dark and evil things in this part of the world and you really should stay away from them,' Vesna's voice rose. 'Evil is all around us, waiting to attack us. The last thing you need to do is invite it into your life. Why can't you find a topic that's uplifting, that will bring light into the world?' She was attracting attention from nearby tables.

'Oh, please, Vesna, don't exaggerate,' said Tamara.

'Exaggerate? Vesna continued. 'What about Milosevic? What about the horrible things in Croatia and Bosnia and here in Serbia that everyone accepts as normal? The Devil has a vacation home here, and he won't leave until we toss him out. Some things are meant to remain hidden in dark places and never see the light of day. Stefan should just leave it alone. It'll only bring trouble.' Vesna stood up, grabbed her backpack and stalked off.

Steven stood up to go after her, but Bear reached out a large paw-like hand and stopped him. 'Let her go. She has her own problems. She's made up her mind and there's nothing you can do about it.'

'She's touchy. All I did was talk about my research,' Steven said.

'It's okay. Sit down and tell us about where you come from in America and what it's like in countries where Slobodan Milosevic isn't running things and where the only vampires are in Hollywood movies,' Bear said.

* * *

Steven had tried to phone Slatina several times, but without success. Due to the wars, phone service was often disrupted, and to get an outside line he had to call the operator, and then wait for a call back. Each time he tried, he was either unable to get a trans-Atlantic connection, or the telephone would simply ring with no answer. He also tried to reach Katarina, but to no avail. He felt increasingly cut off from the world.

With only one letter from Slatina since his arrival, Steven didn't know if his research would meet with the professor's approval. He missed hearing Slatina repeat the phrase 'et cetera, et cetera, et cetera.' He missed talking to Katarina. He missed California, especially the salad bars and guacamole. Some days he looked at the *pljeskavica* and longed for an *In and Out* burger or enchilada.

The next day the mail arrived. This time the postman brought six letters, two from Slatina, one from his parents and three from Katarina. The envelopes had all been opened, and looking at the post marks he could tell that they had arrived in Serbia weeks and even months ago. Steven sat on his bed and read them one by one, savoring each word. Slatina's letters were vague, non-descript, full of general well wishes and greetings with nothing specific, other than a few pieces of university and academic gossip. The professor made no mention of Steven's topic of study, other than to wish him continued success and to urge him to visit Novi Sad at his earliest convenience. His father's neat typewritten letter contained the latest family news and gossip.

He put down his parents' letter, looked at Katarina's photograph and picked up her first letter. It was written in Serbo-Croatian and began with the words *Dear Stefan.* It was full of cheerful banalities about university life, coursework, roommates, the weather, her professors, how different California was from Vojvodina, how much she missed home and her mother, how the Serb émigrés in America were all ultra-nationalists and fascists. She ended the letter by writing *kisses* and a smiley face. The second letter was the same. In the third she told him that one of the boys in her freshman English class had been teaching her to surf. *When you see me next I will be the all-American surfer girl*, she wrote, with a smiley face. She then asked *why don't you write to me*? and ended with *I will come home to spend the summer with my mother in Novi Sad. I didn't have enough money for an airline ticket, but Marko has purchased one for me as an early birthday gift. Kisses.*

Steven began writing responses to Slatina and his parents, and saved writing the letter to Katarina for the very end. His closing paragraph to her was awkward and stilted, but he decided not to change a word.

> *Clouds and darkness lie everywhere. Light comes during the day, but seems strangely distorted, as through a blurred lens, as though something is missing and we are receiving false light. I sought ways to defend against it, to keep from being dragged down into it and overcome by despair. The churches are no help: both Orthodox and Catholics are involved in a war of hatred, using religion to define their enemies. When I enter the churches I feel the devil laughing. The very institutions that should be spreading light are spreading darkness, as though doing the devil's work. The only light I have found is through prayer, and I am now praying at least once a day, even more. Perhaps it's strange, but the terrible darkness has caused me to seek light in a way I never knew I would. Without it I would have lost my nerves long ago and come back to the States. Thank you for encouraging me in this.*

* * *

The following week marked a turning point, when after months of tedious reading, Steven hit the mother lode. On Monday when he requested volume 66 of the Serbian Ethnographic Digest, Gordana the librarian said it was missing. But then she looked again and said it had been placed in a special restricted circulation section the communists had created for ideologically dangerous material. 'But since we are no longer communist, I can give it to you,' she said with a smile, handing him a thick book.

Judging by the dust on the cover, the stiffness of the binding and the crispness of the pages, Steven was the first person to open it. As he turned its pages he came across a piece from 1952, written by Tihomir Djordjevic, a member of the Serbian Academy of Arts and Science. In a 136 page article entitled *Vampires and other beings in our folk beliefs and traditions*, Djordjevic had painstakingly catalogued and summarized the work of all the major 19th and 20th century ethnographers on vampires. It sent electricity through Steven's body as he read the sub-headings: "what is a vampire", "who becomes a vampire", "what makes a vampire", "protection from vampires", "destroying vampires". This was a veritable catalogue of vampirism, scientifically organized and categorized with instructions. 'Everything you always wanted to know about vampires but were afraid to ask,' Steven thought to himself.

He read with elation, taking copious notes, tempted to simply copy the entire book verbatim by hand. By the time the reading room closed at 2:00 p.m. he had taken notes on the first 15 pages.

When he returned the next day he continued taking notes. Just before closing time he thumbed through the remainder of the volume and discovered another article by Djordjevic entitled *The Twelve Mighty Vampires in Legend and Fact.* He noted the bibliographical information and as he returned the volume to Gordana he asked: 'Can I buy a copy of this somewhere or photocopy it?'

Gordana examined it then placed it on a cart. 'I doubt you'll find it in a bookstore. Well, perhaps in a used bookstore, but this was printed in limited numbers, only enough for a few libraries and academicians.' She hesitated, then leaned over and whispered: 'But tomorrow I'll see if I can find a way to photocopy it for you. Come just after opening time.'

'Thank you,' Steven said, sincerely. He vowed to buy Gordana a box of chocolates and flowers.

On Wednesday morning he flew up the smoke-filled stairs and arrived in the reading room completely out of breath and full of expectation, only to find a librarian he had never seen before whose build and dumpy brown outfit made her the embodiment of a bulldog.

'Where's Gordana?'

'She's taken sick leave and won't be back for some time.'

'But she seemed healthy yesterday. What happened?'

'She had a bad night and became suddenly ill.'

So Steven asked for the Djordjevic book. After a few minutes in the stacks she returned and said: 'It's not here,' spittle dribbling from bluish lips.

'But it was here yesterday,' Steven protested.

'Perhaps a professor has taken it. Is there anything else I can get for you?' Her bloated, jaundiced face seemed less than eager to help.

'Do you know when it'll be returned?'

'No, I do not,' she barked abruptly, turned up her pug nose and disappeared into the darkness of the stacks.

Steven waited with growing frustration for the librarian to return. She finally did so ten minutes later, and shot Steven a look of disgust that said 'are you still here?'

'Perhaps Gordana put it somewhere.'

'It's not here and Gordana won't be back for some time,' the librarian huffed with annoyance. 'Is there anything else you need?'

'No. But say hello to Gordana from me,' he said, no longer in the mood to study. He trudged down the smoky stairs and bumped into Professor Ljubovic on his way out.

'Steven, how good to see you. How are you?'

'Well, I'm kind of bummed out. An important book has disappeared and nobody knows where it is. Gordana the librarian set it aside for me, but she's out sick.'

'I'm certain it'll turn up soon. Be patient. Sometimes these things happen. Come with me for a walk. It's a beautiful day and we shouldn't waste it inside.'

Outside all of Serbia was enjoying the blustery spring weather. They walked silently to the Kalemegdan fortress, where they looked out at the confluence of the Danube and Sava below the ramparts. Steven gazed at the two great rivers, swollen with spring runoff, that nearly submerged the forested hulk of the Great War Island under their greenish-brown waters. He followed a hawk as it circled above the lower plain of the Kalemegdan and out over the river towards the concrete-grey forest of New Belgrade's mass-produced communist apartment blocks.

'Do you know much about the Kalemegdan fortress?' Ljubovic asked.

'Some, not much,' admitted Steven.

'You know that Belgrade's a combination of two Slavic words: *beo* meaning 'white,' and *grad* meaning 'city,' due to the white limestone used to build the fortress,' Ljubovic said, pointing at the stone walls. 'In Roman times the city was called Singidunum and the Roman Flavian IV Legion built a *castrum* on this spot. For them the Danube was the line between barbarians and civilization. To the north were the Barbarians.

'But beginning with the Austrians, things flip-flopped and civilization and Europe were to the north in Vojvodina, while here to the south of the Danube and Sava Rivers lay the barbarians. Today we Serbs are deeply divided, and our rivers are a symbol of that. Do you see that tower on that hill across the river?'

'That one over there?'

'Yes. It's in Zemun. Until 1918 Zemun was a Habsburg border town…Semlin. If you'd been here in 1801 everything would have been different. Zemun looks like many other towns throughout Habsburg Europe, from Salzburg to Transylvania, from Zagreb to Prague, and the

Serbs in Zemun looked like and were educated as Europeans. Come with me down to the river,' he said, leading Steven through an old gate, down a steep rock-paved path.

'Back then, Belgrade was a dirty cattle town, a decaying Turkish backwater border outpost that had more in common with Istanbul than Zemun. The last Turkish soldiers didn't leave Belgrade until 1867.'

'In Zemun they ate *schnitzel*, *paprikash* and *Sachertorte*: in Belgrade, *pljeskavica*, *djuvec* and *baklava*. In Zemun Mozart and Beethoven were all the rage: in Belgrade, the one-stringed *gusle* and shepherd's bagpipes. In Zemun people sat on sofas: in Belgrade, on divans. In Zemun wives slept in the same bed as their husbands: in Belgrade they slept in the harem. Women of Zemun wore the latest fashions from Vienna: in Belgrade, ornamented vests and harem pants. In Zemun men wore polished leather shoes and the latest European suits and hats: in Belgrade baggy Turkish pants, curly-toed leather *opanci* and the fez. Zemun had Catholic and Orthodox churches, nuns and monks: Belgrade had mosques and dervishes.'

Steven listened raptly to Ljubovic's interpretation.

'The only things both cities shared were strong Turkish coffee, the Serbo-Croatian language and Gypsies. In the truest sense, Belgrade was where East met West, where two radically different cultural spheres collided. Even today our country has trouble choosing which way to look, which is why we have a two-headed eagle on our coat of arms, with the heads looking in different directions.'

'The Habsburg Empire kept the barbarian Balkans at bay and European culture prevailed, gradually taming the evils that the primitive villagers brought with them from the mountain darkness. After the fall of the Habsburg Empire in 1918, Serbia's kings maintained this civilizing influence and taught the people right from wrong, good from evil, and showed them the path to enlightenment and the modern world. But Serbia hasn't had a king since 1941, and the communists unleashed the primitive instincts that had been kept at bay for centuries. But at least the communists tried to impose order, no matter how faulty or amoral. Today we have neither a king nor communists, but only Milosevic, a man who values neither morality nor culture.'

'What about the Church?' Steven interrupted.

'The Church? Hah!' Ljubovic spat with disdain. 'It's a collection of primitive, half-educated peasants living in a world of myths and half-truths based on poetic memories of a battle lost 600 years ago in Kosovo. They're part of the problem. They teach superstition instead of faith, lies instead of truth, myth instead of history, and state instead of God. And Milosevic has let the Church set the values of the new generation, values steeped in ignorance and based on vengeance, hate, blood lust and superstition. They have unleashed a great evil.'

Steven was surprised at Ljubovic's vehemence. The professor stopped talking as they crossed a road.

'Why does everyone constantly speak of evil as if it's a real force or presence?' Steven asked suddenly. 'The concepts of good and evil were banished from western scholarly discourse long ago. Everything is supposed to be examined within its specific cultural context without making judgments based on our own society's values. Scholars argue that good and evil are relative concepts and that objectively they do not exist. They claim that they are purely artificial constructs based on subjective judgments that emerge from our cultural context. In America, if I were to talk about evil as being real they would laugh me out of the university. Yet everybody I speak with here talks of evil as if it exists and is a palpable presence.'

Ljubovic led Steven along the concrete-lined riverfront embankment. 'It's easy for scholars sitting far across the ocean in the civilized comfort of their universities to speak theoretically of good and evil and deny its existence,' Ljubovic said. 'But I guarantee you that if they lived here for one year, they'd change their minds. The Apostle Paul described these scholars well when he warned his dear friend Timothy of men who are "ever learning, and never able to come to the knowledge of the truth." My advice to you is to ignore scholarly theory, particularly in the Balkans, where you will find that such theory bears little relation to reality.'

'So do you believe in evil as a real concept, as something tangible?' Steven pressed.

'Do you believe in God?' Ljubovic responded with a question.

'Yes, I do,' Steven replied.

'But do you believe God exists? That he's real and tangible and not just some greater cosmic force?' Ljubovic became increasingly serious.

'Yes.'

'What about the Devil? Do you believe the Devil exists? Satan, the Prince of Darkness, Lucifer, Perdition, Beelzebub, the Father of All Lies, the Old Serpent, the Great Dragon?' Ljubovic pressed him further.

'What did you call him?' Steven's interest was suddenly piqued. 'What were the last names you used?'

'The Old Serpent and the Great Dragon,' Ljubovic responded.

'Where did those names come from?'

'From the Revelation of St. John,' Ljubovic looked intensely at Steven. 'You still haven't answered my question. Do you believe that the Devil exists?'

'Oh, sorry. Well yes, but I've never really thought about it except abstractly.'

'Well if God exists, then the Devil must also exist: all of God's holy prophets and apostles testify to this.'

'How do you know so much about religion? Didn't you grow up under communism?'

'Oh yes, and the communists forbade the study of religion. When I was young I was a rebel, and when I saw how morally bankrupt and corrupt the communists were I assumed that anything forbidden was good. As an ethnography professor, I study world myths and religions, so I've read the holy scriptures of all the world's religions. But I find those of Christianity especially compelling. Perhaps it's my cultural background, but the Holy Bible offers me great comfort and wisdom, and I now know why the communists didn't want it to be read. It contradicts everything they teach. It teaches us that we have free agency, that we're children of God, that man has a higher purpose, and that we're not just animals. It contradicts the materialism inherent in communism and replaces it with a spirituality that transcends this world. It also teaches the difference between right and wrong and good and evil.

'But we've digressed. Evil exists. It's tangible and real and here in the Balkans it's all around us. Don't let yourself be fooled by the vain philosophizing of learned men. You must take care that it doesn't seduce you, that you don't unconsciously become part of it. Now, are you prepared for the lecture tonight?' Ljubovic asked Steven.

'Yes. This time there's much more material and I probably won't do it justice.'

'You do what you did last time and you'll do just fine. Come to my office before we start. There's someone I'd like you to meet.'

'Oh? Who?'

Ljubovic stopped and stared at debris floating downstream on the spring flood waters. 'A friend of mine from the University of Novi Sad, a professor of ethnography. I think you'll find that he's not only interested in what you're doing, but that he may also be able to help you in your research. I've invited him here especially to hear you this evening. And Steven, if you still have trouble getting the book you need, let me know next week and I'll intervene with the library.' Ljubovic smiled.

'Thanks,' Steven said, tossing a pebble into a pile of debris that had wedged against a tree at the edge of the embankment. 'The spring run-off has sure carried a lot of logs downstream,' he commented as his pebble landed amid a pile of water-borne plastic bags and bottles.

Ljubovic shaded his eyes and squinted at the river. 'Those aren't logs,' he answered grimly. 'That's from Bosnia.'

* * *

By the time Steven climbed to Ljubovic's office that evening it was already starting to get dark, and the weak neon lighting inside the Philosophy Faculty cast a jaundiced yellow light on everything. On the fifth floor the lights were dark, the empty corridor lit only by the yellowish light that shone through the transom above Ljubovic's office door. From inside came the sound of voices. Steven hesitated before knocking.

The voices stopped talking and Steven heard Ljubovic call out 'Come in.' He entered to find Ljubovic next to a large man in his mid-forties with thick, unkempt hair and a hermit's beard, fiddling with a long white scarf around his neck. The stranger had a slight hunch in his neck and shoulders. 'Stojadinovic, Ljubodrag,' he announced loudly in a deep bass voice, extending a large paw, crushing Steven's hand.

'I've been telling Vlada about your presentation last week. He knew Marko Slatina when he lived in Novi Sad.'

'Marko and I are old friends,' Stojadinovic's smile felt contagious and full of energy. 'It's good to see he's still taking new students. It's a pleasure to make your acquaintance,' his deep voice filled the small office.

'Professor Ljubovic has told me about you too. He said I must meet you when I come to Novi Sad. I didn't know you'd be here this evening,' Steven said enthusiastically.

'No problem. Miroslav has been telling me of your research. It sounds as though you're quite the vampire hunter, the academic Van Helsing of the younger generation,' Stojadinovic's grin was infectious. 'And how is Marko? I haven't seen him for years, although we do write the occasional letter. He didn't mention you were coming.'

'He's doing well.' Steven grinned back. For some reason the presence of Stojadinovic made it feel normal to be researching vampires. 'Yes, yes, and I'll soon start carrying a wooden stake and cross with me wherever I go,' he joked.

Stojadinovic wrapped a large arm around Steven's shoulders in comradely fashion. 'You shall have fun when you come to Novi Sad. The Matica Srpska archives will offer you rich materials.'

'Gentlemen, we'll be late for the lecture,' Ljubovic stood up and reached for his briefcase. 'Let's go.'

A large group of students stood smoking in the hall outside the class room, engaged in anxious conversation. As the three approached, the students took long last drags, extinguished their cigarettes and followed them into the room.

Steven was surprised at the turnout. Whereas there had been only eight at Professor Ljubovic's apartment, there were now almost twenty people, including Tamara, Vesna and Bear, crowded together around tables arranged in a large rectangle. Ljubovic and Steven sat at the head table and Ljubovic rapped his knuckles on the wood to call the meeting to order.

'As you know we like to hold these round table discussions to permit our graduate students the opportunity to share their research with their colleagues in an informal setting where we discuss and share ideas freely.

We have with us this evening my colleague Professor Ljubodrag Stojadinovic from the Ethnography Department of the University of Novi Sad,' Ljubovic gestured at Stojadinovic.

'Our speaker tonight is Steven Roberts, who is visiting from America. For those of you who were not at his first lecture, he discussed manifestations of vampires in the lands of Yugoslavia. Tonight I've asked Steven to share with us more of his research on vampires. Steven?'

Steven cleared his throat, looked around the table and noticed Vesna smiling at him.

'Be nice,' she mouthed at him. He grinned mischievously.

'Tonight I'll discuss the characteristics of vampires. The reason I've chosen to do so is that after examining the collected accounts of Balkan folklore from the 18th, 19th and 20th centuries, as well as examining historical documents, I've come to the conclusion that real vampires bear little resemblance to what we see in films or read in Bram Stoker's book *Dracula*. In fact, pretty much the only thing that Stoker accurately portrayed is that vampires dislike garlic and drink blood.'

'Let's start with the word *vampir*.' He picked up a thick pad of paper covered with notes. 'As you all know this is a Slavic word that has entered many western languages. However, in the lands of the former Yugoslavia…is it okay to use the term 'former Yugoslavia'?' He looked around for approval and Professor Ljubovic nodded his head in agreement as did many of those present.

'In the lands of the former Yugoslavia there are many words for a vampire. They are regional and include *vampir*, *vampirin* in Djevdjelija, *vaper* in Krusevac, *voper* in Ohrid, *vopir*, *lipir*, *lampir* and *lampijer* in other places. To make matters even more interesting, according to folk traditions and beliefs there's no difference between a vampire and a werewolf: they're one and the same creature, an undead shape-shifter that was once human, returns from the grave, feeds on the blood of living creatures and can live forever unless killed. So, in addition to the terms for vampire, we must also include the terms for a werewolf, particularly in Dalmatia and parts of Herzegovina, which include *vukodlak*, *volkodlak*, *ukodlak*, *kodlak*, *kudljak*, *vukozlak*, and *vukozlacina*. There are also other regional terms that describe the same creature. These include *strigun*, *grobnik*, *gromnik*, *tenac*, *medovina*, *prikosac*, *kosac*, *upir*, *upirina* and *lapir*. Regardless of the name, the folk tales all refer to a creature with the same characteristics, no matter the era or geographic location.'

'Now, how do we identify a vampire? What does one look like? Any thoughts?' Steven looked at the students.

Tamara raised her hand: 'they're tall, dark and handsome, have fangs, wear tuxedos with black capes and speak with a delicious sexy accent.' Everybody laughed.

When they stopped, Steven continued: 'Vampires are difficult to tell apart from humans. First and foremost, because they're shape-shifters. Although they can transform their bodies, they typically remain in human form. Other popular forms include a large wolf or a horse, donkey or ox. Evidently shifting shape takes energy and they prefer human form unless necessary. Because vampires are shape-shifters, it's useless to bar a room against a vampire, as he'll simply revert to the shape of a mouse or cockroach and enter that way. Other than shape shifting, the folk tales don't portray vampires as having any other special powers, nor are they superhumanly strong or fast.

'Unlike Hollywood movies, vampires don't usually turn into bats. Rather, they favor butterflies. In folklore if a butterfly or moth enters a home in the evening it means that someone will die from a vampire.'

'Pardon my interrupting,' Stojadinovic said. 'But in our folklore, upon death the human spirit also leaves the body in the form of a butterfly.'

Steven scribbled a note about Stojadinovic's comment and continued. 'When they're in human form, vampires tend to have a specific appearance. Let's start with the face. They typically have goat or cat eyes that are red. Their teeth are made of iron and are also red. They often have a yellowish face and bluish lips, particularly immediately after becoming vampires. But most importantly, vampires don't have flesh. Rather, they're simply large inflated bags of skin, and as they feed they swell up. If they've gone without feeding for long periods of time, then they appear emaciated. So the typical well-fed vampire will appear bloated or inflated.'

'That sounds just like Milosevic and his wife Mira Markovic,' muttered Bear loudly, causing the students to laugh at the thought of the chubby dictator and his plump wife. 'Or Seselj,' called Tamara, sending the room into hysterics with her reference to the puffy paramilitary leader of the neo-fascist Serbian Radical Party.

'You see Steven, even the most mundane ethnographic research has curious implications for modern life,' Professor Ljubovic said. 'Please continue.'

'Vampires also tend to have long fingernails and in some stories they throw flame from their mouth.' Steven stopped and looked seriously at several of the female students. 'I see you have long nails. May we examine your teeth?' There were more laughs. 'Vesna, do you spit fire?' he asked mischievously as everyone laughed.

Vesna wrinkled her nose at him.

'But to return to a more serious…ah…vein. Let's discuss how vampires feed. We all know the classic Hollywood portrayal where Dracula bites the victim on the neck and sucks out all the blood. Well, according to all the folk tales I have found, vampires do indeed live off the blood of living creatures. Human blood is their favorite, and after that they prefer the blood of dogs and cattle, in that particular order. If they feel that feeding from humans attracts too much attention, then they'll resort to other sources. When a vampire enters a village the dogs are always the first to react, howling and barking loudly, as they are the vampire's favorite food after humans. The horses and cattle then react next. And all the folk tales seem to agree that vampires can only feed from the left side of the body.'

'A vampire's power lies in its burial shroud. Almost without exception the folk tales describe vampires as carrying their burial shroud with them at all times, typically draped around the shoulders or wrapped around the neck, or in some instances they drag it behind them. If they lose their shroud, they lose their power to shift shapes. I found numerous folk tales where villagers vanquished vampires by tricking them into dropping their shroud for a few moments, at which point the villagers seized both the shroud and the helpless vampire. Other than the power to shift shapes, vampires are no more powerful than humans, and Balkan folklore contains numerous accounts of people wrestling with vampires.

'For some reason, vampires are averse to water. They cannot cross bodies of moving water, except by a bridge or boat, and the boat must be piloted by someone other than the vampire. They do, however, like to hang out near watermills. Why I don't know, except that in folklore watermills are often associated with the supernatural.

'Some people ward off vampires using garlic, horseshoes, and other wards. In some parts of the Balkans, people bury their loved ones under the threshold or hearth of their homes, or in the front yard, in the belief that the spirits of the dead remain behind to guard the home against evil. Although it's supposed to be effective against vampires, it lowers the resale value of your home.'

Several people laughed.

'Now, how do you kill a vampire?' he looked around the room.

One girl raised her hand. 'Don't you drive a stake through its heart?' she asked.

'Yes, partially. There are three ways that I have identified to kill a vampire. The first is to drive a stake through its heart and then burn its head. But it can't be just any old stake: it must be a stake made from the wood of the Hawthorne tree, which is thought to be the tree from which Christ's crown of thorns was made. The second is to cut off its head and then burn its head and body. The third is to burn it. In any event, it's best if a priest is present to recite prayers while the vampire's being killed.' The audience was listening intently and many were taking notes.

'If I may interrupt,' Professor Stojadinovic interjected. 'The Hawthorne tree has deep roots in mythology and antiquity. But what's most pertinent to this discussion is the fact that the Hawthorne tree emits a chemical called trimethylene, which is also produced by decomposing bodies. Butterflies are attracted to this chemical, which is why they frequently cluster on both Hawthorne trees and freshly dug graves.'

Steven hastily scribbled down the information. 'Now, perhaps the most interesting thing I have discovered is how you become a vampire.' Steven looked around the room, pleased to see that they were so attentive. He was particularly pleased by Professor Stojadinovic's interest. 'I have good news and bad news about becoming a vampire. The good news is that if a vampire bites you, you can't become a vampire. Bram Stoker and all the others got that part completely wrong. The bad news is that if a vampire bites you, you'll die very painfully, either immediately or within a few short days.'

'Then how does one become a vampire?' Stojadinovic asked perfunctorily.

'That's a good question,' Steven responded. 'I'm not entirely certain, except that it's somehow connected to the existence of evil. The folk tales and legends are relatively silent on that matter. The only thing they agree on is that vampires are people who did evil deeds in this life. The folk tales all agree that an honest person cannot become a vampire, so none of us need worry about being bitten and becoming a vampire against our will…just about being bitten and dying.' Several of the students chuckled. 'But there does appear to be a common thread running through the legends that indicates vampires may have made a pact with the devil while in this life or the next. Nonetheless, it's difficult to say. One rarely hears of people becoming vampires who were killed violently or in battle. They're almost always persons who died a natural death. This means that vampires are usually older, uglier people, not the young sexy actors we see in the Hollywood movies. One other common element among all the folk tales is that if an animal, such as a cat or dog or mouse walks over or under the body of a deceased evil person while the body's lying in state in the home, then that person will become a vampire.'

'If I may interrupt you on this matter,' Ljubovic had a quizzical look on his face. 'This explains much about our folk beliefs and practices. How many of you have been in a home where a dead person lay?' Most of the students raised their hands. 'Have you noticed,' he continued, 'how they always fence off the area around the body and make certain that no pets or animals are permitted in the house?' The students nodded. 'Well, thanks to you Steven, we now know why.'

'Is this custom still widespread?' Steven asked. 'Do people still practice it in the 1990s?'

'When my great-Uncle died last year they fenced around his bed,' one student responded.

'My family is from Sombor,' said another, 'and they did the same thing when my grandmother died.'

'You will all note how folklore is a living, breathing thing. Never attempt to isolate it in a sterile academic context,' Ljubovic instructed the students. 'Everything we do today in connection with birth, death, and marriage is constructed on a foundation of past customs and behaviors, whether we recognize it or not. Now, perhaps Steven, you would like to continue.'

'Thank you. Most vampires are discovered and killed by people from their village within the first 100 days after they appear. After someone becomes a vampire he's disoriented and confused by his new state and during these first 100 days they function much like the poltergeist in western European folklore: they invade the house at night, bang on pots and pans and leave a mess behind. One way to overpower them at this stage is to place wheat or barley or rice in their path, and they will obsessively count every grain. If vampires survive long enough, they move away from their village to avoid discovery, live abroad and change their identity. They typically are involved in the following professions: arms salesmen, butchers and traveling salesmen.'

'So what you're saying is that a young vampire is an arms salesman who bangs pots and pans?' asked Ljubovic. The audience laughed.

'Basically, yes. Now this next part is really unusual. According to folklore, some vampires feel remorse for their sins and try to repent. There are even a few rare instances where vampires have achieved redemption, although the stories are vague about the circumstances.'

'Redemption?' Stojadinovic interrupted excitedly. 'What more can you tell us about this?'

'Nothing, really. All I know is that it supposedly happened, but I couldn't find specifics. And now for the fun part. Contrary to what Hollywood and popular authors state, vampires can have sex.' He grinned at the audience. They all sat up and some smiled. 'There are numerous instances of vampires returning to their homes after their death and sleeping with their wives. In some instances the wives became pregnant and bore children.'

'How many of these children ended up looking like the postman or the vampire's brother-in-law?' Ljubovic asked, grinning.

'Good question. In one instance it turned out that the "vampire" lived five houses away from the widow and had helped her poison her late husband. Both received the death penalty. I found a similar account from 1846 in Slavonija where a woman was being "visited" at night in her bed by a vampire, who later turned out to be a neighbor.'

'But these aren't the only instances of people using fears and superstitions about vampires to engage in dubious activities. There are accounts of villages where a rumor spread that a vampire had appeared, and then food and wine began disappearing from local barns and corncribs and cellars. In almost every instance it later turned out that thieves had spread the rumor to scare the peasants into staying indoors at night.

'But let me return to the question of vampires and sex. In addition to the hoaxes carried out so people could sleep with the widow, there do seem to be a number of cases where a dead person became a vampire and returned to have sexual relations with his wife, and in some instances she became pregnant. Most of the children attributed to vampires were born horribly deformed and died shortly after birth, but the few who survived were called either a *vampirovic*, or in Dalmatia – a *kresnik*. The vampirovic acts as sort of an anti-vampire, is clairvoyant and is able to detect vampires, no matter their form. A vampirovic can also kill a vampire more easily than a human, for example with a gun, although the bullet must be made of steel and not lead. When a vampirovic shoots a vampire through the heart, the vampire turns into a puddle of bloody jelly.' Several of the students made faces of disgust at the image. 'A vampirovic can also live forever, similar to a vampire, except that he doesn't feed on blood.

'Most vampires are depicted as nocturnal creatures who return to their graves to sleep during the day. According to the folklore, this is true only of new vampires. There are many examples of vampires who walk around normally during the day, particularly as they grow older and gain experience. So if vampires were among us today it would be very difficult to know who they are,' Steven concluded.

'Don't be so certain,' Stojadinovic interjected. 'Haven't you seen all the black jeeps and limousines with darkened windows? If I were a vampire, that would be the ideal way to travel around during daytime. And I'd surround myself with beautiful, fast women and wear dark glasses.' Many of the students nodded.

Ljubovic jumped in. 'The image of a vampire is indeed a powerful one, that of a mystical being that sucks the life essence from those it attacks. In this regard we might consider Yugoslavia as being under attack by vampires. The symbolism is certainly powerful and appropriate. Any comments or questions?'

A number of hands shot up and Ljubovic spent the next hour conducting a lively discussion on folklore, mythology, symbolism and vampires. At the end of the evening he said: 'I'd like to thank Steven for his presentation,' and began knocking on the table with his knuckles. The others joined in with this polite academic applause. 'Before we leave this evening, I would like to ask Steven if he has any last thoughts or comments for us.'

'Thank you all,' Steven said, relieved that the discussion had gone smoothly. 'There's one thing that keeps popping to mind. That's the origin of the vampire myth. Except for regional variations in names, all the vampire stories are consistent over 600 years. Is it possible that at one time there might have actually been some sort of a biological phenomenon or disease or something that gave rise to vampire stories? Anyway, thank you for paying attention and for coming.'

As the students rose to leave, Ljubovic and Stojadinovic offered their congratulations. 'Truly marvelous, Steven,' Stojadinovic gushed. 'The work you've done is ground-breaking. I'm very impressed.'

'Thank you,' Steven said, floating on a cloud of praise, relieved that his work had pleased the two professors.

'You must come to visit me in Novi Sad as soon as possible,' Stojadinovic added. 'There is much for you to learn there.'

* * *

Slatina's knife minced the tender green basil leaves until they were nearly paste, and then he turned his attention to cloves of garlic, savoring the richness of the scent. His homemade pesto would go on whole grain spaghetti. He glanced at a pan of sliced eggplants, bell peppers, red onions, tomatoes, zucchini, parsley and garlic garnished with olive oil, waiting to be placed in the oven. A salad of rucola, pinola nuts, parmesan and thinly sliced pear brought back memories of home. From the other room an all-news cable announcer droned about the weather in Sri Lanka.

He thought of Steven and wondered what he was up to. He felt increasingly nervous about the sparseness of communication. Was Steven using good judgment in his associations? Was he being careful with his comments? Was he using discretion sharing material with others? The lack of letters and phone calls was worrisome. Increasingly he had begun to question his own judgment in sending Steven with such little preparation. For now, all he could do was hope for the best and trust in Steven's character.

'Can you set the table?' he called.

'Okay, just a second,' Katarina answered. 'I want to hear the news at the top of the hour about Yugoslavia.'

Slatina sighed. He knew there would be nothing good. He heard the music announcing the beginning of the next sixty-minute news cycle, then an announcer's voice:

> *Gun battles broke out today as Serbian forces resumed shelling Sarajevo, attacking the city center, post office, telephone exchange and power stations. At least six civilians were killed and 47 wounded. Serbian aircraft also bombed Croat positions in western Herzegovina, while heavy fighting was reported in Turbe, Derventa and Mostar. Today US Deputy Assistant Secretary of State Ralph Johnson met with Serbian President Slobodan Milosevic in Belgrade. A US official who requested anonymity said that Johnson gave the Serbian strongman a tough message about Serbian responsibility for the ongoing violence in Bosnia and Herzegovina…*

Slatina frowned as he mentally tuned it out, opened a bottle of red wine from the island of Hvar, and poured it into a decanter, noting with satisfaction its thickness. As he sniffed its purple fumes, a smile crept back over his face.

And then Katarina's scream shattered the air.

Slatina dropped the decanter on the floor: glass shards and liquid shot in all directions, sending scarlet streaks across his beige cotton trousers. He ran to find her sitting on the sofa, her knees pulled tightly against her chest, sobbing and moaning. He sat down and placed his arms around her.

'There, there, child, it's okay. It's okay. Tell me what happened,' he said soothingly, rocking her gently. 'Everything will be okay.'

'On the TV… it happened on TV' she breathed rapidly, her voice breaking with emotion. 'I saw it.'

'Tell me what you saw.'

'I…I…was watching the footage of the meeting in Belgrade… just now… in the background, behind the negotiators…I saw it…it was hideous…red eyes that were all wrong…fangs…blackness pouring from its soul…it just walked in back of everybody as normal as can be, carrying papers for one of the Serbian negotiators… and nobody seemed to notice.'

* * *

Interlude IV: The Labyrinth and the Chamber: Monday, 6 May 1940

Two Yugoslav Royal Army officers trudged down the passageway, lanterns in front of them. Each carried a long wooden stake.

'Will we ever find the twelfth?' asked the Lieutenant.

'We haven't heard from him all this time,' the Captain responded. 'Someone must have killed him.'

'The seepage is getting worse,' the Lieutenant said looking around.

'Bad plumbing in the garrison buildings above ground,' the Captain answered. 'Poor quality...cheap materials…the Austrians knew how to build things, but this lot…how I long for good German workmanship.'

They continued through the gloom until they came to an intersection with a marble sign that read *IV/500 Kom. Gall. – Communication Gallery IV/500.* They turned down a side tunnel until they came to the lock embedded in the wall. The Captain faced it, crossed himself, heard a loud click, and turned left towards the far wall. He pressed the wall open and descended the damp stairs, followed by the Lieutenant.

Their descent was halted by a clear stream that covered the bottom of the stairs.

'It's risen almost a meter since last year,' the Lieutenant said.

'They're trapped,' the Captain muttered.

'Perhaps the water has also risen inside,' the Lieutenant said. 'Do you think they could drown?'

'Perhaps,' the Captain answered. He descended the stairs until the water reached his chest, waded to the door in the far wall and examined it. 'The seals are intact,' he called back.

The Lieutenant nodded.

The Captain touched the brick door, his fingers trembling.

Inside the vault all was black, undisturbed by daylight, lamplight or candlelight. No sound penetrated the chamber and all was still. Yet in the dark Natalija saw, and in the silence she heard…silence interrupted by the occasional drop of water falling from the vaulted brick ceiling high overhead into the ever-rising ankle-deep pool that covered the floor. The sound of each drop echoed preternaturally, magnified by silence and stillness.

She felt the captain long before he touched the door and sat up in her coffin in anxious anticipation. She sensed his presence, her heart pounding, as she waited for the door to open. But as before, it remained shut. And then she felt his presence recede.

'Nooooo,' she screamed. 'Take me with you.'

'Your time will come,' the oldest said. 'Patience.'

Natalija lay back down, still awake, thinking of the love that had sentenced her to this torment. 'So this is eternal damnation,' she thought bitterly.

And the water dripped.

And she mourned.

CHAPTER FIVE

BREAKING THE SPELL

Belgrade: 23 April – 2 May 1992

The following day Steven returned early to the reading room, to be met once again by the bulldog librarian, dressed in the same frumpy outfit.

'How is Gordana? Is she feeling better,' he inquired pleasantly.

'I don't know.' Her curt answer and sharp voice clouded the sunlight pouring through the windows.

'Has the book been returned?' He smiled.

'No… It… Has… Not. And even had it been, it's in a restricted category.' Her voice rang arrogantly.

'A restricted category for ethnography books?' Steven spluttered. 'Are you serious? Why?'

'That's unimportant. It's restricted.'

'But I've already seen it. There aren't any state secrets inside,' Steven protested.

The pug nose jutted out across the counter at Steven. 'Don't mock me.

It's a serious matter. You may not see the book.'

'Does that mean it's been returned?' he pried.

She said nothing, and shuffled some papers.

'I thought Serbia was leaving communism behind,' Steven prodded. 'Can folk stories destroy Serbia? What's so dangerous?'

The bulldog snapped at him: 'This library has rules. You obviously cannot respect the rules, so you may no longer use this library. You must leave. Immediately!'

Steven was shocked. 'Why? I haven't done anything wrong. I just want to see a book. Who are you to say I can't?'

'You may not use the library!' The bulldog folded her arms and squinted at him angrily, her eyes reddening. 'Leave, and take your vampires with you.'

'But…' and he stopped just as he was about to continue his objection. Uncertain as to why, Steven suddenly felt he should leave, so he walked out, his head cloudy and muddled, angry, unable to understand why he couldn't get the book, yet unable to understand why he didn't put up a fight. And how did she know he was researching vampires?

'This is idiotic,' he muttered as he left, shaking his head to clear his thoughts, his anger mounting as he walked towards Professor Ljubovic's office. But the office was empty and a note on the door said that he wouldn't be back until the following Thursday.

Steven had lost all will to study, so he stood in front of the Philosophy Faculty, wondering how to get the Djordjevic book again. As he walked dejectedly towards Students' Square he heard female voices call his name.

He looked and saw Vesna and Tamara in the Aristotle outdoor café. They smiled and waved cheerfully. 'Stefan, is something wrong?' Vesna asked.

Steven exploded in frustration. Still standing, he told them what had transpired in the reading room, gesticulating with his hands, his Serbo-Croatian unable to keep pace with his emotions.

'Stefan, it's okay. Just sit down and relax,' Vesna said, pulling him by the sleeve into a chair between her and Tamara, where he sat glumly.

'You should ask Professor Ljubovic to intervene. They can't just throw you out of the reading room like that,' Vesna said. 'There's no reason for a restricted list to exist.'

'What's the book about?' Tamara inquired.

'Vampires, what else?' he answered.

Vesna rolled her eyes and shook her head. Tamara smiled.

'Well, obviously vampires hold the key to Serbia's military success,' Vesna spat sarcasm. 'Letting a foreign spy such as you see the book means Serbia will lose the wars in Croatia and Bosnia. Without vampires to support him, Milosevic will lose power and Serbia might become a normal country. Then they'd stop sucking our blood, and that of course, can't happen.'

'Vesna, what's gotten into you today? You're really negative,' Tamara chided.

'We're killing our own people; inflation is over 1,000 percent; my father's salary is four months late. Just yesterday he finally got paid for December, and hyperinflation meant that all we could afford was two bars of soap, a kilogram of flour, a kilogram of onions, and washing machine detergent. One month's salary! And we're forbidden to withdraw our foreign currency savings from the bank. What are we supposed to live on? If my brother in Frankfurt didn't send us money each month, there's no way we could live. And my parents are dipping into the hard currency they keep under the mattress. Soon we'll have nothing left. The better question is: why are you so complacent? Oh, I forgot, you're in love and your father's a Party member.' Vesna flung the comment at Tamara and lit a cigarette.

Tamara also lit up, clearly offended. They sat mutely, pretending to ignore the tension. Finally Tamara spoke. 'Your presentation last night was excellent!' she gushed. 'Everybody's talking about it! All the graduate students think you're just marvelous, and the assistant professors are all jealous they didn't think of it first and publish something.'

'Yes, it was good,' Vesna admitted. 'Even though I don't like the topic. We were both very proud of you.'

'Well, thanks. I hope you…'

'Oy yoy!' Tamara interrupted, jumping from her chair and grabbing her backpack. 'I was supposed to meet Bear fifteen minutes ago. He'll kill me.' She raced off leaving Steven alone with Vesna.

'She's always forgetting things,' Vesna said. 'Poor Bear.'

She continued: 'Seriously Stefan, you did a very good job last night. You were serious and well organized and your presentation was interesting.'

Steven felt tingles run down his spine as he looked at her wide bright smile, teeth gleaming whitely in a large oval face. Her dark eyes shone through the long chestnut-brown hair that partly covered her high cheekbones and flowed past her shoulders. Her unaccustomed kindness unnerved him.

'Thanks Vesna, but I'm stuck,' he said. 'I don't know what to do next…I think I've pretty much tapped out all the libraries here in Belgrade, and I need a break. I feel trapped here…it's so oppressive sometimes I can't breathe. How do you stand it here?'

'I grew up here, and I can't leave, so there is no use thinking about it,' she said, her face suddenly blank. They studied their drinks awkwardly.

'I have an idea,' she said, suddenly brightening. 'Let's visit used bookstores and see if we can find a copy of that book. I'm certain we'll find one somewhere.' She had an adventurous gleam in her eyes.

Steven's face lightened: 'That's a great idea.' He called for the bill, which came to a little over 15 million dinars, less than 10 cents.

Their first stop was a bookstore at the Serbian Academy of Arts and

Sciences, across from the Philosophy Faculty. It took a moment for their eyes to adjust to the gloomy interior, its dark bookshelves reaching to the ceiling. A man on a ladder sorting books called out 'May I help you?' without looking at them.

Vesna explained what they wanted and he climbed down, tugged at his goatee and pulled a large binder from under the counter.

'Djordjevic,' he muttered as he leafed through the binder. 'Hmm…Tihomir…ah, yes, 1953…hmm. We don't carry it. Only 100 copies were published. It was placed on a restricted list prior to publication… that was a different era you know. Rankovic – Tito's enforcer – was running things. That means all the copies were probably seized by the UDBA and destroyed.'

'UDBA?' asked Steven.

'Yes, the old name for the secret police. I suspect you won't find it anywhere, except in a few select libraries scattered around former Yugoslavia. Even then it may be restricted. I'm sorry.'

'Wow, Rankovic,' Vesna whispered as they walked out. 'That's a big deal. He was the head of the secret police. What's in this book that's so important? Are you sure it's only ethnography?'

'Of course. I saw it with my own eyes in the reading room. It's simply a compilation about vampires in the lands of Yugoslavia. I was able to look at part of it…it's an amazing collection of articles. Djordjevic categorizes vampires and their behavior. It's based on years of scholarship. My presentations were nothing compared to what he did. I need to find that book!'

They spent the rest of the day searching Belgrade's used bookstores. Everywhere they met the same puzzled looks: no one had ever heard of Djordjevic's works, much less seen them.

As they walked back towards the Philosophy Faculty Vesna muttered: 'The UDBA sure did a good job destroying it.' A little further she stopped and began talking to herself, staring off into the distance: 'I'm pissed off,' she said. 'Why did they want to destroy knowledge and keep it from the people? The authorities will respect us only when we stand up to them. They can't keep us down forever. I'll find that book for you, Stefan. I'll do it purely out of spite, what we here call *inat*.'

'Thanks. Although you shouldn't feel obligated,' Steven said, uncertain what had provoked her outburst.

'I'm hungry,' she suddenly announced.

'You want to come with me to the student cafeteria?' he asked. 'My treat.'

'Why don't you come to my place,' she offered. 'My grandmother's preparing lunch.'

'Isn't it too late for lunch?' he looked at his watch. 'It's already 3:00 o'clock.'

'Stefan, how long have you been in Serbia?'

'Four months.'

'Hasn't anybody invited you over to their house for lunch?'

'Well, no…not really…I mean I eat lunch with my host family on Sunday afternoons.'

'Here in Serbia everybody works until 3:00, then they come home and eat, so lunch is typically served between 3:00 and 4:00. We'll be just in time.'

'Okay,' he smiled. As a student he had long ago learned to never turn down a free home-cooked meal.

They fought their way onto the steps of an overcrowded trolleybus that leaned to one side. A large man jammed his armpit into Steven's ear, while Vesna squeezed against him from the other side, her face pressed just below his chin, where he could smell her perfume, feel her hair and feel her skin against his neck. The sensation was arousing.

At the Medakovic neighborhood they squeezed off the bus and walked uphill through a street of apartment flats into a graveyard. The sound of the new leaves rustling in the tall Chestnut trees was music to Steven's ears after the crowded bus, but Vesna hurried ahead.

Steven followed her into a world of death set in stone and bronze…a statue of a youth holding a freshly rolled-up newspaper; a gravestone with an etched photograph of a man standing proudly in front of his Mercedes Benz; a statue of a boxer in his fighting stance. He stopped, fascinated by the celebration of worldly materialism in a place where it no longer mattered.

'Hurry up,' Vesna called. She stood like a statue, hands planted on her hips, legs apart, chestnut hair draped across the shoulders of her black leather jacket. 'I don't like being here.'

'We don't have graveyards like this in America,' he called, and followed her to a residential neighborhood and a house surrounded by a low wall topped by a spiked iron fence. They passed through a gate, decorated with a dried flower wreath and a front door protected by a horseshoe.

'You'll like my grandmother,' Vesna called to him as they entered the house.

He seemed uncertain whether her statement was a prediction or an order.

* * *

Steven lay in bed groaning, trying to recover from the enormous meal. When they had entered the house, Vesna's grandmother had immediately begun fawning over Steven. 'Vesna has told us so much about you,' she gushed, causing Vesna to blush fiercely and avert her eyes. But she continued: 'she told us what a wonderful job you are doing in your research of our folk stories.'

Vesna interrupted: 'Grandma, please.' Then Vesna's mother and father arrived home from work and they all sat at the table and ate. Still the grandmother continued to dote on Steven, offering him food until he felt he would burst, all the time asking him about his family, where he was from, what his parents did, what his interests were. When she asked him if he had a girlfriend, Vesna once again blushed and said: 'Mama, make her stop, she's embarrassing him.'

And then the grandmother asked: 'Don't you think our girls are pretty?' causing Vesna to blush once more.

By the time they finished lunch the sun had set and Vesna walked him to a different bus stop, holding him under the arm all the way there. 'It isn't good to cut through a graveyard after dark,' she said.

He wasn't certain how to react to her hand under his arm. He had seen her and Tamara hold each other like this and had observed other women holding men like this, even though they were only friends. Did she like him, or was it simply a gesture of friendship? She was always so stern and critical of his work. When she placed her hand under his arm he felt a strong attraction to her, which he instinctively resisted. When she kissed him on the cheek just before he boarded the bus, he was pleasantly surprised.

'I like her,' he said to himself.

His reverie was interrupted by a sharp knock on his door. 'Come in,' he called.

Dusan stuck his head around the door. 'Telephone for you.'

Steven said: 'Hello.'

'Stefan, is that you?' He heard a faint female voice in English shouting across an ocean of static and interference. It sent a tingle up and down his spine. 'Katarina, how are you?' he shouted back.

'Good. I can barely hear you. How are you doing?'

'Pretty good.'

Dusan's grandmother looked at Steven from the kitchen, obviously displeased with the level of his voice.

'Marko asked me to call and see how you're doing. He asked why you haven't written.' Her voice barely overrode the static.

He lowered his voice so not to offend the grandmother. 'But I wrote several times, both to him and you. Last week I received two letters from Professor Slatina and three from you, all at the same time. It must be the war. Can you hear me?'

'Yes, I can hear you,' Katarina's voice sounded tense. 'You don't have to shout. That's what Marko was afraid of. How's life in Belgrade? Are you okay?'

'Yes, I'm very busy and I've found lots of information about….'

'Have you been to Novi Sad yet?' she cut him off in mid-sentence.

'No, only Belgrade. As I said, I've found a lot of material about…'

'Marko wants you to go to Novi Sad.' She cut him off once again just before he could utter the word *vampire*. 'He said you should work in the archives and libraries there, especially the Matica Srpska,' she said, referring to the famous Serbian national collection in Vojvodina. 'And visit my mother. I must go now. Stefan, please be very careful of what you say and who you say it to,' her voice sounded worried. 'I miss our talks.'

'I'm being careful. Everything is okay. When are you coming this summer?' But the line went dead before she could answer.

'But am I being careful?' he asked himself. His time with Katarina was now a faint and distant memory, overpowered by his afternoon with Vesna.

* * *

Katarina set down the cordless phone, lay back in the lounge chair, shaded her eyes against the bright noonday sun and squinted at Scripps Pier, the La Jolla Cove, and the hang-gliders flying over the cliffs at Torrey Pines. In the lounge chair next to her Slatina held a volume of Marcus Aurelius' *Meditations*, his eyes hidden behind sunglasses.

'He's getting closer.' Katarina turned to Slatina. 'You must tell him.'

'Yes, yes,' Slatina nodded, pensively, still looking at the book. 'Yet the telephone is dangerous. We must speak face to face.'

A butterfly flew drunkenly across the patio and lighted on Slatina's book. He looked at it curiously and sniffed.

'You really should've told him before he left,' Katarina said, disapproval in her voice.

'Katarina, please trust me,' he said kindly. 'Had I told him the truth he would have thought me a fool or worse, and I would have frightened him off. I would have accomplished nothing.'

'But he's so naïve,' she pleaded. 'He knows nothing…and you know what a good heart he has. As he learns more the risks to him will increase. It's dangerous. Please call and tell him to leave at once.'

'Now, Katja, as long as he knows nothing they will not cause him trouble,' Slatina said.

Both sat silently, staring at the sun glistening off the Pacific.

Katarina broke the silence. 'Promise me you'll get him out.'

Slatina turned and looked sternly at her. 'Katja, please, do not exaggerate the situation.'

'I mean it. Promise me.' Her voice was tense. 'And soon.'

'Does he mean that much to you?' Slatina studied her silent face. 'Very well.' He lifted his sunglasses and looked her in the eyes: 'I promise.'

She looked in his eyes, nodded her head, and then gazed again at the Pacific, as her thoughts turned to her father. The evening before his funeral a butterfly had appeared inside their house, even though the windows were closed. Her mother had looked at it, smiled amid her tears, and said 'Your father's come back to comfort us.' Under the butterfly's watchful gaze, the two of them ironed a clean shirt, socks and underwear, and laid out his best suit, tie and shoes, so that they would have fresh clothes to take to the morgue to dress the body. That night before they went to bed, Katarina turned to the butterfly and said 'goodnight, Papa.' It seemed to move its wings slightly in response.

Slatina interrupted her thoughts. 'You must pray for Steven with all the strength of your heart,' he added, then seemed to whisper something to the butterfly perched on his book.

She nodded silently and watched the butterfly open its wings, take flight from the spine of the book and disappear into the sunlight glinting from the Pacific Ocean's waves.

* * *

The following Thursday Steven knocked on Professor Ljubovic's office door. Ljubovic opened it and smiled grimly at Steven: 'Well, you've certainly stirred up things in the reading room.'

'The new librarian banned me from the reading room. All I did was ask for a book that Gordana had given me earlier.'

'Ah, Steven,' the Professor said. 'Perhaps we should take another walk.' He motioned for Steven to follow him. 'There are too many ears inside the Faculty, too many people not minding their own business, too many suspicious minds.'

'I didn't do anything wrong.' Steven blurted. 'All I did…'

'Listen to me.' Ljubovic interrupted. 'Something strange is happening. Yesterday the DB came by my flat and spoke with me for two hours. They wanted to know who you are, what you are doing, who is financing you and whether you're a spy. Believe it or not, even though this is a police state, they are quite inefficient, and it seems they didn't know you were here in Serbia or what you were doing. I told them about your ethnography research and they seem to have accepted it.'

'But from now on you must be very careful. I think some of the assistant professors may be informers, and perhaps some of the graduate students too. You have nothing to hide…you are conducting legitimate work, so if they call you in for questioning, be truthful with them. Are you registered with the police?'

'Yes, my landlord took me when I arrived.'

'Good, then you have at least followed procedures. You can't get in trouble for that.' They walked briskly out across the fortress and down a steep path paved with rough rocks. 'I asked about Gordana the librarian. She isn't ill. Rather, she displeased someone and they placed her on leave of absence. Her replacement is from the DB and the Dean is very upset.'

'The DB? You're kidding!' Steven exclaimed. 'Am I safe? Should I leave the country?'

'I'm not sure. People are paranoid because of the wars. They don't know how to live without communism. For many people communism was comfortable and they liked being told what to do. For now, just keep your head down. It might not be a bad idea to leave Belgrade until things calm down. Have you thought of going to Novi Sad? Professor Stojadinovic would be delighted to work with you.'

'I was thinking the same thing,' Steven's heart lightened at the prospect.

'Good. Tomorrow is May Day, so there'll be a long holiday weekend. I suggest you relax, enjoy the weekend and then go to Novi Sad.'

'But is there any way I can find the Djordjevic book? It's really important.'

'I can't help you. It would be risky to get it from the reading room. I've asked some friends about it and no one has ever heard of it.'

They walked across the lower city towards a medieval stone tower. 'But I do know a man who might be able to help you. He lives in Sremski Karlovci just south of Novi Sad. They say he knows every book published in this part of the world for the last 300 years. He's Volks Deutsche, you know, the ethnic Germans who were settled in Vojvodina by the Empress Maria Theresa in the 18th century. I will give you his address. Perhaps he can find the book for you.'

As they approached the tower Ljubovic pointed at it and explained its origins. When they reached its base he motioned for Steven to follow him as he climbed through a window into the tower. Once inside, he pulled out a notebook, hastily scribbled down the name and address of the bookstore in Sremski Karlovci and handed it to Steven.

Ljubovic then exhaled deeply: 'The walk has been good for us, no?'

Steven nodded.

* * *

Back at his apartment Steven called Professor Stojadinovic and made arrangements to come to Novi Sad. No sooner had he put down the receiver than the phone rang. No one else was home, so he answered.

'Stefan, how are you,' Vesna's voice flowed softly from the receiver.

He told her his plans to visit Novi Sad.

'Will you stay long? How will you get there?' She asked the questions faster than he could answer. 'Bear has a car…perhaps Tamara and I can talk him into driving you there… can you help pay for gasoline?… then we can have a nice excursion… we all need to get out of here… meet us tonight at 8:00 at the horse statue… we're going out to a movie… tomorrow night we'll stay out all night and celebrate your success and then on Sunday we'll take our hangovers to Novi Sad… okay?'

'Okay.' He liked her voice. 'But can we take the old road? I'd like to see Sremski Karlovci en route.'

'That's a wonderful idea. Sremski Karlovci is beautiful. Did you know they call it the Serbian Athens?'

'Yes, I've read about it. I'll see you tonight at the horse.'

'Yes, tonight at the horse,' she repeated his words to him.

'Your studies are your first priority,' he thought to himself and smiled.

* * *

That evening Steven walked to the Square of the Republic, hoping to release the anxiety caused by the DB visit to Ljubovic. He arrived early, so he walked around window shopping, when he caught sight of Gordana the librarian. She walked past him rapidly into a side street that dropped towards the Danube, carrying a shopping bag. She didn't notice him so he quickened his pace and followed her, trying to keep a discreet distance between them.

She continued downhill into a dimly-lit neighborhood of old buildings and tree-lined streets, her footsteps echoing off the pavement, until she came to the doorway of an old apartment, where she rummaged through her purse.

The street was deserted except for parked cars and Steven approached, calling her name tentatively: 'Gordana, good evening.'

Startled, she looked up at him and blanched as though seeing a ghost.

'Go away,' her voice was shaky. 'I've already had enough trouble because of you.'

A cough echoed down the deserted street from one of the many darkened doorways. 'They're watching,' she hissed. 'Leave! Now!'

'But I…'

'That cursed book has caused me too much trouble,' Gordana spat. 'They'll harm my son if I talk to you. Go away. Leave me alone. Now!' Her voice quivered with fear as she found her keys, opened the door and disappeared inside.

Steven looked around the tree-lined street, shadows covering the pavement where the streetlights couldn't penetrate the foliage.

From somewhere the cough came again.

He turned and walked up the hill to meet Bear, Tamara and Vesna.

When he arrived they were waiting for him. Vesna waved and gave him a small peck on the cheek, which elicited smiles from Tamara and Bear. And then they walked to the movie theatre, Vesna holding his arm.

* * *

He spent much of May Day with Bear and Tamara at Vesna's home, sitting in the back yard and talking to her parents and grandparents while they grilled copious quantities of meat and vegetables. The family atmosphere and Vesna's smile relaxed him for the first time since his encounter with the bulldog librarian. Vesna's father – an engineer – and her mother – a bank manager – had traveled extensively: 'That is, before that ass Slobo came to power,' Vesna's mother said vehemently while her father nodded in agreement.

They spoke eloquently of their ancestors, the Glogovac family, who had left Kosovo centuries before and settled in Croatia. They reminisced of their travels to Asia, Africa, Europe and the United States, and Steven didn't leave until nearly midnight. As he left Vesna kissed him gently goodbye on the cheek, and whispered 'goodnight' in his ear. He floated all the way back to his apartment, while unconvincingly repeating the mantra 'your studies come first.'

Saturday night he arrived early at the horse and made small talk with Bear. 'How's the draft dodging? They still looking for you?'

'Screw them,' Bear spat. 'Yesterday the Military Police visited my sister's home. But they'll have to kill me before I fight for Milosevic.'

'Where are you staying?'

'I'm still at my Uncle's place on Banovo Hill,' Bear said. 'He's an officer, so that's the last place they'll look.' He gestured towards a young man passing by in green camouflage, wearing the wolf's head arm patch of a paramilitary unit, his eyes blank, his movements those of an old man. 'Look at that idiot. They're all drug addicts…you can see it on their faces. They have to take drugs to sleep after what they do on the battlefield. They're all convicts and criminals… killers… Slobo's children.' Bear whispered to Steven.

Bear then whistled quietly, grinned and nodded in the direction of the National Theatre. 'Look at that.'

Two tall women strode confidently across the square arm in arm, both wearing black lace-up high-heeled boots, dark stockings and short dark skirts, topped by dark sweaters and leather jackets, long hair streaming down past their shoulders. Their faces and makeup were perfect, as though they had stepped off the pages of Vogue: lips glittered, teeth sparkled, cheeks blazed with life and eyes glistened excitedly. Both walked in a way that indicated they knew every male eye was on them. Steven stared, only to realize as they drew closer that they were none other than Vesna and Tamara. He caught himself gawking at how beautiful Vesna was.

'Wow, look at you two!' Bear wrapped his arms around Tamara while Vesna kissed Steven three times on the cheeks. 'You know Mariah Carey had a song about you,' Bear commented. 'Vision of Love!' They all laughed.

'Let's go,' Tamara pulled Bear towards the National Theatre and Vesna and Steven followed, Vesna holding Steven's arm above the elbow. They walked slowly to a basement club on Francuska Street that played funk, soul, blues and rock, some domestic, some foreign, the words *Soul Food* above the door. Most of the men stared at Vesna and Tamara as the four of them entered. The décor was thrown-together African ethnic funk, and the place was crowded. They found a spot along a wall, ordered drinks and began to shout at each other over Steppenwolf's *Born to be Wild.*

'When do we leave?' Steven shouted.

'When we wake up,' Bear hollered back. 'Probably around noon or one o'clock. That okay?'

'Can we stop in Sremski Karlovci?'

'No problem. Have you seen Petrovaradin fortress?'

'Only from the train. It was dark.'

'We'll go there tomorrow…you'll like it.'

The girls were dancing together to a Yugoslav pop song about girls in summer dresses, smiling and flirting outrageously with each other and a group of young men that surrounded them. 'Are they okay?' Steven shouted at Bear, aware that he was feeling protective of Vesna.

'No problem, they're friends of ours. We always have fun like this.'

Steven's eyes drifted to Vesna, watching as her skirt raised and lowered slightly over the tops of her thighs, in rhythm to the music. As she danced her breasts swayed gently under the sweater, occasionally straining against the wool. Her movements were hypnotic, and Steven soon joined her on the dance floor, watching her sway rhythmically, her long chestnut hair floating back and forth as she tossed her head.

The music slowed down as a Dalmatian singer implored them to believe in love, and Vesna placed her arms around his neck, drew her body snugly against his, and nuzzled his neck with her nose and forehead. The scent of her perfume was alluring and he placed his hands on the small of her back, which caused her to snuggle in even closer and plant a small kiss on his neck. He moved one hand up her back, gently, towards her neck and she moved against him.

'You are a good man,' Vesna whispered in Steven's ear. And then the music sped up suddenly, they separated and the girls began hopping madly around the room, singing at the top of their lungs to a Croatian rock band: "*we're dancing, all day and night*". Obviously the war did not apply to popular music.

Tamara and Vesna spent most of the night dancing at a frantic pace, while Bear and Steven stood at the side wall and talked about the war, the trip to Novi Sad, the war, the girls, the war, and hyperinflation. After a while the girls pulled them both back out to dance to a Croatian rock song about a black and white world.

Suddenly the music died, the house lights came up and a large shaven headed leatherman flashed a Scorpion submachine pistol and police badge and called for everyone's attention. Other policemen in blue camouflage, combat boots, body armor and helmets blocked the entrance, and others were dispersed throughout the crowd, all wielding Kalashnikovs.

'Good evening, ladies and gentlemen,' the bald man said. 'We're here to conduct a little routine control. Please have your documents ready for inspection.' The police began examining the identity cards of all the men present and searched them. When they came to Steven they perused his passport, asked him why he was in Serbia, seemed satisfied with his response, and proceeded to Bear, who handed them his I.D. card wrapped in a 20 Deutsche Mark bill. Then the lead officer bid everyone goodnight and thanked them for their cooperation. Music played, the houselights dimmed, and the dancing resumed as if nothing had happened.

'Are you okay?' Tamara rushed to Bear's side. 'I thought they might take you away to the army.'

'No problems,' Bear said nonchalantly, but his words didn't match his demeanor, and he was sweating profusely.

'What was that about?' Steven asked.

'They raid the clubs to search for drugs, illegal weapons, criminals and draft-dodgers,' Vesna said. 'It's all just for show. On the streets there's chaos and the police do nothing. They hardly ever find anything, because anyone who does have drugs or weapons will either offer bribes or have his girlfriend hold them in her purse. They don't dare arrest the criminals for fear of retribution.'

'Why didn't they check the women?'

'Come on, Stefan,' Bear said incredulously. 'This is Serbia. We're a patriarchal country. You know what'd happen if they checked women? An uprising.'

By Belgrade standards the night was still young, only 1:30, but the raid had soured Bear's mood. 'Let's go,' he urged the others.

'Why don't you come over to my place for coffee?' Tamara asked. The four of them walked to Tamara's apartment, only a few blocks away from the club. Tamara ushered them into a sitting room, turned on a dim table lamp, put on a tape of Barry White, and went in to the kitchen to fix coffee.

'Bear, would you help me with the coffee?' Tamara called from the other room. Bear left Steven alone with Vesna, who stood examining a painting on the wall. Steven sat on the sofa and gazed at her admiringly as she stood with her back to him. 'She looks fantastic,' he thought.

The table lamp dimly illuminated half of Vesna's figure, leaving the rest in shadow. She turned and glided towards Steven, pulled his legs apart and stood between them, then pulled his head against her stomach so he could hear her heartbeat through her thin sweater. The musk of her perfume – mingled with sweat – entered his nostrils and aroused him. She leaned over, placed her forehead against the top of his head and let her hair cascade over him like a dark, soft waterfall that tickled his skin, covering his face and neck. The physical attraction was strong and the rest of the world increasingly distant.

'We shouldn't be doing this,' he murmured softly, as he reached out his hands and placed them around her waist, drawing her closer.

'Why not?' she whispered breathlessly, wriggling her body against his head.

He felt her heart pound palpably through the fabric of her sweater, and his head clouded with desire. It was hard to think of a reason not to and his breathing quickened.

'We need to stop,' he pleaded, unwilling to push her away. 'We really need to stop.'

'We're stopping,' she said as she pressed him closer.

She knelt between his knees and wrapped her arms around his neck, their heads pressed so closely he felt the softness of her cheek and the warmth of her breath. She rubbed her cheek gently against his and kissed his earlobe, sending tingles across his shoulders and into his groin.

Steven placed one hand across the back of her neck, and another around her waist. He felt her softness, pulled her lips to his and kissed her. Vesna answered with a gentle kiss that quickly turned to fire and soon threatened to devour him.

He embraced her fully as they collapsed backward onto the sofa, lying entangled in each other's ardent grasp. Primordial instincts enveloped them in a cocoon of passion that shut out the room as they clung to each other, desperately seeking salvation from the evil decay about them. As they drank the heat from each other's gasping lips, the world rapidly swirled around, casting off all distractions, until only Steven and Vesna remained.

She grabbed his shirt, untucked it from his jeans and violently pulled it over his head. As she did so his Hawthorne wood cross swung free and bumped against her forehead. 'Take off the cross,' she panted.

Steven stiffened as the cross brought back vivid memories of Katarina and filled him with conflicting emotions, uncertainty and guilt.

'Do it. Hurry,' she gasped between kisses, pulling him down on her.

His head swirled in confusion as his body vibrated with passion. What about his feelings for Katarina? What about his past? Could he stand falling in love and losing again?

'Stefan, please,' she moaned breathlessly.

A loud sound came from down the hallway and Steven jumped.

'Don't worry,' Vesna whispered, panting for air. 'It's only Tamara and Bear. She's a screamer.'

But the spell had been broken.

Steven stood up. 'I have to use the toilet,' he said. He walked down the hall and locked himself in the bathroom, where he splashed cold water on his face and looked in the mirror. 'Get a grip on yourself,' he said to his reflection.

When Steven returned to the living room Vesna was sitting on the sofa, nervously smoking a cigarette. She smiled awkwardly, and he smiled back. He walked up to her, reached out both hands and pulled her to her feet.

'I like you Vesna. I like our friendship. But I'm not ready for anything else right now. Please understand. I don't want to hurt you.'

She nodded, looking down, unable to meet his gaze.

'Are you angry with me?'

She shook her head with a mixture of injured pride and unfulfilled passion, still not looking at him, her face shrouded by her long, dark hair.

There followed an awkward silence.

Then she looked at him, embarrassment and confusion evident in her moist eyes. She placed her finger to his lips and said 'I'm sorry. I had too much to drink. Don't be angry.'

She then gently took his hand and pulled him down a darkened hallway towards the back bedrooms, treading quietly, holding her finger to her lips, smiling mischievously. Outside the bedroom doors she halted, and motioned for him to listen. From behind one door they heard the furious sounds of Bear and Tamara making love. Vesna smiled, pulled Steven down the hallway, out the front door and into the elevator. Only when the elevator door had closed and they were on their way down, did she begin laughing and didn't stop until they were on the street.

A decrepit diesel-spewing Mercedes taxi drove them home. Even though Steven lived in the center, he instructed the driver to take Vesna home first. They sat together awkwardly on the back seat. After a few minutes she turned to him, leaned over and whispered: 'It's a crazy world, Stefan. I don't know what tomorrow will bring, if we'll be dead or alive, or what will happen to us, but I'm glad I met you. I'll help you find your vampires and I won't bother you about them anymore. Things are so crazy now that I feel as if the world is coming to an end, that the apocalypse is…'

He pulled her to him, gave her a hug and held her tightly until they got to her home. Then she jumped out and walked through her gate into the doorway with the horseshoe without looking back.

* * *

Interlude V: The Labyrinth: Saturday, 12 January 1983

The tourists squinted against the glare of the winter sun. They held flashlights in hand and cameras around their necks and chattered excitedly in Japanese as they followed the guide towards a gateway set in the snowy hillside. A long dead hand had engraved the word Minen – German for

"Mines" – above the brick arch in precise Gothic letters on a stone tablet. The guide removed a key and unlocked an iron gate.

'Turn on your lights and watch your heads,' he ordered in accented English. The tourists giggled as they followed him down a dusty brick tunnel, then down steps to another level.

'Today we visit the Great Labyrinth,' the guide said. 'Don't wander off. Several years ago someone got lost and starved to death.' The guide was uncertain how well they understood.

He led them down stairwells, sloping corridors, through tunnel after tunnel, showing them the defenses, powder magazines, ventilation shafts, barracks and bunkers. Their questions annoyed him, but he answered them mechanically. They wanted to stop every few paces and take group pictures, which slowed them down. The deeper they descended, the damper it became.

As they passed a tablet with carefully stenciled Gothic lettering, the guide stopped, turned and addressed them in a bored voice: 'We are now on the fourth and lowest of the underground galleries, and I will share a mystery with you. This red stone cross embedded in the wall is the only Maltese cross found in the entire fortress – all others are either Latin or Orthodox – and it is the only cross of any type embedded in stone in a wall. As you can see by the letters carved underneath – MDCCXXXII – it dates to 1732. No one knows its purpose.' After a group photograph he returned to the main passage and continued a few paces downward before stopping at a portion of the floor where the dirt had been scraped back to expose a layer of brick underneath.

'What is it?' asked one person curiously.

'No one knows, the guide responded. 'Most of the floors on the fourth level are earthen. This was discovered just recently by accident. The dirt had worn away and a colleague of mine noticed these bricks. It could be a cistern for storing water, or the top of another tunnel. However, no one knows where the entrance is.'

One of the tourists knelt on top of the bricks and tapped them with his knuckles, noting the gentle curve of the barrel vault. The rest took photographs of him.

'Don't do that!' the guide said sternly. 'The floor is…'

A loud scraping sound interrupted him in mid-sentence, soft, raspy, as of bricks sliding together. Everyone froze and stopped talking. All shone their lights on the brickwork in the floor.

At once the bricks collapsed from underneath the tourist, and he plummeted feet first into a gaping hole, crying out as he fell. He grabbed and caught hold of the bricks at the edge of the hole, hanging by both hands. One of the bricks began to dislodge, causing him to seek another handhold, and then that brick too began to come loose, just as the guide caught his arms and held him suspended above the void as more bricks fell away. 'Help me,' cried the guide, grunting to sustain the weight of the tourist. Several others rushed to his aid, and gradually they pulled him out of the hole. The rest stood back and took photographs. Yet the brickwork continued to collapse slowly beneath their feet, the hole gradually widening.

'Everybody get back now, it might collapse further,' the guide shouted. 'Back! Get back!' The tourists ran up the tunnel, but the guide stood looking at the hole, now nearly five feet across, shining his flashlight down into the darkness, trying to discern what it held. But he saw nothing. As he edged closer to see into the pit, he heard the scraping noise once again. A single brick fell downward into the darkness, causing him to jump back. For several seconds there was only silence, then the sound of the brick hitting wood, then a splash. And then once again, silence.

'Stay back,' the guide shouted to the others, who had gathered near the junction of the tunnel with the Maltese cross. 'A barrel vault relies on the top bricks to hold it together. The entire vault may collapse with us on top of it. We must leave quickly before we're trapped.'

They ran through the passages and finally emerged into the crisp snow, breathing deeply, steam pouring from their mouths, expressions of excitement on their faces. The guide breathed a sigh of relief.

And then they took a group photograph.

CHAPTER SIX

THE WIDOW'S SUPPER

Belgrade, Karlovci, Novi Sad: Sunday and Monday, 3-4 May 1992

It was almost noon when a bleary-eyed Bear came for Steven in a battered red YUGO 45 that had known better days. 'Is it yours?' Steven asked as he loaded his suitcase in the trunk. 'Yeah. I bought it used,' Bear answered proudly. 'But it's registered under my cousin's name…you know, the army and all that…'

Steven squeezed into the small front passenger seat, while Tamara and Vesna sat scrunched in back. They smiled and waved lazily at Steven, their eyes hidden behind sunglasses. Vesna leaned forward, hugged him passionately and kissed him on the cheek, deliberately grazing his lips with hers as she passed over them. She then leaned back against Tamara and closed her eyes. Steven wasn't feeling particularly alert, although Vesna's kiss and anticipation of the trip had energized him. But now they had to find gasoline, no easy task given that all the filling stations were closed because of fuel shortages.

'Why the shortage?' Steven asked.

'Sanctions,' Bear replied, rubbing his temples to clear his hangover.

'Yeah, it's sanctions, the war, the Croats, the Masons,' Vesna yawned sarcastically from the back seat. 'The Muslims, the space aliens, the Vatican, the CIA, because of everybody except us. It's because Woody Woodpecker didn't report us to the police on time. We never do anything wrong. We're a heavenly people. Come on, the sanctions are a joke. Slobo is using them to hand out monopolies and enrich his cronies.'

'Seriously, why isn't there any gas?' Steven pressed.

'The government does it so that the politicians' cronies can make money smuggling fuel.' Vesna said. 'Then they give kickbacks to the politicians. There's always gas if you're willing to pay. Look at all the cars. Does it seem to you there's a shortage?'

'Slobo keeps prices low so people won't complain,' Bear explained. 'It's okay if we don't have gas, just so the gas we don't have is cheap. Gas costs about 10 cents a liter…that's all people can afford, but you can't find it at that price because Slobo can't afford to subsidize it, so the gas stations run out really fast. I heard there might be some at Autokomanda.'

A mile-long line of cars at Autokomanda signaled that everyone else in Belgrade had heard the same rumor. Bear asked a man at the head of the line what was going on.

'A fuel truck's supposed to come today…maybe this evening,' he said.

'Where do we get gas?' Steven asked.

'Anywhere.' Bear answered. 'But it'll cost more.'

They crossed the Danube to the outskirts of Zemun and stopped at the roadside next to a battered old Volkswagen Golf hatchback, its roof lined with plastic jugs and soda bottles of gasoline. The seller stood with a hand-lettered cardboard sign advertising the fuel being sold while puffing on a cigarette, oblivious to the fire hazard. Bear reached an agreement with the man, Steven paid for the gas in Deutsche Marks, and calculated it had cost more than 500 times the official price and at least four times the price in the U.S.

The girls fell asleep as they drove down a two-lane country road, lined with massive Chestnut trees planted long ago when an emperor had ruled the entire Pannonian Plain from Vienna. Flecks of sparkling sunlight trickled through the leaves, creating a cozy tunnel of shadow and light, green and brown, asphalt and leaves, mixed with white wisps of floating pollen. It made Steven drowsy, and he noticed Bear also seemed to struggle to stay awake. 'Are you all right? Would you like me to drive?'

'I'm tired. I didn't get much sleep last night.' Bear yawned loudly, his mouth gaping open so wide his head almost disappeared.

'I heard,' Steven yawned.

'Yeah? Well, loud equals good!' Bear grinned. The road passed through small towns, each with an old church in the center and Habsburg-era buildings on the main square, and then the trees ended and fields stretched away on either side. It reminded Steven of Iowa: the smell of freshly plowed soil and fertilizer mingling to make the world simple and alive, as earth rejoiced under the rays of a warming sun.

'Is all of Vojvodina flat like this?' Steven asked.

'Yeah except for Fruska Gora.' Another town passed as fields turned into rolling hills, and off to the left Steven could see a range of low mountains.

From the back seat came the sound of snoring. 'It's Tamara,' Bear said. 'She snores, but so do I, so we cancel each other out.'

The car puttered gently up and down the hills, insects occasionally splattering against the windshield. Driving dreamily, the old Yugo rattled along at a gentle pace that defied time. 'Now we're in the Fruska Gora foothills,' Bear said. 'There's lots of monasteries here.'

They passed a long column of drab green army trucks towing artillery pieces, nervous-looking recruits looking out the back. 'That could be me,' Bear muttered half under his breath. 'They're going to fight Slobo's wars and kill their own brothers. Madness…'

Vesna had woken up and began to caress Steven's head with her fingers. She tickled the back of his neck and wrapped both arms around him from behind. He reached up to caress her arms and smiled happily. The countryside became enchanted, each blade of grass, each tree weaving its magic spell just for him. Somehow the war and sanctions disappeared.

They descended a long slope and found themselves with the Danube on their right and the skeletal spires of a church ahead on their left. 'That's unusual,' Steven commented to Bear.

'Yeah. It's the cathedral in Sremski Karlovci.'

Bear gently guided the car off the main road into Sremski Karlovci. They entered the old town center to find time slip backwards as a decaying Austro-Hungarian provincial town arose around them, untouched by modernity, its 18th and 19th century Baroque and neoclassical buildings forming a ring of crumbling neglect around the main square.

Tamara read from a guidebook and explained the town's history, its role as the seat of the Orthodox Metropolitan Bishop, the cradle of Serbian learning and the site of the first Serbian Gymnasium, the rough equivalent of a US High School.

'Karlovci has the nickname "Serbian Athens",' Tamara said proudly. 'Our first educated people studied here, our first printing press was here, and it was a cultural center for Habsburg Serbs. When Serbia threw off the Turkish yoke in 1817 educated Serbs left the comfort of the Habsburg Empire, crossed the Sava River and became the first teachers, scribes, clerks and government officials. They wanted to bring our people out of darkness.'

'Tamara, think of all the money you'd make as a tour guide,' Bear joked. 'Especially with all the foreign tourists we have now.' They all laughed.

They walked up the hill towards the Karlovci Gymnasium, its faded orange and red façade hidden behind tall trees on the west side of the main square. Vesna held Steven's arm as they walked. 'What's that?' he asked, pointing at a square window jutting out from the front of a private home.

'That's a *kibbitz-fenster*,' Vesna answered. 'It's unique to Vojvodina. They're mostly on old German homes, but Serbs also built them. They're made so you can sit in your house when it's cold, but look out and see what's going on in the neighborhood. It's great for neighborhood gossips.' Suddenly a mischievous look came over her face. 'It was also used to search for vampires. When word spread that a vampire was in town, people could stay in the safety of their homes and look up and down the street to see if it was safe to go outside.'

'Really? That's cool.' Steven failed to notice the expression on her face. 'Is there some way to find out more about this? I could use this in my…'

He turned at the sound of the others laughing. 'Ha, ha, very funny,' he said, finally catching the joke.

Vesna put her arm under his, looked up, gave him an innocent look and batted her eyelashes. 'I was just teasing, don't get angry.'

He mumbled something incoherent, she stuck her tongue out at him and smiled, then hugged him.

'We need to find the bookstore,' Steven said, pulling the address Ljubovic had given him from his pocket.

They discovered it behind the Gymnasium in an old Baroque building with a large portal. As they entered, the unfinished bare-wood floors creaked loudly underfoot to announce their presence. As the girls shivered at the sudden drop in temperature, Bear sneezed from the strong smell of maple-flavored tobacco. A small silver-haired man in a sweater closed a book, removed a pipe from his mouth and stood up from behind a desk, squinting at them through wire-rimmed glasses.

'Good day. May I help you?' His wizened smile was ageless and could have been anywhere between 40 and 70.

'Yes, I am looking for Danko Niedermeier, the proprietor. Is he here?' inquired Steven.

'At your service,' he smiled politely and bowed his head.

Niedermeier showed them around the bookstore, its shelves crammed with books in every language of Eastern Europe, from Slovak to Russian, Hungarian to German, and Latin to Ancient Greek, arranged haphazardly. Bear and the girls browsed through the titles while Steven introduced himself and mentioned Professor Ljubovic.

'Ah, and how is Miroslav these days? He used to come here frequently and buy books from me. But now with the war, petrol and books are expensive, and Sremski Karlovci is ever farther from Belgrade.' The proprietor sighed deeply. 'Now, how may I help you?'

Steven told him his difficulties finding the Djordjevic book.

'Restricted you say?' A smile crept over Niedermeier's face as he stirred the tobacco in his pipe bowl. 'Hmmm… I didn't know they still kept books on restricted lists. Well, that will make it interesting. There has never been a book I have not been able to find. I will see what I can do for you.' He picked up a notebook and scribbled down information about the book. 'Please leave me your telephone number and I will call you as soon as I come up with something.' He puffed furiously on the pipe as he attempted to relight it.

'That's not safe,' Steven told him. 'The DB is interested. I'll call you in a couple of days.'

'The DB *and* vampires…oh ho ho ho. How strangely appropriate.' he chuckled softly, blowing large rings of smoke from the pipe. 'I love a good challenge. A bibliophile's life is sedate, and there's nothing like a good search to liven it up. This will be great fun indeed.' He peered out the window, thought for a while, and then turned to Steven. 'You have presented me a challenge. Thank you very much.' He turned away and reached behind the cash register. 'Perhaps I could interest you in a glass of some lovely Karlovacki Bermet. It is a locally produced wine we are quite proud of.'

Steven thought back to the Bermet he had drunk in Professor Slatina's office in September. While he sat and discussed history and ethnography with Niedermeier, the wine's rich taste transported him far across the Adriatic Sea, Atlantic Ocean and the North American continent. Now it all seemed like another lifetime, a fairy tale of normalcy in a country with people who were not scarred by war, atrocities, hatred, hyperinflation and a complete societal breakdown. He sipped the Bermet and thought of Professor Slatina: 'Is he still teaching the second semester survey course?' he wondered. 'Who is his teaching assistant? What's Katarina doing?' Melancholy set in as he thought back to happier times, and he looked across at Niedermeier puffing on his pipe, wearing a contented smile.

'Thank you for coming,' Niedermeier puffed contentedly. 'I will see what I can do about the Djordjevic book. Are you going to visit the Chapel of Peace while you're here?'

'Yeah, we're going there now,' answered Bear.

'Good. Goodbye, and I wish you good health. Please drive carefully. These are odd times. And be careful what you say and to whom you say it.'

Steven was hearing this warning with increasing frequency.

* * *

The Chapel of Peace sat alone in an overgrown hilltop pasture overlooking Sremski Karlovci, a crumbling derelict half hidden by trees, its rust-streaked dome crowned by a small lantern cupola. Time had sent a large crack in the flaking plaster over one of its doors, knocked glass from many of the windows, and rusted the hands of the clocks on the bell tower. A rusty gate and wire fence barred their entrance to the property, and butterflies rested in the tall grass and on the surrounding trees.

'This is my favorite church in all of Vojvodina,' Tamara said. She thumbed through her guidebook. 'It says that in 1699 they signed the Treaty of Karlowitz right here and drew the map of modern Europe, between the Turks, Poles, Austrians and Venetians. It's famous because it's the first time in the history of diplomacy that anyone used a round table for negotiations. Everyone argued where they'd sit and who'd enter the room first. The Turks put up a round tent with doors on four sides so everyone could enter and sit down at the same time and no one could sit at the head of the table. And that's why the church is round.'

They pressed the gate open far enough for the girls to squeeze through, and then Bear and Steven followed.

'It has four entrances,' Bear said. 'One's in back of the altar. And the bell tower has four clocks facing four separate directions. The fourth one's on the inside …you can't see it from here.'

As they approached the chapel they saw that one of the side doors was slightly open, hanging partway off its hinges. Bear gave it a shove, which caused it to fall off the hinges and hit the floor with a loud crash that engulfed them in clouds of fine dust.

'Really, Bear, you didn't have to do that,' Tamara coughed.

When the dust had settled, they walked into the center of the chapel. Natural light poured through the upper windows illuminating peeling robin-egg blue plaster. Other than a carved wooden altarpiece, the church was plain and lacked decoration of any kind.

'It's not round,' said Steven.

'Of course its round, what do you mean?' said Tamara.

'It's not round. It's oval.'

'Round…oval…big deal.'

The narrow wooden stairs creaked loudly as Bear and Steven climbed up to the organ loft and followed a narrow gallery around the chapel.

'So what happened between you and Vesna last night?' Bear whispered to Steven.

'Nothing,' Steven whispered back.

'You should have.' Bear grinned. 'She's hot and she likes you.'

'Yeah, Vesna's a babe, but what'll happen when I leave? If I did something now I'd feel like I'm using her and then moving on.'

'Damn, Stefan, you've got the most over-developed conscience I've ever come across,' Bear shook his head in bewilderment. 'Look, Vesna *wants* you…she told Tamara that she hasn't been with a guy in over a year. And you want her. It doesn't matter if you're together in two months. What's important is now. The whole world's screwed up and going to hell. We might not even be alive in a month, what with the war.'

'Well, there's also someone else I'm interested in.'

'Where? America?' Bear scoffed. 'So what? Have fun while you're here. Vesna's a great girl and who knows, maybe it'll turn into something. You can't tell until you try. And if it doesn't, then you can go back to your girlfriend in America.'

'Well, if I…'

'What are you two talking about up there?' Tamara called, interrupting them.

'Eighteenth century church architecture,' Bear called to Tamara. Then he whispered to Steven. 'Vesna's attractive. Don't be surprised if she doesn't wait around for you. Serbian women make great wives. They're very passionate.'

'Okay, enough about Serbian women,' Steven answered, irritated. 'That's all people talk about, the women. Just back off.'

'Be careful you don't fall and get killed,' called Vesna from below. 'We still have a communist bureaucracy. Just think of all the paperwork we'll have to fill out if something happens to you.'

'Ha, ha. You're sooo funny today,' Steven retorted, smiling.

'Have you two finished up there?' Tamara called out, pacing impatiently. 'I need a bathroom!'

'Mind over matter. Ignore the physical,' Vesna said, from a bench, eyes closed, head tilted back, arms outstretched, as though imitating the crucifixion.

'Remember what I told you,' Bear whispered as they walked down the stairs.

As they left the chapel, Bear and Steven tried to set the door back on its hinges, but its frame was warped and it wouldn't hang properly, so they left it askew as they had found it. They walked down the hill, squeezed through the gate and back into the Yugo and drove off to find a bathroom for Tamara.

* * *

A westerly breeze from the starboard beam wafted the sailboat south towards San Diego's Point Loma peninsula, as the late afternoon sun bleached the teak decking and painted the mahogany trim a deep orange, fired the raised wooden letters on the transom that read *Butterfly*, and infused the taut Dacron sails with the faintest hints of gold. It cast shadows across Slatina's deeply tanned face as he ran his fingers through dark, wind-tousled hair and squinted as the sun moved inexorably lower towards the western horizon.

A group of college students in windbreakers – Katarina among them – sat on the foredeck, chattering animatedly about whatever it was college students talk about. At this moment they seemed to be planning an ice-skating party at the nearby University Towne Center mall. Slatina tensed and frowned as he saw a young man move closer and place an arm around her shoulder.

Slatina tensed, protectively. 'Her father wouldn't approve,' he thought. 'He's a flakey Southern California surfer.' He leaned down to port and slightly inched out a line wrapped around a winch that led to the Genoa. Satisfied with the shape of the sail, he secured the line.

She shrugged off the boy's hand.

'That's better,' he thought, and relaxed, allowing his eyes to glance upward to check the mainsail's telltales.

Once, when he had been her age, he had sailed north from the island of Hvar towards the Dalmatian port of Split. He recalled the voyage vividly, for it was on that journey with his Uncle at the helm, that he had first seen *her*, in front of the ruins of the Roman Emperor Diocletian's palace.

She had stood on the white limestone quay, immobile amidst the bustling crowds, tourists and vendors, like the basalt Egyptian sphinxes inside the palace peristyle. When she looked at him she caught his gaze with opal blue eyes that reached inside of him, seized his heart and pulled him towards her. He raced to the bowsprit, grasping the forestay for balance, their eyes and hearts connected. They stood like that, staring unabashedly at each other as the boat pulled close to the quay. Suddenly, a gust of wind tore a broad-brimmed straw hat from her head and carried it over the water towards the boat, causing a waterfall of hair to cascade to her waist, framing her ivory face in black. As Slatina dove from the bowsprit into the water to retrieve the hat, she turned around and disappeared from view into the heart of the old city.

When he climbed back on deck, the only sign of her was the waterlogged hat. His Uncle only grinned. 'Put the fenders on the starboard side,' he bellowed. 'Make ready the mooring lines fore and aft!'

Only later that evening over drinks on the terrace of the family home on the Marjan peninsula, did his Uncle tell him that he knew the girl's father, that she came from a good family, and that he could arrange for Marko to return the hat in person.

'Look! Dolphins,' someone shouted from the bow, interrupting Slatina's reverie as he looked where they were pointing.

'They'll come to us,' he shouted back. 'They'll surf the bow wave.' And his thoughts turned once again to the first time he had seen her, and how she had changed his life. And how, like Steven, he too had buried his hopes and dreams along with his young wife.

* * *

It was once called the Gibraltar of the Danube, the enormous fortress of Petrovaradin that squatted wide and menacing on a large rock above the great river. Bear's overloaded Yugo struggled to conquer the great fortress, chugging slowly up the steep cobbled brick and stone road that wound up the hill: first over a bridge and through a modest gate that led through a thick brick and earthen rampart, then over another bridge and the impressive Molinar Gate, then across a third bridge and through the ornate Court Gate into a curving tunnel that led out onto the top of the citadel, where they parked the tired car.

They walked around the edge of the fortress ramparts, looked at the green plain that stretched east, north and west across the Danube, the flatness of the green forests and fields interrupted only by the smokestacks of an oil refinery and a distant power plant. Beneath them lay Wasserstadt, Petrovaradin's Baroque lower city nestled amidst massive fortifications. They strolled towards a white clock tower that overlooked the Danube then continued onto a large brick terrace where they found a table under a sun umbrella.

'Professor Stojadinovic should be here shortly,' Steven said, glancing at his watch. 'This is the only restaurant on the fortress, right?'

'Don't worry, it's the right place,' Vesna answered. 'He'll be here.' And no sooner had she spoken than Stojadinovic appeared at the edge of the terrace. Steven stood and waved.

The professor removed his fedora hat and sunglasses to reveal puffy eyes as he tossed his scarf jauntily around his neck. 'Ah, my young friends, how are you? Did you have a pleasant trip?' he asked formally.

After exchanging pleasantries they ordered drinks.

'I am glad we could meet here. Petrovaradin is my favorite place in all of Vojvodina. You know it has a very rich history, don't you?' They all nodded. 'The Celts fortified it in the centuries before Christ, and later Rome used it as a signal outpost to guard the *Limes*, the Empire's northern border. It was considered impregnable and was built according to the manner of the renowned French engineer Sebastian Vauban. Its battlements formed a dam that kept the Ottoman Turkish tide from flooding north into the heart of the Habsburg Holy Roman Empire.' The fascinated looks on their faces encouraged Stojadinovic to add dramatic flourishes.

'Petrovaradin's last battle took place 276 years ago on the morning of August 5th, 1716, when the hopelessly out-numbered Austrian commander

Eugene of Savoy with his 78,000 men, faced the full might of Turkish Grand Vizier Damad Ali Pasha, the Conqueror of Morea, who had at his command nearly 200,000 troops. That morning the fortress's dull red brick and earthen ramparts stood in striking contrast to the Turkish camp, with its splendiferous horse-tail standards and vibrant multi-colored round tents that made the camp resemble an enormous flower garden filled with gardenias, petunias and morning-glories.' Clearly the professor relished talking.

'However,' Stojadinovic continued, as though reciting from memory, 'superior numbers and finer accommodations do not spell victory, and Damad ended up having a rather bad day: troops led by Alexander Würtemburg broke through the Turkish lines in the center and routed the elite Janissaries, while Austrian Cuirassiers and Hungarian Hussars swept the Spahis from the left flank in a magnificent thundering charge of iron hoofs and steel sabers, forcing the Turks to flee and abandon their flower-blossom camp. As Damad's army broke and fled in panic, his heavily-laden treasure wagons sank into quicksand while fleeing Eugene's forces, and he himself received a mortal wound. He died the following day, only to have his lifeless form carried back to Belgrade, where – befitting a warrior – he was interred at the fortress. Perhaps you have seen his mausoleum, the *Turbe* on the Kalemegdan?' They all nodded as he gesticulated.

'But that was a by-gone era, and the muzzle-loading cannon, thick earthen bulwarks, cavalry sorties, trenches, draw bridges and multiple glacis walls that so effectively repulsed the surging Ottoman tide now stand silent, impotent against 20th century technology. No longer do fierce plumed *Yatağan*-wielding Janissaries threaten the Habsburg monarchy. What few cannon are left now serve to entertain young children and tourists. The barracks and stables no longer house Serbian *Freikorps* volunteers, Hungarian Hussars or German officers: their places are now taken by museums, a restaurant, café, and an artists' colony.' Steven listened attentively, fascinated more by the artistry of Stojadinovic's delivery than the actual content.

'You're quite the story-teller,' Steven exclaimed.

'Thank you,' Stojadinovic smiled broadly. 'I cheated. That's actually the script for a documentary film I narrated several years ago. Have you been in the tunnels?'

They shook their heads.

'Petrovaradin has more than sixteen kilometers of underground tunnels and galleries. It took the Austrians 88 years to build them all, and the fortress could hold 10,000 horses and more than 30,000 soldiers. It was truly an engineering marvel, and all of this before your American War of Independence from Britain. A small portion of the underground has been sanitized for tourists, but the really interesting part is the Great Labyrinth in the deep underground beneath the Hornwerk bastion.'

'Can we see it?' asked Steven eagerly.

'That's not too difficult: you simply need to know the right people,' Stojadinovic grinned wryly. 'I myself know it rather well and used to lead tours down there. But then we had an accident.'

'What happened?' prodded Steven.

'Nine years ago I led some tourists through the deepest part of the Labyrinth. I was showing them a corridor where we had uncovered some unusual brickwork, when the floor collapsed out from under us. We almost lost a gentleman from Osaka. I returned later that evening but couldn't get too near the hole for fear of a collapse. I notified the APP – the Association for the Preservation of Petrovaradin – and we began making plans to take a team of specialists from the university to survey it.'

'Several days later a pack of wild dogs savagely attacked and killed a night watchman just inside the entrance to the Labyrinth. Crazy rumors began circulating about packs of man-eating dogs and there was a public uproar and panic, especially when local farmers began complaining that something was killing their cattle. Some people advocated shooting all stray dogs, while others complained that the dog catchers weren't doing their job properly and that it was the mayor's fault.'

'The police responded in typical communist fashion: they placed the entire Labyrinth off limits and went around shooting all the stray dogs they could find. And then the animal lovers protested…it was quite a circus. They kept the Labyrinth sealed off while they carried out an official investigation. The Communist Party had to have someone to blame so they sacked the director of the APP and replaced him with a Party loyalist. He was extremely cautious and limited in his thinking, and he forbade entry to the Labyrinth.'

'Then the economy collapsed and the funds for preservation and research dried up. The director stole most of the budget and inflation ate up the rest, and then after Milosevic's coup against the Vojvodina government in 1988, the APP stopped receiving money altogether. Right now the APP maintains the fortress entirely from rents, the restaurant and souvenir shops. But now there are no foreign tourists, and the artists don't sell as much as they used to, so the fortress is slowly deteriorating. Just recently they appointed a new director of the APP, someone younger and more innovative, but there's no money in the budget.'

'Did you ever return and investigate the hole?' asked Steven.

'No. The new director might permit it, but I haven't really thought about it for some time.'

'Could you organize a tour for us?' Steven asked.

'Mmmm. That's an intriguing thought. I shall look into it. And now, if you have finished your drinks, perhaps I could take Steven and show him where he will be staying in Novi Sad.'

As they walked back to the car for Steven's bag, Vesna hung sadly on his arm. 'You have my telephone number. You will call me, won't you?' she asked. 'And don't forget to come and visit Belgrade on the weekends.'

At the car he kissed Bear and Tamara the traditional three times. Vesna too kissed him the traditional three times, and then unseen by the others, stole a fourth from his lips as she pulled away. 'Hurry back to Belgrade.'

Steven blushed as Vesna turned and walked towards the red Yugo without looking back.

As he and Stojadinovic drove down from the fortress, through Wasserstadt and across the Varadin Bridge into downtown Novi Sad, Steven gazed wistfully out the window of Stojadinovic's Volkswagen Beetle, thinking that it might be all right to let down his guard and open his heart to Vesna.

'I see you have enjoyed your time in Belgrade,' Stojadinovic commented wryly. 'Our women are beautiful, aren't they?'

* * *

The university dormitory assaulted Steven's senses. Moldy carpet, dirty diapers, tobacco smoke and damp concrete hung pungent in the air. As he searched for his room he passed entire families crammed into quarters meant for two or three students: parents, babies, grandparents, children, teenagers, the newly dispossessed Serb refugees from Croatia. He ducked under laundry drying on lines stretched across the corridor and passed old people sitting on stools outside their rooms, talking to each other, smoking nervously. Loud turbo-folk music blasted from boom-boxes and radios as children raced up and down the corridors, yelling loudly. Some held sticks for rifles, playing Partizans and Ustase, their version of Cowboys and Indians.

Passing by one room Steven noticed a muscular shaven-headed youth wearing black jeans, a black t-shirt with gold chains, sunglasses on his bald pate. A black aviator's jacket hung on the back of the chair and he was drinking a yellowish liquid from a water glass, kept company by a bottle of Johnny Walker scotch and a heroin-thin blonde-from-a-bottle wearing tight jeans, high heels and a lacey tank top that was mostly cleavage. The youth jumped up, raced to the door and grabbed Steven with one muscular tattooed arm.

'You're new here.' He didn't ask: he stated.

'Yes.'

'Good. If you need anything, just let me know.' He spoke almost too fast to follow. 'Marijuana, heroin, hashish, changing money, cigarettes, girls, petrol, cars...you name it, no problem!' The blonde smiled at Steven like a cat about to swallow a canary. 'I'm your man. My name is Neso.' He extended a hand in greeting, offering Steven a closer look at the tattoo, a picture of a triumphant Serb in national costume standing astride a dead Albanian in whose chest he had planted a Serbian flag. The caption read *Kosovo or Death*.

Not knowing what else to do, Steven shook Neso's hand and muttered 'thanks.'

'You're not from here, are you?' Neso stated.

'No, I'm from America.'

'Really? Is your family from here?'

'No, my entire family is from America.'

'I'm not from here either. I'm a Serb, but I'm from Bosnia,' Neso said proudly. 'America is good. Look, Ceca, he's a real American,' he said turning to the blonde. 'Do you have a girlfriend? Even if you do it doesn't matter: Ceca likes making new friends.' She smiled suggestively and bent over slightly, displaying her plunging décolleté to good effect.

'Thank you. But no.' Yet Steven found himself staring at Ceca's vulgar display of flesh and thinking about Vesna's kiss.

'You'll change your mind. You Americans have too many Muslims and blacks,' Neso proclaimed loudly, 'they dilute your racial strength. You also have too many Jews and Mexicans. I've got a cousin in Chicago and he's told me everything about America. Do you know him? His name is Radovan Stojilkovic.'

'No, I'm from Utah. It's a long way away.'

'Oh well, no big deal. I like America. I want to move there someday. Americans and Serbs have always been good friends. Anything you need, just let me know,' he shook Steven's hand once more and then let him continue searching for his room.

Steven's dilapidated room housed one other person, an agriculture graduate student from China who spoke no English and poor Serbo-Croatian. His name sounded like Geronimo, but Steven wasn't sure.

Loud voices and music continued to echo down the corridor. Steven sought respite from the noise in the cafeteria, which was depressingly drab and socialist. Cleanliness was a low priority, as was the quality of the food, which consisted of cabbage and bean *pasulj*, submerged in grease and cooking oil. The cafeteria stunk of greasy baked fish, so Steven returned to his room.

The noise from the refugees kept Steven up until after midnight, and then he was awoken twice, by a husband and wife screaming hysterically about who had cheated on whom, and by someone pounding loudly on a door, yelling for Neso.

* * *

Early Monday Steven fled the chaos of the dormitory for the stillness of the Matica Srpska library, its founders' busts lined protectively in front to keep out noise. He perused the archive's catalogues and took note of collections by famous ethnographers, and then came across the name Stefan Novakovic. It seemed familiar, yet he couldn't quite place it, so he reviewed his notes. Then he found it: Novakovic was the scholar who had found the original Flückinger documents about the Austrian Army vampire-hunting missions in Serbia. Excited, he immediately ordered the first two cartons of Novakovic's papers and then went to the reading room to await their delivery.

After fifteen minutes the cartons arrived, and Steven found Novakovic's notes. The handwriting was nearly indecipherable and resembled chicken tracks more than any particular alphabet. 'It's like cuneiform,' Steven muttered to himself as he struggled through it. But references to the Austrian Army were nowhere to be found, so he returned the cartons and ordered the next two. And the next two. And the next two. It was late afternoon before he found the documents he wanted.

Judging from the notes, while working in the Vienna Kriegsarchiv, Novakovic had stumbled upon records from the Kalemegdan fortress. The notes were cryptic, but the more Steven read the more excited he became:

- *3 March 1731, news to Bgd from Medvedja near Jagodina, vampire reported,*
- *7 March 1731, Flückinger sent to investigate with IV KaiGrKo. Commanded by Captain von Zlatinow,*
- *6 April 1731, Flückinger and von Zlatinow return to Bgd,*
- *15 April 1731, Flückinger, von Zlatinow and IV KaiGrKo depart,*
- *11 June 1731, Flückinger and von Zlatinow return with 3 heavy sealed wagons, refuses inspection of wagons, says burned vampire in Medvedja, ashes thrown in Morava,*
- *18 June 1731, von Zlatinow and IV KaiGrKo. to Peterwardein w/wagons, Kalemegdan commander General Albrecht Graf von und zu Meyerling writes complaint directly to Hofburg,*
- *24 July 1731, IV KaiGrKo. and Flückinger return to Bgd via boat from Peterwardein, Meyerling formal protest to Hofburg, von Zlatinow jails Meyerling 3 days, released after promising to cooperate,*
- *28 July 1731, von Zlatinow requisitions provisions from fortress stores, flour, salt, wine, beer, meat, salt, shot, powder, steel bars, twelve heavy wagons, teams of oxen and horses,*

The other entries were similar: news of a vampire; von Zlatinow and Flückinger and KaiGrKo. depart and return at a later date, often with sealed wagons, and then a letter of complaint from Meyerling. The logbook for the next year showed a similar pattern, and Steven realized Peterwardein was the German variant of Petrovaradin.

'What does *IV KaiGrKo.* mean?' Steven asked himself. And then it dawned on him: 'of course, what an idiot I am,' he muttered aloud, slapping himself on the forehead, drawing stares from other readers. '*KaiGrKo*...it's an abbreviation of *Kaiserlich Grenadier Kompanie*, an Imperial Grenadier Company.' But what authority did a lowly Captain, a company commander, have to imprison a General with impunity, and a Count at that? At that time the Austrians were busily expanding Kalemegdan with the intent of making it their main border outpost against the Turks, perhaps even larger than Petrovaradin.

Steven exhausted the Novakovic files shortly before closing time and walked to the high-rise main post office in the center of town to call Vesna, but she wasn't home, so he left a message with her grandmother. He then walked to the university, where he found Stojadinovic still in his office.

'How was your first day in the Matica Srpska?' he asked.

When Steven related his discovery, Stojadinovic's eyes glowed with excitement. 'You may be on to something quite noteworthy. How do you wish to follow up on this information?'

'Well, the fourth Imperial Grenadier Company kept going to Petrovaradin, so perhaps I can get the fortress commander's records from there. But the records for the Kalemegdan were in Vienna, so that means I'll have to go to Vienna to the Kriegsarchiv.'

'Slow down,' Stojadinovic smiled gently. 'The records haven't gone anywhere. There's an important difference between Kalemegdan and Petrovaradin: the Austrians took all the Kalemegdan records back to Vienna, whereas Petrovaradin's records were left behind. So I'm sorry Steven, you'll have to cancel your plans to eat Wienerschnitzel and Sachertorte.'

'They're here? Really? Where?' Steven's excitement grew.

Stojadinovic gave him a broad grin. 'Tomorrow I shall take you to the City Historical Archive in the old barracks on top of the fortress. There you'll find all the records you wish. If you don't mind, I would like to look into this with you, as it is very intriguing.'

'It would be an honor.'

'Oh, and tell your friends I have received permission from the new director of the APP to take you through the Great Labyrinth. If they're interested, perhaps we could visit it a week from this Saturday.'

'That would be wonderful,' Steven answered. 'How many people can come?'

'I thought just the four of you. No one has been there since 1983, and it may still be dangerous, so I don't wish to take too large a group.'

'Great. Now for a stupid question,' Steven said, 'How do I get to Sremski Karlovci?'

'By bus, of course,' Stojadinovic answered. 'It's a beautiful town. Is there a particular reason you wish to go there?'

Steven told him about the book and Niedermeier.

'Ah yes, Danko is a good man,' Stojadinovic smiled. 'I have known him for many years and everyone at the university uses him to find old books. When he puts his mind to something, he always succeeds. If he has promised you the book, then you will get it.'

Steven then walked back to the main post office and called Vesna again.

'I missed you,' she said.

* * *

A warm spring evening was gradually descending over Novi Sad as Steven walked along the tree-lined riverfront towards the Varadin Bridge, the Danube crawling beside him like the body of a dark, undulating serpent without beginning or end. As he started across the bridge he watched the street lights gradually twinkle to life. The scent of pipe tobacco entered his nostrils, the smoke trailing from a lone fisherman in the stern of a slender wooden skiff that drifted on the current under the bridge, until the stench of decaying fish gradually overpowered the receding tobacco.

Across the river, batteries of floodlights bathed Petrovaradin's ramparts in their ethereal glow, inoculating the massive fortress against the darkening gloom until it gradually levitated above the river and hovered over the firmament, irradiant, beckoning and untouchable, straining against the invisible chains that bound it to terrestrial captivity. Beneath it Wasserstadt huddled safely behind the fortress' massive lower walls, its Baroque buildings neglected by time, kibbitz-fensters jutting self-importantly from the upper stories of crumbling facades.

Steven descended the bridge, veered into Strossmajer Street and began checking the Baroque buildings, their street numbers standing emboldened in relief above the doorways, an echo of not-so-distant Habsburg glory. The air and pavement quivered in the dusk as though the spirits of the fortress were racing forth from the tunnel under the clock tower, down the long stairs to restore the town to glory. He walked up the empty street, past a couple of battered Yugos rising forlorn from the uneven cobblestone, bathed in the light of upper windows.

In the gloom he found the number he wanted, a two-story row house tucked against the foot of the hill with the massive Ludwig bastion surging out from above like the prow of a Grecian Trireme. Over the entry he could make out the crumbling letters *R L*, and *anno 1745*: underneath St. George stood in an alcove, busily slaying a dragon.

Steven looked at the presents he carried: a bar of chocolate, some flowers and a small package, sensed they were inadequate, but went ahead and pressed the buzzer that read *Lazarevic.* He waited. And waited. And nothing happened. He pressed the buzzer again, hearing only silence. He stepped back and looked at the darkened house.

'Who are you looking for?'

Steven jumped, startled by a stooped woman in black who seemed to have sprung from the cobblestones. Her eyes peered sternly from leathery wrinkles, framed by scraggly white hair that protruded from a black head scarf. Gnarled hands planted firmly on broad hips gave her the authority of someone who had been born in that street and lived there all her life.

'What do you want? Are you one of those drug fiends?'

'Good evening; I'm looking for the Lazarevic family. I'm a student from America…their daughter Katarina asked me to give something to her mother.'

'From America? You have seen our Katarina? How is our angel? Is she healthy? Is she eating well? Does she have a boyfriend?' Gone was the scowl, replaced with a ragged smile which still held a few teeth. Her years disappeared as if by magic.

'Are you Mrs. Lazarevic' he asked hopefully.

The old woman giggled. 'No, I'm her neighbor. You won't get her by buzzing. The interphone is dead,' she volunteered, picked up a pebble and threw it against a window on the upper floor while yelling loudly: 'Mariana, you have a guest, a young man from America who knows Katarina from the university.' After a few moments a head appeared briefly in the kibbitz-fenster and then disappeared. 'Here she comes.'

All up and down the street curious heads filled the kibbitz-fensters, attracted by the old lady's voice.

The sound of bolts turning signaled that someone had come. The door opened rapidly and a tall woman of ageless beauty opened the door, her face half in shadow.

'He will make a good husband for your Katarina. See how handsome and healthy he looks,' the old lady clucked, pinching his cheek.

Mrs. Lazarevic held out her hand in greeting. 'Welcome Steven, I have been expecting you. Please come in.' As she held the door open for him she said rapidly to the old woman 'Tetka Nada, when I want a matchmaker I will call you. But Katarina is still too young. Give her time.'

'When I was her age I already had two children. She will get old before you know it and you will never see your grandchildren.' Nada stood watching them, hands back to their resting place on her hips.

Steven offered Mrs. Lazarevic the flowers, chocolate and the package he had brought from Katarina. She hugged him, kissed him warmly on one cheek and said: 'Welcome most sincerely to our home. Katarina has told me so much about you. I see she did not exaggerate in her praise.' He blushed.

Without waiting for an answer she shut and locked the door with multiple bolts and led him down a darkened photograph-filled corridor, up a flight of stairs and into a well-lit sitting room with a large, ornate ceramic stove rising all the way up to the high ceiling. A massive china cabinet covered nearly an entire wall, while old portraits and black and white photos covered the others. Next to the cabinet hung what appeared to be an old Habsburg officer's sword and a Turkish *Yatağan* sword.

Mrs. Lazarevic sat him at an oval table laden with food. In the light Steven could see she was probably between 40 and 50, had light hair, blue eyes and noble features.

'It is so good to finally meet you. How is my Katarina? Does she like America? Where is she staying? Is she eating well?'

The evening progressed with his answering questions between mouthfuls of the food she kept offering him. Questions, answers and more questions still, interspersed with a cucumber-tomato-pepper and cheese salad, stuffed peppers, homemade cornbread with young cheese baked inside, bread, ajvar, baked "wedding" potatoes, Wienerschnitzel, and finally some homemade Esterhazy cake. 'For a thin person you eat a lot,' she commented with a smile. 'My Katarina will never forgive me if I don't put some weight on you.'

As he finished his second slice of cake he noticed a portrait that appeared to be from the 18th century of a large man wearing an officer's sword. Next to it hung a portrait of a man attired in the field-grey uniform of a Habsburg officer at the beginning of World War I, a confident look on his face. Both men had green eyes, strong features and large, elongated moustaches.

She noticed his gaze: 'Katarina's father came from an old military family here at Petrovaradin that served the emperor for centuries in the border lands. This house has been in the family since 1745. Katarina inherited the Lazarevic eyes.'

She pointed to a framed black and white photograph of a large man, who looked strikingly similar to the men in the two portraits, holding an infant, standing next to what appeared to be a much younger version of herself. 'That is my late husband Rade, taken right after Katarina was born. He was very handsome and strong and kind.'

'I'm sorry for your loss. Please accept my condolences.'

She looked at him strangely. 'It was inevitable. No one is immortal. We all die and must one day suffer for our sins. Even the best man must do so. No one can live forever…' her sentence faded off. She then changed the topic abruptly. 'So, what are you doing here? How long will you stay? These are difficult times, you know.'

'Professor Slatina got me a fellowship to study folklore and has given me a research assignment.'

She perked up at the mention of the professor's name. 'Ah, yes, you are working for Marko?'

'Yes, researching folklore about monsters…in fact, mostly about vampires.'

She stiffened visibly. 'What does he have you doing?'

'Mostly looking through archival records. Nothing exciting.' Steven stuffed another forkful of cake into his mouth.

She relaxed. 'And what have you found thus far? Vampires, really now…' she huffed. 'Surely you don't believe any of that nonsense.'

'Not really, at least, that is, I didn't before I came. But I think it's possible that there may be something behind the whole phenomenon. I've found lots of information about vampires. In fact, I'm getting concerned because I feel my research is drawing negative attention.' He then told her about the disappearing librarian.

'You need to be very careful,' she cautioned. 'People are suspicious. Use common sense in all you do. Now, it is late. You should go,' she said abruptly. She ushered him out of the house, thanking him for delivering the present from Katarina and changed the subject back to her daughter. As he walked out the front door, she admonished him 'be careful in what you say and do. Be extremely careful with whom you share this information. And watch your back at all times. If anything unusual happens to you, please tell me immediately. Goodnight. May God bless you.' And she disappeared into the house, leaving Steven standing on the darkened cobblestone, alone amidst the silence of the old fortress.

* * *

Slatina picked up the phone on the third ring. 'Hello,' he said, grace and dignity resonating in his voice as he put down his pen and stood up from his desk and stretched.

'You're putting him in danger, you know that?' A woman's voice flowed smoothly over the crackling hiss of the long-distance line.

'Mariana, how good to hear from you,' Slatina answered warmly.

'Don't give me that. You know what you've done. Now make it right,' she snapped and the line went dead.

'Hello, hello?' Slatina sighed and put down the phone.

'Who was that?' Katarina asked, standing in the doorway.

'Your mother.'

'My mother? Why didn't you let me talk to her?'

'Bad connection.' He picked up the phone and dialed a thirteen digit number from memory. After several rings someone picked up. 'Zoltan,' Slatina spoke in fluent Hungarian. 'I will be coming next week.'

* * *

Interlude VI: The Chamber: Tuesday, 15 January 1983

The falling bricks and shouting voices had woken them three days earlier. Yet even now they continued to lie in their coffins, floating in the shallow water, too weak to escape through the hole that beckoned tantalizingly so very high above them in the vaulted brick ceiling. Lacking nutrients or strength, they lay dormant. The first hours after the ceiling collapsed felt like centuries.

'What shall we do?' whispered a faint voice.

'Ssshhh. Patience,' came a barely audible reply.

A third voice chimed in: 'Wait and watch. They'll come to us.'

And so they waited. Then some time later they heard it…the faint sound of movement, tiny feet and claws, a scurrying of life. It came from above, closer, closer.

First a whiskered nose: then beady eyes that peered over the edge of the hole, sniffing the air, catching the strong scent of decaying wood, rusty iron, crumbling brick, mildew, moldy flesh and rotting cloth. It edged closer, seeking a way to crawl down over the edge and into the Chamber, only to lose its grip and tumble into the water. The splash sent ripples throughout the shallow pond. The rat swam towards the nearest coffin, grabbed hold of the wood and clawed its way up the sides onto the top of the partially open lid. It sniffed again, sensed the odor of moldy flesh and rotting cloth from within. It crawled haltingly towards the gap between the coffin lid and the edge of the coffin. A hand suddenly flashed out and grabbed the rat. It squealed as the hand pulled it into the coffin. And then there was silence.

The arm reappeared, flung the rat's carcass away and pushed the coffin lid into the water, sending ripples across the pool.

The rat-eater sat up, an emaciated, deflated balloon of moldy skin, under a dirty mop of long, ragged hair. He wiped the blood from his lips with flesh that hung loose in folds around his hand and arm and picked his teeth with long, yellowed fingernails as his red feline eyes gazed narrowly around.

He looked around the vault, at the other coffins and the hole in the ceiling and began to wail softly, a horrible sound that started low and reached ever higher until the very bricks vibrated, causing centuries of dust to shake free from the walls and ceiling. The sound ended abruptly in a choked gasp, almost a sob. Then the rat-eater collapsed backwards into the coffin.

Minutes later more whiskered noses poked over the edge of the hole, attracted by the wail, and within minutes several dozen more furry bodies had fallen and disappeared into the coffins. The rats continued to come in increasing numbers, now squealing loudly as they poured torrentially from the ceiling into the chamber below, a waterfall of fresh rodent blood for the famished captives, churning the water white and rocking the coffins. And then abruptly the torrent ceased. The eleven grabbed the last remaining survivors from the water and made short work of them, and then gazed at the surface of the small pond, now covered in a blanket of furry carcasses.

All were sitting now, gazing at each other and the ceiling. 'Manna from heaven,' the general, Branko, commented wryly.

'Is it day or night?' asked the youngest, Ivan.

'Does it matter?' answered the eldest, Lazar.

'I suppose not,' answered the pedophile bishop, Mihailo. They conversed in archaic Serbo-Croatian.

'How can we get out of here?' asked Ivan.

'We have fed. Be patient,' said Lazar. 'It is now just a matter of time. We have food, we have an opening, and we need only discover how to get through it. I sense a door, but it is the part of the wall where the water leaks the most. There are too many crosses here…let us think.'

'We are only eleven,' said the baby-faced sweet shop owner, Lynx. 'They must have killed the Vlach. Our quorum is dissolved.'

'No, he is alive. If they killed him there is no reason to keep us,' said the accordion play, Igor. 'He hid well.'

After a while the Montenegrin doctor, Rastko, broke the silence: 'Where are our burial shrouds?'

'I know not,' replied Lazar. 'But if the Venetian burned them I'll hunt him down like the dog he is, and then I'll reach my hand into his bosom, tear his heart out and suck the juice from it fresh while it's still pumping.'

'That sounds quite delicious. But you assume he is still alive…how much time has passed?' asked one of the Bosnian twins, Hasan.

'I've lost track of time. Does anyone know?' Lazar answered. The others shook their heads. 'I wonder who the emperor and the sultan are. Are we in Turkey or Austria or perhaps even Hungary? Perhaps the Hungarians have regained their throne from the Austrians.'

'I hope we're in Turkey…the Turks were such easy prey,' said the small spy, Stanko. 'And the spices they use in their cooking make them taste quite good.'

'Yes, Turks,' chimed in the other twin, Tarik, reminiscing wistfully. 'They taste so much better than the Germans…how can those Schwabies live on a diet of cabbage and pork? They taste bland and I get gas. The Serbs eat too many onions: that also gives me gas…and the Hungarians: all that paprikash makes for horrible indigestion.'

'Everything gives you gas,' Natalija said, laughing. 'If only we had our shrouds we could get out of here.'

'Quiet, all of you.' Lazar was becoming annoyed. 'We need to escape. The Venetian did a clever job constructing this prison. We are floating in water so we can't move about and there are crosses everywhere. We must think.' And he lay down once more and closed his eyes.

A gentle bump against his coffin made him sit up. A small chest was scraping against the wood. He attempted to open it, but the lock held firm, so he tapped the box until he found rot and struck it repeatedly until the wood gave way. He reached in and pulled out an old piece of linen, dark with mold and mildew. 'The burial shrouds,' he shrieked triumphantly. 'He didn't destroy them!'

* * *

Butterflies make almost no noise, even when flying in groups. These eleven were no exception as they fluttered through the hole in the ceiling, up the corridor and past the marker with black Gothic letters that read *IV/500 Kom. Gall.* Not knowing their way through the labyrinth, they did what butterflies do so well – they followed air currents down passageways and up ventilation shafts. After half a day of meandering flight through tunnels and galleries, they came upon a drunken night watchman, slouched against a wall just inside a gateway that led out, drinking freely from a bottle of homemade *sljivovica* plum brandy.

And then they had their first real meal in 253 years.

CHAPTER SEVEN

THE LAZAREVIC STAKE

Novi Sad: 5-7 May 1992

Tuesday morning dawned loudly. The clamor of refugee children in the corridor woke Steven well before his alarm went off and his head swam in a sleep-deprived haze. At nine o'clock he met a groggy Stojadinovic in the town center. 'I'm an inveterate night owl,' the professor yawned drowsily, his puffy eyes hiding behind sunglasses, fedora pulled tightly on his head, as though he wanted to draw the curtains and go back to sleep.

'Did you ever find anything further about the redemption of vampires?' Stojadinovic asked sleepily.

'No. Nothing yet,' Steven replied.

'Tell me if you do. It's an interesting concept.'

A blue city transit bus took them the short ride across the Varadin Bridge to Wasserstadt. They walked uphill past the monastery church of St. George, through a long brick-lined tunnel under the clock tower and out onto the top of the upper fortress to the old barracks, now the city archive, where Stojadinovic introduced Steven to the director, an old classmate of his. After a courtesy cup of Turkish coffee, the director took them to the archive's catalogues and excused himself.

'Let's start with the years immediately before and after the appearance of the 4th Grenadier Company at the Kalemegdan,' suggested Stojadinovic excitedly. 'I'll begin with 1733 and work backwards, and you begin with 1730 and work forwards.' Steven nodded in agreement, every bit as excited as Stojadinovic.

Steven ordered the Petrovaradin commander's *Tagesbuch* – logbook – and occupied one table, Stojadinovic at a different table. As Steven turned the pages of the large leather-bound folio, he could see it consisted of hand-written daily entries on yellowed parchment by the fortress commander, Marquise von Herrenhof, whose meticulous hand had recorded events largely in German, with occasional notations in Latin: construction contracts with local guilds, artisans and tradesmen, contracts for supplying food for the garrison, notes of troop movements and parades, visiting dignitaries, and decorations for distinguished service. Miscellaneous documents, such as instructions from the Imperial court in Vienna, had been pasted to blank pages. It was a dry bureaucratic document.

Steven turned each fragile page with a ruler, careful not to damage the brittle binding. He read of daily life in the fortress: how much food, wine and beer the troops consumed; fights between the garrison's Hungarian Hussars, the Petrovaradin Regiment and the irregular Serbian *Hajduk* detachment; merchants cheating on deliveries; tavern-keepers overcharging the troops; an outbreak of syphilis; complaints about drunken soldiers. Steven quickly lost himself in the minutiae of 18th century fortress life and forgot entirely about the 4th Imperial Grenadier Company's elusive commander Captain von Zlatinow.

'Have you found anything?' Stojadinovic's voice abruptly pulled Steven back to the twentieth century.

'No, not yet.'

'I think I've found something…keep reading…I must find some other documents,' Stojadinovic turned and walked out of the room towards the catalogues.

Steven returned to von Herrenhof's Tagesbuch, spending less time on trivia and more in search of von Zlatinow's Grenadiers. And then he came across a journal entry for Thursday, September 10th, 1730, at the end of which the author had written:

Arrival today of the IV Kaiserlich Grenadier Kompanie via flotilla from Vienna. The boats unloaded substantial quantities of sealed crates. It is a reinforced unit, the men are large, all are veterans and in good health, and have new equipment and uniforms. They are under the command of Captain Marcus von Zlatinow, a

Venetian mercenary. He presented me with a most confidential document written in the Kaiser's own hand, the contents of which I am forbidden to discuss. Suffice it to say that His Imperial Majesty the Kaiser has given von Zlatinow carte blanche to act in His name: Von Zlatinow given highest military rank in the border regions. All fortress commanders, officers and civilian administrators are to follow his orders on pain of death. He is answerable only to the Kaiser. He will undertake a special construction project in Hornwerk. He will also undertake special expeditions into the newly conquered lands. von Zlatinow deposited twenty four large crates of gold bars with me for safekeeping, for which I issued a receipt to him for the Societas Draconis and stored them in the fortress treasury. Each crate can be lifted only by eight men. IV Grenadiers billeted in the Long Barracks separate from the other troops; von Zlatinow and Lieutenant Lazarewitsch billeted in Officers' Quarters.

Steven stared in shocked disbelief. He had finally found von Zlatinow. No wonder Count von Meyerling in Belgrade was so upset; ordered about by a mere captain with a letter from the Kaiser granting enormous authority. And the gold…probably worth a fortune by today's standards, all of it belonging to the Order of the Dragon, which meant that not only was the Order alive and functioning more than 300 years after its founding, but was operating with the blessing of the Kaiser. Obviously von Zlatinow was associated with the Order, and judging from circumstantial evidence, von Zlatinow's mission seemed to be hunting vampires. Steven rested his chin on the palms of his hands and stared at the wall, trying to put together the pieces of this rapidly expanding puzzle. Did this mean the Order had some connection with fighting vampires? But why would this Kaiser and his predecessors devote such significant resources to hunt a mythical creature? he asked himself.

He turned his attention to the September 11th entry from von Herrenhof to the fortress quartermaster to disburse supplies to the 4th Grenadiers from the fortress stores, and to write contracts for procurement of fresh supplies. Nothing unusual there: vegetables and meat, bread, flour, beer and wine, new beds, mattresses and bedding.

The entry for Sunday, September 13th, made only one mention of the 4th Grenadiers. Von Herrenhof had written cryptically: "*the entire Kompanie attend mass together at the Church of St. George*," as though worth noting. Reflecting on this, Steven recalled his discussions with Professor Nagy in Budapest and the professor's words came rushing back to him suddenly: 'why is it called after the Dragon…why not the Order of St. George…especially since the members of the Order wore the cross of St. George at all times…after all, the Dragon represents the evil one, Satan…why name your order after your adversary...they were formed to fight against the serpent himself, Satan.' If Nagy was correct, then it made sense for vampire hunters to have St. George as their patron saint. After all, he slew an allegorical Satan in the form of a dragon. Steven's head spun with the possibilities.

In an entry dated three days later, Steven found another passage:

> *I have discovered that von Zlatinow met in secret with the master of the masons' guild and signed a contract. He has also reached a secret agreement with a master locksmith. Work is to be carried out at the Hornwerk. My officers and I have been forbidden from observing or noting the location of the works under penalty of death or from discussing it with the soldiers. The regular garrison is forbidden from entering the Hornwerk until the works are completed, and the IV Grenadiers now stand guard duty there. This is most unusual and completely out of keeping with all protocol. I have written a letter of protest to the Hofburg and dispatched it by express rider. Von Zlatinow has also requested that we procure three wagonloads of Hawthorne wood.*

Steven devoured every word. So von Zlatinow was constructing something in secret underneath the fortress in the Hornwerk that required brick masons and a locksmith, a secret room or passage perhaps. But for what purpose?

Von Herrenhof next mentioned the 4th Grenadiers on September 25th:

> *Today the wagons of Hawthorne wood arrived. The Grenadiers began sharpening them into long stakes. The fortress blacksmith has been ordered to attach the stakes to pikes with iron bands.*

The arrival of the Hawthorne wood excited Steven. According to all the folk tales, only a Hawthorne wood stake could kill a vampire, and here the entire company was making long stakes. Clearly von Zlatinow and his troops planned to slay vampires.

There were no further mentions of the 4th Grenadiers or von Zlatinow until October 7th, when the commander's entry showed a change of attitude:

> *IV Kaiserlich Grenadier Kompanie has drilled regularly every day since arrival and they march and fire superbly, even over rough ground. Never have I seen tighter ranks and lines or a better formed square, and all without the aid of a drummer. They respond rapidly to Lieutenant Lazarewitsch's commands and do not hesitate in the least. Von Zlatinow commands as befitting a man of noble birth and sets a superb example to the men, not hesitating to step in and demonstrate how things should be done. They are of superior quality with the extremely high discipline and morale one expects from the German soldier, a sharp contrast to my undisciplined Magyars and Serbs. When off duty they do not mingle with the Serbs or Magyars and avoid public drunkenness and quarrels. They are truly a credit to his Majesty. I have written to the Hofburg requesting Imperial Grenadiers be assigned to the*

permanent garrison.

"Lieutenant Lazarewitsch." Could that be one of Katarina's ancestors? Steven was busily scribbling notes in his notebook, when a hand on his shoulder caused him to jump and yelp from fright. Others in the reading room looked at him with annoyance, and he turned to find Stojadinovic standing over him, smiling broadly.

'Come outside, we must talk,' he whispered softly. 'You may leave your materials here. No one will touch them.'

They found a table at the fortress' terrace and ordered drinks, enjoying the view over the Danube and Novi Sad. They basked in the pleasant spring weather and squinted in the bright sun, oblivious to the tremendous human suffering going on in neighboring Bosnia and Croatia.

'Well, I must say that this day has turned out to be one of the most interesting days of my academic life,' Stojadinovic said. 'I have found documents that raise more questions than they answer, and in the process I may have found the answer to a puzzle that has long vexed me. But first, tell me how your work is going.'

Steven excitedly related everything he had found, and then went on to add his thoughts regarding the Order of the Dragon and the Hawthorne stakes. 'Forgive me if I sound ridiculous, but do you think it's possible vampires might once have existed?' he asked Stojadinovic.

'Of course not, don't be silly. But obviously at one time superstition was quite strong, and there can be little doubt that what you have discovered and what I have come across indicates that people were at one time quite afraid of vampirism, much as you in America had your Salem witch trials. Whether this is related to people's fear of death, the lack of faith in an afterlife, or perhaps superstition, I cannot say. But we now have evidence that an Austrian emperor spent significant resources on hunting vampires. Given this, we cannot dismiss the existence of something that the popular imagination referred to as vampires. But the existence of actual vampires? Nonsense! I somehow doubt that those folk-vampires actually had any sort of special powers, or that they went around biting people on the neck.'

'Hmmm, yes,' Steven responded. 'But there's one thing I don't understand. Why does von Herrenhof say that von Zlatinow is a Venetian? Von Zlatinow isn't a Venetian or Italian name at all. In fact, it sounds eastern European, almost Slavic.'

'You are correct. But at that time it was not uncommon for people of different nationalities to enter into the service of the Kaiser. It is possible that von Zlatinow is a Germanized version of an Italian name, perhaps *di Zlotinni* or something similar. But let me share with you what I have found,' Stojadinovic said excitedly. 'As I read the Tagesbuch for 1733 I discovered that several pages had been torn out from the months of January and

February, and judging by the aging of the paper, they were removed contemporaneously, not later. I can therefore only suspect that someone had decided to censor Von Herrenhof's Tagesbuch.'

'That could have been von Zlatinow,' Steven said.

'Yes, it could have been. From what you say he certainly had the authority to do so. In any event, I came across no mention of the 4th Grenadiers after February 1733. What I did find was a minor legal dispute in late March 1733 between a local master locksmith and the fortress quartermaster, who refused to pay the locksmith. I requested the archival documents from the local magistrate's office and found the particulars of the case. The quartermaster claimed there was no record a contract had been made, and that the locksmith had no evidence he had ever been in the fortress, much less installed a custom-made lock. The locksmith then presented a diagram of the locking mechanism as evidence, and stated that he had installed it in the Hornwerk, but that he himself was unable to say exactly where, as he had been led there blindfolded. The court proceedings came to a sudden halt following the intervention of Captain von Zlatinow and the quartermaster immediately paid the locksmith.'

'Wow. So what happened?

'I don't know. I have been able to find nothing further.' Stojadinovic then smiled broadly and looked Steven directly in the eyes. 'However, the magistrate kept the sketch of the lock and I know where it is.' He acted extremely satisfied with himself. 'In fact, it may provide the answer to what happened to my tour group in 1983.'

'Really? How is that?'

'I've seen the lock many times in the Labyrinth, but never knew it was a lock. It's perfectly camouflaged. If you didn't know better, you'd never think to open it. We shall see it when we go there.'

* * *

The next morning Steven was waiting at the Petrovaradin archive when they opened the doors. He ordered more of the fortress commander's logbooks from the period before 1730, but found that he was doing little more than turning pages and trying to somehow distract his thoughts from Katarina and Vesna. After a while he gave up and walked across the bridge to the drab socialist-era lobby of Novi Sad's main post office and sought a booth. Vesna answered after the ninth ring. 'Ciao, how are you?' he asked cheerfully.

'Crazy and unforgettable,' she purred groggily into the phone. 'Ummmm. It's lovely waking up to your voice.' And then she fell silent and he could hear her breathing faintly. Alone in the musty atmosphere of the heavily insulated telephone booth, Steven felt a strong intimacy.

'Did I wake you?' he asked.

'A little…it's wonderful to hear you,' she whispered back. 'Wake me any time you wish.'

Steven told her about Stojadinovic's offer to take them through the Labyrinth the following Saturday.

'That's super,' she said, still half asleep. 'I'll tell Tamara and Bear. What time should we be there?'

'Around 4:30 in the afternoon. Is that okay?'

'Why so late?'

'I don't know. That's what Stojadinovic said. Is it a problem?'

'I suppose it'll be okay. Don't make any plans for that Saturday night. We'll all go out together. I can't wait.'

'Say hello to Tamara and Bear from me. Oh, Professor Stojadinovic said to wear boots and old clothes.'

'So I should leave the Gucci and Armani at home, huh?'

'You'd look great in a flour sack,' he said.

'Yeah, but wait until you see me all muddy and sweaty.'

'You'll probably be even more beautiful.' He kicked himself for saying that, not wanting to encourage her, yet feeling a strong physical attraction.

'Do you really mean that?'

'Yeah.'

'Stefan?'

'Yes?'

'I miss you.'

He didn't answer, fearful of giving her false hope, but his breathing deepened and became louder.

'I hear you breathing.'

'Yeah,' he rasped, thinking back to Bear's advice in the Chapel of Peace.

'And?'

'Yeah, it seems kind of strange without you. Let's talk when you get here.'

'I can't wait to see you. Think of me.'

'I'll see you then on Saturday. Ciao.'

'Ciao.'

He hung up the receiver, stood in the booth for a while, savoring the sound of her voice, and then finally opened the door and walked out, the tobacco air of the lobby refreshing after the booth's mustiness.

He paid for the call, and then made another one, to Danko Niedermeier at the bookstore in Sremski Karlovci. The phone rang interminably, and Steven was ready to hang up after the twelfth ring, when Niedermeier finally picked up.

'Ah, how very nice to hear from you,' Niedermeier spoke rapidly. 'And how did you like your visit to Karlovci?'

'It was very nice, thank you. We visited the Chapel of Peace as you suggested.'

'Ah, that is good, very good.'

'I wanted to see if you discovered anything about the Djordjevic book.'

'Ah, yes, the books. Well, I spoke with the publisher and he still has copies left. I have ordered sufficient for your students.' He spoke so rapidly that Steven could barely follow him. 'The boxes will arrive next Wednesday morning.'

'But I was talking about the Djordjevic…' The line went dead.

Steven clutched the receiver, troubled. Obviously Niedermeier felt he couldn't speak freely about the book. Steven left the phone booth and walked around the corner onto Jewish Street. Lost in thought he wandered through the shade of the large overhanging branches that made this busy boulevard feel timeless and deserted, past the enormous old synagogue.

'First Gordana the librarian, now Niedermeier…everyone's afraid of that book…' He muttered under his breath, unaware that he was attracting stares as passersby looked at the crazy young man talking out loud in a foreign tongue. 'Am I becoming paranoid?' He stopped and turned around suddenly to see if he was being followed, but it seemed that there were only other pedestrians on the street, passing innocently.

He watched the other passengers as he hopped a city bus to the main bus station, trying to see if anyone was following. From the bus station he caught the next bus to Sremski Karlovci, and arrived slightly before noon.

Steven walked across the main square, which even now in the middle of a weekday looked quiet and deserted, and sat on a bench in the shade of the large Chestnut trees standing sentinel before the Cathedral of St. Nikola. The lion heads on the four-sided fountain stared indifferently at him as water trickled from the rusty pipes in their mouths. Wind blew dust from the square's potholed asphalt into Steven's eyes, making him blink, as he again looked around to see if anyone had followed him. He saw only a few old women and men in black on the benches, and young men sitting idly in the café across the square: he recognized no one from the bus.

And then a loud screech of brakes and the sound of powerful motors revving attracted his attention to two black Mercedes four-wheel drive SUVs with tinted black windows that raced down the street from the hill in back of the Karlovci Gymnasium, sending pedestrians and other cars fleeing from their path. They tore across the sleepy square, the front seats occupied by shaven heads wearing sunglasses and dark clothing. Both bore the distinctive blue police license plates.

He stood and walked rapidly up the hill whence the black SUVs had come and found the bookshop, its door standing slightly ajar. Steven suddenly felt his foreboding turn to fear as he pushed the door open all the way and entered, to be greeted by a scene of chaos. Stepping carefully over scattered books, torn posters and fallen shelves towards the back room, he found

Niedermeier sitting in a corner on the bare wooden floor, holding a handkerchief to his face. Noticing Steven he removed the handkerchief and winced slightly: a trickle of blood ran from his nose and the lenses of his glasses were cracked.

Steven stooped to help him: 'Are you okay? What happened?' But he already knew.

'Could you please go in back to the bathroom and fetch me some toilet paper?' Niedermeier asked in a barely audible whisper. Steven did so and handed it to the beaten proprietor, who wiped the blood from his nose. 'Wine…I keep it up by the register…under the floor to the right of the desk.'

Steven lifted a loose floorboard near where the desk had stood and exposed a cache of wine bottles and glasses tucked away among books and papers. He took an already-opened bottle with a cork in its neck and a glass and returned to find Niedermeier still sitting, holding his head in his hands, the veins showing blue through the skin. He poured Niedermeier a glass of Bermet and handed it to him. Niedermeier ignored the glass and took the bottle.

'You're causing a lot of trouble, young gentleman,' Niedermeier whispered from behind the handkerchief. 'You and that accursed Djordjevic book. Let us drink to Tihomir Djordjevic and his elusive book,' he smiled a pained yet determined smile, raised the bottle and clinked it against Steven's glass, then drank deeply.

Steven stood, feeling guilty, wanting to help, but uncertain what to do. 'I'm sorry. I didn't mean for you to get hurt,' he stammered rapidly. 'I didn't know you'd have trouble because of it.'

'Uh. Yes. Well, trouble I have...they carry police badges but they are nothing more than thugs and criminals. We law-abiding citizens need police to protect us from the police,' the wine bottle trembled in his hand. 'Go lock the front door, please,' he gestured and Steven did so.

'And my pipe: can you find my pipe?' Steven walked through the litter of the shop and finally found the pipe, tobacco pouch and assorted tools for it scattered on the floor. He brought them to Niedermeier who, with shaking hands, slowly filled the bowl with tobacco and tamped it down, then lit it and took several deep puffs, which calmed him.

As he sipped his wine, Niedermeier began to speak. 'I have been on the trail of the book since you were here. Really it is not that difficult a matter for me: there has never been a book I could not find.' He was becoming slightly boastful again. 'But as I activated old contacts funny things began to happen. Many refused to talk to me, especially the ones in Belgrade. They had been warned about giving the book to anybody.'

'I did, however, locate a copy in Pirot,' he said, referring to the city in eastern Serbia. 'It is far from Belgrade and sometimes news and official instructions arrive there much slower.' He now had a slight grin on his face. 'My friend snuck it out of the archive and photocopied it. He will send it by bus this evening and it should arrive sometime tomorrow. You can come for it on Friday morning. I will have to charge you substantially more, of course, to cover the transportation costs, long distance telephone costs and damage to the shop.'

'That's no problem. The Balkan Ethnographic Trust will pay for the damages,' Steven spoke confidently to comfort Niedermeier, even though he was unsure whether BET would actually pay.

'When you called our friends from State Security were here asking why I was looking for the book and who I was getting it for…evidently someone told them I was looking for it. Do not worry, they didn't ask about you. I told them nothing, of course, but they were not satisfied and will probably return. It is no longer safe to call me on this telephone.'

'Young gentleman, I have no idea what is in this book of yours,' Niedermeier stared directly in Steven's eyes, 'but if it is important enough to cause the DB to rough up an old bookseller in the middle of a war, then it must contain extremely valuable information. What is this legend of twelve mighty vampires? I have never heard of it before.'

'I have absolutely no idea,' Steven responded returning Niedermeier's gaze with openness, hoping to allay any suspicion he might harbor, 'but it makes me wonder what's going on. In Djordjevic's other article *Vampires and other beings in our folk beliefs and traditions* he stated that vampires like to socialize, but are only able to do so in groups of twelve or less. The more research I conduct into vampires the more I'm convinced that they may have once actually existed in some form or another. I know that sounds silly, but I can't think of any other explanation for the recurring nature and commonalities of the phenomenon.'

'Oh nonsense, don't be silly!' Niedermeier exhaled a cloud of rich maple-scented smoke. 'There are no such things as vampires. There must be some other reason the DB is interested. I dislike it when the strong use force against the weak. It makes me want to fight back all the more. We will get the book and fight back against them. Come by on Friday morning and I will give you the book. By then I will have read it and uncovered its terrifying secrets.'

* * *

Back in Novi Sad, Steven returned to the post office and called Dusan, who wasn't home, but the grandmother answered the telephone and told him Katarina had called the previous evening and asked that he call back as soon as possible. Looking at his watch he saw it was almost five o'clock, which with the nine hour time difference would make it morning in

California. It took several attempts for the operator to get a line, but finally he succeeded and Katarina picked up on the first ring.

'Stefan, how good to hear from you,' she spoke in English. Her Serbian accent was less pronounced. 'I can't talk long or I'll be late for class. Marko is in Europe conducting research and he asked me to tell you he'll be in Budapest next week. He'll be staying at the Gellért Hotel. He said it's important you meet him to review your research.'

'Okay. Your mother said to say hello. I saw her last night.'

'How is she doing? Is her health okay?'

'She seemed okay. She fed me so much that I haven't eaten anything all day. How're you doing? How's California treating you?'

'Great. Peter has taught me how to surf,' she bubbled. 'I think I'm the first ever surfer girl from Vojvodina. We go every morning before class. But I've got to run or I'll be late. I'll talk to you later. Say hello to my mother from me. Bye.'

Peter. Her surfing instructor has a name, Steven thought. He shook his head to clear the emotional cobwebs. A brisk walk back to the dormitory helped, and by the time he arrived, the dread of facing the din within had driven any jealousy from his mind.

He reluctantly entered the refugee-infested building and tripped over children who ran into him full tilt as they loudly chased each other down the hallway. He walked past the watchful eye of Neso, the blackmarketeer, and to his own room, where he shut the door and tried to ignore the noise and read a book. After 20 minutes he gave up and went down to the cafeteria and chose from its selection of depressingly greasy dishes. He poked at the film of thick orange grease that obscured something vaguely meaty, stirred it absent-mindedly and thought about Budapest and how to get there.

Perhaps he could leave on Monday. He would spend several days there, talk to Professor Slatina, maybe meet again with Professor Nagy, and take a breather from Serbia.

The burden of darkness was visible on people's faces as he walked down the streets and in their behavior towards each other in stores and on busses; people snapped at the slightest provocation. Civilized behavior was rapidly disappearing as people fought to survive hyperinflation and the war economy. The break would be welcome.

After gazing once again at the coagulated grease on the surface of his bowl, Steven lowered his spoon and went directly to Neso's room.

Steven heard Neso's profanities well before he saw him. Neso was yelling and waving a Scorpion machine pistol at a thin youth clad in a Metallica sweatshirt. In the background a boom-box blared the mind-numbing electronically synthesized bass and accordion beat of Balkan turbo-folk. From what Steven could understand of Neso's tirade the fellow owed money for drugs. Ceca sat calmly on the bed applying nail polish, while a dark-haired girl in a scandalously short miniskirt sat and filed her nails. The room smelled of acetone as Steven rapped loudly on the open door.

'American,' Neso looked up with a smile and jumped to his feet, 'come in, come in.' Turning back to the Metallica sweatshirt he yelled: 'Get lost and don't let me see you again without the 500 Marks or I'll strangle you with my bare hands.' Neso picked him up by the belt and threw him roughly onto the hall floor. Turning back to Steven, he said calmly: 'How do you like Novi Sad? Are you having fun? Sit down and have a drink…Ceca, get us some juice!' She and her friend jumped up and disappeared from the room, returning moments later with four cups and a carton of juice.

'What can I do for you,' Neso asked boisterously. 'Do you need to change money?'

'No, I just…'

'This is Ceca's friend, Dragana. If you want she doesn't have a boyfriend…and they like to play together,' Dragana leered at Steven while caressing Ceca's arm.

'No.'

'If you don't like girls I can get you a boy,' Neso said matter-of-factly.

'Chill out.' Steven said. 'I need to go to Budapest next week, probably Monday. Is there some way besides the train?' Both girls immediately lost interest and returned to their nails.

'No problem. Just tell me the time you want to leave and I'll have a minivan pick you up and drive you directly to Budapest. It costs 75 Marks, but because you're an American and I like you, I'll only charge you 60. If you're going to Budapest then you won't need Ceca or Dragana,' he laughed. 'You'll find everything you want there. When you go to Hungary perhaps you can bring me back some cigarettes and coffee. I'll give you money for it. You're a foreigner so they'll let you bring in more than usual.'

Steven drained his glass and fled quickly to his own room, where he found Geronimo snoring loudly. No sooner had he sat down on his bed then Neso knocked on the door.

'Listen, I have a great deal for you. If you'll carry a package out for me and bring one back I can get you on the minivan to Budapest for free. You're an American and the customs officers won't search your bag as carefully. In fact, you can even earn a bit of money on a regular basis if you like.'

Steven gulped. 'What would you like me to carry?'

'Oh, nothing really, just some packages. Usually they weigh about a kilo or two.'

'Thanks for thinking of me Neso, but I think not.'

'No problem, no problem,' Neso answered as if Steven had offended him. 'I just thought I could help you a little…you know…do you a favor.'

'Okay. Thanks. I need to sleep.' He closed the door.

You need to get out of here, Steven told himself. Just make it to Monday and then you'll have a week's rest in Budapest. And then back to Belgrade and away from this madhouse. He decided that if he had to stay in Novi Sad any longer, he would find different accommodations.

* * *

The next day Steven told Stojadinovic of his plans to visit Professor Slatina in Budapest. 'Tell him hello from me,' said Stojadinovic.

The DB visit to Niedermeier continued to bother him. He was only doing legitimate research, yet he felt he was to blame for the bookseller getting beaten up. Why was the Djordjevic book attracting so much attention? As the day progressed he became more paranoid. By the evening he was agitated enough to visit Mrs. Lazarevic.

This time he threw a small pebble at the upper window, to avoid broadcasting his presence to the entire neighborhood. When he told Mrs. Lazarevic he had spoken with Katarina she smiled and invited him in. In the sitting room she once again brought out copious amounts of food while she interrogated him about his phone call.

When she had wrung the last possible drop of information from him, she smiled. 'Peter, a surfer. Surely she's not serious about a surfer.' Mrs. Lazarevic looked directly in his eyes. 'What do you think of my Katarina? She is pretty, yes?'

'Yes.' Could she see through him that clearly? What about Vesna?

'Yes, my Katarina is quite beautiful. And intelligent too. She won prizes in mathematics in Gymnasium.' She noted his silence with approval. 'She was also a gymnast until she grew too tall.'

'A gymnast? Really?' An image of Katarina as a gymnast brought back teenage fantasies that he struggled weakly to suppress. He shoved a piece of warm apple strudel into his mouth, savoring the rich scents and flavors of apples, cinnamon and powdered sugar as they melted together on his tongue. He hoped that by chewing Mrs. Lazarevic wouldn't notice the color in his cheeks.

'I probably should not tell you this, but she thinks very highly of you.'

He started, sat up straight, jerked his arm involuntarily and knocked over a glass of milk, while gagging on the strudel. As he fought for air he noticed that Mrs. Lazarevic was busily wiping up the spill with a contented smile.

'I think highly of her too,' Steven spluttered.

'But I have bothered you with my intrusive questions. I must apologize. You are a fine young man. It is too bad there are not more such fine young men in the world today.' Once again, she smiled at him. 'But you came here for another reason. I see you are nervous. What is wrong?'

The chance to unburden his mind calmed him slightly. He told her of the fortress commander's log books and the IV Imperial Grenadier Company. 'Is Lieutenant Lazarewitsch an ancestor?'

'Yes,' she nodded approvingly and pointed. 'That is his portrait.' Steven examined the painting, a large man wearing a white coat lined with scarlet, gold sash around his middle, white trousers, riding boots, cocked hat, holding an officer's cane. The other Lazarevic men in the family portraits on the walls seemed to lean closer in interest.

He noticed the officer's cane had an ornately engraved golden pommel in the shape of a dragon with its tail in its mouth and a cross cut down its back.

'That portrait…when was it painted?'

'I believe sometime in the 1730s when he became captain. Why do you ask?'

'He's holding a cane with the symbol of the Order of the Dragon engraved on it!'

'Oh, really?'

'Yes, do you know what it was?'

'No. Such things do not interest me,' she said abruptly. 'What else did you discover today?'

'The Order used to hunt vampires,' he said.

'Oh, those are just stupid old wives' tales. There're no such things as vampires.'

'So you've heard of it?' he pressed.

'Steven, if you live in this part of the world long enough you'll hear lots of crazy things. Vampires and vampire hunters? Do I bother you with questions about Roswell, New Mexico or Big Foot…or the Loch Ness monster?' she laughed.

Giving up, Steven told her about Niedermeier.

'This is not good. In fact, it is too much. What did Marko tell you about this?'

'I don't understand?'

'What did he tell you about your research? Specifically?' Mrs. Lazarevic became very serious.

'Well, nothing really. He simply asked me to come and research folklore, but everything I touch leads back to vampires.'

'And Katarina? Did she tell you nothing?'

He looked puzzled. 'I don't understand what you're asking…'

She gazed intently into his eyes. 'You really don't know, do you?' Her voice smiled with sympathy where her face did not.

'Know what?' he asked.

'Enough,' she said with a sense of finality. 'Are you wearing protection?'

The question startled him. 'What do you mean?'

'My Katarina said she gave you a cross of Hawthorne wood. Do you wear it?'

He reached under his shirt and pulled it out by the string around his neck.

'Good. Do not remove it. Not even to shower. It has helped protect you up until now. You have read about vampires, yes? You know all about them now, don't you?'

Steven sat dumbfounded.

She walked to the china cabinet once again and pulled out something wrapped in an old dark velvet cloth, which she removed to reveal a thick long stake of highly polished wood, easily half a meter long, sharpened at one end: at the other end a handle had been carved, like a sword. The wood was black at the point, as though stained with much blood. She placed it on the table in front of Steven.

'Please, take this for your own protection. It is from the *Glog*, the Hawthorne tree and has served the men of the Lazarevic family well for centuries. I have no son, so you must wield it for me. Please take it.'

He looked at her, shock and surprise imprinted on his face. 'I don't understand. I mean, certainly it is nice of you, but, I mean, thanks, but…what is it and what do I do with it?'

'You will know what to do with it,' she said taking the object from the table. 'It is very simple to use.' She swiftly thrust with the stake as though with a fencing rapier. 'Straight to the heart.'

Steven picked it up gingerly.

'Take it with you to Budapest,' she insisted. 'Show it to Marko, and tell him that I told him to stop fooling around. Then he will tell you what to do with the stake.'

* * *

Interlude VII: The Exit: Monday, 15 January 1983

Moonlight drifted through the open gate, its pale glow illuminating the eleven gaunt figures that stood over the night watchman's mangled corpse, flesh protruding from shredded clothing up and down the left side of his body.

'Finally, human blood,' said Lazar, the oldest, looking slightly less deflated than before as he wiped his blood-stained lips with the tips of his fingers.

'A mere appetizer…I'm still famished,' griped Ivan, the youngest.

'We all are,' said Mihailo, the bishop. 'Stop complaining, there'll be more.'

Lazar examined the corpse, while the others watched. 'His clothing is quite unusual…his dress is neither that of a peasant nor a noble…from his scent he has bathed recently, I would say within the last day or so…perhaps he's a foreigner… He has most of his teeth, and they are sound.' He pulled at the victim's clothing. 'Look at his coat…it's fastened with brass teeth of intricate workmanship.' He pulled open the front of the winter coat. 'His boots are also strange…the soles are very thick and made from some material that's not leather or wood…it's softer…there are grooves in the soles…definitely foreign workmanship.'

Lazar rifled the body, emptied its pockets, opened the man's wallet and removed the identity card. 'He's a Serb,' he announced. 'Not an Austrian or a Turk. And look at the miniature portrait on this card: he must have been a man of importance to carry this with him. It says here Republic of Serbia, Socialist Federal Republic of Yugoslavia.' He stared at the others in disbelief. 'Is it possible the Serbs have won their independence from the Turks?' He passed the ID card around for them to see. 'And why did Austria let them form a republic? I thought Venice and Ragusa were the only republics. Isn't a monarchy more efficient? And what does this word socialist mean?' No one knew the answers to his questions. The oldest pondered for several moments. 'It must be the work of that idiot priest Krizanic. He was always trying to get the Serbs and Croats to join together in one state. I'll bet somebody was actually stupid enough to read his book and do it.'

Lazar examined the victim's public transit pass: 'this also has a miniature portrait. Look at how lifelike it is! The man must be quite wealthy to afford such luxuries. And it says here City Public Transit Company…what could that mean?' The oldest looked at the others, who shrugged their shoulders. 'Perhaps,' he continued, 'he owns a carriage and freight company.' He passed it to the others. 'And here's something called a Driver's License…with another portrait. Three portraits…and he's licensed to drive carriages…when did they start requiring that?'

He removed cash from the wallet: 'Look at these: bank notes, issued by the National Bank of Yugoslavia. He's carrying millions of Dinars with him. Fortune has smiled on us: we found a rich man.'

'It doesn't matter,' grumbled Igor, the accordion player. 'The rich taste the same as the poor.'

'I wonder how much the exchange rate is between the Thaler and the Dinar?' mused Stanko, the spy.

'We shall soon find out,' answered Lazar. 'And look at this! He's carrying a weapon.' He loosened the man's belt and pulled off the holster, opened it and withdrew an old revolver. 'It's strange craftsmanship…nothing I have ever seen before,' the oldest continued as he pulled back the hammer, opened the cylinder and spun it around. 'It's engraved with the word *Zastava* and the year 1956. We have been locked away more than two hundred years!!' They all gasped.

He accidentally ejected the bullets onto the ground. 'Multiple cartridges…and they have attached the ball to a brass casing…and it loads through the breech. This means no more muzzle-loading, no more measuring out powder for every shot, no more ramming the charge home down the barrel, no more forgetting to remove the ram-rod before firing, no more problems keeping your powder dry. They can probably fire several shots a minute with this. An army with this weapon could rule the world!' he exclaimed gleefully. 'We have truly met with good fortune: our meal is wealthy beyond belief, is carrying large quantities of bank notes on his person, and is possessed of a superior weapon.'

'But where's the flint?' asked Lynx, the baby-faced sweet-shop owner.

'I don't know. We must find out how to use this.' Lazar scooped up the bullets and inserted them back into the cylinder, one by one and passed the pistol around for the others to examine.

They wandered slowly outside onto the darkened brick and earthen ramparts of the fortress overlooking the river. 'The sky is aglow,' commented Ivan, rushing anxiously ahead. He stopped, stunned at the sight that greeted him: and then the others caught up. Upriver to their left, ghostly pale floodlights illuminated a broad white bridge suspended on white steel threads from tall slender towers, while to their right a city blazed with light. Strange carriages with blinding lamps scurried on the road below them and across the bridge, all without horses. A lone barge, its lights glowing merrily, moved slowly upstream against the current. From across the river strange machine-like noises wafted across the water. Could it be music?

'Look at all the carriages…how swiftly they move…surely horses cannot run that fast,' exclaimed Branko the general. 'And the light…there is so much light…almost as if it were day. How many candles and lamps there must be! And the boat is moving without sails or oars against the current...this cannot be real. Are we dreaming?'

'No, we are not dreaming. It looks as though things have changed quite a bit,' Lazar muttered. 'This may be a problem.'

'We must feed again,' said Mihailo.

'Patience!' Lazar admonished. 'We must first consider our situation. Before we move into society we must discover what has happened and who rules this land. Things have changed greatly. In the meantime, we don't wish anyone to know that we've escaped. Therefore, we mustn't attack humans right away. We must restrict ourselves to cattle and other animals until we can discover the best way to feed. I know it's distasteful, but that's the only way for us to build up our strength before we decide on our next move.'

'Who are you to order us about?' Ivan spat back at him. 'We're free now and can do as we wish. I've spent enough time with the lot of you in that stinking chamber. I hope never to see any of you again.'

'Do not be so anxious,' Lazar cautioned. 'I'm certain the Venetian is somewhere, waiting, watching, biding his time. When he discovers we have escaped he'll alert the Order…and this time they will kill us. We must exercise extreme caution. You should do well to remember how he caught you.'

'It wasn't my fault. It was Good Friday, and I had to return to my grave.'

'Then you would do well to move your grave,' Lazar said. 'Are we agreed that we must remain together for now to avoid discovery?'

All the others muttered, grunted and nodded their agreement, except for Ivan. 'What is it to be?' Lazar asked. 'Do you truly wish to endanger us all? Or will you remain with us?'

'Yes, yes. Of course. What other choice is there?'

'There is no other,' Lazar smiled grimly. 'We shall move away from the fortress and the city. Perhaps we can find some cattle. My hunger grows and the power beckons. And we must find the Vlach so we can reform our quorum.'

CHAPTER EIGHT

THE ADVERSARY AWAKENS

Novi Sad, Sremski Karlovci, Budapest: 8-10 May 1992

Steven lay in bed, trying to fall asleep in the darkened dormitory, the refugee children having long since settled in for the night. All was silent, except for garbled profanity emanating from down the hall as Neso argued with Ceca. Steven glanced at his wristwatch every few seconds, unable to sleep, keeping track of the duration of the argument: ten minutes, fifteen, half an hour, forty-five minutes, Ceca launching accusatory diatribes, Neso hurling back angry retorts. It seemed another woman was in question. The argument continued nearly an hour until the sound of a loud slap signaled Neso had ended the argument on his terms. Now the only sounds were Neso's angry monologue, punctuated by several more loud blows and Ceca sobbing.

As Steven listened to the drama, the second and minute hands on his wristwatch slowed to a crawl and then seemed to freeze in place. Every little once in a while one would move ever so slightly forward in its circular procession, first the one, then sometimes the other, with no rhyme or pattern. Sometimes one hand would inch slowly forward, stop, and then wait for the other to overtake it, only to be overtaken in turn. The two hands played this game of temporal leapfrog as the round dial glowed dimly in the gloom, a platter of luminescent tranquility detached from the turmoil inside his head. No amount of willpower could compel the hands forward. Holding the watch to his ear he could hear its faint ticking, a muted metronome disconnected from Steven's reality. Seconds… minutes… hours… the clock softly ticked, but the hands didn't respond.

He gazed at the flakes of discolored paint dangling over his head, petals of enamel unfurling from the dampness of a concrete ceiling, splattered with faded hues of black and grey by the lamppost outside the window: splinters of shadow, fingers of light and blades of dark, probing, crawling and stabbing across the room and ceiling in palmetto-leaf patterns. Light and dark were clearly in league with time, and none seemed to move.

His imagination began to create phantom apparitions from the shadows. A scene from an old documentary film about a great cat in Africa played over and over. He had watched it long ago on television in vivid color, but now it was blanched to black and grey by the night. He couldn't remember if it was a cheetah or leopard, but it crept along slowly and methodically through deep brush at the edge of a thick forest bordering the savannah, waiting for an unsuspecting zebra or gazelle to venture too close. Camouflaged by its velvety coat, the cat bode its time, lurking, crawling and slinking, but never emerged fully to pounce. And throughout that night, as he waited for time to move forward ever so slightly, sleep was like the great cat, lurking always within view, but never coming close enough to take him.

Yet his mind raged wildly, his thoughts and ideas surging like waves. Was Katarina's mother perhaps just a little bit crazy? Had the loss of her husband unsettled her? Why had she given him the stake? And where did she get it? Did vampires in fact really exist? Steven's mind turned to the elusive von Zlatinow…what had he and his unit been doing at Petrovaradin, Kalemegdan and deeper inside Serbia between 1731 and 1733? Hunting vampires? What was the insignia of the Order of the Dragon doing on Lazarevic's cane? What had the Imperial Grenadiers done with Hawthorne stakes? Where was the lock that was mentioned in the log books? Was it a lock to a secret chamber of some kind? And what on earth was he to do with the stake Katarina's mother had given him, which he had yet to remove from his backpack for fear of attracting unwanted attention in the dorm.

'What am I doing here,' he asked himself. 'There's a war going on. The police and DB are probably looking for me. Should I leave? All this talk of vampires is nonsense. Mrs. Lazarevic has a screw loose,' he said, vainly trying to reassure himself.

Then his thoughts raced back four years to the darkest moments of his fall from grace, when everyone in his congregation had turned their backs on him for having disgraced his priesthood and his calling. When his faith had begun to fail, Julie alone had ignored social conventions and seen the goodness within his heart. She had restored his faith in God and himself. She said "I do" to him across the altar two years later. And he had stood over her grave on crutches two weeks after that to lay her to rest...along with his faith.

And then suddenly his mind turned to Katarina, how she too had shown faith in him, and how it had led him to rediscover his faith in himself and God. He thought of his time with her, washing dishes, talking and learning Serbo-Croatian and realized he did indeed have feelings for her.

And Vesna? I like her, and she's here. But I'm not sure I really feel anything for her except physical excitement. Katarina is an ocean and two continents away and… I'm not sure I'm ready for this. I've got to break this off with Vesna before it goes any further, he decided. I'll talk to her when she comes next Saturday.

The conflict in his heart pushed aside his earlier fears about vampires, and fatigue finally set in. Sapped of emotion and energy Steven exhaled a deep sigh, clutched the cross at his throat, and let sleep carry him off like the great cat its prey.

In sleep he dreamt a battered trolleybus. Its doors opened and Vesna stepped down, clad in a diaphanous white gown, the white muslin draping thin upper arms, cascading off the peaks of her bosom, falling down to trace the firm roundness of her stomach and the beckoning junction between her legs. Or was it Katarina? She smiled at him, beckoned him closer and then he saw it was neither Katarina nor Vesna, but a woman of dark beauty, more alluring than any he had ever met. Around her face, thick dark hair framed milky skin, and her feline eyes glowed red, reminding him of the great cat in the documentary film. Urgent physical desire pulled him closer until he took her suddenly in his arms and pulled her forcefully to him, his body trembling with excitement. As he leaned in to kiss her she smiled, displaying sharp incisors between blood red lips.

With a shiver, he awoke. Late for his meeting with Niedermeier.

* * *

Steven stepped off the bus in Sremski Karlovci, backpack in hand. It was already midday in the airless town, the birds muted, the main square deserted. All Karlovci was hushed, its windows shuttered and doors closed as if the townspeople had fled inside, reminding Steven of a showdown in a bad spaghetti-western. As he walked with hesitant step through the main square, the only noise he heard was the raucous beat of Balkan turbo-folk blaring from the deserted café opposite the cathedral, its dark green sun umbrellas casting hollow shadows across empty plastic chairs and tables. He quickly crossed the main square, walked up the hill past the Gymnasium to the book shop, glancing furtively behind to see if he was being followed, nervous with anticipation about seeing the elusive Djordjevic book.

The bookstore shutters were closed, but the portal gates stood open. The door displayed a hastily hand-lettered cardboard sign in Cyrillic that read *Popis – Inventory*. 'How strange,' he thought. 'Niedermeier is Volks Deutsch. Why would he write in Cyrillic?'

As he knocked, the door swung open under his fist, revealing blackness in place of the shop interior. The sight of the splintered doorjamb sent a shock of adrenalin coursing through his veins, causing his pulse to race wildly and his body to freeze in place.

'Mr. Niedermeier,' he called into the darkness. There was only silence. 'Mr. Niedermeier,' he repeated, louder. Still no reply.

Uncertain, he removed the Hawthorne stake Mrs. Lazarevic had given him from his backpack and wielded it in his left hand. 'What am I doing,' he asked himself. He felt around hesitantly on the wall inside the doorway with his right hand, vainly seeking a light switch.

He entered the darkness, his path dimly lit by faint beams of fugitive sunlight that had evaded the shutters. The few rays scattered, making a patchwork quilt of light and dark, barely illuminating torn-down shelves, an ankle-deep carpet of ripped books, paper and splintered wood in which the smell of pipe tobacco lingered faintly. Fragments from a coffee cup lay on the floor near a pile of kindling that had once been Niedermeier's desk, as a small puddle of dark liquid soaked slowly into the wood. Blood perhaps? Or coffee? Steven couldn't tell.

'Mr. Niedermeier,' he called. 'Mr. Niedermeier, it's me, Steven.' No response. His eyes played tricks on him as he looked around the room. He heard the rustle of paper from the direction of the back room, where he thought he saw a human shadow flash across the wall.

'Who's there?' he shouted. 'Who is it?'

He waded through the detritus of the store towards where he had last seen the shadow. 'Mr. Niedermeier,' he called. 'Is that you? Are you okay?'

There was no answer.

'Hello?' he called again.

'Who's back there?' he called, as he walked into the back room, stake at the ready.

Yet the back room and shop were empty: there was no sign of Niedermeier anywhere.

Am I hearing and seeing things? he wondered.

His mind raced. Where is he? Have they hurt him? What if the police find me here? They'll accuse me. What if the men in the black 4x4s come back?

I've got to get out of here before somebody finds me.

Yet something compelled him to stay.

He lifted the loose floorboard near Niedermeier's desk and lowered his face to see if Niedermeier had left anything inside, when a silent fuzzy blur darted out of the hole directly at him. He jumped with fright, shouted and flailed about with his hand, but whatever it was had vanished in the spectral gloom.

His peripheral vision registered a slight movement off to his right, causing him to yell and turn suddenly to face the threat: a butterfly that hovered between light and dark for a fleeting moment, only to disappear into the shadows.

Everything he had learned about butterflies in Balkan folklore came rushing back in a microsecond…the soul of a dead person turns into a butterfly…vampires transform into butterflies. Both ideas set his spine tingling with icy chills. His pulse sped up and a cold sweat trickled down his forehead. Is Mr. Niedermeier dead? he wondered.

He held the stake out, brandishing it as a weapon. 'Who's there?' he demanded loudly.

There was no answer.

What if it's a vampire, he asked himself. Do I stab it through the heart? He shifted the stake in his left hand, reaffirming his grip, all the while staring intently into the shadows where the butterfly had disappeared, his heart pounding rapidly.

Is Mr. Niedermeier trying to contact me through the butterfly? He stood rooted to the spot by fear. 'Mr. Niedermeier!' he cried. 'Mr. Niedermeier, is that you?'

More silence.

'I can't believe I'm talking to a butterfly,' he laughed nervously.

He spoke louder, trying to bolster up his courage. 'I'm being ridiculous. There are no such things as vampires…a person's soul doesn't turn into a butterfly. It was only a butterfly.' He shivered suddenly and could barely swallow.

'There's a perfectly rational explanation for all of this…but what's a butterfly doing under the floorboards of a book shop?'

But if it is a vampire, he thought, how do I kill it? Can I squash it like a bug while it's a butterfly?

Steven's peripheral vision detected movement and he turned. An enormous brown fuzzy insect with black spots on its wings walked slowly along the spine of a fallen book. It stopped and fixed its gaze on him.

Steven held the stake out in front of him with both hands, hoping to keep the butterfly at bay. His hands shook, sweat glistened on his forehead and his armpits were wet. His breathing and pulse were so rapid he feared blacking out.

Wings folded together, the butterfly continued walking. Suddenly it fluttered into the air, disappearing backwards into shadow, only to reemerge and fly directly towards the human intruder, lighting on the tip of the stake. Steven froze, but the tip of the stake shook violently in his hands.

The butterfly began walking slowly up the stake, bit by bit. Reaching his left hand it took a tentative step onto Steven's damp skin, stopped to scent his flesh, unfolded and then refolded its wings as if trying to decide whether or not to fly away, and then continued gradually onward. First to his knuckle, then the back of his hand – it kind of tickled – then up to the gooseflesh on his wrist. The journey from wrist to elbow took forever, and Steven breathed deeply to calm his shaking.

'Mr. Niedermeier?' his voice croaked dryly.

The creature continued its measured journey, from his elbow up towards his shoulder. 'Mr. Niedermeier?' he rasped once more. 'Oh Lord. Can butterflies bite through cloth?'

The butterfly continued towards his shoulder, heading for his neck. And then he remembered that vampires feed…

'From the left side!' he shouted and brushed the creature off himself in panic, then watched it flutter rapidly towards the still-open front door and disappear into the sunlight.

He sank suddenly to the floor, the energy drained from his body. He put his right hand on the floor to steady himself, but it found only air, and he plunged rapidly downward, his arm swallowed up by the hole where the floorboard had been.

* * *

First it was the numbness, and then a massive wave of pain. His neck, head and torso screamed in a chorus of twisted muscle and bruised flesh. Everything remained foggy. He couldn't move his right shoulder but he could move his right hand, which felt strangely detached, floating in air. As he gradually opened his eyes, needles pierced his optic nerves. He couldn't focus: he could only sense pain. 'Slowly,' he said to himself. And slowly the world came back together, piece by distorted piece, out of focus, a mixture of torn paper and splintered wood, the smell of mold permeating his nostrils.

'I…I… Niedermeier's bookstore…' It all came rushing back to him. The store appeared unfamiliar when viewed from the floor. Steven's head was twisted at an unnatural angle and his neck lay across the opening of the floorboards, his right arm hanging in the hole. He felt something in his left hand, and brought it around in front of his face until he could see his fingers gripping the handle of a wooden stake.

'Oooow.' Debris muffled his moan. He dropped the stake and pushed himself up out of the hole, only to quickly lie flat as pain jolted through his body. The right side of his head was sore and tender to the touch, as was his neck. His ribcage felt bruised, the fingers on his right hand were scraped and his left hand was numb from gripping the stake tightly. Everything hurt.

Looking down at the hole that had been the cause of his troubles he saw a scrap of paper. He gingerly pulled out string and a piece of brown wrapping paper creased in the shape of a book, with Niedermeier's address scribbled in pencil on the front, and on the back a return address in Pirot. Folding the paper carefully, he placed it in his pocket, and continued rummaging under the floorboards. He found several accounting ledgers, as well as two unopened bottles of vintage Bermet, but no sign of the Djordjevic book. He opened the ledgers and thumbed through them, but found only columns of numbers and book titles. Nowhere was the Djordjevic book listed.

He replaced the ledgers and floorboard, gathered his things, and walked into the shop's back room, where the cloudy bathroom mirror showed him that his neck and face were swelling on the right side.

He emerged into the diluted sunlight to find the town was still deserted. He hurried down the hill and caught the first bus back to Novi Sad, trying to avoid stares at his injured face.

He watched a large brown butterfly with black spots on its wings flutter alongside the bus until it could no longer keep up. Then it turned aside into a field of yellow flowers.

* * *

Back at the dormitory Neso saw Steven's injured face. 'Who did this to you? Just tell me and I guarantee you he'll never touch you again.'

'Thanks, but I had an accident and fell and hit myself really badly on the floor,' Steven winced.

'Yeah, an accident. If you need me to talk to "the floor" that hit you, let me know. I don't want you having any more accidents.'

'Ooooo, does it hurt?' Ceca cooed, walking up to him, running her fingers gently across his cheek. She too had bruises on her face. His right cheek was so numb that he barely felt her touch. 'Let me get you something cold.' She walked down the hall and returned in a matter of seconds with a bag of frozen peas. 'This will help you.'

'Thanks,' he grunted, wondering who kept frozen peas in a dormitory.

'Do you still want the mini-van for Monday?' Neso looked at him.

'How about Saturday?'

'No problem. It'll be here at 11:00 p.m.'

'Why so late?'

'Because it takes passengers to the airport, and most of them have morning flights, so they need to get there around 6 or 7 a.m.'

Steven nodded and retreated to his room. It was mid-afternoon, so he closed the curtains and lay down on his rumpled bed, the frozen peas pressed tightly against his cheek. His thoughts raced as doubts crept into his mind.

What am I doing here? I thought I was doing research, but now I'm chasing butterflies…or vampires. How safe is it here? Am I to blame for Gordana losing her job? Is her son in danger because of me? Now Niedermeier's missing and his shop is trashed and the DB is involved. Why is that Djordjevic book so damn important? Are they torturing Niedermeier? Is he dead?

He searched the ceiling for meaning, its peeling paint creating patterns he had stared at the previous night. His eyes picked out a zebra; a castle on a hill; the Mona Lisa; a surfboard… But the splotches became less innocent, more eerie: twelve murky shapes; Niedermeier's body floating face down in a pool of water; a vampire kneeling over a body, feeding.

He shook his head to clear his thoughts and muttered to himself. 'Did the butterfly really follow the bus or was it my imagination?'

A strong weight pressed against his throat until it began to constrict his breathing. He struggled against it, tried to lift it, yet couldn't. He tried to sit up and call for help, but no sound emerged.

Abruptly all light fled, driven by a swirling blackness that descended from the ceiling and expanded until it filled the corners of the room. An unseen force overpowered him and dragged him from his bed into a realm of shadow. His tongue was bound and he could neither cry out nor speak as grey mists swirled about and enveloped him. Demonic shades circled round like wolves thirsting for the blood of a lamb, while thick tentacles of shadow held him fast and dangled him above an interminable void, ready to cast him into its maw. Dark winds buffeted him, and then the very jaws of hell surged forward from the void and parted and Evil opened its grisly mouth wide after him. Claws of despair pulled him downward as he fought for breath, knowing he would succumb at any moment.

He knew this was no dream, that he was about to be destroyed by a power more sinister than any he had imagined possible. As thick darkness closed round him, he saw in his mind the small pine cone Katarina had given him in California those many months ago and felt its rough raspy petals on the skin of his palm. At once he felt himself falling, until his legs crumpled to the floor of a dungeon cell and he found himself kneeling in supplication. The tentacles of the unseen adversary still held his tongue hostage, but his heart cried out for deliverance.

No sooner had desire forced the prayer from his heart, then his bands were loosed, the weight lifted from his throat and his tongue freed from the spectral bonds. Light flooded the room and his heart, while deep peace permeated his entire being. Wings of blinding glory lifted him upward, and carried him sailing across bright sunlit lands, protected by sentinels wielding shields of light and fiery swords with righteous arms.

He began thinking to himself the words of an old hymn: '*The morning breaks, the shadows flee…the dawning of a brighter day, majestic rising on the world.*' The words expressed the faint beginnings of a newly rediscovered hope that now sprang up within his heart, and made him feel that perhaps, once again he might find his faith.

Everywhere there was light.

* * *

Steven tossed a pebble at Mrs. Lazarevic's window. He lacked any recollection of walking from the dormitory or crossing the bridge, although he knew he had. All he remembered was a strong burning inside that had driven him from the dormitory and guided him to her front door, throwing up a hedge along his path against his invisible enemies.

She came down, opened the door, took one look at his bruised face and said: 'You will stay the night here.' He did not argue.

The Lazarevic home felt immune to the madness of the outside world. Neither refugees, nor war nor unseen perils seemed to penetrate its walls. As he sat on the sofa, sipping chamomile tea, he felt safe. The thick walls of the old building warded off evil, as did the Lazarevic men in the paintings and photographs on the walls. He vowed to study more closely the various folk talismans placed on the outside and inside of the house, that up until now he had regarded merely as decorations.

Between sips of chamomile tea and mouthfuls of homemade chocolate *palacinke*, Steven told Mrs. Lazarevic what had happened at Niedermeier's bookstore, emphasizing the butterfly. He told her of his struggle with the dark force in his dormitory. She sat listening, asking no questions.

'You have had a difficult day,' she said, her voice soft and comforting. 'Here you will be safe from the powers of darkness. Nothing will harm you.'

'What's happening? What attacked me?'

'The butterfly is troubling,' she looked at the portraits on the walls as if seeking their advice. 'It may have been a vampire or it may have been Mr. Niedermeier's spirit, or perhaps even an ordinary butterfly. From its behavior I can't tell. In any event you have awoken a great evil that dislikes your presence. Something you are doing is causing it to react and attack you.'

He looked quizzically at her: 'I'm not certain I understand.'

She spoke calmly, soothingly. 'The Adversary finds it easiest to do his work if people are unaware of his existence. He uses materialism and moral relativity to lull them into comfortable lives until he gradually dulls their spiritual senses to the point where they have little need for God. When they no longer need God, then for them He ceases to exist. It is a subtle and clever plan. The Adversary will take direct action only when he senses a righteous man is ready to remove his spiritual blinders and break free from his materialistic cocoon. He will then send his minions to defeat the man before the man can gather spiritual strength. Sometimes they will even try to possess him. This will not be the last such attack. Be watchful. Do you recall what you did to overcome the dark force?'

He related his vision of the pine cone.

'My Katarina is wonderful. You see, she did give you something useful.'

'But a pine cone?'

'It is a powerful symbol of your faith. That will be your weapon…your faith. If you are upright and true, your faith will render you invincible in all your encounters.'

'Faith?' he said faintly. 'I didn't think I had any left.'

'Don't be silly. Of course you do. You've only lost faith in yourself, not God. One day you will be a champion of light.'

'A champion of light?!' he sputtered. It sounded like a tacky, second rate, made-in-Japan Saturday morning cartoon. 'What in the world are you talking about?'

'Oh, I am merely talking. But don't worry. You were not attacked by vampires. You were challenged by the Dark One himself. He is too jealous of his power to ever give that much of it to anyone else, particularly to vampires, greedy small-minded things that they are.'

'Is this for real?' He didn't want to believe what he was hearing, but couldn't reject what she was saying.

'We must get you out of Serbia. When are you leaving to see Marko? He'll put everything in perspective.'

Steven sat up, now feeling there was an exit from the dark tunnel. 'I'm leaving tomorrow evening around 11:00 p.m.' He nursed his chamomile tea for some time then looked at her. 'What's this all about?'

She gazed at him a long, long moment, looked around the room at the Lazarevic portraits, and finally returned her gaze to him.

Mrs. Lazarevic stood and walked to the china cabinet, opened it and withdrew an old album, its cover well worn. She set it on the table and slowly opened the discolored cover, revealing yellowed black and white photographs, some of which appeared to be Daguerreotypes from the 19th century. She pointed to one, which showed two youngish men posing formally in the tightly-tailored narrow-waist dress uniforms of the Habsburg cavalry, with calf-high boots, striped trousers, richly braided Hussar tunics slung jauntily across one shoulder and plumed *czako* hats on their heads. Both held officers' swords and wore long moustaches, and one was clearly a Lazarevic. The other reminded Steven vaguely of someone, although he couldn't say who. He wracked his brain, trying to remember the Austro-Hungarian nobility and royal family. At the bottom of the page someone had written: *Wien, 5.viii.1874* in now-faded ink using an elegant cursive hand.

Mrs. Lazarevic turned the page and pointed to another black and white photo of the same two officers, this time wearing open great coats draped around their shoulders. Both wore the World War One field uniforms of the Habsburg *Kaiserlich und Königlich* Army, held officers' swords and sported the same long moustaches. Underneath, the same elegant, cursive hand had written: *Peterwardein, 5.viii.1914*. Steven looked closer at the photo. The second man looked increasingly familiar, but he wasn't certain.

Mrs. Lazarevic simply turned the page and showed him another photo of the same two men, their moustaches as black and full as in the first photo, this time wearing officers' uniforms of the Yugoslav Royal Army. The photograph had been taken on field maneuvers as they stood proudly next to a large artillery piece. On the bottom the same hand had written: *Brcko, 5.viii.1940*. He stopped her and turned the pages back, comparing the photographs. Neither man appeared to have aged in the course of sixty-six years. And then he saw it. The second man bore a striking resemblance…no, it couldn't be…to Professor Slatina!

'Who are they?' His voice was so dry he barely managed to expel the words.

Her unwavering gaze made him deeply uncomfortable. 'You really don't know, do you? He told you nothing? The man on the left is my late dear husband, Rade Lazarevic. A better, more honorable and upright man never walked the face of this earth. The man on the right is well known to you. He is your dear professor, Marko Slatina.'

His vision darkened and his breathing quickened. He steadied himself on the table with both hands, trying to concentrate on the photographs now blurring before his eyes. After several moments he lifted his head in disbelief and looked directly at Mrs. Lazarevic. 'Is this real? Are you serious?'

'Yes. Very real. And I am quite serious. I can't believe Marko is so irresponsible as to send you out here completely unprepared. You could get killed. Or worse.'

He stared at her uncomprehendingly. 'But how can this be?'

'How well have you studied your folklore? Do you know what a *vampirovic* is? Or a *kresnik*, in Marko's case?'

His mind flashed back to what he had read about the vampirovic, the offspring of a vampire and a human that could live forever and hunted vampires. He sat stunned. 'But that's only folklore…I mean, this isn't real, is it. A vampirovic? Come on…' Yet he kept flipping through the pages, examining the photographs. He came to a photograph of a young Mrs. Lazarevic standing between the two men, now without moustaches, her arms around them, next to the clock tower at Petrovaradin, dated 6.viii.1960.

'Are Marcus von Zlatinow and Professor Slatina…'

'One and the same,' she finished Steven's sentence for him.

He scanned the portraits on the walls around him, until a light switched on inside his head. 'Then these are…'

'All of my late husband, may his soul rest in peace,' she answered proudly.

'And are you…'

'A mere mortal, such as yourself.'

Steven sat speechless, looking at the portraits on the walls and the photos in the album. All seemed to smile at him.

'Marko has sent you on a fool's errand and placed you in grave danger,' she said. 'You must take great care what you do, with whom you speak, and what you write down. Already you have attracted unwanted attention.'

'I don't understand.'

'Use your head. If Marko and my husband are *vampirovici*, what does it mean?'

'Come on, they're just folklore, old tales,' he protested.

'What does it mean?'

'That vampires exist…'

'That vampires exist,' she said. 'Marko didn't send you on an academic voyage. He sent you as a scout.'

'A scout?! What are you talking about?'

'I'll let Marko tell you everything in Budapest. Better you hear it from him than from me. Please, take care of yourself. But if you have any problems, come see me, and I'll help you as best I can.'

Steven sat stunned.

'Marko has always been a strong, good man,' Mrs. Lazarevic said. 'But he is a fool when it comes to matters of the heart.'

'Excuse me?'

'Never mind. We shall speak only about what is important, not gossip.' Her voice was now more severe, and she seemed to say it more to herself than him. But then she decided to enlighten him a little.

'I have seen the signs, Steven… They feed… I feel it, sense it, in the air, in the wind, in the trees, in the soil. It is they who brought this darkness to the land. Even now they think they are undiscovered. As long as they believe this, you are safe. Yet nature abhors them. Their very presence is an open wound on the face of the land, and nature screams out in pain.'

'They fear Marko will come for them again and finish the job, as he must, and this time he will not be soft-hearted as before. For them there will be no redemption, nor will there be an Emperor to show some foolish notion of mercy. But they have grown careless and complacent, gorged and bloated on the freshly-spilled blood of innocents. For now they focus on Niedermeier. For your sake, I hope he is discreet,' she fixed him with an accusing stare. 'And,' she added, 'alive.'

She resumed: 'You have partaken of new knowledge, much as did Father Adam and Mother Eve. Like unto the fruit of the knowledge of Good and Evil, it can kill. You must be extremely careful with this knowledge and mention nothing of it or your research to anyone, even your professors and most trusted friends. For in the day they partake, they shall surely die.'

Steven stared in his tea then turned to her. 'So you really believe vampires exist?'

'Oh Steven, how young you are. After all these years of communism I find your innocence refreshing. It gives me hope for a better world. Yes, vampires really do exist. But for this evening you shall be safe from them. Come, you will sleep in Katarina's room for the night. And when you see Marko, tell him the Emperor's pets have escaped and that it's time he return and finish the job.'

Mrs. Lazarevic had turned Katarina's room into a shrine to her daughter, and Steven fell asleep surrounded by Katarina smiling at him from countless picture frames.

* * *

Steven waited until the operator called his name, then he entered the musty booth, picked up the receiver and heard the phone ring distantly. Even now there was static on the line. Someone picked up the phone and the line suddenly became clear and he heard Katarina's voice as though she were in the next room. He had forgotten the nine hour time difference and had woken her at two in the morning.

'It's me,' Steven said.

'Where are you calling from?' she whispered, her voice still groggy.

'Novi Sad.'

'Are you okay?'

'I'm okay…I think.'

'I've been worried,' she said. 'Do you need anything?'

'I don't know.' He hesitated. He wanted to escape from Serbia to the warm feeling he had when he was in Katarina's presence. 'I…I just needed to hear your voice.'

There was silence. Finally she said: 'I'm here.'

He listened to her breathing softly over the line, wanting to say something. But the words wouldn't come out, as though he feared that the invisible force that bound him to her would disappear.

'Do you still have the cross?' she asked.

'And the pine cone,' he answered.

A wave of silence washed over them.

'I have faith in you,' she whispered.

After a long silence he asked: 'Do you?'

After an equally long silence she answered 'Yes.'

'Thanks.' Steven could hear her breathing become gentler.

'I look forward to seeing you again,' she whispered faintly, almost asleep.

'Good night,' he said. 'Sleep well.'

He hung up the phone.

* * *

They came for Steven two nights later in a dark late model mini-van with mud-covered license plates. The time was shortly before midnight and lightning slashed across the heavens, its intermittent streaks revealing the undersides of murky clouds, billowing and roiling behind a cloak of darkness, while chains of gut-wrenching thunder shook the dormitory windows and set the walls humming. Black rain cascaded down as they entered the dorm.

Steven had fallen asleep early, exhausted by the stressful events of the week and was roused from slumber by male voices that matched the resonance point of the concrete, causing the surrounding walls to vibrate with eerie tonality. An unusually deferent Neso said: 'Yes, yes, the American. He's in the room down there. Knock on the door. He's probably sleeping. I'll show you.'

Steven slipped from his bed in fear and grabbed the stake from his backpack.

The sound of hard-soled boots drew closer, until they stopped in front of Steven's door, and then Neso politely said 'he's here. He's a good kid, be nice to him.'

A fist pounded heavily on the door and a gruff male voice called out: 'Mini-van for Budapest.'

Steven breathed a sigh of relief, hid the stake and opened the door. The driver carried Steven's suitcase out to the van, along with a small package Neso had slipped him in return for a fistful of Marks. Ceca smiled coyly as Steven said goodbye, while Neso insisted on kissing him three times on the cheeks. 'If you need anything in Budapest, I mean anything, call this number.' Neso handed him a piece of paper.

Heedless of the downpour, the dark van rushed through an even darker countryside while Steven stared through fogged-up windows, nicotine-blackened condensation dripping down the glass. Most of the passengers slept, their bodies contorted into unnatural positions against the seats and windows, while a nervous businessman in the rear puffed putrid cigarettes all the way to Budapest.

Steven stayed awake all the way to the border, thinking about everything that had happened since his arrival: the war, vampire ethnography, Gordana the librarian, Vesna, Niedermeier, the attack of darkness, and now Mrs. Lazarevic's revelations about her husband and Professor Slatina. He would finally have the chance to leave it all behind, decompress and clear his head for a few days in Budapest. But he also felt apprehension about his impending reunion with Slatina. What would he say to the professor? What would the professor say to him?

Was Mrs. Lazarevic really to be believed? Were both her late husband and Slatina really the quasi-immortal vampire-hunting offspring of vampires – the vampirovici of the old folk tales? Could a person really live that long? Was Slatina really the enigmatic Captain Marcus von Zlatinow from the fortress commander's log books? The names were certainly similar enough, but the commander had referred to von Zlatinow in his log book as a Venetian, whereas Slatina claimed to be from the island of Hvar in Croatia. What would a Venetian have been doing in the service of the Habsburg emperor? If Slatina really is a vampirovic, why did he send Steven on a scouting mission? Why not come himself? Looking at his dim reflection in the foggy glass Steven asked himself: 'Am I losing my sanity along with everyone else in this country?'

If everything Mrs. Lazarevic had said was true – and he had no reason to doubt her, other than the fact that it was completely outlandish – then the professor had a lot of explaining to do. Or was Mrs. Lazarevic simply a crazy widow suffering from loneliness, whose only child had gone off to America leaving no one to keep a lid on the mother's fantasies?

After the border, he relaxed with the knowledge he was outside Yugoslavia and fell into a contorted sleep, only to awake disoriented on the outskirts of Budapest. Dawn's first faint light was beginning to creep over the horizon when they reached the Budapest airport, where all the passengers alighted, except Steven.

The van then took him into the city center, through 19th century Pest, across the Danube to Buda via the gaunt skeleton of the emaciated Szabadsag Bridge to deposit him in front of the Hotel Gellért, an imposing *fin de siècle* building sitting heavily on the banks of the Danube. The lobby was deserted but for a middle-aged desk clerk with greased-back hair, chatting with two tired-looking ladies-of-the-evening. The desk clerk jumped up when he saw Steven, shooed away the girls with a wave of his hand, and rushed behind the reception counter.

'Pleassse, may I help you,' the clerk's heavily accented English and lisping "s" gave him all the charm of Boris Badenov in the Bullwinkle and Rocky cartoons. Slightly giddy from lack of sleep, Steven fought to keep from laughing at the mental image.

'I'm looking for a guest, Professor Marko Slatina,' Steven said, keeping a straight face.

'Pleassse, one moment, pleassse.' The oozing clerk ruffled through some papers. Unable to find what he was looking for he opened a drawer and ruffled through more, and then another drawer. He shrugged his shoulders. 'Pleassse, we have no guessst by that name. May I help you in sssome other way, Mr.…?'

'Roberts, Steven Roberts.'

'Ahhhh, yesss, pleassse,' he rummaged again through more papers. 'Thisss isss for you,' the clerk handed him an envelope and disappeared into the back room.

Surprised, Steven opened it and found a piece of hotel stationery with a street address on Uri Utca. Not knowing where that was, he brought down his hand on the silver bell on the counter, filling the empty lobby with a loud metallic ring. The greasy-haired clerk reappeared hastily and clasped his hand over the bell to dampen the tone.

'Yesss pleassse, how may I help you pleassse?' The clerk's forced politeness was infuriatingly servile, yet he was clearly annoyed and his use of the word "please" bordered on obdurate.

'Where is this address?'

'You may take a taxi, pleassse. One isss waiting right outsssside the front door, pleassse.' He gestured towards the entrance with a dramatic flourish of his arm. 'Pleassse, it isss on *Várhegy*, Casssstle Hill.' The clerk watched Steven walk from the lobby, suitcase in hand, and then picked up the telephone and dialed a number.

As though immune to speeding tickets the taxi driver raced his aging Skoda north along the Danube and up Castle Hill. The rickety suspension banged against the uneven cobblestones as they zipped through the castle walls and past a massive palace, testimony to the bygone grandeur of the Habsburg imperial court. The taxi clanked over the cobblestones as it turned into Uri Utca and the driver slammed on the brakes, throwing Steven against the dashboard. Steven paid the driver, who rattled off as though late for the starting flag of a Formula One race.

In the deserted street the only sound was the tweeter and chirp of birds waking to the new day as the sun's first rays began to brighten the tops of the houses, bathing the pavement in radiance, drenching the tightly-packed two and three storey Baroque buildings in pastels.

The blue building stood against the western wall, a patron saint on timeless watch in a second floor niche above a stone archway large enough for a coach and horses. Steven approached and knocked at a small door set in the massive gate. After waiting a respectable interval, he knocked again. Then he pounded hard. 'Come on, open up,' he muttered.

Exasperated, he finally tried the door latch and it sprung open. He stepped into a gravel courtyard filled with unexpected greenery: a large tree, a flower garden and a multitude of bushes, all shimmering with hordes of butterflies, taking Steven aback. Towards the rear a green door opened, and a stocky elderly man emerged, dressed in overalls and a workman's apron.

He walked past Steven, shut the door in the gate, picked up Steven's suitcase and walked into the building, taking no notice of Steven whatsoever. Steven followed him up a flight of stairs to the first floor, where the man set the suitcase on a bench in an austere room that resembled a monk's cell, with a small bed, a writing table, and a plain wooden cross on the wall. From the window Steven could see the ramparts of the medieval city and valley. The old man showed Steven the bathroom, led him back to the room, said '*schlafen*' in badly accented German and left.

Steven headed for the bathroom to bathe. Staring back at him from the mirror he saw a scraggly Che Guevara look-a-like, whose bleary, bloodshot eyes would have looked at home begging at a freeway off-ramp.

After bathing, Steven lay down. Four hours later he awoke to find a tray of food on the table. After eating, he opened the bedroom door to find the old man sitting on a chair in the hallway, reading a book.

'*Komme*' he said to Steven, once again in barely intelligible German, and Steven followed with his backpack. The old man took him out into the courtyard, through another door, then down into a musty cellar with vaulted brick ceilings, where he turned on a flashlight.

'*Komme*,' he repeated, as he led Steven through another door, then downward into another, even deeper cellar, then through a veritable labyrinth of corridors, tunnels, cellars, and more tunnels.

Steven was completely disoriented. He followed the old man through the underground warren, until they came to a series of staircases that led up and finally out into a different courtyard, this one painted in a bright orange that magnified the midday sunlight, causing Steven to shade his eyes with his hand.

'*Komme*,' the old man repeated once more as he led Steven quickly inside the building to a spacious and airy upper room filled with a massive dark wood dining table that appeared to have been left from medieval times.

They continued out onto a terrace above the city wall, bright sunlight reflecting from the white stone buttresses and arches of the neo-Gothic parliament directly across the glittering Danube. They had crossed the entire width of Castle Hill via the cellars and were now on the eastern-most river side. Steven squinted and blinked as his eyes struggled to adjust to the brilliant glare of midday.

The silhouette of a man approached, grasped him firmly by the hand and shook it heartily.

'Welcome to Buda,' Professor Slatina exclaimed warmly.

* * *

Interlude VIII: Backa, Salas 431: February - April 1983

It was a typical *salas*, an isolated Vojvodina farm consisting of a whitewashed one story house with a corn crib and other outbuildings sheltered under clusters of tall Linden, Maple and Chestnut trees, with fields spreading out endlessly on all sides.

The eleven arrived unannounced for supper late one frosty February night, when snow blanketed the roads, cutting the *salas* off from civilization. The flickering light of the television and embers of a dying fire cast jittery shadows across the whitewashed tobacco grey walls, while a dim 45 watt light bulb struggled to defeat a thick yellow lamp shade. The parents had sent the children to bed early, and then retired to the old overstuffed furniture of the sitting room with the grandparents to watch a television documentary on humpbacked whales. The men and the mother smoked and drank beer. After the humpbacked whales had finished mating, everybody trundled off to bed, the mother remaining behind to tidy up. She opened a window to air the cigarette smoke from the room.

Unseen, two large hairy butterflies entered through the window, and fluttered to the ceiling lamp, waiting until the mother had shut the window and turned out the lights. Then followed what Ivan the youngest artlessly termed 'a wonderful six course meal.'

The eleven watched the flickering picture box in rapt fascination, learned of electricity, studied all they could from documentary films and what few books and magazines lay around the house. They lived off the farm animals, slowly taking blood from one after another. From the television they learned of Tito's Yugoslavia, communism, Brotherhood and Unity and Workers' Socialist Self-management. In February they discovered that starting the farmer's battered car – an old *Fica*, the Yugoslav copy of the tiny Fiat *Toppo Giggio* – was not as easy as they had seen on television. They saw that the world they had once known had changed dramatically. No longer did a Kaiser sit in Vienna, a Sultan in Istanbul or a Tsar in Russia. At first they were baffled by communism and democracy, concepts unknown in their time. But the language of power stays the same, no matter which age, and they quickly grasped the essentials.

Using the *salas* as a base, they traveled throughout Yugoslavia to places long forgotten, valleys long flooded, fields long built over, mines long abandoned and old watermills still churning. Slowly, bit by bit they collected the vestiges of their once substantial fortunes and compared notes. They sought out the Vlach but could not find him. Nor could they find any evidence he had ever been killed.

And when they finally decided the Vlach was dead and their quorum would not be reformed in its full capacity, one by one, they left the *salas* and rejoined the world.

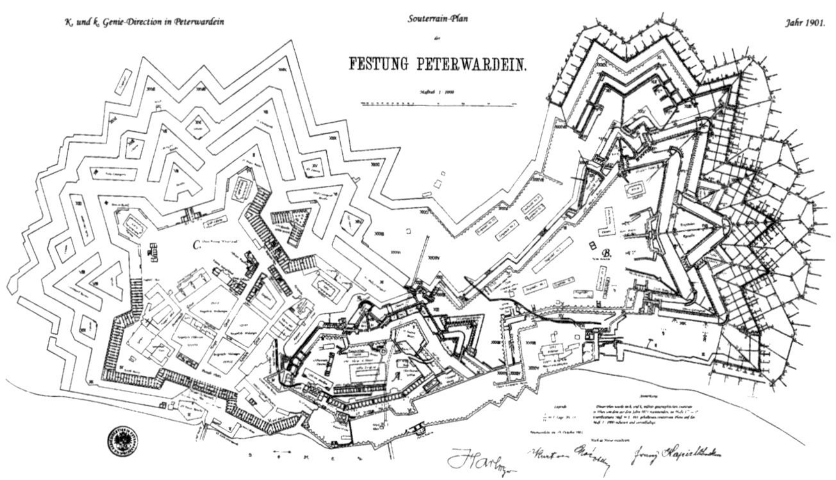

CHAPTER NINE

THE TRUTH WILL OUT

Budapest, Petrovaradin: 10-15 May 1992

Slatina was fashionably attired as usual, looking every bit the high society Italian playboy in a beige linen suit and matching crocodile belt and shoes. 'Perhaps he could be the mysterious Venetian,' Steven thought. But he looked no older than his early thirties.

'My dear Steven, how delightful to see you once again,' Slatina placed his sunglasses on his head, hugged and kissed Steven on both cheeks. 'Thank you so much for coming. I trust I have not inconvenienced you with these alternate arrangements. After all, precautions must be taken.'

'Where are we?' Steven demanded irritably.

'But of course, of course, there is much to discuss and you must have so many questions.' Slatina's disposition matched the midday sun. 'Come, we shall talk and you shall tell me of your research and of my good friends in Belgrade.'

Slatina motioned for Steven to sit in a cushioned wrought-iron garden chair. Slatina sat while Steven remained standing and the elderly man brought a tea pot and sandwiches.

'Afternoon tea is yet one more proof of the magnificent cultural heights achieved by the English,' Slatina purred gracefully, sniffing the aromas from the teapot. 'Would you not agree?'

Steven muttered and remained standing.

'So tell me, young Roberts, how is your research progressing?'

Steven responded by opening his backpack, removing the wooden stake and laying it brazenly on the table. 'Mrs. Lazarevic gave this to me.'

Slatina started at the sight and spilled his tea, clearly recognizing not only what but whose it was.

'She said I was to tell you…' Steven fumbled in his pocket and pulled out a piece of folded paper, 'that the Emperor's pets have escaped…and it's time you return and finish the job.' He placed the paper face up on the table for Slatina to see.

'And she also told me a great deal more,' Steven folded his arms on his chest. 'A *kresnik*?' He let the word hang in the air and looked expectantly at Slatina.

For the first time since Steven had known him, Slatina appeared at a loss for words. The smile disappeared as the professor picked up the stake, hefted it and rapped it hard against his open palm. 'I haven't seen this for a long time,' he mused. 'You know, of course, that it belonged to Katarina's father.'

'What in the hell is going on,' Steven exploded. He no longer cared about his fellowship from the Balkan Ethnographic Trust, nor did he care for his relationship with his mentor. He now felt like walking away from graduate school and his Ph.D. entirely, simply to get away from Slatina. 'I thought I was going to Yugoslavia for ethnographic research, but instead I find out you've sent me on some weird vampire hunt, where I don't know if I'm the hunter or the hunted.'

His loud voice attracted the attention of the old man, who came out onto the terrace. Slatina waved him away.

'What is the Balkan Ethnographic Trust? What are you using me for? I don't like being manipulated!'

'Yes, yes, of course.' Slatina remained sitting and looked Steven up and down, clearly taken aback. 'I must apologize most profoundly for my failure to communicate to you the circumstances of your position. Due to the sensitive nature of the matter I felt it best to not inform you fully until you had gained further knowledge and I was certain you could be trusted. Certainly you have earned the right to many answers. Please calm down and tell me what you have done thus far.'

'No,' Steven said defiantly. 'First *you* tell *me* what's going on. I want to know what *you've* gotten *me* mixed up in.'

'I must once again apologize,' Slatina said sincerely. 'I should have been more forthcoming with you prior to the start of your journey. Yet I feared if I told you, you would think me deluded, or that you would fear the dangers involved. Either way you would not have gone, and I knew no one else of sufficient moral stature and maturity who I could entrust with…'

'Trust with what,' Steven interrupted.

'Steven, I shall be very blunt with you,' Slatina said. He stood, grasped Steven by both shoulders and looked directly into his eyes, unblinking.

What Steven saw made him gasp, for the professor's eyes reddened until they were a deep luminescent scarlet, and then his irises altered their shape to resemble those of a large feline. Steven saw power and strength in them, as well as a brief flicker of a soul that had comprehended the depths of human darkness and was haunted by it.

Then in a heartbeat the scarlet eyes sprang and burst through his own, crawling into the core of his soul as Slatina's gaze clutched Steven in an iron grip. Steven watched powerless as Slatina reached inside him, ripped out his heart and handed it to the jackal-headed Anubis, who placed it on a golden balance to be measured against a glowing feather. A hideous beast with a crocodile head and hippo hindquarters crouched at his side, growling and salivating in anticipation of devouring Steven's pulsating heart. As Anubis lowered the heart on the balance Steven felt chills course throughout his body. He watched in horror as the balance began to dip downward, only to gradually halt its movement and then ever so slowly ascend until it was level with the feather. And then the feather inched downward as the heart rose ever so slightly. The growling beast roared with dismay and vanished, and suddenly Steven was back on the terrace, looking into Slatina's gentle smile.

He felt violated and naked, ashamed to look at the professor. An uncomfortable silence followed, in which Steven stared at the tile flooring.

Finally Slatina spoke. 'You have the heart of a good man, Steven Roberts. What I shall share with you…you must never divulge to anyone. Otherwise you will suffer your life to be taken.'

Steven could see this was no idle threat: Slatina, he was now sure, had clearly carried it out on previous occasions and would not hesitate to do so again.

'And by accepting this information you shall bind yourself to me in a very difficult quest,' Slatina continued. 'Is this what you want?'

Steven stood, silent and uncertain. Uncertain whether he wanted to enter further into Slatina's strange world, and whether he fully comprehended the choice he was about to make. 'What kind of a quest? What're you talking about?'

Slatina's eyes maintained their eerie glow: 'Good against Evil, Light against Dark, a quest that could end with you losing your soul and your life, or perhaps saving the souls and lives of others.'

Steven looked at him for several moments, frightened by the eyes and the power that lay behind them, unsure of himself and Slatina, unsure of the wisdom of what he was doing.

And then he nodded his head affirmatively, although still uncertain.

'Do not nod your head. You must say it. You must give me your spoken word,' Slatina looked directly at him with those unearthly cat eyes, now a dark crimson.

'Yes,' Steven's voice emerged uneven.

'Very well. I know you to be trustworthy and a man of honor and conscience. The light you nurture within your heart is strong…' Slatina's voice trailed off. He smiled at Steven, his eyes now reverting to their normal shape and color.

Slatina approached the wrought-iron rail of the terrace and looked down. He sniffed the air from habit. 'Sit down, drink your tea, eat a sandwich, and permit your old professor to share with you a tale unlike any you have ever heard.'

Only now did Steven notice the railing was covered with butterflies. They moved aside as Slatina approached, making space for him.

'I fought on these very battlements when we drove the Turks from Buda in 1686,' he exclaimed wistfully. 'We lost many good men and destroyed the entire city in the process. But that is another story, one which I shall tell you on another, perhaps less serious occasion.'

Steven looked at him and listened, uncertain whether to believe Slatina's claim about fighting in a battle at this very spot over 300 years ago. After all, the professor looked so young. Steven sat down, picked up a sandwich and realized he had lost his appetite.

'Now, where shall I begin,' Slatina asked as he stood at the railing, both hands firmly grasping the wrought iron, staring across the river over the rooftops of Buda and Pest into space, as though transported back through time. 'I was born in 1640 into a patrician family on the Dalmatian island of Hvar, to a goodly mother, kind and wise. Her family married her off at a young age to the heir of the Slatina family, a rogue by the name of Hektor, ten years her senior, may God abandon his soul to the fires of Hell. Have you ever been to Hvar, young Steven? It has the oldest indoor theatre in all Europe and is really quite beautiful. We are proud of it… But I digress.' His eyes shone as he recalled his home.

'My mother was beautiful, pure and gentle with a strong faith in God. My father was a wastrel, whose life was given to pursuing worldly pleasures: gambling, women, wine and exotic powders and pastes from the Orient, what we today call narcotics. She brought with her a dowry of several servants, slaves, vineyards on the north side of Hvar and on the island of Vis. The family press made a rather good *Vugava.* You do know about *Vugava*, of course…' his voice trailed off as he wandered through distant memories.

'*Vugava*?' Steven was confused.

'Yes, our white wine, raw, primitive and powerful, and it is made only on Vis. It won the name "Queen of Wines" from the Greeks, and was exported throughout the ancient world: Cyprus, Crete, Rome, et cetera, et cetera, et cetera… As a wine it is not for everyone…but I digress yet again.'

'To feed his evil habits and cover his gambling debts, my father traded with the Turks and the Genoese contrary to the laws of Venice…'

'Venice?' Steven asked, intrigued. 'What did he have to do with Venice?'

'Venice? But of course you know that Hvar was a Venetian possession at the time.'

Steven kicked himself for forgetting Balkan history. 'So, are you the one they called the Venetian?'

Slatina looked surprised. 'How did you know that? It was my nickname when I served the Habsburg Emperors.' His tone showed newfound respect for Steven.

'When my mother bore him only daughters my father quickly became bored and moved to Venice itself, where he could more easily indulge his vices, leaving her behind on Hvar to languish and make do as best she could.'

'When he had squandered his family's fortune my mother refused to let him spend her dowry. He turned to piracy against Venetian vessels, disguising himself first as a Turk, then later as an Uskok corsair. As a pirate he committed crimes and deeds most heinous and vile, that only the blackest heart could conceive, and he bragged that he had set a curse on God himself, if such a thing is possible. The Turks called him Kara-Hektor, or Black Hektor.' On one voyage he was taken with disease. He returned to Hvar, where he quickly died and was buried in the graveyard on the hilltop overlooking the harbor.'

'But his story didn't end there. Several weeks after his death he was seen wandering near the graveyard at night. Wickedness combined with happenstance, and he had become a vampire. One evening he visited my mother to satisfy his vile lusts, and I am the result. Twenty one years later I tracked him down in a lagoon at the mouth of the Neretva river where he was hiding. I killed him,' He looked around, brushed some imaginary dirt off his suit coat, and turned again to stare over the Danube. Several butterflies fluttered in the air and came to rest on his shoulders, as though comforting him.

Steven sat numbly. 'I'm really sorry. I didn't know that…'

'Do you know what it is like to kill your own father? No, of course not. But I must say, under the circumstances it was quite liberating. He had blackened the family name, besmirched my mother's reputation and terrorized all Dalmatia in search of blood to feed his unquenchable thirst.' Slatina's hands clenched the railing tightly.

'So you are a vampirovic. I mean a kresnik,' Steven stared at Slatina's back, waiting for confirmation.

Slatina turned, leaned back against the railing and smiled kindly. 'Yes, young Roberts, I am. And a worse fate I could not imagine in life, except that which awaits my adversaries.'

'Your adversaries?'

'Yes, my adversaries. You call them vampires.'

'Vampires,' Steven repeated without emotion, overwhelmed by Slatina's tale.

'Vampires,' Slatina stated emphatically.

'Vampires,' Steven repeated. 'But…I mean…'

Slatina waved his hand. 'Please permit me to continue.'

'My family's patrician status enabled me to enter the service of the Serene Republic, Venice, and I commanded a contingent of *Stradioti* light cavalry near Spalato, or Split, as they call it today. I eventually won my spurs in the *Cavalieri di San Marco*, Venice's only chivalrous order,' he said with evident pride.

'So you're a knight,' Steven looked at him, still skeptical.

'It's not all that it's cracked up to be,' Slatina smiled. 'So, did you look into the Order of the Dragon?'

The sudden change of topic surprised Steven. 'The Order, yes, of course. Why?'

'Have you discovered its purpose?' Slatina asked.

'Well, not really.'

'Well, you know, of course, that a vampirovic has special…how shall we say…talents,' He smiled at Steven, who shuddered at the memory of Slatina's eyes and the interrogation of his soul. 'Talents that enable him to track and kill vampires with great expediency. Mine came to the attention of the Order.'

Steven's curiosity had driven most of the anger from him, and each new revelation made him more curious. 'Were you in the Order of the Dragon?' he blurted.

Slatina smiled again and nodded. '*O quam misericors est Deus, Justus et Pius.*'

'O how merciful is God, Just and Faithful,' Steven translated.

'Yes. I was in the Order. In fact, I believe I am all that is left of it. You must understand what we faced. The mountains in the Balkans contain vast riches of ores and minerals that man has mined since antiquity. But under those hills lay a darkness placed there by the Adversary at the foundation of the world to corrupt man. This latent evil was uncovered by Roman miners who worked the hills at *Argentium* in Bosnia, and at Novo Brdo in Kosovo and other places. The Order was created to repulse it.'

'This great wealth provided half of Europe's silver during the Middle Ages and financed the rise of the Serbian Empire, the Bosnian Kingdom and the city-state of Dubrovnik, while Bavaria's House of Fugger and their bank grew fabulously wealthy from it.'

'I was inducted into the Order while serving the Austrians. We used the natural barriers of the Danube and Sava Rivers to keep this evil from the heart of the Empire. While in the Order, I met another vampirovic, a Serb by the name of Rade, who's father Lazar had terrorized his native village in Kosovo for many years before Rade killed him. Rade was serving in one of the border units garrisoned at Kalemegdan when I first met him. I had him transferred to my command and we became the Emperor's sword and shield in the fight against this plague. For over 200 years, we were bosom companions and best friends.'

'Just a second, now,' Steven interrupted. 'The folk tales I read all say that a vampirovic is supposed to be immortal, just like vampires. So how did Lieutenant Lazarevic die? And why are you still alive?'

'Immortal,' Slatina once again smiled wistfully. 'Well, I would hesitate to say for certain, as I would need to live to see the end of what we call time to make any such pronouncement with certainty. I can, however, state that we do seem rather long-lived and it is damned hard to kill us if we don't wish to die.'

'But why did Katarina's father die?'

'Because of a woman,' Slatina said wistfully, 'As true a love as ever captured a man's heart. You see, should a vampirovic decide to reproduce, he loses the essence of his immortality. As he passes on new life, he becomes subject to all the frailties and infirmities of mortality. Unfortunately, my dear Rade had taken quite a fancy to schnapps and cigars over the centuries. Before he met Katarina's mother it meant nothing, but his habits stayed with him after Katarina's birth, and the accumulated centuries of tobacco, alcohol and meat-eating caught up with him quite rapidly.'

'I'm sorry,' Steven said.

'Now, have I not told you enough crazy stories for one day?'

'But why'd you send me to Serbia?' Steven asked. 'And what did Mrs. Lazarevic mean when she said that "the Emperor's pets have escaped"?'

Slatina looked at him as if deciding whether or not to continue, then sat down and took a sandwich. He motioned to Steven to do the same.

'It is simple. I cannot travel to Yugoslavia. I needed someone I trusted to gather information for me.'

'But why can't you travel there?'

'Steven, you see, Rade and I were the only vampirovici in the Order, and since we could destroy vampires far more easily and effectively than the others, the Order gave the two of us a free hand and focused more on social and political activities. The Order dwindled in size until the reign of Franz Joseph I, when there were only a few active members who had joined largely to be close to the throne. And then the Great War began.'

'After two disastrous campaigns in 1914, our Army finally occupied Serbia in October 1915, and Rade and I continued our work. For the first time we were able to work unhindered throughout Macedonia, Kosovo, Serbia, Sandzak and Montenegro. When Franz Joseph died in 1916, the new Emperor Charles was busy with the war and trying to keep Hungary in the Empire: He treated the Order as a relic of a bygone era and did not replace fallen members. Several died on the Carpathian Front and a couple of others of old age. After the war Serbia established the Kingdom of Serbs, Croats and Slovenes, which as you know was later to become Yugoslavia. The Prince Regent, Aleksandar Karadjordjevic enlisted substantial numbers of former Habsburg officers in the army of the new country, and Rade and I switched sides. We met with Aleksandar and informed him of the existence of the Order. He became its new patron upon becoming king in 1921 and permitted us to continue our work.'

'During the Second World War we first sided with the royalist forces, but then withdrew from the fight, as all sides engaged in the most unimaginable forms of brutality against each other. We watched this curse spread unchecked from *Argentium* to the rest of the country, and soon found ourselves working day and night to keep the evil under control,' Slatina's face hardened as though recalling particularly unpleasant memories.

'After the war Rade and I faced new problems. As former Yugoslav royal officers we were under suspicion by the communists. Having served under the Habsburgs we were doubly suspicious. Because of my high birth and social status I was considered a class enemy and was forced to flee the country to avoid prison, while Rade, of humbler birth and lower rank, was able to avoid such difficulties. I was able to return for a brief time in the 1960s, but had to leave to avoid the police. You see, even now should I attempt to return I will most certainly be arrested.'

'So you sent me instead,' Steven pushed further. 'To do what?'

'Ah, that is where things become difficult. You have been to the great fortresses at Kalemegdan and Petrovaradin, no?'

'Of course.'

'Well, you know that there are extensive tunnels under those fortresses, yes?'

'Yes. Professor Stojadinovic has offered to take us underneath Petrovaradin on Saturday.'

'Stojadinovic…Ljubodrag Stojadinovic?' Something about the name puzzled Slatina. 'I haven't heard from him for a couple of years. I heard he had a serious heart attack and assumed the worst. They say he was quite the *bon vivant*…prone to excesses, alcohol and…hmm…female students.'

'Well, he's very much alive and speaks highly of you,' Steven said.

'I am glad to hear he is doing well. Please give him my regards. Back in 1733 Rade and I did something that at the time we thought clever. However, it now appears to have been a mistake.'

Steven eyed him quizzically. 'A mistake? What kind of mistake?'

'Well, it appears we may have left some vampires behind.'

'What do you mean "it appears"?'

'Ah, yes, well, you see…ahem,' Slatina cleared his throat: 'We interred eleven vampires in an underground tomb.'

Steven sat, dumbfounded. 'Eleven vampires in an underground tomb? I found references to you constructing something at the Hornwerk at Petrovaradin. Is that where they are?'

'Ah, you have done good work, young Roberts, good work.'

'I also came across an article about twelve vampires by an author named Tihomir Djordjevic,' Steven said hesitantly. 'But you only had eleven.'

'So you did find it,' Slatina exclaimed. 'I was uncertain you would. And? What do you think? It's all true.'

'I haven't actually seen it yet,' Steven replied, and then told him about the disappearing librarian and Niedermeier.

Slatina looked concerned. 'Come inside, I fear we are getting too much sun.'

'But why twelve if there were only eleven?'

'Ah, yes. There was a twelfth, but we never found him. He is still out there somewhere. We caught his scent again during World War Two, but were unable to pursue him.' Slatina said as he led Steven into an expansive drawing room where two large life-sized, full body oil portraits hung side by side on a wall, one of which appeared to be a young Slatina wearing the colorful garb of a late renaissance Venetian nobleman, and the other of a tall, slender and strikingly beautiful raven-haired girl on the cusp of womanhood clad in a flowing dark green velvet dress. Slatina motioned for Steven to sit on a post-modern white leather sofa. The old man followed and brought them both glasses of mineral water.

'Who is she?' Steven asked, noticing the girl's resemblance to the red cat-eyed woman from his dream of the trolleybus.

'Her name is Natalija. The portraits were commissioned by her father as a wedding gift to the two of us,' Slatina said absently.

'I didn't know you were married.'

'I lost her immediately after my wedding…like you I had to bury my wife.' He stared at the portrait intensely.

'I had no idea,' Steven blurted in shock.

'But that was long ago, young Roberts. Life goes on, and we should best follow the admonition of our Savior and let the dead bury the dead. We should not dwell on the past. It is best you move on from your grief and let yourself love again.'

'But let us move on to the twelve. Where should I start,' Slatina muttered partly to himself. 'The article was actually a part of Rade's diary that was confiscated by the communists. Djordjevic received access to it and published it more as a curiosity than anything else.'

'You must understand, young Roberts, when a person first becomes a vampire he is very confused. He has just been in the after-life for a short period of time, seen the torment that awaits him, made a pact with the Devil to sell his soul, and then had his soul abruptly returned to an already decaying body lying in a closed grave. Usually it takes a vampire about 100 days to come to his senses. During this time he is unaware of his powers, is disoriented and unable to act rationally, while an overpowering thirst for man's life essence overwhelms him. Young vampires are extremely vulnerable and careless, led by their lusts, and peasants kill most of them at this stage.

'If a vampire makes it past the first 100 days it begins to collect its wits and becomes far more dangerous. By that time the vampire has learned to understand the hunger gnawing within its belly and is able to exercise greater self-control. This is when the vampire begins to recognize its powers. To survive the wrath of local villagers it moves to areas where it is unknown, typically to larger cities where it can hide among the morass of humanity and practice its evil.'

'What are a vampire's powers,' Steven inquired. 'I've read lots of folklore, but I'm not certain what's real and what's myth.

'They shift shape. A vampire typically appears in one of several forms. You will see them usually in their human form, which is their normal appearance, or as a lycanthrope, what you call a werewolf.'

'A werewolf?' Steven's eye widened.

'A werewolf,' Slatina responded.

'It's just that, you know…this is all so…'

'Unbelievable,' Slatina finished his sentence.

'Unbelievable,' Steven nodded.

'Now, where were we?' Slatina sipped his mineral water. 'I have forgotten where I left off…vampires…vampirovici…the Order of the Dragon…the Twelve…oh yes: lycanthropes.'

'Werewolves,' Steven added.

'They can be quite an intimidating sight, what with all the hair and teeth and claws and growling.' Slatina made a face and tried to imitate a werewolf, which made Steven laugh. 'But a werewolf is only more dangerous because there are more sharp pointy bits to watch out for. They also metamorphose into just about anything you can think of, cats, dogs, wolves, horses, et cetera, et cetera, et cetera. But for some reason they favor butterflies. Shifting shape drains them of energy, and they can only do so a limited number of times before they need to rest and feed.'

'Oh.'

'Their other power is that they can mesmerize the weak-willed, the simple-minded and uneducated and those who are unaware.'

Steven thought back to the bulldog librarian. Was she a vampire?

'You asked about the Twelve. Vampires cannot gather in groups larger than twelve. We tried once to put fourteen of them together in the same room and they all turned to jelly in a flash,' he snapped his fingers, his eyes twinkling with macabre delight. 'Imagine that. We did it several other times just for fun.'

'When twelve vampires band together of their own free will, then they wield far greater powers. Fortunately, they are selfish and egocentric, and although they like to socialize, they dislike cooperating, so a quorum is extremely rare. We heard of one such quorum led by a Vlach…'

'A Vlach?' Steven interrupted.

'Yes, from Wallachia. We captured eleven of them – all powerful and mature – who, at the Emperor's orders we interred under the fortress in a special chamber, but we never found the twelfth. The bloody manner in which Yugoslavia is breaking apart suggests not only that they have escaped but also that they are the driving force behind the bloodshed. If so, then they have hidden themselves in the government, police and army, as well as powerful institutions in society and surrounded themselves with mortals of equally evil design, willing to do their bidding for material reward. These mortals probably don't know their masters are vampires.'

'Which fortress did you bury them under?'

'Why Kalemegdan, of course,' Slatina said matter-of-factly.

'Kalemegdan? I thought you built something at Petrovaradin,' Steven was surprised.

'Oh, did I say Kalemegdan? You are so right, I meant Petrovaradin. These memories have distracted me. Please forgive me.'

'Vampires underneath Petrovaradin? Well, Stojadinovic will just have to cancel his little excursion. I'm not going near that place,' Steven said emphatically.

'But you must, Steven,' Slatina said gravely. 'I need you to ascertain if the seals on the chamber are still intact.'

Steven stared at him in disbelief. 'You want me to go crawling through tunnels to find a chamber full of vampires!? Are you out of you mind?'

'Now Steven, it is not as dangerous as you may think,' Slatina said reassuringly. 'If they have escaped, which I believe they have, then they will be long gone. If they are still there and the seals on the chamber are intact, then you will not enter. In either event, there is little danger.'

'You can't be serious,' Steven said incredulous. 'Do you really want me to go check on a room full of vampires?'

'You are large and strong, yes? You played American football and wrestled, yes?'

'Yes.' He was taken aback by Slatina's change of topic once again. 'But that has nothing to do with it!'

'Excellent! Wonderful! Then you will have no trouble defending yourself against a vampire,' Slatina continued. 'Simply fight a vampire as you would another human being. But do not let him bite you on your left side, or he will paralyze you and begin to drain your life's essence.'

'Now hold…'

'If you don't let them bite you, they are no more powerful than an ordinary human being,' Slatina cut him off before he could even begin his sentence. 'Even the lycanthropes aren't that difficult to combat. They just look fierce, although their teeth and claws do make things a bit more difficult. But they are not invisible or exceptionally fast or strong. Their power lies in their ability to shift shape, command lower animals, immobilize humans with their bites, and drain a man's life essence, et cetera, et cetera, et cetera. Other than that, they are no different from you or me. Once they are discovered, they become vulnerable, so they do all they can to maintain secrecy.

'Most importantly you must remember that a vampire's powers lie in his burial shroud. If you can take that from him, he cannot shift shape or flee, and you will have him at your mercy. Some vampires will even stop struggling entirely, get down on their knees and beg for their shroud back. Therein lies the essence of their immortality. If you burn the shroud, you are left with a weak, bloodsucking leech in the shape of a human with little ability to fight back, other than its fists. As long as you know what you are facing, you will be safe. Simply do not let them gang up on you.'

'Are you really serious?' Steven asked. 'Do you really expect me to return to Serbia, go into the tunnels under Petrovaradin, find some secret chamber and see if it's full of vampires? There's no way!'

'Not just that. If the seals have been disturbed you must enter and retrieve an item for me.'

'Retrieve an item? You're crazy!' But curiosity got the better of him and he added: 'What kind of item?'

'Nothing really, simply a small package,' Slatina said elusively.

'What's in the package? You've already sent me out once without telling me what was happening. If you think it's going to happen again, then forget it.'

Slatina looked at him carefully.

'It is my journal.'

'Your journal? Then why don't you go get it?'

'I cannot. I will be arrested.'

'What's so important about your journal?' Steven asked.

'These twelve were clever and powerful and had mostly disappeared from view. A smart vampire moves far away and blends into his surroundings making him nearly unnoticeable. He may run a business by day, surround himself with lackeys who protect him, and use his wiles to kill his victims in a manner attributable to everyday violence. Yet we found their Achilles heel. A vampire must return to its grave every Good Friday. We found their graves, and – if you will – staked them out,' he chuckled at his pun.

Steven winced and rolled his eyes.

'I recorded the final resting places of the eleven. If they have not moved their graves, it will be a useful tool to recapture and kill them, especially those who are concealed.'

'But Easter's almost a year away,' Steven said.

'It will not be easy. It took us nearly four years to round up the twelve. Some were hundreds of years old when I captured them and had amassed substantial fortunes. If they are free they will recover their treasure and use it to re-enter society.

'This is a struggle against darkness, against the Adversary. I am asking you to help me revive the Order of the Dragon and fight the kingdom of the Devil. I need your goodness and your honesty. I need the strength of your faith.' Slatina gazed directly into Steven's eyes, but this time without his eyes turning feline red.

A long silence followed, during which Steven heard every tick of his own wristwatch.

'Is there no one else?' he asked.

'I need someone right now who is honest, with a good heart, and who understands what is at stake,' Slatina replied. 'I frankly do not have the time to find and train someone else. Too much is happening far too quickly. If they have escaped, then I fear they may try to reunite their quorum under the command of the Vlach. Something has torn apart the once-proud Yugoslavia with ease and is feasting on its life's essence. If it is them, they must be halted before the scourge spreads further.'

Steven looked at his hands for a long time before again looking Slatina in the eyes.

'Then I will help you. But who is the Vlach?'

'Ah,' Slatina smiled grimly. 'He is known to you as Vlad Dracula.'

* * *

That evening, as they sat on the terrace watching the lights of Budapest and drinking wine, Slatina said matter-of-factly: 'Steven, I must rebuild the Order, and I would like your help. Throughout its history the Order always had a monarch as its patron. But now there are no longer emperors or kings, nor are there great powers willing to intervene. As long as the chaos lasts the vampires will profit. It is in their interest to prolong the chaos, as it makes their lives easier. The resulting wars will see more people infected with this evil. The Order must be restored to its former power and influence, or the curse will spread upon the face of the earth.'

Thanks to investments made on behalf of the Order hundreds of years earlier, Slatina had enormous wealth at his disposal, money invested throughout the world, via a network of holding companies. Yet money could not buy what he sought: a sovereign as patron who could place the full power and might of his state behind the Order. Approaching a foreign intelligence service was ruled out, as he knew that the Order would end up being manipulated. Forming a special corporation would do no good, as it would have no credible reason to enter the war-torn region. He could turn to the Vatican, but the current Pope had sided with the Croats and had no real power even in Croatia. A small mercenary army could not operate openly in Bosnia, Croatia, Kosovo, Montenegro or Serbia without attracting the attention of the local forces or the United States, Russia and the European Union. He felt stymied.

During the next several days Slatina taught Steven more than he had imagined possible. Steven listened raptly and enjoyed the myriad digressions the professor made as every little thing sidetracked him into some long-lost memory. Slatina liked to walk while talking, and in this manner they covered much of Budapest. Slatina taught Steven how to open the locks to the chamber under Petrovaradin and began training him to fight vampires. Steven discovered that for this, being left-handed was a useful gift.

'In a fight, a right-handed person leads with his left,' Slatina showed him, as they stood in front of a large punching bag. 'A left-handed person leads with his right hand, so it gives you an advantage and keeps the left side of your body away from their teeth. When you fight a vampire, just remember everything you learned in wrestling, and don't let it sink its teeth into you.' He also helped Steven recognize some of the external signs, particularly the bloating.

Every evening they watched CNN, BBC and Sky News on television. Slatina paid rapt attention to the stories coming from the Balkans that showed besieged Sarajevo, refugee camps, and most of all, the politicians and warlords. On one occasion, he drew Steven's attention to a baby-faced paramilitary commander who passed briefly across the screen in back of a group of politicians and said: 'That one is a vampire.' When Steven asked how he knew, Slatina said simply: 'I can tell.' Then added: 'War brings out the noblest and basest instincts in man. It is a perfect breeding ground for the spread of evil. We have much work ahead of us.'

Slatina wondered how Steven would face the challenges ahead. The darkness was now encompassing Bosnia, as the terror left no human life untouched. Each day they listened to gruesome and horrifying testimonies of ethnic cleansing, mass murders, mass rapes and the wanton destruction of entire villages. Steven's mission took on a new sense of urgency and he became anxious to leave.

'There is something else you must do,' Slatina said. 'Today we shall purchase a television and video recorder for you to take back to Serbia. I want you to tape the news and talk shows. I must see whether vampires are present in public life.'

'How can you tell who's a vampire?'

'As I told you, I have special talents…they cannot hide from my gaze,' Slatina said grimly.

Steven wondered about his other special talents. The two homes on Castle Hill seemed overrun with butterflies, and on several occasions he could have sworn he had seen Slatina whispering to them.

* * *

After a week of brainstorming the Order's reincarnation and learning about vampires, on Friday Steven bade farewell to Slatina. By mutual agreement Steven would travel to Petrovaradin, examine the vampires' chamber, retrieve the journal, and then proceed to Belgrade, where he would tape the local television news and talk shows for Slatina to scan for vampires. Steven would stay for two weeks and then return to Budapest. Slatina had instructed him to get a map of the Petrovaradin underground from Mrs. Lazarevic and to find out from her how to access the chamber. His final words to Steven were: 'Trust no one.'

Steven took the mini-bus back to Novi Sad on Friday. Although the television and VCR attracted the attention of the Serbian customs officials, a twenty Deutsche Mark banknote resolved the issue quickly. 'I'm learning, Neso,' Steven said to himself.

He arrived at Mrs. Lazarevic's home shortly after mid-day and she greeted him warmly: the first question she asked was: 'What did Marko tell you?'

After lunch she brought out a large flat map case, from which she withdrew a sprawling yellowed diagram on thick parchment, over a meter long and half a meter wide. At first glance it appeared to be nothing more than an intricate series of star-shaped geometric lines with interconnecting and crisscrossing diagonals. But an intricate hand-stenciled legend read *Souterrain-Plan der Festung Peterwardein, in Dermahlen Befintligen Stant Nebs. Denen Mayerhoffen und Umbligenden Schantzen, anno 1797*, with a scale of 1:4000. It was a map of the fortress' defenses and underground corridors from 1797. 'You will copy this,' she said.

She drew his attention to the markings. 'The fortress has four underground levels in the Labyrinth, and each intersection has a marble tablet or marker stating the name of the corridor. The lettering on the tablets is color-coded: red for the first level, green the second, blue the third and black the fourth. That way you can keep from getting lost, if you know which level you are on and have a map. If you don't, then you could starve to death down there if your batteries die. So you must have a guide.'

'Professor Stojadinovic will lead us. He says he knows the underground galleries well.'

'No one knew them better than my Rade,' Mrs. Lazarevic said. 'He was stationed here as a soldier until the outbreak of World War Two, and he could find his way around the tunnels in the dark. There is also a fifth level. My Rade and Marko built it long ago, and it is unknown to anyone else…you read about that in the archives.'

'Yes. And Professor Slatina told me about it in detail.' He studied the map more closely. 'But the fifth level isn't on this map.'

'Do you see this passageway here, where it says *IV/500 Kom. Gall.*, and then it leads to *IV. H.G. 507*?'

He stared at the faded print in the maze of intersecting lines. 'Yes.'

'In this passageway lies the entrance to the fifth level,' she stated matter-of-factly, 'where they interred the eleven vampires.'

'Have you been there?'

'Yes, many times. But the ground water rose and flooded the entrance to the lower chamber, so neither Rade nor I have checked the seals for more than fifteen years. Now even parts of the fourth level are flooded.

'What's it like, this chamber? What's in it?'

'Just vampires in coffins. If they are still there, then they are very, very hungry. And angry.'

'Are they still there?'

'I think they escaped years ago,' she said with a polite smile. 'When you go tomorrow, make certain everyone stays together. Have Professor Stojadinovic lead you to the entrance to the fifth level, but make certain he doesn't know that you know. I will tell you how to open the lock. If the seals are intact, just leave them as they are.'

'Is it safe?' Steven asked.

'Yes. Marko has always been a strong, good man, but he is a fool sometimes when it comes to women. It is because of a woman that this is happening.'

'A woman?'

'Never mind. We shall speak only about what is important, not gossip,' Mrs. Lazarevic said, reprimanding herself again. 'You will be safe.'

'Are you sure?' Steven said, his voice uncertain.

'Yes. If they escaped there is no reason for them to linger in the Labyrinth. They will have moved to another location. Take Marko's journal and leave.'

'Are you sure I'll be okay?'

'Steven, if I let you do anything dangerous my Katarina would never forgive me. Now, make certain you take a dry pair of socks and a warm jacket. It's chilly down there, and I don't want you to catch cold. And I will make some fresh apple strudel to take with you…'

She reminded him of his mother, and he smiled.

'Now, I shall make you a warm supper. I hope you like garlic.'

* * *

Interlude IX: Vakufgrad, Bosnia and Herzegovina: April 1992

The Serb-controlled Yugoslav People's Army had encircled the town two days earlier and begun lobbing artillery shells indiscriminately into the town center every so often, simply to frighten the inhabitants. From inside there was no contact with the outside world. All phone lines had been cut, there was no electricity or running water, and army roadblocks prevented the residents from leaving the terror of the bombardment. The town was defenseless, the only weapons at the residents' disposal being a few scattered hunting rifles. People huddled in their cellars or on the ground floors of their homes seeking refuge from the incoming shells.

Their Serb neighbors had all left a few days earlier, and the remaining members of the town council sent a delegation to the army to announce that the town was open and undefended. But the army maintained the roadblocks and the cordon around the town, while continuing to sporadically lob shells on the defenseless inhabitants.

Low clouds and a heavy mist descended on the town as the weather turned everything murky, the only color coming from the fires started by artillery. Buildings shuddered with the impact of high explosives on concrete, brick and plaster. A few bodies lay in the streets, persons unlucky enough to be caught in the open when the shelling started. The artillery tore apart cars, peppered street-lights and light posts with shrapnel, demolished storefronts, shattered and cracked windows and rained dust everywhere. The townspeople found themselves caught in a hell they could not flee.

At dusk the artillery fire lifted and a small convoy of dark jeeps and military trucks approached the army roadblock to the east of town, a black Mercedes SUV in the lead. A tinted window lowered and the commander looked at the regular army officer manning the roadblock.

'You have orders to let us pass.'

The officer in charge nodded grimly, recognizing the face in the Mercedes as belonging to a man whose nickname – *Ris* or Lynx – instilled fear in the hearts of all who heard it. 'We've softened up the town for you. There'll be no resistance. Just send them out to us and we'll send them to refugee camps.'

'How we do our job is none of your business,' Lynx said arrogantly, shifting his silenced Heckler & Koch MP5 machine pistol in his hands as he petted a small wolf cub on the seat beside him. He disappeared behind his tinted window and the convoy drove on towards the town center.

The Wolves descended on the village at nightfall, wool balaclavas covering their heads, their shoulders sporting a patch with a ravenous wolf's head, jaws open, teeth glistening. They waved large Bowie knives, Kalashnikovs and German Heckler & Koch MP3 rifles as they rousted people from their homes and lined them up in their yards, shooting indiscriminately. One Wolf formed ten captives in a line, let his men place bets, then pressed his pistol against the skull of the last man and pulled the trigger. Three fell over dead and the winner collected his jackpot.

They herded the inhabitants into the local high school auditorium. The Lynx walked among them, patted the children on their heads and gave them candy. He then left them without food, water or the use of toilet facilities for the next four days, the men on the right side, the women and children on the left. They took the more attractive women and girls to a local motel, where the Wolves satisfied their lusts in a non-stop orgy of gang-rape that lasted until the women passed out, and continued even after.

They came for the men individually, starting with the mayor and town councilmen, then local business leaders and anyone with a university degree. The Wolves bound their hands behind their backs with wire and dragged them from the auditorium as their wives and children screamed and protested. The screams and shrieks of the tortured echoed down the school hallways day and night, filling those in the auditorium with terror as they awaited their turn. Sometimes the Wolves would throw a lucky survivor back into the auditorium, too badly beaten to walk or crawl. More often than not, they were never seen again.

Lynx took over the mayor's office. The Wolves brought him a prisoner every several hours, hands bound. After inhumanly loud sessions of torture, Lynx would throw each victim's bloodless corpse out the window into the parking lot below.

While he feasted, the increasingly bloated commander ordered his troops to strip all the homes and buildings of anything of value: jewelry, toilets, hot water heaters, stereos, televisions, washing machines, sinks, door and window frames, electric fixtures, personal possessions, even books. They loaded everything onto trucks that disappeared in the direction of Serbia to be sold on the black market. Those cars still able to run were also taken. When everything of value had been stripped from the homes, they were put to the torch or demolished with explosive charges.

On the third day a Wolf brought a man to Lynx, bent with age over a gnarled cane, born – he said – when a Sultan still ruled Bosnia. 'He says he has information that he'll give only you, boss.'

The old man stood hunched before Lynx, lifted his eyes and stared the commander in the eye. 'I know what you are,' he said knowingly, pulling a Hawthorne cross from his shirt. 'And I know what you want.'

'Don't waste my time, old man,' Lynx growled.

'The Vlach…I know where he hides.'

Lynx jumped to his feet. 'The Vlach?! Where?' He shrieked, grabbed the old man and lifted him off his feet. 'Tell me before I break all your bones and suck you dry.'

The old man stared at him impassively. 'You can do nothing to me that time has not already done.'

'What do you want?'

'Freedom for my children and grandchildren and great-grandchildren and their safe passage to Hungary.'

'You ask for much.'

'I offer much.'

'How do you know such information? How do I know you can be trusted?'

'We are Saxons. My ancestors came as miners and constructed his lair.'

'Tell me where he is,' Lynx snarled furiously, shaking the old man again. But he said nothing.

The next day the Wolves turned over most of the surviving women and children to the Army for processing and transfer to refugee centers. The most attractive ones were taken away to be sold as sex slaves. The surviving male prisoners, their hands bound behind their backs, were loaded in trucks and driven away to a special detention camp, or as Lynx so artlessly put it: 'food storage.'

Lynx left Vakufgrad with an elderly passenger beside him on the seat of his SUV, while two trucks full of men, women and children and their belongings headed for Hungary.

CHAPTER TEN

THE CHAMBER OF CROSSES

Petrovaradin, Belgrade: 16 May 1992

Steven sat in front of the old officers' club on the Petrovaradin terrace and looked across the Danube, apprehension etched on his face as distant, towering banks of black thunderclouds drove a strong wind before them. From their base threads of lightning darted earthward, chasing the scent of rain and fresh ozone. Frantic waiters scurried across the wind-swept terrace, chasing runaway tablecloths and tumbling sun umbrellas. He felt the occasional large, isolated drop of rain fall from the light grey clouds overhead.

'How was Budapest?'

Steven jumped at Stojadinovic's voice and slammed his knee against the table. Only Stojadinovic's quick reflexes kept Steven's glass from falling to the ground, but the professor winced in pain as he caught the glass. 'Damn it,' Stojadinovic said. 'My back.' He sat down gingerly, across the table from Steven. 'It's an old injury.'

'Sorry.' Steven was jittery. 'You scared me.'

'No problem. Steven, I don't wish to be rude,' Stojadinovic said. 'But you smell of garlic.' He wrinkled his nose in disgust.

'I ate dinner at a friend's house. Her mom fixed meat with garlic, garlic mashed potatoes, baked peppers in oil with garlic, garlic soup and fresh salad with garlic. And for dessert there was an onion pie.'

'Yes, I can tell from over here.' Stojadinovic winced, pulling his scarf over his nose. 'Waiter, double scotch,' he called, then turned to Steven and grinned sheepishly: 'Hair of the dog…so how is Professor Slatina? What'd he say about your research?'

'Not much. He's okay,' Steven said.

'What's that?' Stojadinovic inquired, pointing to the hand-drawn map on the table.

'It's the Petrovaradin underground. I traced it.'

'Where'd you find it?' Stojadinovic was suddenly quite curious. 'In all my years of research I've never seen such a detailed map.'

Steven hesitated, not wishing to lie, yet remembering Mrs. Lazarevic's advice: 'Trust no one.' He chose his words carefully. 'It's from a friend. She's from an old family here in Petrovaradin. The daughter's in the US, and they let me copy it.'

'That's the problem with Serbia: all our best families and people are moving abroad and taking priceless heirlooms with them,' Stojadinovic muttered angrily. 'A map that valuable should've remained in the country and been placed in a proper archive, but then the archives probably wouldn't know how to take care of it. There are few reliable maps of the Petrovaradin underground remaining, and this one looks more accurate than any I've seen.'

Relieved, Steven didn't correct Stojadinovic's incorrect conclusion.

'What's this you have marked on the map?'

'It's a section I want to see. I heard there's a Maltese cross on the wall.'

'You're in luck. That's exactly where I'll be taking you today, because that's where I think the lock is and where I had that trouble in 1983. I even brought some rope, so if anyone's interested they can climb through the hole and see what's under the floor.' He opened his backpack to show Steven, who shivered in anticipation of what they might find. 'But I'm afraid I won't be able to do much, not with my back acting up…it's between the fourth and fifth vertebrae,' he added.

A large drop of rain hit Steven on the forehead, and he quickly folded the map.

'Haallooooooo....Steeefaaan.'

Steven turned to see Vesna run across the terrace, dressed in blue jeans, dark hair falling across her old flannel shirt and dark blue windbreaker. Her smile dispelled the darkness of the gathering clouds. She ran up and hugged him, kissing him on the cheeks.

'Blyak!!! You smell like garlic!' she exclaimed, smiling. 'Your breath is awful!' And then she moved in and hugged him again, this time a little longer. 'This is horrible,' she said. For a brief moment all thoughts of vampires and his commitment to his studies disappeared.

He didn't notice Bear and Tamara as they walked towards them. 'Hi Stefan,' they said. 'Hello Professor Stojadinovic.'

'Stefan is Mr. Stinky.' She hugged him tightly around his waist and laid her head against his chest, smiling at the others.

They walked the length of the fortress to the Hornwerk section, ignoring the sporadic, yet increasingly frequent drops of rain, Vesna holding Steven's arm while Bear and Tamara listened to Stojadinovic explain the Fourth Imperial Grenadier Company. Finally they came to a high arching brick vault in the steep grassy hillside at the edge of the St. Elizabeth Bastion, barred by a massive wooden door. Steven noticed an orange and black butterfly perched above the arch on the stone tablet with the word *MINEN* carved on it. The butterfly opened and closed its wings several times as Steven regarded it warily, then decided it was not the one from the book store and relaxed, all the while asking himself if he was crazy for fearing a butterfly.

'It's the *Vanessa cardui*, what the French call "la belle dame",' Stojadinovic gestured at the butterfly, then removed his sunglasses, revealing bloodshot eyes and a puffy face. 'I believe in English they call it the Painted Lady. We have them everywhere.' He took a key from his pocket and pulled on the padlock that held the door shut. As he did so the entire door fell against his shoulder. Steven and Bear jumped to his aid and grabbed the heavy door, wrestling it away.

'Damn! My back,' Stojadinovic winced. 'Someone's been here and removed the hinges.'

Steven touched his backpack, reassured by the stake inside.

'Pay attention now,' Stojadinovic said. 'This is the second largest fortress in Europe, after the fortress at Verdun in France. But Petrovaradin has more underground tunnels than Verdun, and it was not destroyed during the First World War.'

They turned on their flashlights and climbed down a narrow stairway to a vaulted tunnel of brick covered with flaking white plaster. A crunching noise echoed up as they trod on broken glass, plastic bags, condoms and animal bones that carpeted the dirt floor. Their flashlights revealed graffiti-covered walls: "Mirko was here," "Nikola is a fag" and "Red Star #1".

The yellowish flashlight beams played tricks with the darkness, as shadows appeared and disappeared suddenly in the most unexpected places, the light darting and flowing. Colors seemed less crisp to the eye, faded and bleached by the flashlights. They continued down a long, sloping passageway until

Stojadinovic's flashlight illuminated a three-way junction defended by a bunker with musket ports.

'Everyone remain together,' Stojadinovic called. 'Make certain you know who's in back of you, and if they're not there, then yell loudly and we'll go back for them. If you get separated, yell loudly and stay put. And Steven, because you stink of garlic you may bring up the rear.' As the others laughed, Stojadinovic turned left, followed by Bear, Tamara, Vesna and Steven.

Suddenly they felt a faint rumbling shake the earth. 'Thunder,' Stojadinovic said as he looked at the floor.

'Will the tunnels flood?' Bear asked.

'No. Ground water rises slowly: sometimes it takes a year for a one centimeter rise,' the professor answered.

As they continued down more tunnels, ramps and steps, Steven traced their progress with difficulty on his map. Everywhere his light shone on graffiti, cigarette butts and beer bottles.

'Is there a café in here?' Bear joked, making them laugh.

When they reached the second level Stojadinovic turned off his flashlight and motioned for them to do the same. They stood in the dark for some time, until he mumbled something to himself and then turned on his flashlight. 'Did you hear anything?' he asked.

The four shook their heads.

'Sometimes people come down here with a mind to do mischief. I've never had any problems, but its better we surprise them than they surprise us. You'll notice there's no light here whatsoever.' He motioned for them to follow.

They now felt the temperature drop substantially and they could see the vapor from their breath waft across the beams of their flashlights. Then they descended another level, or so Steven assumed, because of the blue lettering on the tablets.

'Ow, my ankle,' Tamara cried, stopping to lean against the wall.

Steven shined his light at her feet to see that the floor was no longer smooth, but was now littered with wet, slimy bricks, strewn haphazardly. As they proceeded, cobwebs clung to their faces and hair, as the ceiling lowered, forcing them to stoop in places.

'This is gross,' Vesna said, wiping grey cobwebs from her mouth.

'Anyone ever play Dungeons and Dragons?' Steven asked.

'Yeah.' Bear's voice came from the front. 'I'll buy a scroll of mapping.'

'I'll sell you mine.' Steven answered with a chuckle.

'You're such geeks,' said Tamara.

'The bricks,' Stojadinovic interrupted, 'are here because of the French.' He stopped to check that everyone was still there. 'During the Napoleonic Wars the Austrian Emperor sent the Imperial Treasury here to prevent

Napoleon from stealing it. To this day rumors persist that it's still hidden under the fortress. People come seeking gold…they tap on the walls, and when they hear what sounds like a hollow spot they tear out the bricks in hopes of finding the Austrian Imperial Treasury. Of course it's silly, but this leads to tunnel collapses and cave-ins and is slowly undermining this magnificent fortress.'

The journey seemed to lack direction, and lacking outside reference, time lost all meaning as they followed Stojadinovic down galleries and passageways, all intersected at angles by other tunnels that mimicked the star-shaped fortress' geometry. At one point Stojadinovic stopped and again motioned for silence. He shined his powerful flashlight down the corridor to their rear, but there was nothing to be seen except the empty tunnel trailing off into darkness.

After resting, they continued past passageways leading off at regular intervals. In one gallery, miniature stalagmites rose from the floor: in another, a small stalactite drooped from the ceiling. A rustling from the inter-floor ventilation shaft drew their attention to a family of bats, hanging upside down.

'Bats give me the creeps,' Tamara moaned. 'Let's keep moving.'

'Wouldn't it be cool if there are vampires here?' Bear asked. 'Wouldn't this be the perfect place for them?'

'Bear, stop it right now or Vesna and I will leave!' Tamara said her voice trembling.

'Stefan stinks so badly of garlic that he's scared off every vampire within a kilometer of us,' Bear said. Vesna and Tamara laughed a little too heartily, trying to cheer themselves up.

If they only knew, Steven thought to himself as he felt the stake through his backpack, then pressed Katarina's cross to his throat.

'Shhhh.' Stojadinovic motioned once again for silence and doused his light. The others did the same and they all heard a faint noise behind them, possibly emanating from one of the side tunnels. All held their breath and waited in a total absence of sound: but the noise was gone. Stojadinovic exhaled and whispered 'I think we're being followed. Let's wait just a bit longer.'

They sat, and as they became accustomed to the stillness they heard water drip. Vesna cuddled closer to Steven and laid her head on his shoulder, while Bear and Tamara began kissing. After what seemed like hours, the professor switched on his light. 'Let's go,' he said. 'We're getting closer.'

They followed him down one more level where the lettering on the tablets changed to black. 'Is this the fourth level?' Steven asked.

'Yes. Stay together,' Stojadinovic answered brusquely, turning and looking back to make certain everyone was there.

Steven touched a wall, felt the damp and slime: dripping water and mold.

His light revealed several flooded side-tunnels, some to a depth of only a few inches, while others sloped downwards until the ceiling descended below water-level. They then entered a part of the tunnel that had been widened into a tiny chamber with pointy Gothic arches. Stojadinovic examined a massive wooden door set on barrel-hinge posts that jutted from the stonework and tried it, but it was locked.

'This is strange.' Steven said, pointing to the arches. Their lights revealed a chamber that had once been blood-red, but was now faded orange, discolored by streaks of black mildew running down the walls. 'Why the Gothic arch and red walls? So far everything's been white plaster or red brick,' he said.

Stojadinovic answered: 'That's a good question. Some think this section of the tunnels, which is the deepest, is also the oldest. Yet that would be unusual, when you think that they typically dug the tunnels from the top level down. Why would this have been built first? Steven, I think we may have found answers in the archives, and they lie with the Fourth Imperial Grenadier Company. This may be their handiwork.' He withdrew a large iron skeleton key, slipped it into the lock and pulled the heavy gate open to reveal a tiny faded-red junction chamber with Gothic arches and iron hinges, passages branching off to the left and right. He shined his light on a marble plaque with black lettering: *IV/500 Kom. Gall.*, Communication Gallery 500, level four. The marble plaque on the intersecting corridor read *IV. H.G. 507.*, Listening Gallery 507, level four. But Stojadinovic continued forward.

'Professor, isn't this the tunnel with the cross?' Steven asked.

Stojadinovic spun around and walked back to look. He shined his light on the hand-drawn diagram and the marble signs. 'I haven't been here in many years and all the tunnels start to look the same after a while. I do believe Steven is right. Is everyone here? Yes? I shall go first.'

Stooping, the others followed him down the low tunnel to the left, trying to avoid small piles of bricks and shallow puddles of water that dotted the muddy floor. As they climbed over several mudslides flowing from side alcoves where treasure-hunters had removed bricks, they became increasingly muddy.

After 25 meters, Stojadinovic illuminated a red stone Maltese cross embedded in the right hand wall between two small round stones. 'I believe this is the famous lock we have heard so much about. The problem is to figure out how to open it. Of course, after all these years, and with all this water, it's probably rusted or jammed. Or it may not be the lock we are looking for. Steven, would you care to try it?'

Steven squeezed around Vesna, Tamara and Bear and approached the cross. 'Don't break it,' teased Vesna.

He pushed the upper tip, which gave way slightly, stiffly. 'It moved!' he cried excitedly. He began pressing each end of the cross, upper, left, right, lower, and each gave way slightly, only to pop back. Nothing else happened.

'Use a hammer,' Bear joked.

'Be gentle,' Vesna whispered playfully.

Steven pressed slowly at the very top of the cross, then the very bottom, then on the tip of the left arm, then the tip of the right arm. Then he pressed the middle. Then he pressed the round stones on either side, simultaneously. A loud pop from the passageway's end caused everyone to jump. Vesna and Tamara both yelped and grabbed Bear's arms, while Stojadinovic shone his light in the direction of the noise. 'Be careful, we don't wish to disturb anything or cause a cave-in. If this is the oldest section of the fortress, then it may be fragile. Everyone, please stay behind me.'

With the professor in the lead, they walked bent over until they met a solid wall.

'Where'd the sound come from?' Bear asked.

'From here,' Stojadinovic tapped the wall. It sounded solid, but as he pushed it, it gave way slightly. Everyone gasped. He pushed again, and this time it opened further. 'We've found something,' he said excitedly. We've really found something.' His face glowed animatedly.

Steven's heart raced. Would the seals be intact?

The professor pushed once again, and the wall swung completely open to reveal a stairwell, broader than the passageway, descending in a spiral to the right. They all crowded into the opening and Stojadinovic led them cautiously down the stairs, one hand on the faded blood-red wall.

'This is a major discovery,' Stojadinovic exulted. 'I must return with a camera.'

Tamara gazed intently at the plaster. 'Allegorically, the color red makes it seem as though we're making a descent into Hell, sort of like Dante's Inferno.'

'There you go again…too much literary criticism,' teased Bear. 'Read something worthwhile, like comics.'

As they wound their way down, their flashlights reflected off a pool of still crystal water that covered the steps, blocking further progress. 'Flooded, damn it!' the professor cursed loudly.

Steven let out a heavy sigh of relief. No vampires today, he thought. The seals are under water.

'I wonder where it leads,' said Tamara.

'Obviously there's a fifth level to this fortress,' said Stojadinovic. 'And I think there might be another way to get there.'

A different way? Steven felt an uncomfortable sensation in the pit of his stomach. Neither Slatina nor Mrs. Lazarevic had mentioned another entrance.

But Steven followed Stojadinovic as they returned to the top of the stairwell and pulled the wall shut. 'We don't want someone else finding this and vandalizing it,' Stojadinovic said.

They returned to the red Gothic junction chamber and followed Stojadinovic left about a dozen meters down Communication Gallery 500 until they came to a depression in the floor where the earth dropped several inches.

'Everyone stand back,' Stojadinovic warned them. 'This is where the floor dropped out on my group in '83. It's fragile and could collapse at any time.' As they shone their lights at the spot, the earthen floor turned suddenly to nothingness as gaping darkness spanned the width of the tunnel. Crossing would be difficult, if not impossible.

'It's much larger than I remembered,' Stojadinovic said. 'Let's lower the rope and see what's down there.' He returned to the junction chamber and tied the rope around an iron barrel-hinge post protruding from the stone door frame, unrolled it until it reached the hole and then tossed it into the darkness. After about six seconds they heard a splash echo back and forth from below.

'Whatever's down there, it's wet,' Stojadinovic said. 'I can't climb down with my back. Who would like to go see what's down there?'

Steven suddenly found himself volunteering. 'I'll go.' Only he knew the secret of the chamber and he felt responsible for the others. 'I did this all the time in Utah…rappelling, rock climbing, you know…it's no big deal.'

'I'll go too,' Bear chimed in. 'Girls, do you want to come with us?' Both shook their heads.

'Are you certain you know how to do this?' Stojadinovic asked. 'I don't want you getting injured down there.'

'It's okay,' Steven answered.

Vesna hugged Steven. 'Be careful, Stinky,' she whispered worriedly in his ear. 'I'll be up here waiting for you.'

Steven adjusted his backpack tightly around his shoulders, clipped his flashlight to a lanyard around his neck, grasped the rope firmly in both hands and approached the opening head-first, peering slowly over the edge into the darkness below. He shined his light into the hole: 'It looks like a large room,' he said. 'I can't see much…there's water at the bottom…it's at least seven or eight meters down, maybe nine, I think…there's a bunch of large rocks in the water.'

Rocks? Or were they coffins? The hair on the back of Steven's neck stood on end. The chamber was breached! Had the eleven escaped? What if the vampires were still inside? Was Slatina's journal still there? He shined his flashlight around the chamber, uncertain whether to proceed further. His small light illuminated only bits of the murky void, but curiosity and a sense of duty drove him on. 'Bear, you better stay and protect the ladies,' Steven said, only half joking.

He swung around and lowered himself feet-first down the rope, his flashlight hanging from his neck. 'Can you shine your lights down here?' he called. 'It's hard to see.' The others obliged. Steven slid down the rope into a large, round domed chamber.

He shinnied further, his legs wrapped tightly around the rope, his flashlight shining downward. A drop of water fell and hit his head. He looked up and saw Stojadinovic, Vesna and Bear looking into the hole after him. He stopped and looked directly down. 'It looks shallow,' he called up to them.

'Be careful in the water,' Stojadinovic called back. 'It may be muddy or there may be a hole. You don't want to slip and drown.'

Steven lowered himself until the soles of his boots were just above the surface. The water was perfectly clear and absolutely still, except for small ripples sent out by the rope wiggling serpent-like in the water. Again he inched down the rope until his boots entered the water; then his jeans. He immediately began to shiver.

'It's cold,' he called up. A few more inches and the water reached his crotch, just as his feet touched a solid surface.

'I'm on the bottom,' he called. He let loose the rope and unhooked his flashlight from the lanyard. He breathed rapidly, his heart pounding from the adrenalin and cold.

Steven shined his light around the chamber's dome and walls, which seemed uneven, undulating. It must be the gloom, he thought, as he gazed at the mold-darkened crosses jutting in ragged relief from the red-orange plaster walls, interlaced with splotches of white hedgehog fungus and long, thick mushrooms, their shafts dangling downward from the ceiling like tumescent phalluses.

As Steven waded, his feet stirred up a thin layer of silt from what appeared to be a paved stone floor. Close by a reddish-black cross rose straight from the chamber floor. He could see that mold obscured an inscription of some sort.

Bear splashed down loudly beside Steven, sending waves through the chamber. 'Damn, its cold!' he said. Both looked up at the professor. 'You should see this!' Bear called up with excitement. 'It's amazing'!'

Stojadinovic smiled. 'What do you see?'

'Coffins,' Steven said loudly. 'Eleven coffins. And a large cross.'

'Coffins?!' exclaimed Tamara. 'We should leave. Bear, come back. Right now! I want to leave!'

'Don't panic. We're okay,' Bear assured her. 'We're just going to look around a little.'

Steven's heart quickened as he approached the first coffin. Through its partially open lid he saw it was empty, save for the skeletal remains of numerous rodents. As he approached the next coffin he felt a grotesque crunching underfoot as though treading on egg shells. He shined his light in the water and saw dozens of rodent skeletons on the chamber floor.

'There're rat bones everywhere.'

'Yeah, here too,' Bear called from the next coffin. 'This is gross.'

After the eighth empty coffin, Steven waded over to examine the large cross, relieved that Mrs. Lazarevic was right and that the vampires had indeed gone.

'No vampires down here,' Bear called up to the girls. 'Just empty coffins and lots of dead rats.'

'Ooowww, that's sick,' Vesna said, her voice echoing off the water.

Steven rubbed at the mold on the cross with his sleeve. 'There's an inscription… it's in Latin,' he called out. 'It says… wait… something… something… *miseri*… *Deus*… *tus*… *et*… *ius*…Okay, I got it.' He continued rubbing at the mold. 'It says *O quam misericors est Deus, Justus et Pius.*' Steven didn't say that it was the motto of the Order of the Dragon.

'Interesting,' Stojadinovic said.

Steven walked around the backside of the cross and glanced up. High in the center of the cross-piece he found what he had come for: a small votive statue of St. George. He stood on tiptoes, reached behind the statue and felt a waxy package. Was it Slatina's journal?

'Have you found anything?' Stojadinovic called.

Steven hesitated. 'Trust no one,' he told himself, once again repeating Mrs. Lazarevic's advice. 'Nothing,' Steven said.

'Hey, look at this,' Bear said from across the chamber. 'There's a cross here that looks just like that secret lock.'

'What kind?' Stojadinovic called, shining his light towards Bear.

'Maltese, just like the other one.'

While the two were distracted, Steven quickly removed the package. The waxed surface was slick and it slipped from his fingers, bounced off his chest and fell. He bobbled and caught it quickly, just before it hit the water's surface. Making sure no one was looking, he slipped it in his backpack.

'This water's freezing',' Bear said with a shiver.

'Bear, come back now!' shouted Tamara. Her voice was panicky. 'I'll warm you up. Hurry!'

'How about you Stefan?' Vesna called. 'Do you need warming up?'

Steven noticed one coffin riding lower in the water than the others, its lid still in place. Was it still occupied? If so, was it a vampire? His stomach churned. 'Bear, give me a hand,' he called. Steven pulled the stake from his backpack as he approached the coffin.

'What the hell is that?' Bear asked as he waded closer, sending small waves through the water, rocking the coffins. 'Did you come to kill vampires?'

'Pull back the lid,' Steven said brusquely.

'I'll give you some light.' Stojadinovic's voice echoed down from above. Then he saw the stake in Steven's hand: 'What are you holding, Steven?'

'Just a stick I found.'

Bear wrestled with the lid, trying to get a firm grip on the slick, moldy wood while Steven's adrenal glands kicked into high. Bear pulled the lid back suddenly with a single powerful movement.

Steven looked into the coffin, doubled over and began retching in the water.

'Stefan, are you all right?' Vesna shouted.

'Bear, what's going on? Answer me now!' Tamara's voice screamed.

Bear looked in the coffin, paled and turned away gasping for air. 'Lord God, this is sick. This is so...oh God!' He looked at Steven, who was still doubled over, gagging. 'What the hell's going on?'

In the coffin lay a man's body, stripped naked and white from lack of blood, his throat brutally torn open to expose the jugular vein and vertebrae. His genitals had been torn off and shoved in his mouth and other signs of torture were evident. It was Niedermeier, the bookseller.

Steven's vomit had discolored the otherwise clear water and portions of lunch floated on the surface. The smell of garlic-scented stomach acid pervaded the chamber. 'Oh dear Lord, oh dear Lord,' Steven repeated, breathing rapidly. 'Tell me this isn't happening.'

'What is it?' shouted Tamara, now hysterical. 'What's going on? Climb out of there at once. At once, do you hear me? Come back right now!'

Vesna's calmer voice also penetrated the chamber: 'Are you all right Stefan? Do you need help?'

Steven stumbled to the stone cross and held on for support.

Then suddenly there was a splash. Bear and Steven spun around to see the rope slowly coiling downward to the bottom of the pool.

Above them, Steven and Bear saw nothing except the edge of the hole and dim shadows from flashlights playing erratically off the tunnel wall above. They heard Tamara shout hysterically: 'What are you doing, you creep?' And then she screamed. 'You freak, get away from me!'

Vesna too began screaming, but it sounded somehow distant as though she was further away from the hole. 'Oh my God!! No!! Oh Lord have mercy! Oh, Lord have mercy.' It was both a scream and a desperate prayer for help. 'No, No! Oh my God, please help!' Her voice was hysterical and frantic.

Bear and Steven waded directly under the hole. 'Professor! Tamara! Vesna!' they both shouted loudly. They heard only the girls' panicked screams of terror and stood there, helpless.

Both girls fell silent, and the only sound came from the frantic breathing of Bear and Steven.

Then Stojadinovic appeared at the edge. As he looked down at them he smiled wickedly, his incisors elongated and sharp, blood dribbling down his chin.

'Ha…ha…ha…very funny,' Steven said. 'Did Vesna put you up to this?'

'Good one, Professor,' Bear called, picking up the rope. 'Catch.' He threw it up, but Stojadinovic made no move to grab it.

Stojadinovic licked his lips, raised his sleeve and wiped the blood from his chin.

'Professor,' said Steven. 'Please, not now.'

'Tamara, it's not funny,' Bear shouted. 'It's cold down here and there's a dead body. Stop fooling around.'

'Vesna, come on,' Steven called. 'Niedermeier's dead and this place is really starting to scare me.'

Stojadinovic simply stared.

'Professor,' shouted Steven angrily. 'Get us out of here. It's really not funny anymore.'

'Oh, my. You are in trouble, aren't you?' he taunted.

'Tamara, Vesna,' Bear shouted.

There was no answer.

Stojadinovic continued to watch them, nary a word leaving his lips. Then his eyes turned cat-shaped and began to glow red, like fiery coals.

And suddenly Steven understood everything: the professor's scarf, his night-owl behavior, his aversion to Steven's garlic stench, his apparent death a few years previously, and why Niedermeier had been convinced someone was feeding information to the DB.

'Oh, good Lord!' Steven exclaimed. 'you're not really…'

'Oh, but I most certainly am,' Stojadinovic chuckled. 'I apologize for leaving you here, but supper awaits. I'll return for you later when the garlic is out of your system. You shall make a lovely dessert.'

'Wha….?' Steven's shock was so thorough he couldn't even get the word out.

But Stojadinovic only grinned down at them, his incisors glistening moistly.

'Mother of God!' exclaimed Bear, his jaw open in disbelief. 'He's not really…I mean…there aren't…I mean…what the hell is going on?' he grabbed Steven. 'You've got a stake. Is this real?'

'Stop playing with your food,' a female voice commanded from somewhere above in the tunnel, then laughed in tones that froze the marrow in their bones.

Stojadinovic joined in the laughter. 'Poor Steven…so naïve…so trusting. I must go now. Supper awaits. Enjoy your stay down there. Bye-bye.' And then he was gone.

Again the female voice echoed from above as it said something unintelligible to Stojadinovic.

'But…' Steven spluttered, his jaw open, paralyzed with the realization that he had just seen a vampire.

'What the hell is this? Is he a vampire?' Bear demanded, shaking Steven.

'How the hell am I supposed to know?'

'You're the expert! You're Mr. Vampire. You know everything. You're the one who brought us here. What the hell is going on? Answer me! Is he a vampire?'

'Yeah,' Steven answered vaguely, as in a trance, staring at the hole above them.

Shaking his head, Bear began mumbling the Lord's Prayer: '*Oce nas, koji si na nebesima...*'

'The lock,' Steven said pointing to the wall and shaking Bear. 'Maybe we can open it.'

'Where?' Bear asked.

'Over there.' Steven waded rapidly towards the wall, pushing waves of water with each stride. 'It's just like the lock on the top door.' He waded quickly to the Maltese cross and pressed it as before: top, right, left, bottom, middle, then the two round stones. Nothing happened.

'Hurry,' urged Bear. 'He's killing them!'

Steven's hands trembled as he tried the combination again. 'Nothing!' Maybe he had it wrong. Top, left, right, bottom, middle. Again nothing.

'Stojadinovic, you son of a whore, I'll screw your mother and your father and your whole family in order!' yelled Bear. 'Come on Stefan, come on!' He shook Steven by the shoulders. 'Remember! You can do it!'

And then Steven remembered Slatina's instructions. He pressed the combination in the opposite sequence of the top lock: middle, bottom, left, right, top.

There was a small silent pop from behind the wall. Bear grabbed Steven, hugging him tightly. 'You did it, you did it!'

Without warning the brick wall burst open with tremendous force, propelled by a surge of water that ripped the hidden door from its hinges and sent a large wave across the room. The wave caught Steven and Bear in its grip, sweeping them under towards the center of the room. Steven held his breath and tried to paddle as best he could, but the stake in one hand and flashlight in another made swimming difficult. The weight of his clothes, backpack and boots dragged him down and the chilled water slowed his muscles. He finally struggled to his feet, gasping for breath. The water was chest height and rising rapidly. He made his way half-swimming, half-bouncing towards the cross in the center of the chamber.

Bear, with no stake or backpack to weigh him down, was already at the cross. Water continued to surge through the doorway. Bear held out a hand and pulled Steven towards him. The water was now almost six feet deep and still rising. Clinging to the cross, they watched the top of the door disappear under water. Soon they were sitting on the crosspiece, then kneeling, then standing.

Several inches below the top of the cross, the water stopped rising. Steven and Bear looked at each other, both breathing heavily and shivering.

Attracted by the noise, Stojadinovic appeared above the hole, the lower part of his face a mask of blood. 'Oh, my, what have you done? Please don't drown before I'm ready for dessert,' he snickered and then disappeared.

'Stojadinovic, you treacherous son-of-a-bitch,' Steven yelled loudly. 'I swear I'm going to kill you with my bare hands!'

'If you do anything to Vesna or Tamara, so help me God…' Bear yelled.

The ceiling was at least three meters above them and a coffin bumped into Steven.

'We can get out,' Steven said. 'The water's stopped rising, so it's reached equilibrium with the staircase. If we swim through the door we'll get to the staircase.'

'Okay,' Bear grunted. 'But I'm not sure my flashlight is waterproof like yours.' Already the bulb seemed dimmer.

Steven placed his stake and backpack on a coffin. They pushed the coffin towards the wall, hanging on its sides for flotation. At the wall, Steven looked at Bear, murmured 'Good luck,' took several deep breaths and dove down towards the doorway, his flashlight dim in the silty water, and pulled the bulky pack behind him as he furiously breast-stroked and frog-kicked. His buoyancy pushed him towards the ceiling, which quickly began sloping upward. It was slow going as he pulled the heavy pack through the water. He had swum ten meters and his lungs were about to burst, when his head finally broke the surface of the water and he felt air against his face. He gulped deep breaths of fresh air and paddled furiously towards the steps, where Bear sat, waiting.

'Hurry!' Bear said, his flashlight now flickering dimly.

Steven quickly removed the stake. 'We've got to kill Stojadinovic,' he said grimly.

They ran up the curved staircase, pulled the brick wall open and raced into the tunnel, Steven first, stake in hand. They came to the junction, turned left down Communication Gallery 500 and stopped, unprepared for what met them. There lay Tamara, Stojadinovic kneeling over her, gnawing the left side of her neck.

'Get away from her you bastard!' Bear shouted, unable to get around Steven in the narrow tunnel. Stojadinovic looked up, startled, as he wiped Tamara's blood from his lips. He rose to his feet, his body bloated from feeding.

'You think to challenge me while I feed? Do you not know what I am? Do you not fear my power?'

In the gloom of the tunnel behind Stojadinovic a shadowy figure knelt over Vesna. Startled by the commotion it looked up. Its long raven hair framed a pale face and lips tinted red by Vesna's blood. Steven thought he had seen the face before, but it couldn't be…in a portrait on the wall of Slatina's study in La Jolla…in his dreams…on the wall of Slatina's house in Budapest…a woman whom Slatina married more than 300 years ago…a woman who should be dead…yet here she was, sucking the life from Vesna's throat.

'Natalija!' blurted Steven in disbelief.

Her red feline eyes blazed with shock at being recognized, then struck Steven with a gaze that rooted him to the spot. He was stunned by her beauty and something else, as she rose, slender and graceful. 'Take them!' she commanded in a hissing voice.

Instantaneously Stojadinovic's face elongated as long hair sprouted from his skin, until it metamorphosed into a blunt canine snout with glistening razor-sharp teeth in an open mouth. Thick fur covered his skin and his fingernails elongated and thickened to become sharp claws. His stature remained the same, but fur now protruded from his shirt collar and shirt cuffs. The mane of newly-sprouted fur nearly covered his red eyes.

Steven froze as fear gripped his sinews and stopped his heart. Then something inside snapped and took control of him. As though propelled by an unseen power he rushed forward and grabbed the werewolf by the throat with his right hand. The suddenness of Steven's charge took the lycanthrope by surprise, driving it backwards until it tripped over Tamara's prostrate form and fell to the ground with Steven on top. Steven clenched it by the throat and raised his left hand high overhead, the stake ready to strike.

Growling, Stojadinovic fought furiously, grabbed Steven's left arm and stopped the stake from descending. His sharp claws ripped Steven's shirt and flesh, leaving painful gashes on his arms and chest. But Stojadinovic, repelled by Steven's garlicky stench, didn't try to bite him. Flailing claws made it painful for Steven to maintain his hold on the werewolf's throat, so he let go and jumped off.

Stojadinovic arose and swatted at the stake, growling: 'I'm going to disembowel you, boy!' He then screamed in pain as his paw touched the Hawthorne wood of the stake and his fur sizzled.

Steven parried the blow, wielding the stake rapier-like. He feinted a thrust, and as the werewolf lunged to swat it away, Steven kicked it firmly in the crotch. Stojadinovic dropped to his knees, clutched his groin with one hand and clawed blindly at Steven with the other, while emitting a horrible high-pitched yelp. The professor struggled to his feet and lashed out wildly. Steven feinted again with the stake, causing the hairy beast to step backwards towards the hole and lose his footing. As Stojadinovic teetered on the edge, paws wind-milling wildly, Steven thrust the stake at his chest. Sensing an opening, Steven quickly snatched Stojadinovic's scarf with his right hand and pulled. The loose scarf slipped easily off the werewolf's neck.

The werewolf howled loudly and instantly transformed back into human shape. Steven thrust directly at Stojadinovic's sternum. This time the stake penetrated the skin slightly, making a noise like a heated brand on cattle hide as smoke arose from the sizzling flesh. Stojadinovic screamed, stepped backwards, lost his footing, flailed his arms violently and toppled backward into the hole. There was a loud splash.

Steven looked around for the female vampire, only to see an orange and black butterfly with white spots flutter upwards into a ventilation shaft. Was it the same one that had been at the tunnel entrance? Had she transformed into a butterfly?

Behind him, Bear gently lifted Tamara's head, cradled her in his arms and began to sing her a lullaby in between sobs, as he tenderly rocked her lifeless body. 'You'll be okay,' he whispered, reassuring himself. 'You'll be okay.'

Steven rushed to Vesna and felt her pale neck for a pulse, bent over her mouth and listened for breath. Nothing. The vampire had sucked all life from her. He hugged her as anguish and guilt harrowed up his soul for bringing his friends down here and exposing them to this horror. 'Why didn't I come alone,' he asked himself. 'Why'd I drag them down here with me? Why'd I do this to Vesna?'

He stood, walked to the hole and shined the light down on the water to find that Stojadinovic had climbed into the casket with Niedermeier's body. Upon seeing Steven he cried out: 'My shawl! Give it back to me!'

Steven looked at him coldly. 'What's it worth?'

'Anything you desire, anything!'

'Where's Natalija?' demanded Steven.

'I can't tell you.' Stojadinovic wailed. 'She'll kill me if I do.' There was fear in his eyes.

'Who's Natalija?' Bear whispered.

'I'll kill you if you don't,' Steven threatened, ignoring Bear.

'First give me my shawl. I'll give you all my wealth.'

'I'm not naïve.' Steven sneered at Stojadinovic. 'If I give you the shawl you'll turn into a butterfly and fly away. Bear, have you got a cigarette lighter?'

'Yeah,' Bear handed him a silver Zippo. 'Why?'

Steven held the scarf above the hole for Stojadinovic to see, and then he lit the lighter and moved it close to the scarf. 'Where's Natalija?' he demanded. 'Tell me or I burn it.'

'No, please, I beg of you. No,' Stojadinovic implored. 'Please stop. She's at

Debauchery. Go to Debauchery and ask for her. Please, don't burn my shawl. Pleeeeease!'

Steven looked at Bear. 'What's Debauchery?'

'A night club.'

Steven turned to Stojadinovic. 'Where are the twelve?'

'What twelve?' Bear looked at Steven, bewildered.

'Where are they?' Steven repeated, ignoring Bear once again.

'Nooo. Give me back my shawl. I told you where Natalija is. She's one of them. Ask her.'

Steven set the scarf alight, causing Stojadinovic to writhe and howl in the coffin. 'Stop it. Stop it. Nooooooooo.'

Stojadinovic's scream sent chills through Steven's and Bear's hearts. When the shawl had burned nearly up to Steven's fingertips, he dropped it and watched the last glowing remnants as they wafted towards the water.

Steven looked at Bear and said: 'He's not going anywhere. Vampires suck in water.' Stake in hand, Steven jumped feet-first through the hole, landing with a splash. He plunged deep under the water and when he broke the surface he saw Stojadinovic in the coffin only a few feet away, rocking in the waves. He quickly paddled towards the coffin, gripping the stake. Inside the professor lay weeping and trembling.

Steven reached the edge of the coffin and grabbed the side for leverage. 'Why'd you burn my burial shroud?' Stojadinovic sobbed self-pityingly, immobilized by the trauma of his loss.

'This is for Vesna and Tamara!' shouted Steven angrily as he braced himself against the side of the coffin, raised his left hand and plunged the stake into Stojadinovic's bloated chest and through his heart. As the sharpened wood met flesh, a large geyser of blood spurted upward and sprayed Steven's face, while a column of smoke, ripe with the stench of seared flesh rose upward. Stojadinovic's dying shriek echoed interminably and sent dust falling from the ceiling, rippling the dark surface of the water. The Hawthorne tip had pierced the professor's back and the rotted coffin bottom beneath.

* * *

'Stefan,' Bear called down. 'Are you all right?'

Steven shuddered. Was he alright? He had just killed a man…if Stojadinovic could be called that. Or had he? Had he murdered Stojadinovic? Or a vampire? He struggled with what he had just done, still unable to believe vampires existed and that he had just killed one with a stake.

'Stefan?' Bear called again.

Steven looked up and nodded, then looked back at Stojadinovic. 'I'm not sure he's dead,' he called up to Bear.

'Huh? What do you mean? You just drove a stake through his heart. He's dead.'

'Yeah, but all the folk tales say you have to cut off the head and burn it.'

Bear's eyes widened. 'That's sick.'

'But what if he really is a vampire? What if the folk tales are right?'

Bear shuddered. 'Then do it. If the folk tales were right about the existence of vampires, then they're right about how to kill them.'

Steven began shaking from the cold and the trauma of killing a person that – until just a few moments ago – he had considered a friend and mentor. Yet he pulled a large knife from his backpack. 'Just in case,' Mrs. Lazarevic had said when handing it to him before he set out. 'Just in case.'

He flinched at the first cut, unable to watch. Then he sawed at Stojadinovic's neck, cutting rapidly through the flesh. The knife sliced easily, but slowed when he came to the vertebrae in the neck.

Steven hacked furiously, but the fresh human bone was resilient. Blood and scraps of flesh flew everywhere, coating Steven's face, hands and clothing. He pulled Stojadinovic's head back by the hair, stretched the neck, and then attacked a gap between two vertebrae. Finally the knife cut through and he held the head victoriously overhead, blood dripping from the severed jugular down his hand and sleeve to his shoulder. Steven withdrew the stake from Stojadinovic's chest and placed it, along with the knife and head, into his backpack and swam from the chamber.

Bear had placed both girls side by side and was kneeling over their pale bodies. Stojadinovic had savaged Tamara's neck, leaving the jugular gaping open. In contrast, the female vampire had left Vesna with two small neat puncture marks.

'They killed them,' Bear said in shocked disbelief. 'I can't believe they killed them. Those were real vampires.' And then he turned accusingly at Steven. 'You knew about this, didn't you? You knew vampires exist. You knew they'd be down here. That's why you brought the stake and ate garlic, isn't it? Answer me! How'd you know about the vampires?'

'Bear, I don't know...look, I'll…I'll explain later. It wasn't supposed to be like this. Let's get out of here before they come back. Can you carry Tamara? I'll get Vesna.'

Bear picked up Tamara's flashlight and looked around. 'Are they coming back?'

'I don't know,' said Steven. 'But I don't want to wait to find out.'

Bear picked up Tamara with a grunt, tossed her over his shoulder and headed back the way they had come. 'The door's locked,' he shouted as he reached the junction room.

Steven picked up Vesna, slid her over one shoulder and turned to follow Bear. Her body felt cold and her muscles stiff. He walked with deliberation, trying to convince himself that he couldn't have known…their tunnel expedition should have been simple and safe. Lost in these thoughts he felt a faint breath of warm air on his neck. Vesna moaned imperceptibly and then again a little louder.

'She's alive!' Steven shouted. 'I think she's alive.' He kissed her neck and whispered 'don't give up' in her ear.

Bear turned to see and smiled grimly. He placed Vesna's head between his large hands and kissed her gently on the forehead. 'How do we get out?' he asked.

'Stojadinovic didn't have a map. He just learned about this place by wandering around. There's a shorter way.' Steven pulled out the waterlogged map. 'Give me some light. My batteries are dying,' he said.

'Mine too,' said Bear. 'We need to conserve.' He switched his off and pulled out his Zippo lighter. They pored over the map and decided on a direction.

From the junction chamber Steven led them in the opposite direction of the secret door and through a maze of tunnels, using only one light to conserve batteries. Finally they came to a long tunnel that sloped upward. Steven and Bear sweated and struggled under their loads as they trudged up the slick, brick-strewn slope. They finally came to a junction with blue letters on the sign that told them they were on the third level.

Steven was almost as large as Bear, yet carrying the girls through the narrow, cramped tunnels was tiring, as he had the added burden of Stojadinovic's head and Slatina's journal in his backpack. He had to keep shifting Vesna to consult his map, all while holding the stake. From the third level Steven found a direct tunnel up to the second, and then a stairwell to the first. As they stopped to rest, Bear grabbed Steven and motioned for silence. Both stood there, puffing.

'Down here,' a hard male voice called from a tunnel to the right.

Steven motioned to Bear and both staggered into a bunker, hiding behind a wall with loopholes for muskets. They laid the girls on the floor and switched off their lights.

'Where now?' came another voice this time, nearer.

'Keep going straight. They're here somewhere.' The two friends heard the heavy tread of boots approach their hiding place. 'Keep your ears open. There are four of them…two guys and two chicks.' The footsteps neared the bunker and light from flashlights flickered through the loopholes. From the sounds there were at least half a dozen.

A low moan emerged from Vesna's lips, and Steven quickly clamped his hand over her mouth.

'Did you hear something?' asked one of the men.

'Yup, it's probably a ghost,' laughed another nervously.

The light flickering through the firing ports illuminated Vesna's face. Her eyes opened briefly and looked at Steven as she tried to form words with her mouth. But no sound emerged and she closed her eyes. Steven bent closer to her face until he could feel the faint breathing from her open mouth. She felt so cold.

From the other side of the firing port came the sound of someone opening a metal lighter. 'Cigarette break,' said a voice. More lighters opened and closed and the smell of tobacco wafted into their hiding place.

'What are these holes for?' someone asked. 'What's behind them?' An arm reached through one and fingers fluttered inches from Bear's head. He flattened against the wall to avoid them.

'They're for firing muskets,' another voice answered. A flashlight shone directly through one of the loopholes, illuminating the wall just above Steven's head.

'Let's see what's behind this…'

'What the hell are you doing?' a new voice interrupted. 'Move your lazy asses down to level four. The boss wants those kids found. Now!'

There was angry grumbling as boots stomped out cigarettes. One glowing cigarette flew through a loophole and landed on Vesna's jeans leg, smoldering. The boots marched away heavily, accompanied by grumbling. 'We don't even have a map. Where are we going?'

After the sounds had echoed away, Steven switched on his light, only to be met with a faint beam. 'It's dead,' he muttered.

Bear switched on his. It too flickered dimly and began to die. 'Damn,' he said, pulling out his Zippo.

With Bear lighting the way, Steven led them along a tunnel in the opposite direction, which they followed for more than a hundred yards, with frequent stops for the lighter to cool off. They struggled up a sloping tunnel that turned into steep stairs. At the top of the stairs a large wooden door barred their way. Steven and Bear set down the girls and threw their shoulders into it, splintered the wood around the hinges and knocked the door down with a dull thud. Fresh air rushed at their faces, and beyond the door they saw the night sky, lit by a brilliant full moon… and something else.

A hundred and fifty meters away the headlights and revolving gumball of a dark blue Zastava police car illuminated five dark SUVs parked near the powder magazine of the St. Elisabeth bastion, near the main gate to the Labyrinth. A policeman stood guard, keeping back gawkers. Bear and Steven set the girls down and rested, watching as more police cars pulled up and discharged their occupants into the tunnel.

'Where's your car?' Steven asked Bear.

'Over there,' Bear motioned in the opposite direction of the vehicles. Under cover of darkness they carried the girls to Bear's Yugo and loaded them awkwardly into the back seat. Steven was about to get in when a very loud and bloodcurdling shriek came from inside the backpack.

'Stop!! Stop!! You over there,' the policeman at the tunnel entrance shouted. 'Stay where you are!'

'Drive,' Steven yelled as he jumped in. The backpack shrieked again and Steven dealt it a heavy blow. The shrieking stopped.

Bear stepped on the gas as the policeman came running towards the Yugo. The clutch wouldn't engage and Bear jiggled the stick shift frantically. The policeman ran closer and drew his pistol. 'Halt!' he cried.

Bear finally threw the car into gear and started forward, accelerating as quickly as the old Yugo could manage, bouncing across the grass. The policeman was gaining and he fired a shot, missing.

'Go!' shouted Steven.

'Where?' Bear shouted back. 'Those SUVs mean we're screwed.'

The Yugo had reached gravel and was now putting distance between itself and the policeman, who stopped, out of breath and fired off several more shots, all missing the Yugo. He turned around and ran back towards his car.

'Faster!' Steven shouted. 'And turn on your headlights or we'll hit something!'

Bear accelerated, pushing the Yugo to its limits as they raced towards the fortress gate.

'Drive down to Wasserstadt!' Steven said. 'I'll show you where.'

As Bear gunned the old Yugo down the bumpy cobblestone road towards the bottom of the hill a column of black SUVs raced up the hill directly towards them, blue lights flashing through their grills, followed by old blue Zastava police cars with rotating lights.

'We're dead!' said Bear.

But the SUVs ignored Bear's battered old Yugo and continued up the hill onto the fortress.

'Faster!' cried Steven.

'It's going as fast as it can. It's a Yugo, not a Lamborghini!'

At the bottom of the hill Bear made a quick left and trod heavily on the gas, the small motor racing at top speed.

'The cop's coming down the hill,' Steven said looking back. 'I can see his lights.'

As Bear steered the old Yugo through the Belgrade gate into Wasserstadt the police light disappeared from view. He quickly swung into a narrow side street and cut the motor and lights. Both he and Steven ducked down and waited. After 20 anxious seconds, flashing blue lights illuminated the surrounding buildings. When they had passed, Bear sat up, and then immediately ducked again, pushing Steven down, as more flashing blue lights appeared and then disappeared.

And then the road was clear.

* * *

Interlude X: Belgrade: 17 May 1992

Ten sat on the terrace of the White Palace in the leafy Belgrade suburb of Dedinje, enjoying the view across a still-dark valley in the waning hours before dawn as Igor played a mournful tune on his accordion.

'Where is she?' demanded Rastko, the doctor from Montenegro, dressed in the garb of a New Age mystic. 'She's kept us waiting all night.'

'She will come,' said Tarik, now a secret policeman for the Bosnian government. 'Have patience. What do you have that's so urgent? Naptime?' The others chuckled.

'Screw you,' Rastko replied.

'I have something new regarding the Vlach,' Lynx said.

They all looked at him.

'I have a hostage who claims he knows his whereabouts. I'll let you know if he has anything useful.'

'You know how many of these false alarms we've had,' muttered Mihailo, fingering the reading glasses on his nose.

'Yes, but this one knew what I wanted before I asked.'

A large glass-paneled door swung open and Natalija walked onto the terrace.

'You're late,' said Rastko.

Lynx jumped to her defense, his baby face glistening. 'Shut up,' he growled. He stroked a baby wolf on a leash by his side.

'We're eleven,' said Stanko, now a DB official. 'Tell us what happened.'

'Our secret is discovered,' said Natalija.

There was an uproar among the eleven as they hurled questions at her in rapid order. 'What? How did this happen? Who? Didn't we cover our tracks…'

'Stop, stop! One at a time,' Natalija's manner was haughty, as though born to privilege. 'Let me tell you what we know. It started with a university student from America…he claimed to be here to study ethnography, but he showed an unhealthy interest in Djordjevic's works and we had to cover our tracks and remove the book.'

'And the librarian,' added Igor, now attired in the uniform of a Croatian Army general.

'And her son,' exhaled Mihailo.

'We thought that was the end, until the bookstore owner became too nosey. So we had to deal with him. But the American still kept poking his nose in things, so Stojadinovic lured him and his friends into the Labyrinth. Somehow the American had a complete map of the underground. I don't know where he got it, but he had it. He found the upper entrance to the chamber and he knew how to manipulate the lock. He carries a Hawthorne stake.' This last remark caused another uproar and looks of consternation.

'May I continue?' she asked. 'Yes, a Hawthorne stake. It looked old, as though used many times. I need not remind you that such a weapon gains power with each kill. He impaled Stojadinovic…Wait, wait…Stop talking… He killed Stojadinovic…and knew to cut off his head. He has taken it with him and I assume he has burned it. Prior to killing him he took his shroud and taunted him, then burned it. He clearly knows what he is doing.'

'No!' Ivan said, shocked.

'You shouldn't have let Stojadinovic have the bookstore owner,' said Branko, wearing the uniform of a general in the JNA. 'He was too crude and hungry. He lacked talent. That is the problem with young…'

'Let me finish,' Natalija said. 'Stojadinovic drained one of the girls, and I started on another, but she still lives…her blood calls me and I must finish her.'

The others nodded in assent.

'But who are they? Who is this American?' asked Stanko. 'Is he a vampirovic?'

'I think not, otherwise he would have discerned Stojadinovic long ago and killed him. But he has discovered our secret and is dangerous.'

'Who sent him?' Stanko asked. 'How did he come to this knowledge?'

'I am uncertain. Stojadinovic thought the American was getting instructions from his professor in America, so if you can have your DB look into that it will help. I don't yet have the professor's name, but we'll find out. Go to the university and the apartment where the American lived and find out where he is and who he associated with. We must hunt them down.'

All nodded their assent.

'Is the Venetian behind this?' asked Lynx.

'We've had no sign of him or his Order since we broke free,' answered Branko. I can't imagine he is still alive, but then again, a vampirovic is immortal, unless he fell in love in the meantime…'

'Which would be exactly like him,' snapped Natalija.

'What do you think, Natalija,' asked Lazar, who until now had remained silent. As he stood an SPS party lapel pin glistened in the moonlight against his expensive Italian suit. 'You know him best. Is the Venetian behind this?'

'Somehow, the American knows my name and…please, calm down! Only Marko could have told him this. So there is no doubt that Marko is behind it. The question is how? I know Marko and the way he operates. It is so like him to send someone in his place. If it is Marko, he will remain in hiding until the end and will never expose himself unless absolutely necessary.' She looked around the group intently as the sky began to show the first streak of grey on the horizon.

'We must smoke him out,' said Stanko, a large Cuban cigar and a snifter of cognac in his hands. 'You must set a trap.'

She nodded.

CHAPTER ELEVEN

THE HILLTOP GRAVE

Novi Sad, Sremski Karlovci, Belgrade: 16-18 May 1992

Mrs. Lazarevic clapped a hand over her mouth when she saw Steven and Bear carrying the girls, but quickly ushered them in.

'Vampires,' Steven blurted as he carried Vesna in his arms. 'We were attacked by vampires in the tunnels.'

'Dear Lord have mercy! Place the girls there,' she motioned them towards the sofas in the sitting room. 'And this one?' she looked at Tamara and saw the remains of her savaged throat.

'She's dead,' Bear intoned emotionlessly.

'Oh no, poor thing,' she exclaimed, rushing to help Bear with Tamara. 'What happened?'

'Stojadinovic was a vampire,' Steven panted, out of breath. 'And he had help…from Natalija.'

'Natalija? She was there?' Mrs. Lazarevic gasped. 'Then they have escaped. I should never have let you go down there. Were you followed?'

'No. We got away. They killed Mr. Niedermeier,' Steven continued, flustered. 'We found his body down there…then we had to run…the police and DB are after us…we're in big trouble.'

'What about the girls?' Bear interjected gruffly.

'Leave them to me. Steven, go clean up immediately! You too, young man, whatever your name is!'

'This is Bear, my friend,' he said. 'Can we help?'

'Go clean up!' She ordered. 'This is my job and you know nothing about it.'

'Do you have a grill? I need to burn something.'

'Pardon me?'

Steven dumped Stojadinovic's head onto the sitting room table and watched it roll across the white lace tablecloth, splattering behind it a trail of gore and body fluids, its eyes open and alert. Mrs. Lazarevic started at the sight.

'Not on my good tablecloth!' she shouted angrily. 'My Rade always ruined my tablecloths like that, and I won't have you doing the same. Take it down to the cellar immediately! There is a furnace my Rade used for that sort of thing. You will find wood and coal. Then wash off in the downstairs bathroom!' she ordered, as though severed vampire heads rolled across her sitting room table every day. 'We shall discuss this when you return. Now go!'

* * *

The furnace sat in a corner of the vaulted brick basement, its mouth gaping open, waiting to be fed. They tossed wood inside, started the blaze, and placed coal on it. When they were satisfied the temperature was hot enough, Steven pulled Stojadinovic's head from his backpack by the hair. At once the head cried out: 'No, not that. Please, I beg you. If you kill me they'll only come after you.'

'Shut up,' Bear said, now clearly enraged.

'It's not my fault. I didn't want to become a vampire. You must believe me,' he pleaded. 'I'm really not like the others. I died two years ago…had a heart attack and my family didn't protect my bed while I lay waiting to be buried. It's not my fault.'

Steven looked at him skeptically. Bear approached and knocked the head from Steven's hand with a blow that sent it spinning across the dirty floor into a corner.

'You son of a bitch! You killed Tamara! And now you want to make good?'

'I'll give you anything you ask,' Stojadinovic's voice was muffled, his head mouth-down on the floor. 'I have money. I know where the others keep their treasure.'

'Treasure?!' shouted Bear. 'Treasure won't bring Tamara back.' He kicked the head into the wall.

'Careful,' Steven said.

'Ow,' Stojadinovic whimpered, 'that hurts! Great treasure, hidden by the Twelve throughout the ages. I can lead you to it. Gold, gems and silver. They've even added bearer bonds and cash…lots of German Marks, Swiss Francs, British Pounds...You could be fabulously wealthy.'

'Listen, you slimy low-life,' Bear followed the head across the room. 'I'm going to stomp you to death.'

'Won't work…you've got to burn him,' said Steven, his voice cold as he nudged the head gingerly with his foot.

'You think everything has a price, huh?' Bear said. 'You can't pay for human life.'

'Really, I can make you rich,' Stojadinovic pleaded. 'I can lead you to treasure.'

'And what do we have to do to get it?' Bear asked.

'Simply return my head to my body. Then I'll lead you to it.'

'First you tell us.' Bear drew his leg back as though readying to kick again.

'Stop! If I tell you first, then you'll kill me and take the treasure. You have nothing to fear from me. You have already burned my shroud…I'm powerless.'

'But you killed Tamara.' Bear said.

'Yeah, and Vesna.' added Steven.

'They made me do it. I didn't want to. They made me. I have the power to bring your girlfriends back, both of them. Don't you want them back?'

'How?' Bear asked skeptically. 'We burned your shroud. You yourself just said you have no more power left.'

'I can't believe we're talking to a head,' Steven said. 'Anyway, he's lying!

'How about eternal life,' cried Stojadinovic. 'Immortality? I can offer you…' and then he screamed horrifically as Bear picked him up and tossed him through the open door into the maw of the furnace. Stojadinovic's shrieking head landed with a splash of sparks on the bed of coals and began melting, the hair and skin dripping and burning away as though made of flammable gelatin. In less than half a minute the head was gone and the drippings burned off.

Steven and Bear looked at the furnace for some time before Bear said: 'it's hot in here. Let's wash up.'

* * *

They looked in the mirror of the large white-tiled downstairs utility bathroom. Bear was covered in mud, his hair and face streaked with sweat.

Steven's arms and chest still bled from the gashes left by the werewolf's claws and he rubbed his hands over his hair, face and beard, trying to remove traces of Stojadinovic's blood and the mud of the tunnels. It was clear why Mrs. Lazarevic had been shocked by their appearance.

Bear sat on the toilet seat and watched silently as Steven began washing his face. 'You owe me answers…you knew there were vampires...you brought a stake…ate garlic. You came prepared. Why didn't you tell us? Tamara's dead and Vesna's going to die and they'll both turn into vampires. What the hell's going on?'

Steven continued washing without answering.

'I can't believe it…vampires…are we on drugs?' Bear asked.

Steven remained silent as he looked in the mirror and tried to figure out what had happened over the past few hours, unable to believe that vampires actually existed. Even when confronted with proof, it still seemed so incredible as to defy reason. Had he actually killed one? And with a stake? Even now the thought sent shivers down his spine.

'Come on,' Bear prodded. 'You've been Mr. Vampire since you came to Belgrade. You killed Stojadinovic like a pro. What are you, a vampire slayer? I mean Tamara's dead, for God's sake. She's dead.'

Steven turned to face Bear. 'A vampire-hunter? Me? Hah! Do you really think I know what the hell I'm doing? I'm definitely not a vampire-hunter…or maybe now I am…I don't know any more. What I'm trying to say is that I'm still trying to figure it all out.'

'Stefan, those were real vampires!' Bear said adamantly. 'Stojadinovic changed into a werewolf and the other one changed into a butterfly.'

'Yeah, I saw,' Steven agreed as he sat on the edge of the bathtub. 'But was it wrong for me to kill Stojadinovic? I mean…I killed someone.'

'Are you kidding me?' Bear sputtered. 'He killed Tamara, he tried to kill us, he was a vampire and a werewolf…it was self defense.'

Steven looked at him for a long while. 'I'll tell you what I know, but first you've got to promise you won't say a word. To anyone.'

Bear grunted affirmatively.

'No, say it. Promise.'

'I promise.'

Then Steven told him about the Order of the Dragon, Slatina and the twelve vampires. 'When I came to Yugoslavia I didn't have a clue what I was getting into. I honestly didn't think we'd find vampires down there. They told me it was safe. And I had absolutely no idea about Stojadinovic.'

'You've got to be kiddin' me,' Bear exclaimed. 'Twelve vampires?'

'Yeah, that's what Slatina said. You saw Stojadinovic. You saw what happened to Tamara and Vesna. You saw Stojadinovic's head. We're mixed up in something really big, and I don't have any idea what to do or where it's going to take us.'

'I can't believe it…this is crazy…but it does explain what's going on right now in Yugoslavia,' Bear exhaled, looking Steven in the eyes. 'Are you a member'?

'Of the Order? No. It's fallen apart. But I think they may restart it.'

'I want to join.' Bear said suddenly. 'I want to avenge Tamara.' He stood up. 'Give me the soap.'

* * *

Mrs. Lazarevic sat next to Vesna's limp figure and tenderly rubbed salve into the wound on her throat with one hand; in the other she held Vesna's hand as she half-chanted, half-sung in an obscure tongue. Three candles on the table cast amorphous shadows on the wall above the sofa. Mrs. Lazarevic ignored Bear and Steven as they entered.

'Where's Tamara?' Bear asked softly.

Mrs. Lazarevic turned and fixed him with a stare that indicated silence was in order, and then gestured with her head towards the back rooms.

Bear found Tamara in a bedroom, arms folded peacefully across her chest with a cross in her hands, large gold coins over her eyes. Mrs. Lazarevic had wrapped a white scarf around Tamara's neck to cover the wound and placed herbs on it, but blood had begun to seep through. An icon sat above her head and small wood carvings had been placed around the room as wards. Bear stepped over the makeshift barrier of tables, chairs and chests that had been constructed around Tamara, then fell on her body and began to sob uncontrollably. Over and over he asked her forgiveness, professed his undying love and vowed to avenge her death. He then began to sing lullabies.

In the sitting room Mrs. Lazarevic placed Vesna's hand in Steven's and continued chanting, while the sound of Bear's lament drifted in from the other room.

Mrs. Lazarevic taught Steven the words to the chant and said: 'You must keep repeating that.' She stood and walked to her china cabinet, removed glass jars filled with herbs and grasses, opened several, sprinkled their contents gently on Vesna's throat, and rubbed them into the wound. The puncture marks glowed red and angry against Vesna's pale skin.

Vesna moaned softly, then opened her eyes and looked at Steven with a vacant stare, as though unable to focus. Her mouth tried to form words, but no sound emerged. He leaned closer and whispered 'Vesna, please come back.'

'Stefan…' she whispered in barely audible tones.

Steven took her hand and kissed her gently on the forehead.

'Vesna…I've been…are you all right? I've been so worried.'

'I feel cold and my neck burns,' she murmured. 'What happened? Where are we?'

Steven hugged her. 'You're safe, very safe, and I will warm you,' he whispered as he hugged her gently. 'I thought we had lost you.'

'I'm so sorry,' she whispered faintly. 'This wasn't how I planned on spending our first night together…' she smiled weakly as her voice trailed off and her eyes closed.

'Keep chanting,' Mrs. Lazarevic said.

'But she's…'

'Keep chanting if you want her to live.'

He chanted in time with Bear's sobbing lament, their voices blending in hope and anguish, healing and death, to fill the entire house. A warm spirit entered, settled over both of them and brought comfort as they raised their voices against the evil that permeated the land. Mrs. Lazarevic listened to their strange duet, a smile of longing and hope on her face.

* * *

Sunrise found Bear asleep on the floor beside Tamara's body and Steven in the sitting room slumped next to Vesna, her hand in his as he mumbled the chant in his sleep. Mrs. Lazarevic entered the sitting room carrying coffee on a tray, then returned bearing another tray loaded with fresh bread, cheese, tomatoes, and a jar of jam. She roused Bear and Steven, marched them to the table and sat them down. 'Eat,' she commanded.

'Tell me what happened last night,' she ordered sternly.

Between mouthfuls of food the two told her of their discovery of the secret door, the flooded stairway, the hole, Stojadinovic's betrayal, the appearance of the female vampire and their escape from the Labyrinth.

'It was strange,' Steven said. 'Somehow I knew what to do. The vampire thing was bad enough, but when he turned into a werewolf I freaked out. Yet somehow I knew what to do.'

'Yes, you did. You held Rade's stake,' she said. 'The more times a stake kills a vampire, the greater the power it confers on its bearer. You were fortunate that you had a venerable stake to guide you. But you have stirred up a hornets' nest. This morning on the RTS news they reported that Mr. Niedermeier had been kidnapped, tortured and killed by a ring of drug addicts…and they put Steven's picture on the television as ring-leader and called him a foreign spy. They seem to know only Steven, otherwise they would have put all your pictures on TV also. For now, Bear, Vesna and Tamara are unknown, but the DB will start asking at the university to find out who your friends are. I hope they find nothing, but if they do, then your families will be at risk.'

'What do we do?' asked Bear.

'You must leave the country.'

'But what about Tamara? Is she going to turn into a vampire?'

'Probably not. She has led a good life, no?' she looked at Bear for confirmation and he nodded.

'And I built a barrier and placed wards around her body, so I see no reason for her to turn into a vampire, provided we give her a proper Christian burial in holy ground with a priest.'

Bear looked relieved.

'Will her family be a problem?' Mrs. Lazarevic asked.

'Maybe not, at least for a while,' Bear said. 'Her parents are divorced. Her mom's in Sarajevo and can't leave because of the siege; her dad's some big shot communist who lives in a big new apartment in Novi Belgrade with a new wife Tamara's age… sometimes they don't talk for months. Tamara lives by herself in her mother's apartment…'

'Any family who'll miss her?'

'She has a sister in South Africa and an Uncle in Australia.'

'Because this is on TV, I don't know how we can find a priest who will let us bury her on holy ground or who will conduct a service,' said Mrs. Lazarevic.

Silence followed as they looked at each other.

Steven finally broke the silence. 'I'm a priest… I could do it.'

'You're a priest?' Bear looked at him in shock.

'Yes, it's a long story…and I know where we can bury her.'

'I knew there was something special about you,' said Mrs. Lazarevic with a faint smile. 'Then we must bury her immediately, while it is still the Lord's day.'

'How? We need to wait for nightfall or someone will see us,' protested Steven.

'If you bury her after dark then she might become a vampire. It must be during the daylight!' Mrs. Lazarevic was adamant.

'This will be a problem,' said Steven.

'Vesna will be a bigger problem. The vampire now knows the taste of Vesna's essence and will not be satisfied until she has taken the rest of it. They are compulsive, you know…once a vampire tastes your blood it cannot rest until it has finished. Natalija will do all in her power to track Vesna. And because she has Vesna's blood inside her she will be able to sense Vesna's whereabouts. If Natalija is in the vicinity, then my wards can no longer conceal Vesna. We must get her out of the country. Only distance will conceal her.'

'We could kill her,' Bear suggested.

'Kill Vesna?' exclaimed Steven. 'Are you crazy?'

'I meant the vampire.'

'You? Kill her? I doubt it,' Mrs. Lazarevic said. 'If it was indeed Natalija then she is one of the twelve and is too powerful. The three of you must leave the country at once.'

'But she's at Debauchery,' Bear objected. 'Stojadinovic said so. We've got to…'

'Don't chase Natalija.'

'I need to go back to Belgrade,' Steven said. 'I left most of my things at the Popovics.'

'Forget your things! Your life is more important! You may not go to the Popovics. Nor may you call anyone you know.'

'I want to kill her, damn it!' Bear shouted.

'Stay away from her!' Mrs. Lazarevic said sternly. 'Do you understand?'

'Hell no!' Bear exclaimed, but nonetheless nodded reluctantly. 'Who's Natalija?' he asked.

'She was Marko's wife. They were madly in love with each other, but their love and her beauty were fatal. She was young, immature, spoiled, vain, jealous and unable to control her passions. Less than a week into their marriage she became suspicious of a servant girl and accused Marko of cheating on her with the girl, and killed her, so Marko's mother and Uncle annulled the marriage and sent Marko away on a voyage to the Levant. It created quite a scandal, but because she came from a noble family everything was hushed up. Nonetheless, rumors spread and no other family would consider her for their sons. She died shortly thereafter under unclear circumstances. Some say she was strangled by her father to restore the family honor. In any event, she became a vampire. Marko still harbors an irrational affection for the girl. Rather than kill her as the Order instructed, he became convinced he could find a way to reverse the process of vampirism. He was the one who convinced that foolish Emperor to imprison them under Petrovaradin, all so he wouldn't have to kill Natalija. He has spent much of his life searching for a cure for the curse.'

'Who's Marko? What Emperor?' Bear asked.

'I'll tell you later,' Steven answered.

'Bear,' Mrs. Lazarevic said as she fixed him with a strange look. 'What is your real name?'

'Simic, Teofil,' Bear answered sheepishly. Steven started. All this time and he had never learned Bear's real name.

'Okay then, Teofil, do you have a passport?'

'Yes, in Belgrade. But they won't let me leave the country until I've served in the army.'

'We shall fix that. First you must go to Belgrade and get your passport and Vesna's. And you must do it quickly before they discover your identities. Steven, you will go with Teofil to get Vesna's passport.'

'But how will we get to Belgrade without being caught? They'll recognize my car.'

'Did they get a good look at it?' she asked.

'I don't think so. There are thousands of Yugos on the street. But they'll be looking for us. There are military police everywhere rounding up military-aged men…they'll catch us for sure.'

'No one will arrest you. Leave it to me,' she said authoritatively. 'I shall make arrangements for the three of you to leave the country unseen.'

Both nodded.

'Now, let's bury Tamara.'

* * *

Vesna shivered under the blanket as she leaned back against the trunk of a large tree and thought of warmth, love, and the life that had so nearly been drained from her. Mrs. Lazarevic sat next to her and held her hand as they watched the sun glisten off the Danube's brown waters to paint the speckled patchwork fields across the river a late afternoon orange. Tamara's body, wrapped in a rug, lay next to them in the waist-high grass of the hilltop pasture surrounding the Chapel of Peace.

In front of the church's main entrance a large stone slab the size of a coffin lay flat in the grass, its mossy surface covered in Latin inscriptions commemorating a Venetian diplomat buried during the 1699 peace conference. The late afternoon sun beat down on Bear and Steven as they attacked the slab with shovels, prying it up on its side. They dug underneath it until the hole was about five feet deep. Neither said a word as Steven and Bear unwrapped the rug and lowered Tamara's body in the grave. Mrs. Lazarevic stood at the edge, sprinkled herbs and handed Bear an icon to place next to Tamara. Steven climbed out and watched as Bear knelt next to Tamara, said a prayer, crossed himself and kissed her one last time. Steven offered his hand and pulled Bear from the grave.

The sun was beginning to set as Steven pulled out a folded, yellowed piece of paper and began to read nearly verbatim the words he had read two years earlier over a frozen grave. 'Dearest Tamara, your life was taken by the evil serpent, the son of darkness, in an act of monstrous violence. But what one serpent has taken, another will return. The Apostle John told us that "as Moses lifted up the serpent in the wilderness, even so must the Son of man be lifted up. For God so loved the world, that he gave his only begotten Son, that whosoever believeth in him should not perish, but have everlasting life." This everlasting life awaits you, Tamara, not in the corrupted form of a vampire, with which the Dragon has cursed this land, but as something higher and purer.' He looked at Bear, who knelt on one knee, his head bent over the grave.

'The Apostle Paul,' Steven continued, 'tells us in his first letter to the Corinthians that "the dead shall be raised incorruptible, and we shall be changed. For this corruptible must put on incorruption, and this mortal must put on immortality. So when this corruptible shall have put on incorruption, and this mortal shall have put on immortality, then shall be brought to pass the saying that is written, death is swallowed up in victory. O death, where is thy sting? O grave, where is thy victory?"'

Bear sobbed softly.

'Dear Tamara, I promise you that everlasting life awaits you, with God and his holy angels. I bless your grave that it will be hallowed up to God, that it will be a place of repose and rest for your mortal remains. By the power of the priesthood which I hold, I consecrate this ground and bless you that you will arise in the resurrection of the dead, to have your corruption clothed with incorruption, your mortality with immortality. For the prophet Job told us "I know that my redeemer liveth, and that he shall stand at the latter day upon the earth: and though after my skin worms destroy this body, yet in my flesh shall I see God".'

'Tamara, you will live once again to see the face of God and those who love you. I bestow this blessing on you in the name of our Lord and Savior, Jesus Christ. Amen.'

'Amen,' murmured Bear softly as he rose to his feet and crossed himself. 'Amen' whispered Vesna from where she sat. 'Amen' said Mrs. Lazarevic.

Bear reached down, picked up a clump of earth and threw it into the grave.

After they had filled in the hole and replaced the heavy stone slab, they stood silently, watching the sun's last glow from over the hill to the west. Bear stared at the dark stone slab for a long time, then whispered 'I'll see you again.' They all walked slowly down the hill, Steven carrying Vesna in his arms as a brilliant full moon rose slowly over the Danube to illuminate the night sky and the dark land beneath.

* * *

'They've escaped,' the woman said, her voice dampened by the heavy insulation inside the phone booth.

'Escaped!' said a male voice on the other end of the telephone line. 'How?'

'The ceiling collapsed.'

'When?'

'I don't know. It's been a while.'

'All of them?'

'Yes.'

The line crackled with the static of a bad international connection.

'Was anybody hurt?' he asked.

'Yes. One girl was killed and another bitten.'

'Who did it?'

'Stojadinovic.'

'Damn! I should have guessed.'

'He's dead. Steven killed him.'

'He's a good lad. Where is he now?'

'Tomorrow they go to Belgrade to get his girlfriend's passport.'

'A girlfriend? Good for him. Do you think he can handle one of our women?' he asked with a chuckle.

'Just because you couldn't doesn't mean he can't,' she taunted.

'That's not fair.'

'It's very fair, Marko. This is happening because of your stupidity.'

'Mariana, you don't understand...'

'Don't lecture me on love, Marko. You will always lose that argument. You don't lock someone you love in a casket for three hundred years and throw away the key. If you really loved her you would have killed her and ended her suffering. This is about your selfish perception of love, not real love. When you love as strongly as Rade did, then you can say something. He loved me enough to sacrifice his immortality, which is more than you ever did. And that's why I married him and not you.'

A long silence followed.

'So Natalija has escaped?' he asked eagerly.

'She attacked one of the girls in the tunnels. Or at least Steven thinks it was her. How would he know who she is?'

'He saw her picture at my place.'

She sighed deeply.

'Will Steven be safe in Belgrade?' Slatina asked.

'I've disguised him well. And he has a girlfriend who survived the attack, which means you have another recruit. They need to leave the country.'

'Can they get to Ram?'

'Ram?! You're playing with fire.'

'It's the main smuggling point and the only way we can be certain they aren't being followed.'

'You'll need to arrange asylum for two, Vesna and Teofil.'

'I'll start on it right away. When can they cross?'

'In two nights.'

'I'll send a boat to pick them up.'

Again the line crackled.

'What will you do with them?' she asked.

'What I should have done years ago. The Order must be restored, and they will help me. I have asked Katarina to assist.'

'Please Marko, take care of my Katarina. She's all I have left. And make certain she marries a good man. There are so few of them left. I had hoped that Steven would find her interesting, but apparently not.'

'Patience, Mariana. You need to…'

'Don't tell me to be patient. I'm mortal and will one day die.'

'Katarina is still young and is enjoying the innocence of life in America. I will care for her as though she were my own daughter. I swear on my mother's grave.'

'She would be your daughter if you had been more of a man!'

'That's not fair, Mariana.'

'Marko, I must be going.'

'Mariana, it was good talking to you.'

'Likewise, Marko.'

'Do you need anything? Medicine? Money?'

'No. I have sufficient.'

Mrs. Lazarevic hung up and stepped from the telephone booth, wiped the sweat from her brow with a handkerchief and went to the counter to pay.

* * *

'You will cross the Danube at Ram,' Mrs. Lazarevic told them. 'Go to the landing at midnight two nights from now. A boat will come for you.'

'But why there? Isn't it easier to cross the border somewhere else?' Bear asked.

'Ram has been the main crossing point between Serbia and Romania since time immemorial. The people there are experienced in the river smuggling trade and will turn a blind eye.'

'Okay.'

'There are two ways to get to Ram. You should take the longer road. It is worse, but safer. It goes through Kisiljevo.'

'Kisiljevo?!' Steven exclaimed. 'That's where they had that famous vampire incident in 1725. Is it safe?'

'How do you know?' asked Bear.

'I read about it in my research.'

'More vampires?' blurted Vesna, clutching her throat. 'Please, can't we go another way?'

'For you it will be safe. For those who follow, perhaps less so.'

'What do you mean?' Bear asked.

'The villages around Ram always had problems with vampires…Kukljin, Kisiljevo, Klicevac, Kurjace, Zatonje… Dracula used to visit Ram every year and gaze in sorrow across the Danube at his beloved Wallachia, knowing he could not cross. He always lashed out in frustration at the villagers. But long ago Marko showed them how to defeat him. You'll be safe there.'

'What are you talking about?' Steven asked. 'Are you sending us into something dangerous again?'

'My dear Steven, the path that you and your friend have chosen means that you will be in danger for the rest of your lives,' Mrs. Lazarevic answered soberly. 'But for now, the danger to you comes from man, not the supernatural. The supernatural will help you.'

'What do you mean?' asked Bear.

She ignored him. 'Do you remember the motto of the Order of the Dragon?' she asked.

'*O quam misericors est Deus, Justus et Pius*,' Steven answered. 'O how merciful is God, Just and Faithful.'

'If you encounter trouble, simply repeat the motto.'

'But what's this all about? What type of danger are we getting into?' Bear was agitated.

'Just get to the landing at midnight,' she answered calmly. 'Marko will send someone to pick you up.'

'Something doesn't feel right about this,' Steven muttered.

'Tell me about it,' said Bear. 'We're trying to escape from vampires by going to Romania.'

* * *

The next morning two military policemen walked into the main post office near the Federal Parliament in downtown Belgrade and asked to use a telephone booth. A crew cut and clean shave had removed Bear's wild mane and bushy beard, making him a new man, while Steven too had received a crew cut, shaved his beard and colored his hair and eyebrows black. The uniforms and distinctive *VP* Military Police armbands made them feared figures, and people glanced away when they passed, especially military-age men. When Bear had asked Mrs. Lazarevic where she had gotten the uniforms, she had only smiled and said 'Petrovaradin is a military town. If you live here long enough you make friends.'

Steven placed the first call to North America. The connection took some time getting through, so he waited while Bear made a local call to Vesna's parents.

After a long while Bear emerged from the booth, sweat dripping down his face. 'Her dad's totally pissed off and her mom's losing her mind. They promised not to call the cops 'til we explain what's going on, so we need to visit them. When we get there, let me do the talking.'

Steven nodded.

They took a taxi out to Vesna's place and rang the buzzer. Her father opened it after the second ring and looked at them with surprise. 'Yes,' he smiled stiffly. 'How may I help the Army do its patriotic duty today?' His tone was cynical.

'Mr. Glogovac, it's me, Bear…and Stefan.'

Mr. Glogovac's jaw dropped as he stared in disbelief. 'Teofil…what has happened to you? Nada, it's them,' he called loudly, 'Simic and the

American.' He ushered them into the sitting room, where they remained standing.

Mrs. Glogovac entered, furious. 'Where is my Vesna?' she demanded. 'What have you done with her? I told you she shouldn't get involved with a foreigner,' she huffed at her husband. 'I…oh!' She started at their appearance.

Bear interrupted. 'Good day Mrs. Glogovac. Vesna is safe and recovering with a friend in…'

'Recovering?' shouted the mother. 'Recovering from what? I want to see her now! What did you do to her?'

'Where's my daughter?' the father bellowed, standing toe-to-toe with Steven, looking him in the eye.

'Vesna's fine. She's doing well. But she's not well enough to travel. She's safe in Novi Sad and is…' Steven said.

'What happened to her?' thundered the father.

Bear looked at Steven, who nodded. He then looked Mr. Glogovac in the eye and said 'She was attacked by a vampire in the tunnels under Petrovaradin.'

'What?! Do you really expect us to believe some half-assed story like that? Where the hell is she?'

'It's the truth,' Bear said. 'He bit her in the neck and started sucking out her blood.'

The mother whimpered and swooned.

The next two hours consisted of tense explanations and heated exchanges with the parents, during which Vesna's mother fainted twice more, the first time on hearing of Tamara's death, the second on hearing the details of Stojadinovic's. As Bear explained, Steven marveled at his coolness. Finally, after several shots of rakija for the father and some Xanax for the mother, Vesna's parents calmed down and agreed not to call the police.

Still, Mr. Glogovac remained skeptical. 'You can't really expect us to believe this vampire nonsense!'

'When Vesna arrives tomorrow,' Bear assured them, 'she'll tell you everything.'

The father grumbled, shaking his head.

'We think they only know who Steven is. If that's the case, then we need to remain anonymous,' said Bear. 'But the police are in league with them, so whatever we do, we can't let them know.'

'Can we talk to her?' pleaded the mother. 'I need to hear her voice.'

'Yes,' said Bear. 'But you must call from a post office in case your line is being tapped.'

'When?'

'Now,' said Bear. 'I'll come with you.'

Steven waited with Vesna's father while Bear left with the mother. He sat across from Mr. Glogovac, shifting nervously during the awkward silence. Finally, Mr. Glogovac spoke. 'You know my daughter likes you, don't you?'

Steven looked him right in the eyes. 'She's a dear friend. I'll do everything to protect her from evil. Everything.'

The father looked at him skeptically.

'Mrs. Lazarevic says that Vesna will be okay,' Steven offered. 'We just need to get her away from here so the vampires don't find her again.'

'You don't really expect me to believe this vampire story, do you? What really happened?'

Steven stood up, opened his backpack, pulled out the stake, its tip still fresh with Stojadinovic's blood and handed it to Mr. Glogovac. 'This is what I used.'

Mr. Glogovac took it, hefted it, and examined it closely. He looked at Steven, then at the stake. 'We have stories in our family of an ancestor who had one of these. Will you take her to America?' Mr. Glogovac asked. 'That's a long way away, you know. We won't be able to visit very often, especially with the war.'

'I think we're going to Budapest at first,' Steven responded. 'After that, I don't know.'

'You realize you are taking my daughter from me.'

'I didn't want this to happen to her or Tamara or us. But there's nothing I can do now.'

'This is all so ironic,' the father muttered.

'How do you mean?'

'In olden times the groom would steal the bride and then send his best man to treat with the family and barter for the bride's price. He would offer sugar, oranges, socks, towels, coffee, gold…this is all somehow strangely reminiscent of that.'

'But we haven't stolen Vesna…I mean…' he blushed furiously.

'You haven't even offered to pay me for Vesna. She is worth much more than a kilo of oranges or some new socks or a kilo of coffee. How much will you give us for her?'

Steven tensed, alarmed at the sudden turn the conversation had taken.

'Relax, I'm joking,' the father smiled grimly and slapped Steven on the shoulder. 'Vesna is my only daughter. Take care of her. What is important is that she's happy and safe. If something should happen to her I'll hold you responsible and will not rest until I've found you, do you understand? If any harm comes to her, you will suffer. Now promise me you will take care of her.'

Firmly, Steven said: 'I promise.'

'I will hold you to that promise. Now, did you know that our family name, Glogovac, means Hawthorne, like your famous writer. Legend has it that the family name comes from an ancestor who was a famous vampire hunter. He killed them with a Hawthorne stake…like this one.'

The door burst open as Mrs. Glogovac and Bear returned. 'How is she?' asked Mr. Glogovac as his wife ran up and hugged him.

'She's eating and sitting up and Mrs. Lazarevic – oh, she's such a nice woman that Mrs. Lazarevic – she said that Vesna will be able to travel tomorrow and will come by train…'

As Mrs. Glogovac related her telephone call with Vesna, Bear grinned at Steven and gave him a thumbs-up.

Steven nodded back. To his horror, Bear mouthed the word "Debauchery Club."

* * *

Interlude XI: Belgrade: 18 May 1992

The proud paddle-wheeler sat moored at the confluence of the Danube and Sava Rivers, across from the Kalemegdan fortress. Once it had seen better days as a luxury river cruise boat, but its engines had long since been removed and a slapped-on coat of white paint covered its rust.

The eleven gathered on the deserted mahogany dance floor around a large table as waiters brought out bottles of champagne and elegant wines. Lazar, Stanko and Lynx lit large cigars. When the waiters had been dismissed, Lazar called the meeting to order.

Stanko said: 'My men have been active. We brought in Professor Ljubovic and his wife and are holding them for questioning. We also brought in the Popovic family, except for their son, who has disappeared. He's a draft-dodger, you know.'

The others nodded their approval.

'Ljubovic claims to know nothing, but he'll respond when we question his wife. The Popovics are fools…the grandparents feel it is their patriotic duty to assist the state in all matters…they're good communists. We need more citizens like them.'

'Our informants at the University have inquired about the American's friends, but so far it seems he lived a hermit's life. We can't even find out who the dead girl is…he's done a good job concealing everything. We have ascertained that the American's professor is a Marko Slatina from the University of California…'

'The Venetian!' gasped Igor, looking at Natalija.

'Yes, the Venetian,' Stanko replied. 'And it seems he trained this student to come and hunt us down and kill us.'

'So that means the Order is still flourishing,' said Branko.

'Nonsense,' blurted Natalija. 'If it were flourishing he wouldn't be hiding half-way around the world in California.'

'Perhaps he's trying to get away from you,' said Rastko.
'Shut up,' growled Natalija.
'We're examining all telephone calls with California,' Stanko continued.
'Do you have any more information about his associates?' asked Lynx.
'Nothing yet,' answered Stanko.
'Anything yet on the Vlach?' Lazar asked Lynx.
'Srebrenica,' Lynx responded.
The others stared at him.
'He's in Srebrenica.'

CHAPTER TWELVE

THE BUTTERFLY'S LAIR

Belgrade: 18-19 May 1992

The taxi ride from the Glogovac home to Bear's cousin's house on Banovo Hill had consisted of Bear repeatedly mouthing "Debauchery" and Steven repeatedly mouthing "no." When they entered the apartment a heated argument erupted.

'You heard Stojadinovic,' Bear said. 'Natalija's at Debauchery.'

'Don't be stupid! You heard Mrs. Lazarevic.'

'It's only a woman vampire,' Bear chided.

'What if there're others? I had beginner's luck with Stojadinovic.'

'Come on, we'll eat lots of garlic,' Bear teased. 'And you bring the stake along, just in case.'

'No, no, no and no! We don't know what's in there.'

'I've been there before.'

'Good. Then you don't have to go again.'

'Come on, it's just criminals and businessmen and some old fart singing

Sinatra and Tony Bennett.'

'Don't be an ass! My picture's all over TV.'

'I just want to see. We need to know if it's really her.'

'It's too dangerous,' argued Steven.

'You're chicken,' Bear taunted.

'Damn right! And if you're not, then you've got pig-brain jelly in your head.'

'Natalija killed Tamara. Are you going to let her get away with it?' Bear goaded. 'Don't you want revenge?'

'Yes, but not now. We don't know what we're up against.'

'So you're going to forget Tamara, just like that?' Bear grabbed Steven by his shirt front, shoving him against the wall. 'I want revenge. Do you understand?'

'You're crazy…'

'Stefan…'

'Bear…'

They looked at each other. Then Steven relented.

'So what's going on with you and Vesna? You seemed real weird towards her in the tunnels.'

'Bear, back off. It's none of your damned business. Vesna deserves better than for me to hurt her, especially now. What she needs is a good friend.'

'You already hurt her when you rejected her advances.'

'I'll hurt her even more if we start something I don't believe in just because we're both horny, especially when she's vulnerable. Women take relationships a lot more seriously than men, and she's already introduced me to her family.'

Bear shook his head. 'You're the first guy I've ever met who turned down such a beautiful girl. You sure you're not gay?'

'Not everybody thinks with his dick like you,' Steven was becoming angry. 'Drop it, unless you want trouble.'

'Oh, the big American's threatening me. I'm really frightened.'

'I mean it,' Steven said, advancing until they stood toe-to-toe. 'I'll kick your ass faster than the Nazi's did in 1941. Try me.' He stared Bear in the eye and tensed his muscles.

'You're touchy today,' Bear said, backing away. 'Forget I said anything.'

Late that evening Bear and Steven walked through the darkened Tasmajdan Park, wearing civilian clothes they'd borrowed from Bear's cousin on Banovo Hill. They passed the imposing Cathedral of St. Marko and the tiny Russian Orthodox chapel, crossed an elevated concrete walkway to a low, non-descript building at the park's edge and entered a drab glass lobby to find a shabbily dressed man smoking at a desk in front of dark velvet curtains. 'Admission is ten Deutsche Marks,' he said without looking up, his voice almost drowned out by the sound of a jazz ensemble playing "Fly Me To The Moon" behind the curtains. They paid, he parted the curtains and a King Kong look-alike frisked them for weapons.

They descended a broad staircase into a dimly-lit imitation of a 19th century Viennese bordello, booths around a dance floor, velvet curtains on the walls. A jazz combo backed a mummified retiree in a tuxedo whose stage smile had frozen in place, exhorting them to let him "see what life is like on Jupiter and Mars". A waiter showed them to a booth and they ordered drinks.

They looked around them at the playground of Belgrade's *nouveau riche*. Men who only a year before were the dregs of society now displayed expensive Italian suits and ostentatious wristwatches, while haughty young women in designer jeans, miniskirts and cocktail dresses flashed their wares. Some were buyers, others sellers: it was difficult to distinguish who was who. Bear and Steven were definitely underdressed.

'Is this it?' asked Steven. 'I expected…I don't know, something more…uh…'

'Look at all the gold-digging *sponzoruse* at the bar.' Bear muttered. The girls sized up the two, decided they weren't worth the effort and turned back to their drinks.

As their drinks arrived the singer began a tribute to Edith Piaf. People moved in and out of focus through the thick tobacco haze, the tide of men and women ebbing and flowing between the tables, as couples swayed self-indulgently on the dance floor. In this night club, in this city, in this country at war with the world and itself, everything was fleeting, and the patrons seized whatever pleasures they could, conscious they might be their last.

Bear glanced about curiously while Steven squirmed like a schoolboy in a confessional.

'She's not here,' Bear said.

'Hey Bear, if it's May 1992 in Belgrade, what time is it in Washington?'

'Huh?'

'Haven't you watched Casablanca? Never mind…this was a stupid idea. I've got to pee and then let's go.' Steven stood and headed for the bathroom.

While Steven was gone, the mummy began crooning 'Oh the shark has, pretty teeth babe...' and a commotion erupted at the top of the stairs.

Everyone in the club turned to look at six hard, shaven-headed men attired in black: shoes, trousers, t-shirts, and aviator jackets that barely concealed Scorpion submachine pistols. They flanked a young woman of perhaps 22 in a black silk cocktail dress with spaghetti straps and a single strand of pearls around her neck, a flashy scarf draped over bare shoulders. Her striking features and dark eyes were emphasized by dark hair that had been pulled back. It was Natalija.

As she appeared at the top of the stairs, head held high, the band suddenly stopped in mid-beat and launched into an enthusiastic version of "Hello Dolly," except that the mummy belted out 'Hello, Natalija' with gusto in heavily-accented English.

The clientele stood and applauded politely as she strutted slowly down the stairway, a modern-day empress making her ceremonial entrance, holding her bodyguards' elbows for support, captivating the room with her dark beauty. Halfway down the stairs she bent over to adjust the strap on her stilettos, showing the top of her thigh-high black silk stocking and marble-white décolletage. With the liquid grace of a lioness she glided towards a reserved booth, waving in acknowledgement with one hand, a glittering Louis Vuitton clutch in the other. She sat in the center of the booth and sniffed the air slightly, her entourage forming a protective cocoon. People approached Natalija's table, said hello and exchanged air kisses. Others sought an audience.

Emboldened by his disguise, Bear motioned to a waiter: 'I'd like to buy a drink for that lady over there.'

'Excuse me sir, but I don't know if that's a good idea,' the waiter said.

'Just do it.' He slipped 20 Deutsche Marks to the waiter.

'Yes sir.'

The waiter returned to the bar and said something to the barman, who looked briefly at Bear, shook his head disapprovingly, and set about making a drink.

Steven returned from the toilet and said: 'let's go.'

'Look over there,' Bear gestured at Natalija's table.

'That's her!' exclaimed Steven.

'And her apes are DB,' Bear said.

'Let's go!'

Bear shook his head. 'Just a little longer. Let's see who she meets and where she goes afterwards.'

'We know she's here. Now let's leave.'

'Just a little longer,' Bear pleaded.

'She'll recognize us,' Steven whispered.

'How can she? She hardly saw us in the tunnels, and we looked completely different then,' Bear said confidently. 'No one has any idea who we are. Did you bring the stake?'

'Of course not. Where would I hide it?'

'You didn't bring the stake?!' Bear was furious.

'Let's go.'

'Wait. I just bought her a drink.'

'You what?!' Steven exclaimed. 'Have you lost your mind? You're completely different since Petrovaradin.'

The barman placed a gin and tonic on a tray, which the waiter placed in front of Natalija. He whispered something to her and pointed at Bear. She acted surprised, looked across the room at them, smiled tentatively and raised her glass. Both returned her salute, Bear smiling, while Steven avoided her gaze.

'See, she didn't recognize us,' Bear gloated.

'I can't believe this.'

'Calm down…wait just a little longer. But don't pay any attention to her. It drives women crazy when you ignore them.'

'She killed Tamara and almost killed Vesna and now you're flirting with her?'

'It's just reconnaissance. You got a better idea?'

'Yeah! Let's get the hell out of here. You know what her apes will do to us if she suspects? She'll drink our blood through a straw for Happy Hour.'

'Stefan, we're okay. Just act cool. We'll leave in a bit.'

Steven hung his head in his hands and stared at the marble table top, unable to believe what was happening.

They ordered more drinks, sat through the end of the set, and generally did their best to ignore Natalija. During the break another round of drinks helped Steven loosen up, and they bought drinks for a table of *sponzoruse*, and flirted openly.

By the beginning of the next set the parade of petitioners at Natalija's table had evaporated. She lit a long, slender Cuban cigarillo and looked around with a bored expression.

The waiter approached with a note on a tray. 'From the Lady,' he said.

Bear opened it. 'Would you care to join me for a drink?' it said in a flowery hand. He handed the note to Steven and looked across the room: she smiled at them, her cigarillo clutched between her fingers.

'What do we do?' asked Steven, panicked.

'Keep your mouth shut and let me do the talking,' Bear said.

When they sat down on either side of Natalija her presence and perfume intoxicated them and she smiled so beautifully that all thoughts of Tamara and Vesna disappeared from their minds.

'Good evening. My name is Natalija,' she said as she raised a hand with ruby red nails.

'I'm…mmph!' gulped Steven as Bear kicked him under the table.

'Such a tremendous pleasure,' Bear responded, as he lifted her hand and kissed the air above it. 'Please pardon my cousin. He's from Chicago…you know how uncivilized Americans are.' His voice was crisp and firm. 'I am Vlada and this is Nenad. Thank you so much for inviting us. We watched you all evening…'

'What about your little friends?' she motioned jealously towards the *sponzoruse*. 'Wouldn't you rather sit with them?'

'They're kids,' Bear said dismissively. 'You…are a real woman.'

Her face glowed with satisfaction as she turned to Steven. 'An American?

How interesting. Tell me Nenad, are American women as beautiful as our women?'

'Miss Natalija, no one even comes close to you, not even here in Serbia,' he smiled flirtatiously.

Bear grinned at him and winked.

'So, Nenad American, what are you doing in Serbia?'

'I came to…'

'He came to defend the homeland,' Bear interrupted. 'When he saw what the Ustase and Balija were doing, he joined Seselj's Eagles.'

Steven glared at him.

'And he just got back from Bosnia. He was in Bijeljina, you know.'

'Oh, a genuine hero,' she fawned.

Steven thought back to the police in the train station when he first arrived and said: 'I'm just doing what every patriotic Serb should do when his country is attacked.'

Bear looked at him proudly.

'You have such a sweet accent,' she purred. 'Were you born in America?'

'Yes, but my parents are from Belgrade.'

'And you Vlada, what do you do?' she asked.

'I work in the Army General Staff building…on the Seventh Floor,' he winked knowingly.

'Oooooooh,' she smiled back at him. 'Such a strong young man, so fit and ready for combat,' she squeezed his arm, 'and with a desk job…someone's daddy must be a big shot.'

'It looks like yours isn't too bad off either,' Bear parried.

'Touché,' said Natalija.

'Where are you from,' Steven asked, his head becoming hazy.

'All over,' she laughed.

'Where is "all over"?' Steven pursued.

'Mr. Nenad American, you are quite curious. Don't be, it complicates things. Why don't we dance?' It was an order masquerading as a question.

Mesmerized by her beauty, Steven said: 'Sure, why not?'

Bear bit his lip, unable to restrain him as she led Steven on to the dance floor. The band struck up a tango with Hungarian Gypsy overtones.

She moved immediately into Steven's arms and pressed her body close to his, humming softly. The skin on her bare back was soft, smooth and cold, as was her hand. Her body proved strangely compliant as he guided her with the beat, yet she pushed with her hips, directing his every step with her loins. Steven became aroused and for a second he remembered Vesna and Tamara. Yet Natalija's closeness swept all thoughts of guilt from his mind as her humming became an opiate that deadened his senses and caused the other dancers to disappear in a haze.

As Natalija's thick dark hair brushed against his cheek, he tried vainly to conjure up an image of Vesna or Katarina or Julie, but Natalija pressed her face against the left side of his neck, nuzzled him and purred. He inhaled deeply. Her perfume – a rich musky-sweet mélange of decaying fruit – entered his nostrils and left him disoriented. Cold lips left frosty kisses along his throat, then drew slowly apart as her tongue darted out to trace a small circle around his Adam's apple.

Deep within his subconscious the thought occurred that he was dancing with a vampire and that she had her mouth against his throat. Yet her loins reached out through her thin silk dress to overpower his resistance, while her outward submissiveness drowned his remaining willpower. Time faded and soon the world became theirs alone. She moved her lips slowly up his throat with tentative nibbles until she reached his jaw.

She sniffed his scent, kissed her way up his jaw line to his earlobe, bit it gently and whispered: 'Mr. American, are you sure you're there? I can't sense you at all. Do you sense me?'

'Yes, I feel you,' he gasped hoarsely, his heart pounding rapidly in his chest.

'Let's go somewhere else,' she purred as she pressed herself against his chest. 'My place?'

Was it a question or an order? Steven no longer cared, completely in her thrall. He followed mutely as she led him by the hand back to the table. The room had emptied of guests and Steven vaguely remembered Bear.

'Where's my cousin?'

'He left,' said a bodyguard.

'Oh,' Steven nodded dully, uncertain anymore as to who Bear was and why he should care.

Natalija picked up her scarf and purse and led Steven out to a large black SUV. On the back seat she leaned against him and placed his hand on her lower stomach so he could feel her heart pulse through the thin silk of her dress. The SUV took them to the old city center and stopped in front of a stately old triangular building with a mansard roof across from Toplicin Park. The bodyguards chaperoned them through the lobby and inside a small wood and glass elevator. As they entered, Natalija dismissed the bodyguards and pulled the elevator doors shut.

She used the narrow confines of the old lift to press herself shamelessly against him, pushing him back against the wall with her pelvis, breasts and stomach.

Her apartment occupied the entire top floor of the old building, its elegant high-ceilinged salons decorated with overstuffed modern beige furniture. She removed her heels, stretched languidly, walked slowly across the room and placed her scarf and purse on the bar. 'Do you like my place?' she asked as she turned on a local radio station. She was much shorter now, barely five feet six inches.

A clock on the wall said 4:05. Already the night sky was becoming less black as Chet Baker began to sing:

I get along without you very well,
Of course I do,
Except when soft rains fall…

He stood, admiring her lithe figure and hair, breathed deeply and then walked to the bar. She walked to a window and opened it. 'It's stuffy in here,' she said as she let her raven black hair fall to her waist.

As the physical distance between them increased Steven's thoughts became less muddled, and suddenly it struck him: who she was, where he was and the predicament he was in. How did he get here? Where was Bear? He began to panic, realizing she had used her powers to mesmerize him.

'You're tall. I like tall men,' she smiled flirtatiously and walked towards him, a self-satisfied look on her face. As she approached he struggled against the aura of her power, which strengthened the closer she came.

Although Steven thought of Vesna, Tamara, Slatina, the haze inside his head thickened.

She ran her fingers down one arm as she looked him in the eyes. 'You're so strong.'

He shook his head as he struggled against the tentacles wrapping themselves around his soul, choking his free will.

'I can't wait for what comes next,' she cooed.

'What did come next?' he thought. His thoughts were clouded and muddled and he couldn't focus or concentrate. And then he thought of Katarina and the pine cone and at once he found the mental clarity he sought, the memory dispelling the haze.

'You witch!' he yelled, grabbing her upper arms. 'If you didn't steal Vesna's blood you'd be nothing but a withered old bag of bones.'

Her eyes widened in surprise and began to change to the now familiar feline red. She struggled fiercely to free herself, but he held her tight. She kicked, but yelped when her bare toes missed him and hit the bar. Suddenly she stopped struggling and looked him in the eyes.

He looked away to avoid her gaze.

'So, it was you at Petrovaradin,' she said calmly. 'Congratulations. You're quite cunning. Are you wearing a Hawthorne cross?'

He smiled without answering.

'Of course, that's why I couldn't sense you on the dance floor.' Her tone changed suddenly: 'But now you've really ruined my night,' she shouted. 'Do you know how damn hard it is for me to get laid? Do you?' She smiled revealing the two incisors that had drunk Vesna's blood. 'Most men are afraid to approach a beautiful woman, and the ones that do are usually jerks…like you.'

She suddenly calmed again and tried once more to move her body closer to his. 'But you have captured me and I am yours,' she smiled cat-like and batted her eyelids. 'What are you going to do with me? Will you impale me?' She tried to grind her hips against his, but he held her away as he fought the magnetic pull coming from her loins and inhaled deeply, only to be attacked by the elixir of her perfume.

'I didn't bring my stake with me tonight,' he grunted.

'I wouldn't say that,' she laughed naughtily, staring suggestively at his crotch.

'Stop it! I want answers,' he shouted, trying to concentrate and avoid her gaze.

'Young man, you are trying my patience,' she sounded exasperated. And then in an instant he found himself holding a large black cat that scratched his arms, jumped from his grasp and ran across the room and hopped on the sofa in front of the open window.

He quickly picked up her scarf.

Equally quickly, she transformed back into a human vampire. 'Careful with that,' she called from across the room. 'It's my favorite.'

'I'm sure it is,' Steven smiled, certain he now held the upper hand. He pulled Bear's Zippo from his pocket, lifted the scarf and said: 'if you want this, you'd better give me some answers.'

'Don't be annoying. Put it down!' she said coldly.

'Who are the twelve?'

'Put it down or I'll get really angry.'

'Tell me or I'll burn it.' He flipped open the lighter and held it under the scarf.

'You fool. You really think you know what you're doing, don't you?' Her voice rang with furious exasperation.

He lit the scarf and let it fall into the bar sink, where flames consumed it.

'You idiot!' she shouted. 'Now you've really pissed me off.'

'So, you don't like it when someone burns your burial shroud, do you?' Steven gloated triumphantly.

'Burial shroud my ass! That was my favorite Hermès scarf, and it's quite expensive.'

Steven's eyes widened with surprise. 'It's not your burial shroud?'

'Of course not. Do you think I'm a novice like Stojadinovic? Now sit down and talk to me before I get really mad.' She pointed at the sofa by the open window. 'No need to fear, I won't hurt you. I'm not hungry tonight…all I wanted was a good lay. I bloat when I feed…if I wasn't watching my figure your girlfriend would be dead. She was tasty, by the way. You should try her sometime.'

Steven lunged at her, but she was nimble and dashed out of the way as he tripped and stumbled on a divan.

'But now you've screwed things up. Men! You're all alike! Give me a man who can… Oh, never mind.'

Steven stood behind the sofa and looked out the open window. It was five floors down. Outside the horizon lightened as dawn approached.

'Can I get you something to drink?' her voice became suddenly hospitable.

Steven was taken aback. A vampire who had killed his friend was offering him a drink? Balkan hospitality was not to be underrated. 'Just mineral water, thanks.' He needed his wits about him.

She fixed herself a gin and tonic and poured him a mineral water, walked over to where he stood by the sofa and handed it to him. She remained standing for a moment and then sat down on the sofa. 'Come, sit down. I'm not going to bite you…now,' she chuckled, patting the cushion next to her.

He sat.

'Tell me about yourself, Mr. American. Why did you come here? What do you want? Who sent you?'

'Who are the twelve?' he blurted out.

'Please don't be annoying. I'm being nice: you should too. How did you know my name?'

'I saw your picture.'

'My picture?!' The drink fell from her hand and she cursed. 'Dammit! My sofa.' She jumped up and ran to the bar for paper towels. As she bent over to clean up the drink the front of her dress fell open revealing her alabaster bosom and flat stomach. Steven averted his gaze. She looked up at him and smiled knowingly, her eyes no longer red or feline, but opal blue, moist and feminine.

When she finished wiping up she mixed herself another drink and sat down again. 'You saw my picture? Where?'

'Hanging on a wall.'

'Don't play games with me,' she hissed as her eyes reverted to feline red.

'Your husband showed it to me,' he said.

'My husband? Marko? Damn him to hell!' she screamed, flung her glass at the wall, jumped to her feet and began cursing.

In a flash her face became an elongated furry muzzle, her mouth gaping open to reveal canine incisors. Short, golden fur made a strange contrast to the black cocktail dress and pearl necklace and her claws were still clad in ruby red nail polish.

In her wrath she advanced on Steven, who sat frozen on the sofa. With a horrible growl and salivating jaws she turned away, knocked over a lamp and shredded a large love seat with her claws. Her necklace caught on a claw and burst, showering pearls across the floor and behind furniture cushions. She smashed the bar and shattered the mirrors behind it, broke several more chairs and then turned her attention to the rest of the furniture. She picked up her stilettos and hurled them at Steven, but he ducked and they flew out the open window as she transformed back into human shape, her rage expended. She panted and trembled, fangs extending from her mouth. Blood trickled down her chin from where she had bitten her lower lip and tears ran from her eyes. 'My Christian Louboutin-Dior shoes. I'll kill Marko for that.' She was sobbing deeply.

In spite of his revulsion and anger over Vesna and Tamara, Steven felt desire well up inside him. Unable to understand why, he stood up, walked towards Natalija and raised a handkerchief.

She recoiled.

But he waited, looked directly in her cat eyes and tried once more.

This time she permitted him to dab gently at the tears running from her eyes, trembling under his touch. As he did so, her incisors receded into her mouth and her eyes reverted to their human form and color. When he had wiped her cheeks, he dabbed at the blood on her chin.

Steven then raised his finger and wiped the last droplets of blood from the puncture wounds on her lower lip, stared directly into her eyes and placed the bloody finger to his own lips, tasting her essence: lavender mixed with hints of wild mushrooms and rosemary.

For a twinkling, they stared in each other's eyes, bound together and adrift in a moment between night and day, dawn and dusk, 1992 and the timeless eternity the immortal damned are cursed to haunt. Suddenly the wounds on her lip disappeared and she broke the spell with a right round-house blow to his face that left him holding his nose.

'How dare you?!' she shouted, her eyes reverting to their vampire form.

She launched herself at him, metamorphosing into a werewolf in mid-leap. Her sudden charge knocked him backward and he hit his head on the hardwood parquet floor. He lay stunned, a golden short-haired werewolf straddling his chest, its jaws slathering over his face, his arms pinned to the floor.

'No more games, American. Where is Marko?' Natalija growled as she moved her jaws closer towards his neck. 'Tell me now!'

Her breath smelled of rotten meat and Steven wanted to vomit. He stared directly in her eyes for a tense eternity until her breathing slowed and she calmed down sufficiently to metamorphose back into human shape. She let go of his arms, and stood up, directly over him. Under her dress, her marble thighs emerged from her stockings and disappeared in gloom, towards a shadow resembling a butterfly's folded wings.

After a moment's pause, she walked towards the window and turned around, silhouetted by dawn's brightening glow. 'What do you want?' she demanded.

Steven pulled himself carefully to his feet in anticipation of her next violent mood swing and clutched the cross on his chest. His arms were scratched and bleeding and he felt blood trickle slowly from his nose where she had hit him onto his lips.

'Do you want to impale me like you did Stojadinovic?' she asked quietly. 'Do you want to cut off my head and burn it?'

He stared at her, still overpowered by her beauty, yet terrified of her power and the evil residing inside her.

'Please kill me,' she pleaded plaintively.

He stood there, licking the blood from his lips.

'Go now and find a stake,' she begged Steven fervently. 'My darling husband drove a stake through my heart centuries ago, before I ever became a vampire, and the pain still lingers. Here…' She ripped furiously at her silk dress, tearing it until it was no more than a pile of rags at her feet. She walked towards him, bare except for her stockings, reached out and placed his hand on the cold flesh over her heart. 'Right here…is where Marko pierced me. For centuries I have lived with the pain of a lifeless heart that cannot die. If he were to impale me now I would thank him for the release.'

Then her mood snapped again: 'I damn his soul for all eternity for what he did to me,' she shrieked. 'May he burn in the darkest fires of hell: I will be there waiting for him. When you see Marko, tell him that I will drag him down into the same hell he placed me in. All he has that is precious, I will destroy. I wish to see him suffer as he made me suffer. Tell him I shall await him in Srebrenica, and there we shall see the face of the Dragon. Together.'

She stood on tiptoes, wrapped her arms around Steven's neck and kissed him on the lips, tasting his fresh blood, drinking in his essence. The passion of the kiss chilled the marrow of his bones. He felt hot breath from the back of her throat and tasted his own fresh blood on her tongue. Her ardor broke his will and he crushed her to him, returning her kiss with equal fury, passion and lust for nearly a full minute before she broke away, gasping. She looked up at him, slowly licked his blood from her lips, and shuddered.

'I will have you,' she said softly. 'Not now, but in another time and place where none of this matters, where there will be time for us.'

She turned and walked towards the open window, the first rays of the rising sun splintering around her bare figure like shards of broken glass. She spun around suddenly and looked him in the eyes once again. Steven strained to see her against the sun's direct rays.

'One more thing, Nenad American…tell Marko I love him.'

Steven squinted as her body suddenly disappeared, and an orange and black butterfly with white spots flew out the open window.

* * *

Steven staggered to the elevator, confusion marring his thoughts. The power of Natalija's kiss and body, combined with her stunning physical beauty had left him shaken and uncertain.

What had just happened? Why had he responded the way he did? How could he have felt, much less shown compassion for the vampire that tried to kill Vesna? Why was he attracted to her, against all reason? Had she mesmerized him again? Or had he kissed her of his own free will?

Stumbling from the elevator, he collapsed against a large tree in the middle of an empty sidewalk café and began to sob. He felt that by showing compassion for Natalija and by kissing her he had betrayed all his ideals, as well as the people closest to him…Vesna, Tamara, Katarina, Slatina, Mrs. Lazarevic…that he had fallen from grace…that God himself had turned his back on him in disgust. He was a disappointment to himself and those around him. He wanted to pray, but didn't feel worthy to approach God.

Yet the taste of her blood lingered tantalizingly on his tongue, etching itself deeper into his senses with each passing moment. As he rolled his tongue in his mouth, her taste left him wanting more: more of her beauty, more of her scent, more of her essence. His loins and chest screamed for her. Strangely, he sensed her nearby, felt that she was in close proximity. He looked at the trees, but the foliage was too thick to see if the branches concealed an orange and black butterfly with white spots. And then she was gone. Just like that, as suddenly as the first flash of morning sun. He felt it.

Suddenly Steven understood the obsession that had consumed and driven Slatina the last 260 years. Natalija had gotten into the professor's blood, just as she had now gotten into his. At some point Slatina had tasted her essence, and had let her become a part of him. Would the feeling ever cease? And then it dawned on him that the only way to cleanse himself of it would be to take her or kill her.

* * *

Interlude XII: Belgrade: 18 May 1992

'If the Venetian is active, then we must reconstitute our quorum,' said Lazar, the eldest. 'Together we shall be stronger. We must find the Vlach.'

'But the Muslims hold Srebrenica,' said the doctor, Rastko.

'How soon can we take it?' Lazar looked at the general, Branko and Lynx.

'My army will seize it by the end of next month,' boasted Branko, brushing cigar ash from his crisply pressed uniform.

'The Muslims are encircled, without food or electricity,' said Lynx. 'They have few weapons and are nearly defenseless.'

'I've longed for Srebrenica. Its call is powerful,' said Mihailo. 'We should've known he'd be there.'

'Do we really wish to wake the Vlach?' asked Ivan. 'You know how insatiable he is, without bounds or reason. That's what drew the Venetian's attention and got us captured in the first place. And he's probably hungry…his appetites could again attract attention to us.'

'There's a war underway,' scoffed Lazar. 'No one will notice if a few thousand people go missing. When you wake the Vlach, make certain you have a good meal waiting.'

'I know just the thing,' said Branko. 'But what if he wants more? What if he becomes too ambitious and tries to take over from us?'

'He won't do that,' said Lazar with assurance. 'Ruling requires work, and he has long ago become too fond of worldly pleasures. That's what made him one of us. I know: I watched him become a vampire. I was there.'

'Then Srebrenica it is,' said Branko. 'I'll leave tomorrow for the front in Bosnia. I have to begin preparations for the capture of Srebrenica.'

'Likewise,' added Lynx.

'Much as I would like to stay and find the girl,' Natalija said, 'I too must leave for Croatia.'

'I'm also off to Croatia,' said the youngest, Ivan. 'You need someone to fight against.'

Branko and Lynx smiled.

'And we're leaving tomorrow for Sarajevo,' said Tarik, rubbing his shaven head.

'But I don't want to be the one to wake him,' Branko said. 'What about you, Lynx?'

Lynx shrugged indifferently: 'Sure, why not? My men need a change of pace from playing with civilians. And who knows…some of them might even survive and have a story to tell their grandchildren. It's not every day you get to wake up Vlad Dracula.'

CHAPTER THIRTEEN

THE WALLS OF RAM

Ram: 19 May 1992

Atop a high bluff at the Danube's edge, Steven, Vesna and Bear sat huddled in the ruins of the castle of Ram, its crumbling towers and walls long ago overrun by the tall grass that besieged it. Across the river they could see Dracula's Wallachia, mysterious and gloomy, nearly obscured by low-lying clouds and rain.

Early that morning Steven had found Bear unconscious on a park bench in front of Debauchery.

'Everything hurts,' Bear had said, squinting at the morning sun. 'Sorry about last night…leaving you with Natalija...they put something in my drink. What happened?'

'Nothing. We danced,' Steven said, knowing he would take the events of that evening with him to the grave.

At the Glogovac home they met Vesna, who had arrived by train with Mrs. Lazarevic.

The trip from Belgrade to Ram had been uneventful. Vesna's mother had gone to the basement and returned with long strands of braided garlic, the kind peasants hang to dry on the outside of their homes in the late summer and autumn. She draped a strand around each of them, which they removed and put in the car trunk as soon as they were out of sight of Vesna's house.

Vesna lay on the back seat, while Steven and Bear, attired in Military Police uniforms, sat in front as they started off on what all knew would be their last road trip in Bear's red Yugo.

'It seems strange without Tamara,' Vesna commented as she fidgeted nervously with the scarf that covered the puncture marks on her neck.

Bear coughed and stared stoically ahead, saying nothing, while Steven nodded and muttered 'yeah.'

Vesna sat silent, sullen and angry. 'Because of you I have to leave my home and parents and abandon my studies,' she lashed out at Steven. 'I didn't want any of this. I only want to live normally, and now I'll never again be able to do that. Why'd you take us under Petrovaradin?'

Steven stayed silent, unable to answer. He wrestled with a conscience besieged by feelings of overwhelming guilt: for exposing his friends to the dangers under Petrovaradin; for starting a half-hearted relationship with Vesna when his heart clearly sought unobtainable Katarina; at betraying Katarina, with whom he wasn't even certain he had a relationship. But most of all, guilt for what he had done last night with Natalija, permitting himself to be lured into the situation, to drop his guard and allow animal instincts to overpower him. He felt horrible and ashamed about the encounter and could not look either Bear or Vesna in the eyes. He distracted himself by wiping condensation off the inside of the windshield so Bear could see.

Bear stared ahead at the road, pretending he wasn't there, lost in his own thoughts about Tamara and their lost future.

The trip passed in silence as they drove eastward through the countryside, until a small yellow sign with faded lettering alerted them to the turnoff for Kisiljevo. As they veered onto a crumbling asphalt road, they saw a decrepit blue police Zastava appear from the rainy mist, one cop asleep inside, the other sitting on the hood in a rain poncho, puffing on a cigarette. The smoker flagged them down.

'Good day,' he said arrogantly. And then he saw their uniforms and became friendlier. 'Where are you headed?'

'There are some draft dodgers in Ram,' Bear responded, fidgeting with the gear shift.

'And the girl?'

'A hitchhiker.'

Vesna smiled formally at the policeman.

'A hitchhiker?' the policeman winked lewdly. 'Well, be careful. Part of the road isn't paved. And hurry back. Strange things happen in these parts after dark.'

The rain had swept Kisiljevo's only street clean of humans.

'The first modern vampire came from here,' Steven said.

Vesna shuddered.

Through the foggy car windows they saw engraved marble plaques set in the façades of houses.

'Look at that,' Bear pointed at one house.

'Yeah, over here too,' Vesna added.

'Tombstones. I read about these,' Steven said. 'They bury people in the house to protect them from evil, you know…under the threshold, under the hearth, in the yard in front of the gate, that sort of thing. It's an old superstition…if evil approaches, then the spirits of the dead family members will rise and protect the home.'

'That's sick, burying a dead person in your house,' said Vesna. 'It's primitive superstition.'

'Yeah,' Bear nodded. 'But maybe that's what Mrs. Lazarevic was talking about when she said the supernatural would help us.'

'Maybe,' Steven agreed, although he saw no connection.

The next village was as ghostly as Kisiljevo, and then they entered Ram to find more of the same: a lifeless, rain-swept street, tombstones in the walls. Other than the policeman, they hadn't seen a soul since leaving the main road.

'This is spooky,' Vesna said. 'There's no one here.'

'Of course not,' Steven said. 'They're all inside.'

They drove to the top of the bluff, abandoned the Yugo deep in the high grass at the base of the castle ruins, draped themselves in garlic and took shelter from the rain inside a crumbling tower.

'We've got about five hours,' Steven said, looking at his watch. 'Where are the sandwiches?'

As darkness fell they ate and spoke in hushed tones about events of the last three days.

Steven related how Slatina had talked him into coming to Serbia and how his research kept leading back to vampires. 'But I didn't really believe they were real until Stojadinovic attacked us,' he said. 'If I'd known, I never would've gotten you involved in this. I swear. I mean, who thought vampires existed?'

'Yeah,' said Bear in the monotone that had now become *de rigueur* since Tamara's death.

'But now that we know they're real, we can't really ignore them and pretend they don't exist,' Steven continued. 'I mean, if you really think about it, the whole premise of sin is that you know the truth and choose to act against it. If we turn our backs and refuse to fight against them, then wouldn't we be committing a great sin?'

'Yeah, that's the whole Holocaust thing,' Bear agreed. 'The Nazis were doing bad things…killing Jews…genocide…all that…and the West knew about it but didn't do anything to stop it. In fact, the people who were around it every day knew about it and didn't try to do anything to stop it. People like us. No one wanted to be put out or have their life disrupted. A little bit of evil goes a long way, and complacency goes even farther.'

'Yeah, that's our situation now,' Steven agreed. 'Because we know, we have to do something. If we don't, we'll have blood on our hands.'

'What do you think, Vesna?' Bear asked.

'It doesn't matter what I think. I have no choice. Tamara didn't have a choice either,' she said, fingering the strand of garlic draped around her shoulders.

'Vesna, I'm sorry, I really…' Steven began to apologize.

'Tamara has nothing to do with this,' Bear exploded angrily. 'Leave her out of it. Stefan didn't know it would be dangerous. I didn't know. You didn't know. I mean, come on, who believes in vampires anymore? If you hadn't been attacked would you believe? Stop acting spoiled. We've got to move on. If we stay behind we die. That's the simple truth, so enough self-pity. It's time to grow up and stop pouting.'

They sat in awkward silence, listening to the rain patter on the grass and stones. Through a gaping hole in the crumbling tower they watched the boats and ferries that lined the landing at the end of the village's only street. Lights from a café twinkled through the rain, the only sign of life in the village. The downpour lightened to a drizzle and a light fog arose from the water to cover the river's surface.

Steven broke the silence. 'Bear, do you believe in God?'

'Yeah, I do,' Bear answered.

'I mean, everyone always asks if God exists. Well, do you think He knows we exist?'

'Stefan, don't get philosophical on me.'

'Bear, since I've come to Serbia I've spent a lot of time trying to find a reason to stop doubting, trying to believe God listens when I pray or that He even knows I'm alive. I've been looking for answers, without really knowing the questions.'

'It doesn't matter whether you think God exists,' Bear answered gruffly. 'Because He does. And do you know how I know? Because we've seen the face of the Devil, and if the Devil exists, then it means God exists. It's the whole Yin and Yang concept. It would be stupid for there to be Evil if there was no Good. Without Evil, the whole idea of Good loses all meaning.'

'You sound like a Gnostic or a Bogomil,' Steven said.

'I'm serious. We just saw the face of the Devil, and it saw us,' Bear said softly. 'If the Devil knows we're alive, then God must too.'

'Wait a second,' Steven interjected. 'If we can see the face of the Devil, why can't we see the face of God? If we're fighting against the Devil, then logically, we're doing God's work. But how can God let imperfect beings do His work when we're not worthy to see His face? The Devil lets those who serve him see his face and he takes those who are like him, corrupted and evil. But people who do God's work almost never get to see His face, and few can ever hope to become like Him and attain perfection.'

'You've got it all wrong,' Bear said. 'Most people who do the Devil's work aren't evil, but are simply ignorant or too complacent to learn the truth, or they're too lazy and comfortable in their everyday lives to rock the boat. And those people almost never see the Devil's face, because the Devil knows that if he revealed himself it would scare them out of their complacency and turn them to God. The Devil's like a vampire…he's most effective when no one thinks he exists and only shows his face to those who resist him.'

'So what you're saying is that both God and the Devil use normal, imperfect human beings to achieve their aims?' Steven asked. 'But how can we…'

'Stefan, three days ago I was just another draft-dodging university student,' Bear interrupted impatiently. 'I had my parents, my friends, an apartment, Tamara, I thought I'd be a student forever, my parents always gave me what I needed…now everything's changed. It's as if my life as I know it is coming to an end. Everything that mattered is now gone or unimportant. I'm fleeing my homeland for I don't know what. I don't have any money…once I leave I'll be officially branded a traitor and I'll never be able to return. I don't know what I'll do, where I'm going, or what's going to happen.'

'Once we're across the river, Slatina's going to get us to Hungary,' Steven offered. 'He'll take care of things.'

'You don't understand,' Bear rebuffed him. 'You're an American. You can travel anywhere without a visa. You come from a normal country. You aren't leaving your whole life and family behind. Your family and university are in America and your country isn't being destroyed by war or vampires. You can always go back home. But I can never return. This is the end for me. I'll never see Serbia or my parents again.'

Steven nodded silently.

'Do you know what my life will be like?' Bear continued. 'It's like I'm a refugee. So quit complaining about whether or not God exists and whether or not you can see His face. He's there. He hasn't forgotten you, anymore than you've forgotten Him. Have you forgotten Him?'

'No.' Steven admitted, looking at Bear's dim silhouette.

'I miss Tamara,' Bear murmured softly.

Vesna began sobbing and Steven reached over to put his arm around her and comfort her, but she shrugged him off.

They sat alone with their thoughts until Bear said: 'What about the twelve?'

'There were only eleven coffins at Petrovaradin,' Steven said. 'Slatina thinks they're looking for the twelfth, and if they can reunite their quorum then they'll become tremendously powerful.'

'Why wasn't the twelfth at Petrovaradin with the rest?' Vesna asked, sniffling.

'Because Slatina could never track him down. He thinks he's hiding somewhere in Bosnia, in the mountains. When I was fighting Natalija she said we'd see the face of the Dragon in Srebrenica, in Bosnia. Maybe he's there.'

'Who is he?' Bear asked.

'Dracula.'

'Dracula?! You're kidding me!' Bear exclaimed. 'How are *we* going to stop *him*?'

'I don't know,' Steven answered. 'Slatina will tell us.'

'Oh dear Mother of God,' Bear rolled his eyes. 'I can't believe this.'

'But why us?' Vesna moaned.

'Why us? Because we know, that's why,' Bear answered. 'And because it's the right thing to do. I won't let Tamara's death be in vain.'

'I don't know exactly what Slatina has planned,' Steven said. 'But I think he wants us to stake out their graves next Easter Sunday…each year they have to return and spend one night. He said he did it before.'

Steven pulled a package from his backpack and shined a flashlight on it. Faded scarlet ribbons, fixed by a large red wax seal with the Order of the Dragon's insignia held it shut.

'What's that?' Vesna asked.

'I took it from that stone cross in the chamber under Petrovaradin. It's Slatina's journal…he asked me to retrieve it. He said he kept a record of the vampires' burial places, so it makes catching them easier.'

'Let's see what's in it,' said Bear.

'I don't know if we should,' Steven hesitated. 'I mean…'

'Go on, open it,' urged Bear. 'What's going to happen?'

'Well, I… okay.'

Against his better judgment Steven broke the seal, removed the ribbons, and began gently to unwrap the waxy oil cloth, but it had stiffened with age and proved difficult. As he did so, small wooden and metal charms placed in the wrapping fell out. Inside lay a leather volume with a locking metal clasp.

'Maybe we should just leave it,' Steven said.

'Come on,' Bear urged. 'Open it.'

'Steven's right, leave it alone,' Vesna said. 'We don't want any more trouble.'

'Go on,' Bear goaded.

Steven forced the latch with a pocket knife, his hands trembling. As he opened the cover the book shimmered briefly, mirage-like, and then returned to normal. He felt a tingle run up his spine as warmth flooded his bosom.

'Did you see that,' Steven asked, breathing unevenly.

'See what?' Vesna responded. 'Did something happen?' She clutched protectively at her throat.

'I don't know. I just thought I felt something.'

'What's that,' Bear asked, pointing at the frontispiece.

Strange symbols leapt from the paper, trapezoids and triangles affixed to mangled bicycles and eyeglasses.

'It's the Glagolitic alphabet,' Steven exclaimed excitedly.

'Glagolitic? Can you read it?' Bear asked.

'Uh… not easily. Last time I saw Glagolitic it took me three days just to read two pages.'

Steven flipped through pages of Glagolitic inscriptions, sketches of geological formations, grave sites, churches, people, vampires, witches and fairies and several clusters of symbols that made little sense to him, as well as what appeared to be occult markings.

'It looks like Slatina was investigating alchemy, witchcraft and black magic,' Steven said.

'What's that?' Vesna grabbed Steven's arm and pointed at the village.

Bear and Steven looked, yet saw nothing.

'I thought I saw something move down there…it looked like a ghost.'

They watched further, yet saw nothing.

'You're probably seeing things,' Bear said. 'Just hold on, only two hours to midnight.'

Steven's tongue began to tingle and his mouth to water as a faint acrid taste of lavender, wild mushrooms and rosemary wafted across his taste buds, and warmth crept into his chest and loins. The sensations felt distant, yet somehow familiar. Then his pulse and breathing quickened as adrenaline flooded into his bloodstream, and he recalled these same sensations from that very morning outside Natalija's apartment.

Looking about wildly he pulled the stake from his backpack, jumped up and frantically shined his flashlight around the inside of the dark tower.

He saw only shadow.

Vesna yelped and clutched her neck. 'It's burning,' she whimpered. 'It's burning.'

'Natalija,' Steven called loudly. 'I know you're here.'

'Natalija? Where?' Bear jumped to his feet, shining his flashlight around.

'Show yourself,' Steven called, his voice steady and strong, belying the fear gripping his chest. 'You can't hide from me. I feel your presence.'

'Nooooo,' Vesna pulled her knees to her chest and whimpered. 'Make it stop,' she begged. 'Make it stop.'

Bear and Steven stood back to back forming a protective cocoon around Vesna.

The sensations on Steven's tongue grew stronger until they overwhelmed his taste buds, while the heat in his chest and loins caused him to break out in sweat.

'Natalija,' he shouted.

'Natalija,' Bear yelled.

But the ruins and overgrown grass swallowed their cries, leaving nary an echo among the deaf shadows that danced darkly around them.

From the edge of town they heard town dogs begin to bark, barks that quickly modulated into wild howls.

Steven and Bear turned in the direction of the howls and saw the glare of unseen headlights reflect off wet asphalt, then the headlights hove into view over the top of the hill: a dark Mercedes SUV, three Army trucks and a tanker truck. The vehicles drove down to the landing, and the trucks pulled onto a ferry and cut their motors. Steven and Bear shut off their flashlights and barely made out the silhouettes of a man and woman who emerged from the Mercedes, followed by a short, stocky figure. Heckler-toting paramilitaries in camouflage jumped from the trucks to form a perimeter, guns at the ready, balaclavas over their heads.

The man sniffed the air, then walked into the café, a wolf cub at heel on a leash beside him. The woman stood alone on the ferry. She too sniffed the air, stood still, sniffed again, and then looked directly up at the castle ruins, her eyes glowing red against the blackness of her face.

Although he couldn't distinguish her features, Steven knew instinctively it was Natalija and that it was her energy that had surged through him and Vesna. And he knew that she too had sensed them. The red eyes now stared directly at Steven and he felt them burn a hole in his heart.

He began to tremble and sweat and his vision blurred as a strong desire to run to her swept over him. He wrestled against it and gasped deep breaths until finally her eyes stopped glowing. Suddenly she turned and walked deliberately toward the café, followed by the short, stocky figure.

'It's Natalija,' Steven gasped for air as the force pulling him towards her waned. He could only imagine what Vesna was feeling. He walked over and held her as she sobbed, immobilized by fear and pain. He tried to comfort her, all the while fighting his urge to run to Natalija.

'Did you see that guy?' Bear asked. 'It's Lynx, the paramilitary commander. He's a born murderer…you wouldn't believe the stories of what he's done in Croatia and Bosnia. I'll bet he's a vampire too.'

The thought made Steven shiver. This time he wouldn't be fighting just

Natalija, but also a trained killer and soldiers.

'I won't let them hurt you,' Steven assured Vesna in a whispered voice. 'I won't let her get near you, I promise.' But deep inside he wondered how strong he would be in Natalija's presence. Would he betray Vesna to Natalija? And how would he handle Lynx and his paramilitaries? He clutched the Hawthorne cross at his throat and began to pray silently, seeking strength as he thought about the pine cone Katarina had given him.

'How'd they find us?' Steven asked. 'How are we going to get to the boat without them catching us?'

'I don't think they came for us,' Bear answered, as a low rumbling wafted across the water.

The noise of marine diesels grew louder and soon a darkened prow without running lights emerged from the mists, then the long low cargo hold of a barge, and finally the superstructure. It slowed, then strained gradually against the current until it rested next to the ferry. Deck hands quickly secured it as a small deck light came on outside the bridge.

Lynx and the stocky figure emerged from the café as paramilitaries began tossing large plastic-wrapped bricks from the trucks up onto the barges.

'Heroin,' whispered Bear.

In the dim light Steven made out the stocky figure's face. 'It's the substitute librarian,' he exclaimed. 'The one who kicked me out of the library. She's one of them!'

When they finished loading the heroin, the deck hands began offloading large cardboard boxes with writing on the sides, which disappeared into the Army trucks. Others ran a hose from the barge to the tanker truck.

'Cigarettes and gas,' whispered Bear.

The deck hands worked quickly and in no time they had closed the tarps on the back of the trucks, filled the tanker, extinguished the deck light, and cast off the barge.

'What time is it?' Steven whispered to Bear.

'11:30,' Bear answered. 'They're going now.'

The librarian went inside and came back with Natalija. The three had a brief conversation, and then Natalija pointed up towards their hiding place in the ruins.

Lynx looked up and his eyes glowed red in the shadow of his face, as did the eyes of the librarian. Lynx lit a cigar, gestured to the paramilitaries, said something unintelligible, and pointed up towards the ruins. The paramilitaries began trotting towards the narrow lane that led up to the castle.

'Vampires and paramilitaries,' Bear muttered. 'Now we have trouble.'

Steven and Bear watched in astonishment: as the paramilitaries passed each house, the wall fluoresced ever so slightly around the tombstones, sending luminescent tendrils wafting outward to form small butterflies that fluttered gently in front of each home. They were barely visible and their luminescence was slight, yet there they were. Evil had woken the spirits of the guardian dead from their resting places to protect the lives and homes of their descendants. Soon these ghostly shades filled the village, fluttering silently, watching the paramilitaries pass. Upon seeing these apparitions the paramilitaries hesitated, stopped, and looked about uncertainly.

'That's what Mrs. Lazarevic was talking about,' Bear whispered, watching the guardians emerge from their slumber.

'Go on, move your sorry asses or I'll come and plant my boot in them,' Lynx angrily shouted. 'They won't hurt you if you leave them alone.' The paramilitaries began to move cautiously, glancing warily about.

'We can't stay,' Steven said. 'They know we're here.' He lifted Vesna and pointed across the lane from the castle towards a small chapel surrounded by a four meter stone wall with battlements. 'Vampires can't tread on holy ground.'

Bear grabbed Vesna's other arm and they half pulled, half carried her through the churchyard gate, garlic garlands swinging awkwardly from their shoulders, their feet slipping on fallen leaves that oozed the scent of decay. The chapel was locked, so they picked their way through a sea of waist-high stone crosses toward a large tree trunk in a back corner, away from the gate and crouched down.

The crunch of boots on gravel echoed up the lane, drawing ever nearer as Steven, Bear and Vesna huddled together in silence. They heard a static crackle and a man's voice, followed by the electronically distorted speech of a walkie-talkie. Then the noises began to move towards the castle ruins until they gradually faded from earshot. Occasionally their ears picked up the odd sound coming from the ruined fortress, the crackle of a walkie-talkie or boots on stone, but the churchyard embraced them in a protective cloak of silence.

'What if they're not vampires,' Bear whispered. 'They could come in here.'

Steven shook his head, mentally kicking himself for not thinking of that. The gate was their only way out.

'Damn it!' they heard the voice echo loudly through the ruins, followed by more voices, the sound of the walkie-talkie, then quarreling.

And then a new pair of boots crunched up the lane.

As the crunching neared, butterflies riding luminescent tendrils exploded from the gravestones around them. They hovered silently above each marker, then fluttered toward the three friends. Vesna closed her eyes, whimpered softly and began to shake.

Bear crossed himself and whispered loudly 'Holy Mary, Mother of God, and all the Saints, have mercy.'

Steven clapped his hand over Vesna's mouth to prevent her moans from giving them away and waved the stake in front of him, but the glowing apparitions took little notice. They fluttered gently in the night air and began to close in around the three, hemming them in on all sides. These weren't vampires, and nothing Slatina or Mrs. Lazarevic had said had prepared Steven for this.

Steven felt Vesna trembling as she tried to swallow her fear and he kept his hand tightly pressed over her mouth. He wielded his Hawthorne cross, which at first seemed to bewilder the butterflies, but then the apparitions tightened in a circle around them.

'What did Mrs. Lazarevic say?' whispered Bear frantically.

Steven thought back to Mrs. Lazarevic's words: 'the supernatural will help you.' He faced the apparitions and whispered softly: '*O quam misericors est Deus, Justus et Pius.*'

The butterflies halted.

'*O quam misericors est Deus, Justus et Pius*,' he repeated.

Then the butterflies washed over the friends as a cascade of blowing leaves, fluttering in wild abandon around their arms, legs and faces, swirling and dancing. Some clustered on Steven's Hawthorne stake and one began crawling towards his hand. He had a flashback to Niedermeier's bookstore and shuddered, but remained still while the glowing insect moved rapidly onto his goose-bumped skin. More of them swarmed over his arms, tingling wherever they touched him. When they finally lifted, the wounds from his fights with Natalija and Stojadinovic were healed, the skin glowing slightly.

Bear stood, awestruck, his arms and face completely covered, while Vesna looked like a human glow stick, her entire body covered in butterflies from head to toe, only her eyes, lips and nostrils visible. For the first time since Saturday she was smiling.

The new boots passed and continued towards the ruins, followed by the smell of cigar smoke. 'You sons of Gypsy whores,' a voice cursed. 'Can't you even find three drug-addled kids?'

'Lynx,' Bear mouthed to Steven.

'You useless faggots,' Lynx yelled. 'Quit playing with each other's peckers and find them.'

Boots scrambled over stone and gravel.

'Fan out, cover the hillside,' Lynx directed. 'They're here somewhere. I want them alive or I'll roast your shriveled balls like I did that Imam's in Bosnia!'

And then Natalija beckoned him. Steven tasted her once again on his tongue and struggled for air as his chest compressed and loins burned. The sensations overwhelmed him with the urge to run to her. Vesna shuddered, clutched her throat and fought the pain as the butterflies scattered from her.

'Breathe deeply,' Steven whispered, feeling his own pulse race wildly, one arm around the tree trunk to steady his resolve.

Vesna began shaking violently, and Steven and Bear grabbed her. Blood dripped from her lips where she had bitten them, and she breathed loudly.

'Hold on, just a little longer,' Steven urged, shaking his head to clear Natalija's tendrils from his mind. He fought, and for the first time, he felt himself winning. This victory, however small, brought hope.

Then Vesna screamed.

'They're in the churchyard, you idiots,' Lynx called. 'Bring them out.'

Running boots approached the gate and then stopped.

'What are you waiting for? You're acting like a bunch of eunuchs. Get in there.'

'Boss… it's full of those things.'

'You spineless dick-head. They won't hurt you… leave them alone and they'll leave you alone. Now get in there and bring me those kids before I skin you alive.'

'But boss, they're ghosts and…'

A silenced gunshot thudded dully, a body hit the ground.

'Either you faggots get your puckered assholes in there and get them, or you'll end up like him!'

Boots moved hesitantly forwards and the gate creaked open. As it did, the butterflies flew rapidly towards it and blocked the gateway.

From behind the tree Steven and Bear could see eight paramilitaries, with Lynx standing in back, his bloated baby-face glowering at them. The first paramilitary placed one foot gingerly into the churchyard and stopped.

'Go on, get in there,' Lynx pushed the man.

As the paramilitary set his other foot in the churchyard, the butterflies darted forward and enveloped him entirely, swallowing him with their luminescence. He screamed shrilly and his arms wind-milled wildly as he tried to fight them off, but the butterflies raised his body off the ground and his feet kicked helplessly. He discharged several rounds into the air, only to have his submachine gun slip from lifeless fingers as his desiccated corpse crumpled to the ground. The ghostly guardians remained, hovering at the entrance to the churchyard.

The paramilitaries fled as one, their boots pounding down the gravel lane.

Lynx cursed after his men, his words echoing down the lane after them. 'Faggots! Cowards! May goats screw your mothers!' As the paramilitaries ran down the hill, the friends heard their screams of fright turn to shrieks of pain and then die out altogether.

Lynx turned and looked at the three behind the tree-trunk, his eyes scarlet and glowing. He raised his Heckler and Koch MP5 submachine gun and a red dot appeared on Bear's forehead. At once the butterflies surged towards Lynx.

Lynx dropped his Heckler and cigar, and in a twinkling metamorphosed into a large dappled stallion. He bolted down the lane, hoofs scattering gravel as butterflies from the churchyard and neighboring houses converged and chased the vampire-stallion down to the main road and out of the village, hooves clattering on the wet asphalt.

Bear and Steven stood and lifted Vesna to her feet, then half-carried her out of the churchyard and past the bodies of the two dead paramilitaries. Bear picked up Lynx's Heckler and snuffed out the still smoldering cigar with his boot, then they walked down the lane, passing house after house with glowing guardian butterflies.

'I wish these damn dogs would stop howling,' Bear said.

At each house a guardian approached, only to stop as Steven recited the Order's Latin motto. Butterflies swarmed the three, enveloping them, crawling over flesh and clothes, dancing wildly about in a radiant whirlwind as they passed the desiccated corpses of the remaining paramilitaries, none of whom had made it back to their trucks. Steven picked up a Heckler and ammunition clips from one of the corpses and proceeded on, stake in one hand, submachine gun in the other.

'How does this work?' he asked Bear.

Bear rolled his eyes. 'If you don't know how to use it, stick with the stake. It'll be safer… and probably more useful.'

Through the stillness of the dark village street, they slowly trudged toward the landing. All was dark, the villagers having decided that on this night they would let their ancestors guard them. Yet on the asphalt, trickles of rainwater glistened with reflections of the luminescent Lepidoptera, the glow twinkling softly in the watery sheen coating the street.

'They're so nice,' Vesna whispered to Steven, looking once again like a large glow-stick. 'They make me feel so good… all the bad goes away.'

'Yeah, just so they don't attack us,' Steven answered, then resumed repeating *O quam misericors est Deus, Justus et Pius* as more butterflies approached.

As the three friends stepped onto the ferry, the cloud of butterflies halted at the water's edge, refusing to go further. Some milled around near the shore, while others turned back and flitted aimlessly through town, as though seeking to ferret out any remaining evil. The Mercedes and trucks sat empty on the ferry.

'What's not right with this?' Steven asked himself. He looked around, saw nothing, and then realized it wasn't what he didn't see, but what he felt. Natalija. The sensations in his chest and loins had not abated since the churchyard, and dogs continued to yip nervously.

'She's here,' he whispered to Bear. 'I feel her.'

'What do you mean?' Bear asked, looking about.

'Can you feel her too?' Vesna asked.

'Yes. She's here. Everyone stay together.'

The ferry lay heavy in the water as wavelets slapped against its hull. They stood at its far edge, their backs to the river, drizzle gently caressing their faces and moistening the metal deck plates.

'Keep your eyes open,' Steven held his stake at the ready.

'It's midnight,' Bear glanced at his watch. 'When's the boat supposed to come?'

'Now.'

'Look,' Bear pointed as two butterflies fluttered from the back of the truck closest to the landing, alighted on the ferry deck and in a twinkling changed into human form – the dumpy librarian and Natalija.

Vesna screamed, clutched her throat and collapsed into a fetal position. The butterflies on the shore surged towards the vampires, but stopped at the water's edge, as though obstructed by an invisible wall.

A chill ran down Steven's back as he hefted the stake firmly in his left hand, dropped the Heckler on the ferry's glistening deck plates and stood protectively in front of Bear and Vesna. Seeing Natalija this close overwhelmed him with a desire to taste her lips once more, to feel the heat at the back of her throat and touch her alabaster skin. He fought the urge to step towards her and willed himself to resist.

While Steven struggled to clear his thoughts and catch his breath, Bear raised Lynx's silenced Heckler and emptied the entire magazine at the librarian. As each bullet struck, she jerked spasmodically like a rag doll until the magazine was empty, then looked at Bear, scorn in her eyes, and laughed softly.

Steven felt his resolve weaken. Suddenly, he staggered forward a single step, propelled by desire. With the stake wavering in his hand, he clutched the Hawthorne cross at his throat and fought for his soul, barely able to breath.

'Stefan,' Vesna cried.

Bear grabbed Steven from behind.

'Get back,' Bear shouted at Natalija. 'I'll kill you, I will!' he grabbed the stake from Steven's hand, picked up Steven's Heckler from the deck and emptied it futilely at Natalija, with no greater effect than on the librarian. Behind Bear, Steven fought furiously to overcome Natalija's hold, using every ounce of strength he could muster merely to stay in one place.

The red of their eyes glowing on their glistening fangs, the two vampires advanced. Then Natalija halted, leaving the librarian to continue her advance alone. Natalija lowered her head for a moment, and when she looked up, her eyes no longer glowed and her fangs had receded. Her hold on Steven's heart eased, and he began to breathe more freely. Natalija stared past Steven, out into the fog.

Steven turned and looked, but saw only grey.

The librarian stopped, turned and looked at Natalija, a puzzled expression on her face.

Then from the fog on the Danube, a loud report rang out. The librarian jerked violently, as though hit with a sledge hammer in her chest, and crumpled to the deck. She began melting into a glowing puddle of jelly that sizzled on the deck plates until it evaporated in a stench that spoke of putrid organs and diseased pollutions of the soul.

Natalija gazed somewhere into the fog as her eyes began to glow redder than Steven ever recalled seeing them, and she bared her fangs like a cornered cat as the muted murmur of muffled motors drifted across the water, drawing nearer.

As the three turned to follow Natalija's stare, invisible hands parted the mists and a long dark Zodiac boat appeared. In its bow, a tall dark figure with scarlet cat eyes held a long flintlock rifle.

'Marko,' Natalija gasped and froze.

'It's Slatina,' Steven cried with relief.

Steven could see a smaller figure with long dark hair flowing from a cap at the helm. Could it be Katarina?

'Get in,' Slatina commanded as the Zodiac pulled alongside the ferry. Bear pulled Vesna toward the boat and Slatina helped her in. Steven looked longingly at Natalija, hesitated, again fought off the urge to run to her and bolted across the ferry deck towards the black boat. As he jumped in the helmsman called 'Stefan.' It was Katarina.

He cringed at her voice, confused by his uncertain emotions for her and Vesna, his conscience burning with shame over the previous night's encounter with Natalija. Katarina rushed to Steven and wrapped her arms tightly around him, not saying a word as she buried her face against his neck.

Slatina rapidly reloaded the flintlock with well-rehearsed motions, rammed the ball and wad home, raised the rifle and took aim at Natalija. She stood rooted to the deck plates, her chest rising and falling in quickening breaths, looked directly at Slatina, her eyes growing redder with each passing second. Unwavering, Slatina held the flintlock's sights on her, his face the determined mask of a professional soldier, his eyes the color of the blood both he and Natalija had shed across the ages.

'Do it, Marko,' Natalija called in an archaic Dalmatian dialect. 'Do what you should have done centuries ago.'

Slatina's aim held steady on her chest.

'I'm waiting,' she said, voice trembling.

Slatina stood immobile, his crimson eyes glowing fiery off the gun metal. Part of Steven hoped Slatina would pull the trigger and kill her, while another part wanted to jump up and wrest the musket from the professor's hands. Only Katarina's arms around him and the smell of her hair in his nostrils kept him in place.

'Please, my dear Marko,' Natalija called plaintively. 'I pray of you, show me your love and the mercy you have withheld from me these centuries. Please, release me from this curse, this un-death.'

Slatina's breathing deepened and his hands began to tremble.

'Do it, Marko,' she sobbed. 'Torture me no longer.'

Slatina spoke in a still, soft voice that carried to her. 'Natalija, redemption is at hand. I have sought it for you these many centuries and it draws closer.'

'Damn you and your redemption! Prove your love and kill me.'

Slatina lowered the musket and climbed from the Zodiac, his footsteps echoing off the steel deck plates as he approached Natalija, a Hawthorne stake in hand. Seeing his approach, she closed her eyes in anticipation of the lethal blow and dug her fangs into her lips until they bled. Steven recalled their kiss in her apartment and began to tremble with arousal. Katarina placed her lips against his ear and sighed soft strange words he could not understand, yet somehow comprehended they were ancient. As she did so, his trembling stopped.

Steven, Bear and Vesna watched in disbelief as Slatina reached Natalija and encircled her in his arms, pulling her tightly towards him. She hugged him and began to cry.

'You gave up on me,' she sobbed. 'Locked me in a casket for 260 years… you abandoned me to a living death.'

'I never gave up on you,' Slatina whispered tenderly, wiping her tears with his finger. 'I convinced the Emperor I could find a way to redeem vampires from their fallen state. I had no other choice, except kill you and lose you forever. After all these centuries I am close to finding the path to redemption. I am so close…'

'But you left me,' she cried, gasping air in great gulps. 'Just as you left me after our wedding night. In that coffin I lost my mind a thousand times each day. Time and again I felt you draw near, then leave, and each time I prayed you would end my torture.'

'My dearest Natalija,' he stroked her hair gently. 'Everything will be all right… I will make it all right… hush.' He pressed his finger against her lips.

And then Natalija reached up and kissed him for the first time in nearly three centuries.

'Natalija, my love,' Slatina gasped as he surrendered hoarsely to his passions.

Steven felt his blood boil jealously as his body convulsed in silent struggle.

'Stefan, peace, peace be with you', Katarina whispered in his ear, clutching him all the more fiercely. But Stefan didn't answer, consumed by his own fight.

Suddenly, Slatina pushed Natalija back, both breathing heavily, their faces smeared with blood from her cut lip that matched the color of their eyes.

'You love me?' Her question was also a statement.

Slatina nodded ever so slightly. 'Eternally.'

She placed her arms around his shoulders, her face against the left side of his neck, opened her mouth and sank her incisors deep into Slatina's jugular. He stiffened, then she withdrew her teeth, placed her lips against the open wounds and began to drink. As she drew his life from him, he closed his eyes with pleasure. She stayed that way for several seconds, drinking in Slatina, ecstasy written across her face, then withdrew. They stood and gazed into each other's eyes for a long, long moment with an understanding that surpassed perception.

Then without a word, Slatina – in a lightening-quick movement almost imperceptible to the human eye – drew back his arm and swiftly plunged his stake through her heart and out her back.

Natalija's eyes widened in surprise and pain and her body stiffened. Her flesh sizzled around the stake, and blood gushed from the wound. She looked him in the eyes, opened her mouth and gasped: 'You do love me,' then fell limp in his arms.

In a twinkling, Steven felt a thousand butterflies course through his veins, rush from his chest, through his throat and into the night air as the taste of lavender, wild mushrooms and rosemary dissipated from his tongue. His knees buckled and his heart cried out as darkness enveloped him and he collapsed unconscious in the bottom of the boat, exhausted from the struggle, as Katarina knelt beside him, calling his name.

Vesna gasped audibly and sat up straighter, as though a weight had been removed from her shoulders. 'It's gone,' she whispered, tears of relief flowing from her eyes. Bear jumped up and shouted: 'For Tamara.'

In Ram the dogs fell silent and the guardian butterflies, sensing there was little reason for them to be out, drifted slowly across the rain-slicked street, back to their gravestones to stand sentinel.

Slatina collapsed to the ferry's deck plates, Natalija's corpse in his arms. He held her limp flesh, the stake protruding from her back, and rocked her tenderly, pressing his face against hers as a sound came from within him, muffled by Natalija's thick tresses. Then another… Then another… Each louder and louder. Then he tipped back his head and let anguish burst from his throat with a wild roar. It was the cry of past love denied, life taken and hopes crushed. It was the cry of knowing he had just annihilated three centuries of an irrational hope, love, longing and desire. It was the cry of Marko Slatina – a man doomed to a solitary eternity.

Slatina's cry echoed south through the village and across the fields into the heart of Serbia, north out over the misty waters of the Danube to Wallachia, and upwards through the cloudy skies to the heavens, where he hoped that God listened and would one day answer his prayers.

And then there was stillness, broken only by the river lapping at the sides of the Zodiac.

Silently, Slatina picked up Natalija's corpse from the deck and carried her to the Zodiac, the stake protruding grotesquely from her body. He set her gently in the stern, causing the three friends and Katarina to cringe, as they huddled in horror in the bow. Slatina looked at them, then muttered: 'She deserves a Christian burial,' under his breath, as if trying to justify holding on to her that much longer, as though each moment spent with the lifeless clay might somehow make up for the centuries spent apart.

Then, without another word, he placed his hands on the helm and pushed the throttles forward, propelling them into the mists.

* * *

Fog lay thick upon the face of the waters, cloaking the river from curious eyes. It pressed ponderously on the Danube's murky surface, stretched clammy tendrils into the dense undergrowth on the darkened shores and billowed after the craft surging upstream, rushing in to fill the void created by the boat's passage. Its thick vapors quickly smothered the muted growl of motors that chased the craft, as dark pearls of condensation formed on exposed skin, drifted into nostrils and lungs, crept under coats and jackets and tugged at ears, whispering faint warnings of the evil that had encompassed the land.

Beneath the boat flowed murky shadows and vaporous hallows that had coursed down the Danube from the shattered shell of Vukovar, past the massive ramparts of Petrovaradin; down the Drina from the vales of Srebrenica; down the gloomy narrows of the Bosna River's tributary valleys; across the Sava's fertile plains. They strained at the water's surface, seeking to rise and engulf them in their dark tide.

At the horizon where vapor caressed the river's surface, Slatina thought he saw the faces of phantom spirits stare searchingly: the ghosts of those felled by the armored blade, the souls the reaper had cut down with his scythe, like unripe wheat. He thought he recognized some of the faces... shades of those left behind… those who had sown and never reaped… specters whose abandoned corpses the winged scavengers had defiled in the blood-drenched mud. They were the seeds of the harvest of blood that Vlad Tsepeş had sown half a millennium earlier in Srebrenica. Once planted and watered by blood, they had taken centuries to grow. And now the fields were once again white, and now was the grim hour of the harvest, the mower and the reaper in which many souls would be cut down, in which a two-edged sword would rend asunder joint and limb as a great and terrible work came forth among the children of men. Now was the new hour of reckoning, and Slatina was sure in the knowledge he could no longer bury it underground to wait another quarter millennium.

Slatina stared coldly ahead into the cloud, his still-smoldering eyes piercing the mist with a crimson glow, as he fought to forget what lay behind him in the stern. His hands tried to coax the throttles past their stops, hoping to outrace the memories that pursued. Yet, like Jonah of old, some things he simply could not outrun, no matter how swift his flight.

He glanced at the four youths huddled in the bow: at Bear enveloping a shivering Vesna in strong arms, comforting her; at Katarina, her hair wrapped in a scarf, tending to Steven, whose motionless head she held tenderly against her bosom.

A quarter of a millennium earlier Slatina had lacked the conviction and courage to kill Natalija and the other ten. To satiate his heart and save one woman's soul he had preserved terrible forces that were just now unleashed, destroying a country and millions of lives. Because of his love for Natalija, many would suffer.

Tonight he had killed the first of the twelve, and as his thoughts turned to the remaining eleven, he began to plan his next steps. Yet his mind and gaze kept returning to the one, the dark figure lying splayed behind him with a stake protruding from her chest and back. He contemplated the darkness around her. Can it be transformed into light, he wondered. Do I possess the faith and strength to continue the fight against these evil forces?

He glanced again at the figures huddled close in the bow, then back into the enveloping fog. He wept as he stared ahead into the murky night, searching for the light that eluded him, yet firm in his stubborn conviction that he would one day find that light, no matter how thick the darkness that enveloped him.

As he thought of the future, his mind turned to the thick gloom that loomed around, thicker than any he had heretofore faced. Then, dense shadows broke over his soul in a tsunami of foulness that engulfed the depths of his heart and whispered a single word: Bosnia.

And when they had receded and fled, he knew that Bosnia awaited.

Historical Note

The characteristics attributed to vampires in this book – which differ radically from popular stereotypes – are based on genuine Balkan folk tales as recorded by ethnographers in the 18th, 19th and early 20th centuries. As a result, this book deals with authentic vampires as described in the folklore of those peoples most closely affected by them.

This book has been placed in as accurate an historical context as possible. This includes accounts of battles and historical events. The Vojvoda of Wallachia, Vlad III, Tsepeş, also known as Dracula, visited Srebrenica in 1476 and conducted a bloody massacre. The physical description of Dracula is accurate, taken from an account written of Vlad III by the Papal Legate Niccolo Modrussa in 1466. The description of Dracula's Srebrenica massacre is taken from the eyewitness account of Gabriele Rangoni, another Papal Legate. Vlad II, Dracul, the father of Dracula, was a member of the Order of the Dragon, as were the Serbian Despot Stefan Lazarevic and the Duke of Spalato, Hrvoje.

The 14th century Law Code of Tsar Dusan contains Article 20, which forbids digging up graves and destroying bodies by "witchcraft". King Sigismund of Hungary and his unfairly maligned wife Barbara are real historical characters. The Dubrovnik Bishopric conducted vampire trials of people from the island of Lastovo in the 1700s.

The description of the gravestones in the walls of homes in the villages around Ram is accurate, as is the recounting of the 1725 case of Petar Plogojovic from Kisiljevo. The Austrian Army did send military units – accompanied by the regimental surgeon Johann Flückinger – into Serbia in 1731 and 1732 to hunt vampires. The result was Flückinger's 1732 book *Visum et Repertum* (*Seen and Discovered).*

Most of the historical documents mentioned and their references to vampires exist or existed. These include the 15th century Glagolitic manuscript in the Archive of the then Yugoslav Academy, now renamed the Croatian Academy of Arts and Sciences; the 16th century chronicle of Georgius Sirmiensis; the court records from Ston in 1666; the 17th century Orthodox Church Nomocanon; the Orthodox Church Council of 1730 in Belgrade; the Dubrovnik Court records from 1736-1744; and the decision of the Austrian Imperial Court War Council of 23 October 1748.

The Djordjevic book *Vampiri i druga bica* – *Вампири и друга бића* (*Vampires and Other Beings*) exists and constitutes a veritable treasure trove of Balkan vampire lore. It provided much of the material for this book's descriptions of vampires as well as hints for where to look further. The only document that is entirely fictional is the Djordjevic book about the twelve. To the best of my knowledge, no such book exists.

The tales surrounding Petrovaradin's tunnels – the giant serpent, hidden treasure, etc. – are accurate, as is the *Sign of the Elephant* tavern and its owner, Hans Georg Siegel. So too are the descriptions of the Maltese cross and mysterious passages under the fortress, as well as the description of the warren of tunnels under Budapest's castle hill. All descriptions of Balkan wines and viticulture are accurate.

Slobodan Milosevic and Vojislav Seselj are real. Both were indicted by the International Criminal Tribunal for the Former Yugoslavia in The Hague (ICTY) for war crimes, crimes against humanity, and/or genocide. Milosevic died during the course of his trial while in custody.

This is entirely a work of fiction, and with the exception of historical personalities, all the characters in this book are fictitious. Any resemblance to persons living or dead is purely coincidental.

CPSIA information can be obtained at www.ICGtesting.com
Printed in the USA
LVOW05s1747130114

369234LV00034B/2713/P

9 781483 921358